SUITE FOR CALLIOPE

"This writer is adventurous . . . images are splendidly suggestive . . . witty stories, jubilantly told."
— Nadine Gordimer

"An extraordinary first novel that, in its remarkable inventiveness, intelligence, and charm-struck humanity, should draw—and more than richly reward—readers of almost every inclination."
— *Kirkus Reviews*

"[An] intricate, fluid, and gritty tale of hidden evil painfully brought to light and conquered . . . at times joyous, always right and riveting."
— *Library Journal*

"A story about human frailties and unusual talents, about family ties and disagreements, about sanity, insanity, and the irregular line between the two. The author must be endowed with an imagination as big as a calliope keyboard and as diverse as the carvings on a circus wagon."
— *Tampa Tribune Times*

"An exuberant debut. For this performance, Hunnicutt deserves a drumroll, bright lights and, above all, the cheers of a standing ovation."
— *The Plain Dealer* (Cleveland)

See you at Gilles!

SUITE FOR CALLIOPE

A Novel of Music and the Circus

ELLEN HUNNICUTT

For Kathy Larson,
With all good wishes,
Ellen Hunnicutt
I W U
1989—

LAUREL

Published by
Dell Publishing
a division of
Bantam Doubleday Dell Publishing Group, Inc.
666 Fifth Avenue
New York, New York 10103

ISBN: 0-440-50088-5

Reprinted by arrangement with Walker and Company

Printed in the United States of America

Published simultaneously in Canada

February 1989

10 9 8 7 6 5 4 3 2 1

W

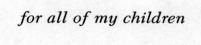

for all of my children

The author is pleased to acknowledge receipt of a Literary Arts Fellowship from the Wisconsin Arts Board. She also wishes to express acknowledgment and appreciation to Philip Turner of Walker and Company.

SUITE FOR CALLIOPE

A Novel of Music and the Circus

1

JUST BEFORE daybreak the old lioness stirs in her bed of sweet clover hay under the low eaves of her wooden stall. Her anguished bellow shakes me awake, rockets over the caved-in giraffe barn, and cannonballs out across the vacant winter meadow. Monumenta! Queen of the veld. Every morning I come back from nameless dreams by way of Africa—foot by cheek, leg by arm, stiff as icicles, nose red—to the blue-brown, ice-patched emptiness of Indiana.

Africa is probably no worse than the other places I've been, but the thrill of that roar astonishes me at five A.M., even though I am a seasoned traveler, alert to thieves and sudden jolts. I still sleep with my money in my sock, even here with Belle, who would not rob me. Belle is an ally, has seen my kind before; the plain pale girl alone in the back of the bus, the drinker of all-night-coffee, the walker with thin-soled shoes. Here I could relax—but I don't.

"Monumenta cries for the good-time years," says Belle rising in the darkness like an old ghost to tend her, "for the people screaming and the smell of the elephants." Belle has lived sixty-eight of her seventy years without my help, does not ask it now. Yet I feel duty-bound to crawl from my cot and trail after her into the sharp, gray, brutal air.

When Belle approaches with the bloody meat, Monumenta's ancient milky eyes glide open, and her nose quivers as prettily as a house cat's. "Feed a lion only meat," says Belle gravely, "and always with the bones in, chuck and neck bones, or they eat it down too fast and sicken. The bones make them suck and nibble." Monumenta sucks and nibbles with her stumpy teeth like a noisy old woman at her bowl of soup, hunkers down and moves grudgingly to let Belle change her bedding. "I'll have no ordinary straw touch her skin," Belle says, putting in the clover. "Lions have delicate skin. You can ruin a lion's skin as easy as that!" Belle's old black eyes snap to show how easy it is.

"Why doesn't she eat you, Belle?" I ask.

"Why should she?"

"She will some day. Some day they'll come and find nothing but your bones, sucked clean."

For answer, Belle raises one bloody hand and flutters it daintily in total disdain of danger, just as she must have done fifty years ago from the trapeze at the very top of the tent, when her pale pink hair blazed red as flame against the canvas, as it does in her pictures, poster pictures she now uses to close out ratholes in the old farmhouse, to cover broken plaster, to stop the January drafts that burrow around the loose, rattling windows. I plan vaguely what I shall do on the day Monumenta sinks her teeth into Belle's crepey old throat. Call for help across the vacant meadow? There is a pistol in the house but it is filled with blanks, a rusty show-business relic.

"Before you go, Norma," says Belle, who knows me by no other name—she is still dancing her reddened fingers in the icy air like a dazed victim wandering off from a hideous accident—"I wish you'd come down here to the barn and play some music for her. Monumenta always liked music. It roused her so. I'll bolt the door and you can play right through the bars, safe as in your own bed. On your violin. A little violin music." She gazes at the lioness fondly, with the half mad smile of saints in old paintings.

"Where am I going, Belle?"

Both bloody hands flutter up now for emphasis. "A nice young girl like you? Anywhere! Anywhere." This theatrical gesture shows Belle to her best advantage. Her small, tough body is still taut and straight, her waist as lean as a young boy's. "You'll be traveling on. When my girls come in the spring I'll need the room." Belle looks out of the barn window at the rusted, abandoned trapeze rig in the side yard. No young girls come in the spring to train anymore. Not one has come in the two years I have been here, but Belle does not recall this, or, in this grim winter dawn, chooses not to acknowledge it. By some agreement I do not fully understand, she has the use of this small farm for her lifetime. At her death, it will become part of the circus museum that sits half a mile away, buildings and grounds closed to tourists now and secured against winter.

The museum exists because many American circuses began in Indiana, wintered here regularly. They stayed until the warmth of Florida and improved transportation lured them south. This place was the womb of crazy farm boys with bravado and dog tricks, freaks and beasts, hard-assed girls and slick boys fifty feet above the ground —sixty, seventy. All of this history is recorded in the museum's archives. Outside of these carefully preserved records, facts are harder to come by. The situation here is fluid. Born of nostalgia and funded by philanthropy, the museum is under the care of two dozen circus veterans, most of them as old as Belle. Like Belle, they are wintered in, spotted about the countryside in old farmhouses and reconditioned summer cottages. Some of them are in house trailers that are half hidden by bales of hay laid up on every side for insulation. In the nearby town there is even a boardinghouse operating, Belle explains, in the old style. Boarders gather around a long table for meals, and men go out onto the porch afterward to smoke, even in winter. "They observe form," Belle says primly each time she tells this tale. Ritual. Operative folklore real as the smell of camels, the taste of peanuts. Form canceled gravity, stayed the teeth and claws of beasts, beat the odds. When form was observed, Belle could not fall. Every mishap could be accounted for, traced to a breach of etiquette.

Near the boardinghouse is the original home of a famous circus family, faithfully preserved. The museum and half of this small town now exist in a tangle of trusts, bequests, tax write-offs, easements, and rent forgivenesses that is beyond ordinary understanding. Circus people were quick to capitalize on this confusion. There are two or three times as many men and women in residence as the museum directors originally intended. Everyone has taken in a friend; jobs are shared like food. Each small paycheck is stretched to provide for these vagrants. This is a clandestine encampment of refugees. I am one of these refugees; so is Monumenta. I am a musician, nearly as good as a circus veteran. Monumenta's claim to hospitality has more validity, a long life of performing in the ring. Many faithful old friends stop by to visit her: "There's the girl!" "That's our baby!" "Sweetest love!" "Pretty thing!"

Sadly, these are summer people, followers of the sun, lovers of bare arms and spangled tights. Winter is their adversary, more cruel than all the remembered sheriffs who revoked their playing permits, confiscated their illegally imported animals, or ran their shows out of town. Their winter garb is often whimsical: layer upon layer of summer clothing, pieces of ancient costumes, horse blankets. This is affectation, not necessity. This is protest.

Summer is much better. In summer, a small circus plays on the museum grounds under canvas twice a day for visiting tourists. It is staffed by a mix of elderly veterans and fresh-faced beginners. There are animals, sideshows, souvenir stands. There are tickets to be sold and taken, there is popcorn to be hawked.

On the museum grounds my steam calliope (I call it mine) is installed in medieval splendor across one end of a great gaudy hall that was once an animal barn. This hall also houses circus memorabilia and provides museum management the opportunity to sell yet another ticket to visitors. The building is opulent, baroque, with a vaulted roof higher than the spire of the town's Methodist church. From its interior walls great blisters of art leer down on all sides, gilt cherubim and griffins, posters and photographs striped with venerable circus names— O'Brien, Cooper, Sells, Cole, Gollmar. There are costumes on dressmaker forms, a life-size ringmaster with hollow, frightened eyes, the artwork of wagons, the trappings of show bands, all snatched and salvaged from the whimsical debris of circuses.

I am overqualified for my job. The calliope is not a difficult instrument to play. With its brief two-and-a-half octave keyboard, it is a dim-witted giant, a dwarf-brained, overmuscled ear bully. I could be replaced by a second-year piano student who would work for minimum wage, who would not have to be wintered over; but circus people are sentimental, love cripples and two-headed calves, see them as proper parts of the world. I know an old circus crone who still cries tears over the ravages of Hitler, not for the Jews and Gypsies but for the midgets who perished at his hands. When I mount the steps to the calliope dragging my bad leg, showing my inelegant face, gaunt and spectral, in brutal contrast to the brilliant gilt heraldry of the instrument's facade, tourists feel a small thrill of distress, but circus people feel satisfaction, justification. They have made me welcome. At the keyboard I sometimes feel I am Bellini's high priestess Norma to this clutch of Druids. I have no shield of Irminsul to strike, but I churn out introit, anthem, and postlude on valved whistles that carry to a range of five miles.

* * *

Back in the kitchen, Belle washes up at the single cold-water tap, stirs the fire. "The coffee's ready!" she cries. This fact seems to amaze her every morning, morning after morning. She is graceful in every attitude and I cannot catch her off guard. She is not got up for any audience. She has broken her bones thirty-one times, had eleven operations, yet everything mended perfectly. Obtuse, wrongheaded optimism holds all of her parts together. Even in sleep she is poised, shoulders straight, fingers slightly curved. She is on top of things. Monumenta would eat me in the wink of an eye.

My history can be told in houses. This one, with its uneven floors and wavy, distorting mirrors, is a fun house. In it youth and age are reversed. I've hurried all my living into twenty years. Belle at seventy is just beginning. As she pours out our coffee, her dry lips pucker into a fragile blue bud; her eyes dart about impatiently. She is eager for the next hour's mischief. This morning it is a newspaper article she stabs with one accusing finger. "This is you," she says. "This one's you, I know it. Look at the picture. Say something in Spanish, Norma."

"Bullshit."

Belle has expected no other response. "It says this girl is seventeen and half Mexican. They don't say what the other half is. They've been looking for her for six years. The mother still believes she's alive. That's probably the Mexican half. The last name doesn't sound Spanish. Once I worked with a man in Pittsburgh who said he was Spanish. A catcher. But he was Mexican. He lied about it. I think he was mostly Indian because his skin was very dark, even in the bends of his elbows. That's how you tell." Belle, who is Italian, prizes the whiteness of her own skin, still possesses a closetful of ancient hats and parasols she puts into service each spring to protect her from the sun. A flyer, she is an aristocrat. In performance, her distance above the ground was the measure of her superiority over others. It was earned nobility, bought by rigorous training, but she no longer remembers this. Now, examining the whiteness of her own arms, she believes she was born a lady. This certain knowledge carries her through all difficult times.

With a small scissors Belle clips out the newspaper piece and adds it to her collection of articles about missing persons, which she keeps in a large candy box under her bed. This is motherly concern on Belle's part, motivated by kindness, tied to some outlandish scheme to rehabilitate me and set me on my way. She no longer expects me to confide in her.

There are many boxes under Belle's bed. This kitchen is only a small part of her world. The clippings keep her in the middle of things. She's connected to the mainstream, invites herself in. She buys stacks of outdated magazines and newspapers from a salvage dealer, ten cents a bundle. Her busy scissors cuts them to pieces. She sorts, boxes, and stores articles and advertisements about hotels, trains, world cruises, restaurants, accidents of all sorts. She's keen on the subject of animals, especially their mistreatment. Her collection of articles on cruelty to animals is largest of all. She has it all documented. Something big is coming, wait and see, when the right people find out what's really happening (says Belle). There is so much to do every day.

Winter is a time for repair in the circus. Popcorn Joe now rattles up the driveway in a dilapidated pickup truck, en route to a carpentry job on the grounds, and spreading the news as he goes. Joe refurbishes circus wagons, will take on all odd jobs, is considered an adept craftsman. "Teddy MacKay has a cancer on his lip," says Joe, barely in the door, arriving in a rush of wind and drifting barn smell. He is a slight, agile man with small bright eyes and large sensuous lips. His skin appears varnished. His slick black hair is cut with neat sideburns and dressed with black shoe polish. Past seventy, he still stands straight and manages to look a little like photographs of Rudolf Valentino. He pulls off a series of jackets and warms himself at the stove. "The doctor did a lab test."

Belle pours out a third cup of coffee. "They'll take it off. That's nothing if it hasn't spread." Belle also collects medical articles. Teddy MacKay, the subject of this exchange, shows trained dogs. He is fortunate; his age—perhaps seventy-five—does not affect his profession.

Popcorn Joe is not persuaded by Belle's argument. "It'll disfigure him for life," he counters stoutly. His hands are stained a dull gray from smoothing his polished hair. "Smack in the middle of his face." He pats his already smooth hair with one gray hand, grateful that his own good looks are still intact.

At one time Joe held an interest in nearly every popcorn concession in the circus business. He made money in popcorn. His methods were devious. He was also a jumping and leaping clown, and a tap dancer. But his real business was elephants. His specialty was buying up bad-tempered elephants and selling them off to small shows. He was good with elephants. Belle confirms that Joe was the only man in the business who could ride bareback all the way around the ring standing on an elephant. The trick never caught on because it didn't look hard, but it was. An elephant's skin is loose. As soon as the animal begins to move, the skin starts shifting and becomes slippery as mud. Joe could ride an elephant bareback while standing on one foot.

He has now reformed, bristles with virtue, cheats no one. He cannot clearly remember when he lost his money and tells the story in various ways. He believes the wife who divorced him many years ago is dead. He has a son in Sarasota who sells insurance, but the boy's mother set him against Joe. The two are estranged. Once Joe went to Sarasota and secretly photographed his grandchildren playing in a yard. He displays a wrinkled picture of two solemn little boys looking up at the camera with surprise and suspicion.

Popcorn Joe has really come this morning to tell Belle of a horse she can get free from a nearby farm for Monumenta. Keeping the lioness fed is a constant concern. Sometimes it is a frantic nightmare. All of the circus people do what they can to help. Monumenta seldom receives the elegant diet of chuck and neck bones Belle prescribes for her.

"Is it sick?" Belle asks warily. "Did you see it move? Walk?"

"He'd already shot it, yesterday."

"It's full of sickness; I know it already."

"Belle, I'm only telling you."

Belle knows she has no choice. She gathers up her butchering knives and an assortment of tubs, pails, and canvas bags. A dead horse is more easily transported in pieces. "At least the cold will keep the meat," says Belle.

"You want me to run you out there now?"

Breakfast forgotten, Belle is already getting her coat. As I locate my cornflakes, I see the teakettle simmering on the back of the stove. On a nearby shelf, a tall glass waits. It has been polished past our usual state of cleanliness, polished beyond hygiene, beyond courtesy. Belle's faculty for warfare is impressive. The glass sits like a challenge on the exact center of a paper napkin. It suggests the burnished barrel of a loaded gun. "Is Alexander coming this morning?" I venture.

For answer, she thrusts one arm into a sleeve with more than usual vigor and faces me with wide, innocent eyes. She seems scarcely able to remember this name. Her expression moves through several modes of condescension. "He will want to know about the flyers who are coming this season," she announces at last. "Tell him they are Italians, Florentines. Tell him to tune his trumpet to Italy—and keep it there." She pauses, casting about for a final denunciation, and then finds it. "If he throws the girl off her swing with his outrageous music, her innocent blood will be on his hands."

"Italy," I say between mouthfuls of cereal. "I'll tell him."

Together, Belle and Joe load the butchering equipment into the truck.

When they have gone, I set about my day's work. When I am not helping to care for Monumenta, playing the steam calliope, or doing simple chores, I repair musical instruments. In my two years here, I have gained a small but steady group of customers. I do not advertise. My reputation has spread by word of mouth. I believe my patrons say, "Take it to the crippled girl out on the circus farm. She's cheaper than the shop in the city." And like all handicapped people I sometimes receive praise I don't actually deserve.

"Her affliction, then . . . it doesn't affect her brain?"

"It probably does, but it's made her better with her hands."

"Yes, they compensate. Like blind people improving their hearing. But she looks like a witch."

"Don't believe that. Don't believe everything you hear. Take your guitar out there. You'll see. Nobody says you have to make friends with her."

With my small income and Belle's mysterious resources, the two of us could live comfortably, were it not for the strain Monumenta puts on our purses.

This morning I will glue a new neck into a violin. The old neck is warped beyond repair. With a small sharp knife I will cut through the glue joints, clean the cavity, and insert the new neck. Then, because my customer is frugal, I will remove the fingerboard from the old neck and attach it to the new one. The fingerboard is cheap pine painted black to imitate the traditional ebony. I will strip off the cheap paint and replace it with a superior black coloring made from a formula more than two hundred years old. I prepare it by boiling horse chestnut wood and mixing the broth with ground copperas. I have tried all of the new products and procedures, and returned to the very oldest. My predilection for using ancient methods and recipes in my work has led to the accusation that I practice witchcraft. I learned these methods from my father.

My best violin varnish contains an ingredient called "dragon's blood." This is actually a substance obtained from a palm grown in India, but the sight of my little jar, with its bright yellow label, sets people's teeth on edge. Nor are they especially reassured at seeing containers labeled Gum Lac, Copal, and Spirits of Wine. I see myself as part of a long and venerable tradition. The violin has always been associated with the devil. Nineteenth-century violinist Niccolò Paganini played so well a rumor circulated through Vienna that he was the son of Satan; no mortal could play so brilliantly. Paganini's mother was compelled to sign an affidavit stating that his father was a mortal man. But I live in an enlightened age; my witchcraft is tolerated.

As I work, I compose music—mentally, silently. I try out dotted eighth and sixteenth notes, whole, half, and quarter notes, syncopation, cross rhythms, duple and triple meters, polytonalities, chord clusters. These grow into rondos, arabesques, gigues, allemandes, courantes, sarabandes, rhapsodies, tone poems, impromptus, fandangos, canons. Most of these creations are unworkable and are immediately abandoned, for I am composing program music, music with a subject. In it there is little room for idle speculation. My music is really my history, or that part of my history that most impels me. It is protected from prying eyes by the convenient codes of music notation. It is unlikely that anyone, except possibly my father, could translate my measures and phrases into actual events. Still, I keep the pages hidden.

2

RICHMOUNT, INDIANA, a few miles east of Indianapolis, has several claims to fame. It was the birthplace of Single G, a famous racehorse, a trotter. The roller skate was invented in this small city. It is the home of Pendle College, a Quaker liberal arts school. Of greater practical interest than all of these, to most Indiana residents, is the fact that the state mental hospital is located in Richmount. The phrase, "They sent him to Richmount," heard across the state, never refers to racehorses, roller skates, or Quakers.

My first house was a neat white saltbox on the National Road in Richmount. The sun came into our small living room through square windows and warmed the carpet where I sat with a doll named Dooney. Grace, my mother, took me on her lap and crooned, "Here is Ada's chin, here is Dooney's chin; here is Ada's nose, here is

Dooney's nose." The doll's hair was made of brown yarn that clung to my lips when I kissed it.

My mother gave me cloth books that would never tear. On their pages were pictures of fruit, a table set for breakfast, a boy in a yellow shirt holding a large American flag. My mother sang, "When Johnny comes marching home again hurrah!" Johnny was the boy in the picture.

The pages of the books tasted like dust. Reynard, my father, said, "Don't-put-things-in-your-mouth-germs-are-everywhere." When my mother read her own books she took copious notes in school tablets with a yellow pencil and my father said, "Grace, cheap paper's hard on your eyes. At least write in ink."

When visitors came to our house they said, "So this is Ada! Are you as clever as your parents?" I knew my mother and father were important people.

When the upholstery on our couch wore thin, my mother threw a heavy green window curtain over it as a slipcover and my father said, "That's beautiful, Grace. You have a knack for things."

I seem always to have known I was not a pretty child. My dark hair was thin and stringy; my long narrow face was also thin and my body angular. Even when I smiled, my eyes looked out over my bridgeless nose with a melancholy peer.

Beside our house was a large mock orange that was nearly a tree. Shaggy bark, sheltering boughs, low-grown, climbable. In blossom, its heavy fragrance lay in my throat like honey, swam into my nostrils, seemed to warm the black bare earth beneath it. There I dug into the dirt with a toy spade and the scent of blossoms was a vapor curling up from the soil. I pressed my bare toes into my small excavations and sang the song of the place: "Bug, bug, ladybug likes the dirty dirt." Then a chorus of humming. I could locate the hum against the roof of my mouth and send it vibrating along the edges of my tongue in an ecstasy of tingling.

In the backyard was a large apple tree that had outlived its productive years. Each summer it formed yellowish nubbins that fell to the ground half grown and rotted into a rich brown mush. A carpet of green and blue flies formed and reformed endlessly a few inches above the ground. I walked straight lines into the slush with my bare feet, and only when I had reached the end of a line did I permit my hands to brush the creeping flies from my legs.

My father had hung a swing from a branch of the apple tree. In it, I performed a dozen clever stunts every day for an invisible, admiring audience. I could push out from the tree with one foot, move through a graceful arc, and stop myself again against the trunk without touching the ground. When my father pushed the swing high he said, "Now don't you come back here!" Again and again in an amazed, wicked voice. A riot of joy. Then my feet touched the lowest leaves and the sky through the branches was greenish white, the color of buttermilk.

On my account, our yard was completely enclosed by a high wire fence. Sturdy gates with child-proof locks were set at front and back. "Dogs," my father told my mother, "carry every kind of filth and disease there is. Besides, they mess in the grass and Ada would step in it." One day when I was two or three, Reynard inexplicably opened the front gate and coaxed in a thin old stray hound. My heart pounded with fear, for I had been taught to despise all animals. To my amazement, my father fondled the dog with real affection and rolled him onto his back on the grass. "There's a good old dog," he said. He took my hand and placed it on the animal. The fur on its belly was soft and warm, and beneath I could feel the dark rippling of its guts.

I began to giggle. "It's baloney!" I cried with delight. "It's an old baloney dog!" For days afterward, I hung on the fence waiting for the dog to come back, but he never returned, and no other dog ever entered our yard.

My father was also a dedicated enemy of cats. "The dog and cat population of this country eats enough to feed China," he declared. Stray cats did not survive in our neighborhood for more than a few days. My father lured them, lay in wait for them, seduced them. He captured them with saucers of cream, bits of liver, syrupy words. Then he put them into the trunk of the car, drove them into the country, and released them. Occasionally, they returned and the process had to be repeated. One day he drove a persistent yellow cat all the way to Cincinnati.

"On your way back," my mother said, "go by that little creamery and bring cottage cheese. It's on the way."

"The green onions are ready in the garden."

"Then don't get chive."

"I won't," my father promised.

The boundary lines of the fence did not restrict my mother's spirit. Sometimes she picked me up and pointed to the west. "The National Road is connected to California. Before they built the big highways, this was a very important road." It seemed unlikely, looking at our quiet, tree-shaded street.

At this time my father had established a music studio on our sunny enclosed porch. He'd already had many teaching studios, in many places. This one, in the house on the National Road, would be his last. His behavior, always peculiar, now became increasingly bizarre. Despite this, he continued to function fairly well for several more years. He was a violinist with the Indianapolis Symphony, a post he held until I was fourteen.

Other people must have found our sun porch very odd. To me, of course, it was home, and seemed completely ordinary. Reynard had laid a bright blue linoleum covering on the floor and papered the walls between the windows with a green-striped wallpaper. He felt these made the room cool and calm. Near the ceiling at either end of the room, he had cut large holes through the wall to the living room to increase circulation, and installed electric fans in both openings. I don't know why the humming of the fans did not annoy him, as he was very sensitive to sound. A sink with a liquid soap dispenser and a supply of paper towels stood near the entrance. Students were required to wash their hands before beginning lessons. My father washed his own hands as often as fifty times a day, sometimes until the skin was raw. He could not bear to have anyone touch his hands.

Reynard disliked any solid mass in a practice room because it absorbed sound. For this reason, the only furniture on the sun porch was a small grand piano and an assortment of wooden lawn chairs that had no padding. His concern for acoustics also caused him to reject the succession of curtains and drapes my mother attempted to hang at the windows. In the end, they were left bare. I remember children passing to and from school on the sidewalk outside, staring into the room with round, white faces.

Sunlight fell across the red-brown lid of the piano in wide, warm, dusty stripes. Despite the air tumbling from the fans and the empty, echoing space, the sun porch was a close, oppressive room. The air tasted dry. It clamped the throat shut with impossibility and frustration.

If my mother's written account is to be believed, Reynard began my lessons before I was two, on piano.

"Don't make the fingers do it, let them do it. Arch the hand, up, up! Wrist rotation, there's a girl, there's a girl. Balance the penny on the back of your hand. Do you want to keep the penny? Don't make me take the penny away. The ends of your fingers are pretty little pillows. Look at the pretty little pillows!"

I did not know for a long time that my father was a short man. He had powerful shoulders and arms that seemed misplaced on his slender lower body. He resembled a man who had exercised too much and in the wrong fashion. Courteous and gentle, he afforded students the same respect he gave to adults. He was an earnest man, but he could also be merry, often changing moods without warning. His hair and eyes were dark. The fierce, rather sad face that looked out from his publicity photographs, chin drawn in resolutely and pressed against the white tie of his dress clothes, was faintly oriental. It was something in the line of his eyes and a certain gold tone in his skin.

Some fragments of my memory are perfectly intact.

By the time I was four, theory and harmony were a part of my daily studies.

"There's a lovely natural minor. See how happy Papa is for the nice scale? Now we shall have the harmonic minor. Hear the raised seventh? It's a tickly sound in Ada's pretty little ear. Now the cadence chords . . . inversions . . . in arpeggios . . . blocked . . . broken . . . parallel motion . . . contrary motion . . . augmented . . . diminished."

It was summer. I wore a ruffled sunsuit, pink, with a faded pattern of trailing vines. The skin on my bare legs turned warm and moist and stuck painfully to the varnish of the unpadded piano bench.

"Name the forms of the minor scale."

"Natural, harmonic, melodic."

"Which is the most common?"

"The harmonic."

"What are the perfect intervals?"

"Unisons, fourths, fifths, and octaves."

"Why are they perfect?"

"They do not shift from major to minor when inverted."

"A major third inverts to . . . ?"

"A minor sixth."

"Now play the Hanon."

"From the beginning, Reynard?"

"Yes, from the beginning."

I do not recall when I began calling my parents by their first names.

Besides teaching, my father repaired instruments, and his skills were not limited to the violin. His repertoire included all strings, from the smallest violin to the largest bass viol, with guitars, mandolins, banjos, dulcimers, and harps making occasional appearances in our home. He loosened recalcitrant valves and mouthpieces on brass horns, cleaned sour and gummy clarinets, realigned injured trombone slides. He rehaired all varieties of bows, restored wounded drums, straightened and polished flutes.

His workshop—only now does it seem curious to me—was our large bathroom. He worked standing at an old-fashioned walnut chest that also served us as a cupboard. Alternate drawers held bath towels and my father's supply of wood; sheets and blocks of the highest quality maple and spruce. Extra violin necks and hanks of bow hair might be found anywhere—neatly stacked with bars of soap, shoved between tubes of toothpaste, piled on top of boxes of Band-Aids. A toolbox holding his small, dainty tools—chisels and knives, spatulas and clamps—was shoved beneath the chest. The top of the chest was nicked and scarred from hours of carving and chiseling. A set of blueprints, the *Stradivarius Series for Stringed Instrument Repair,* roved freely through our house. The drawings, with their precise measurements, were often on the kitchen table, but they might also be found in the bathtub.

For gluing wood, Reynard used old-fashioned horse glue; he did not trust modern adhesives. The glue came in powdered form, silvery-brown crystals. It had to be mixed with water and heated in a double boiler. The rancid smell of the cooking glue was heavy and unpleasant. After using it, Reynard set an electric fan to blow through the house and then burned scented candles. "It will be gone in a moment," he assured my mother and me.

At this time my mother, Grace Simmons Cunningham, was a columnist for the Indianapolis *Star*. She was the author of two novels and a history of Indiana. She had also written a biography of my father that was never published. Through her writing, she had achieved some stature as a historian, the first regional writer in Indiana to be noticed since Gene Stratton Porter invented the saga of the girl of the Limberlost. From time to time, both of my parents taught classes at Pendle College, a few blocks from our home. My father's classes were studio lessons, master classes for small groups of violin students. My mother's were loosely organized talks that by her own admission wandered freely between journalism and history. "It's really entertainment," she told my father. "They bring in my daily column or one of my books and we talk about things."

"But you're teaching them to think," my father answered solemnly. He adored my mother. "Everything you say is worth hearing. It's good for them."

My mother was an inch taller than my father, fair and plump with reddish hair and soft green eyes. She was the undisputed head of our household. Although she played many roles and always presented my father in the best possible light, often to her own disadvantage, she was always in charge. This arrangement suited Reynard.

Grace was warm by nature. She appeared jovial and had a wide circle of admiring friends, but at close range she was nearly as intense as my father. Behind her public smile she was determined and devious. The first objective fact I learned about my mother—perhaps the only clear fact I ever learned about her—was that she made little attempt to separate reality and fantasy. From her point of view, she improved upon the facts. Out of her imagination she sometimes created interviews with people who did not exist and wrote them up for her column.

"Is this man real?" my father asked. These children, this deaf-mute, the long-ago drowning, the desertion, the faith healing, the corn crop, the premature baby, the clairvoyant, the Good Samaritan?

"Of course not."

"It's a wonderful story."

"Thank you."

These pieces were often received by her readers with greater enthusiasm than articles based on real events, which she researched with great care. When a subject interested her, she was capable of meticulous research. She was not unable to distinguish fact from invention, right from wrong, rain from sunshine, and eventually sanity from madness, but she dipped her brush in both pallets, all hues and textures.

This could be seen most clearly in her biography of my father, which I found in her desk after her death. There were two manuscripts. The first was the true account of my father's impoverished youth. It related the stories Reynard himself told, tales and episodes I had heard from earliest childhood. In the second manuscript, Grace had rearranged the facts to Reynard's advantage. Each mishap that befell him brought enlightenment. Dishonesty was redrawn as cunning. His small successes were seminal, linking him to the greatest musical figures of the day. His failures were poignant, the fault of others. The second manuscript was never finished. I believe Grace abandoned it when she finally accepted the fact that my father would never achieve the success she envisioned for him. My mother's disdain for the truth has made me suspicious of every historical account I have ever read, regardless of the reputation and stature of its author.

Several times a month my father drove to Indianapolis for orchestra rehearsals and performances. My mother and I often attended his concerts. By the time I was three, I had heard most of the standard orchestra repertoire.

But most of my father's days were spent at home. Because his students did not come for lessons until after school, he was free most days until three in the afternoon. He spent much of this time doing housework and cooking. I think these tasks were the activities that provided him the most pleasure.

"Look Grace, if I pin the pillow slips to the clothesline open end up, the wind billows inside of them and dries them faster."

"They're so soft."

Reynard loved to cook and bake. "Half a cup of orange juice is the best tenderizer for round steak."

"It's delicious," my mother always said.

Our dining room was the setting for many adventures and an occasional disaster.

"What is it?" Even in the most trying situations, my mother never lost her composure.

"Okra."

"It's different," said Grace, dubious but endlessly optimistic. She watched over my father carefully. I was Grace's friend, ally, sister.

"Ada, isn't Reynard's applesauce nice?"

"Mmm!"

"Did you ever see a prettier pink, Ada?"

"Pink!"

Reynard was her true child.

I believe my parents decided I would be a prodigy before I was born. Grace announced my birth to the readers of her column with enthusiasm, and thereafter provided periodic reports on the progress of her prodigy daughter. These pieces were clever, warm, witty, and freely laced with psychological dicta on child rearing. I believe she invented her theories on parenting as she went along. The articles suggested that all children had enormous potential. Hopeful parents and grandparents read them avidly, and her reader mail, always in generous supply, grew to huge proportions following an Ada column. According to my mother, I had scarcely appeared on earth before I began reading, both English and Latin, and my reading skills were put to good use. With alacrity I read most of the classics, not only in literature but in history and philosophy as well. In no time at all, Grace reported, I was playing violin and piano and composing music.

Most of it was a lie. I lived in the half-light of Grace's imagination, knowing that the child in the columns was and was not me. My first suspicion of outright fraud came when it occurred to me that my photograph never appeared with the columns. I was four, perhaps five years old. "We must protect our privacy," Grace insisted when I raised the question. "It would be like running my own photograph." But I knew the importance my mother placed on pictures, the diligent efforts she made to secure a photograph she wanted for a column. And in fact, she had frequently run her own photograph. She was actually a bit vain about her looks.

Still, it was a long time before I came to see myself as a bona fide impostor. I was perhaps twelve, and Grace had been gone for several years. I was reading a biographical account of pianist and composer Clara Wieck Schumann, an undisputed prodigy of the nineteenth century. Robert Schumann, several years her senior and not yet her husband, had written of her, "She gives us the most interesting things of the most recent times with the least delay." The ambiguity of the statement seized me. It was a delicious puzzle. I saw an image of the young Clara seated at an old-fashioned piano, one hand extended in some show of generosity. Prodigies were charitable? Open handed? Then I reached past the image and brought forth the idea that had stopped me in my reading. Prodigies were self-directed. Some private sun smoldered in each and burst forth unbidden. Despite the manipulation they were often subjected to, they preserved intact a miniature intelligence that was completely their own. "She gives" was in fact "she knows." I could find in myself not a shred of this primary and privileged sensibility. I had learned because I had been taught, never moving out of the traces, never bounding ahead on intuition, always passing off obedience as wit. Staring at the picture of Clara Schumann, I tried to recall the facts of my early life. I knew I had been able to read English and recite simple Latin phrases by rote before I learned to read music. What I really remembered was Grace's reading to me endlessly. My father, rigid and compulsive, would never have permitted me to compose. He believed there was already too much music in the world, sometimes growing heated on the subject. Our consciousness was fragmented, said Reynard. We no longer had a community of belief. The twentieth century belonged to technicians, not composers. I recalled no desire to compose in any case.

But at this time our existence without Grace was complex and precarious. I knew Reynard and I would have to go on as we were.

The articles Grace wrote about me eventually were collected into a book entitled *Ada Learns.* It made a little money, as most of my mother's other books had not. My parents, who lived always in genteel poverty, were able to pay off the loan on the family car.

Grace died suddenly when I was eight, collapsing on the street in Indianapolis. Frantically, Reynard drove us to the hospital. He dodged traffic with maniacal abandon while singing in a pinched, eerie voice, " 'What wondrous love is this, oh my soul? What wondrous love is this, oh my soul? That caused the Lord of bliss, to bear the dreadful curse, oh my soul, oh my soul, oh my soul!' "

Weak and scarcely alive, Grace lay motionless in the high hospital bed. For a moment, I could not look at her white, stricken face. On the wall of the room hung a print of a picture I would later know was Millet's *The Gleaners,* three kerchiefed women bending to their work, a deep landscape stretching out behind them. I studied the picture and it seemed to me the women were tending graves. I understood my mother was about to die. When I looked at Grace, I saw that her lips were moving. Reynard held her hands and bent to catch the whispered words. Then a nurse appeared and gently

ushered us to chairs in the hall. "What did she say, Reynard," I asked.

But if my father understood my mother's last words,
he never divulged them. He sat in silence, studying the
palms of his hands as if they were objects he had never
seen before. Within the hour, Grace had slipped into a
coma. Two days later she was dead of a cerebral hemor-
rhage.

3

I PLAY music with six fingers. The fourth and fifth fingers on both hands are dysfunctional. Of less concern but troubling is my left leg. It is lame and stiff.

Pianists consider the thumb as the first finger and number the fingers outward from it for a total of five on each hand. String players operate a bit differently. Because the thumb is used to support the neck of the instrument, only four fingers remain for fingering. The index finger is one, the others are numbered outward from it for a total of four. This variance created problems when Reynard, a violinist, began to teach me piano, an instrument he did not play well himself. "For theory and visual orientation we will begin on piano," he said. For some time, the issue of fingering obscured the fact that my hands were crippled.

"The morning hours are best," my mother said. "She'll

be freshest then. But the two of you can really have all day. It's an excellent situation." Grace approved fully of the music lessons. She greeted my protests with a bemused smile and complete indifference. After a time, I protested no more.

A tireless worker herself, Grace saw nothing wrong in discipline, schedule, hard work. What were a few tears? We were all caught up in something so fine, so redeeming, that pain was incidental. The future would justify everything.

With Reynard, the situation was very different. He was basically a lazy man, prepared at all times for capitulation and defeat. A stunning natural talent had brought him early recognition without much effort on his part. He could have achieved more than he did, had his disposition and health been different. Sometimes he practiced frantically for hours on end, but often his violin went untouched for long periods of time. I believe he was sympathetic to my plight and suffered during our sessions nearly as much as I did. It was Grace's persistence that made him continue.

In any case, fingering problems created great frustration. When I failed to follow Reynard's instructions he suspected his tongue had slipped, that he had given me directions for the violin. And in fact, his explanations wandered freely between the two numbering systems and two different techniques.

"Did I say first or second finger? Repeat exactly what I said to you."

"I can't."

"You can't say it or you can't do it?"

"I can't."

"Try it again. Slowly."

I think for a long time Reynard and I were both certain that at any moment we would break through this barrier of confusion, this puzzle of numbers, and emerge into a bright blue world of proficiency.

Grace never relented. "It sounds better today. It sounds fine, really so fine."

Reynard operated out of a base four system. He was attempting to teach me a base five system. And I, like all cripples, maximized what function I did have. Unconsciously, I developed a base three system, using my six good fingers. In performance, I am told, I look like someone playing with great agitation.

Reynard watched my peculiar finger crossings with consternation. "I don't know how this can happen."

"It sounds fine," Grace insisted.

"Of course it sounds fine! She plays the right notes! Grace, you aren't a musician. How can I explain it to you?"

My system actually works fairly well, and I cannot remember a time when I was not fluent in it. Except for octaves, certain highly technical passages, and very large chords, I can play most piano music as it is written. When I cannot, I reduce the music, omitting notes and maintaining the harmonic outline. These skills, learned out of necessity, have made me adept at arranging. Perhaps Grace would eventually have found a career for me in that field.

I can easily play all triads in root position. I can play all sixth and seventh chords, sometimes inverting them in order to cover two keys with one finger. I can play all scales, all arpeggios, and my own version of all cadence chords.

I have never considered my problems especially unique. All musicians are embarrassed by their hands. Anthropologists may rhapsodize about the design of the human hand, the miracle of the opposing thumb, the individual shape and function of each finger. For musicians, hands are a source of endless misery, because musical instruments are designed to be played by mallets of equal length and equal strength. Keyboards, fingerboards, and rows of horn keys are uncompromisingly level. To these, the musician brings a sorry assortment of tools. The thumb is a stiff, stubby, foreshortened appendage that must be strained beyond its natural design to strike a key with precisely the same force and in the same period of time as the much longer, stronger middle finger. In no other way can a satisfactory legato be obtained. The middle finger is overstrong and must be restrained. It must also be trained to function at a height lower than that directed by its own design. If fingers were all the length of the middle finger, the hand could float about a half inch higher above the instrument than it does. All musicians labor and scheme to improve hand function.

In the baroque period, some keyboardists did not play with the thumb, considering it too short to be worthy of use in performance. One day, years after my music lessons had stopped, I found a book of baroque keyboard finger exercises in the music library of a university. The four-finger system of playing resembled my own three-finger system in several ways.

When the tension on the sun porch became unbearable, Reynard, in frustration, switched me from piano to violin. I was almost four. The tiny fiddle, ordered from Germany, arrived packed in a box of shredded newspaper. I drew it from the box and lifted it into perfect position the first time. "She's learned everything already, from watching my students," said Reynard triumphantly. This was partially true. ·

Still, my fingers refused to work.

"Only exercise is needed," Reynard said, producing the first Wohlfahrt book. Within a few weeks, I was playing adequately, with a fair vibrato and a strong bow arm. My thumb was now required to hold the neck of the violin. I developed a base two fingering system.

Because my father was a symphony player, bulky orchestra scores were everywhere. Reynard now undertook to make me an orchestra player. "Here is Mahler."

"That's a B-flat cornet part."

"I can't find the fiddle score, Ada. All transposing instruments sound their name when playing written C."

"If I have to transpose, let me play from the French horn part."

"The horns don't have the melody here."

"Then let me play the fiddle part from the conductor's score." I became an orchestra player who had never played in an orchestra.

But with the violin, Reynard was on familiar ground and could no longer evade the truth. My hands did not function properly. There were tense, whispered conversations between my parents. The lessons ceased. The little fiddle was laid away. A black sadness settled over the house.

My new freedom was more terrifying than the lessons

had ever been. Grace continued to read to me, but I sat
silently much of the time in a small rocking chair and
wondered if I would soon die. Had my parents always
known of my disabilities, or was it a new discovery? I sat
now with my lame leg tucked under me, hoping they
had not yet noticed it.

Grace took me to Children's Hospital in Indianapolis.
For this outing, she dressed me in a red and white striped
dress and hung her own ivory cameo around my neck on
a black grosgrain ribbon. In the oval mirror above her
dressing table I resembled a pale, solemn candy cane.
Sorting through her drawer, she found a bracelet made
from Australian coins. She had found it on the street one
day in Indianapolis. The bracelet was hung on my bony
wrist. Reynard forbade nail polish. Any student who appeared for a lesson with the faintest trace of color on the
nails was immediately sent home. Grace found a bottle of
crimson enamel and painted my fingernails. I sat on the
vanity bench, hands extended, while she blew on the
polish to dry it. It seemed to me the ends of my fingers,
glowing like ten wet, red cherries, were the most beautiful objects I had ever seen. I thought, She has painted my
fingernails so the doctors won't chop off my crippled
hands. No one would dare destroy anything so lovely as
my glittering red fingernails. When the polish was dry
she brushed my hair and fastened red ribbons in it.

Then Grace put on a red satin dress with puffy sleeves
and nearly every piece of jewelry in her drawer. She
wore a ring on each finger. She was fiercely elegant, the
courageous defender of my crippled hands and lame leg.
Young as I was, I knew we were not appropriately
dressed for a visit to the doctor. Dishonesty was every-

where in the small bedroom. We were shamans confronting the medical world with magic.

At the hospital, a nurse put me on a table and stripped away my clothes, then a doctor came in and rolled me about like a sausage. "The dysfunction is identical in both hands?"

"It appears so." Grace was not yet prepared to make any concessions.

"But only one leg is affected?"

"Yes." Grace patted my good leg as if offering proof.

I lay naked and disconsolate, thinking that the gray worm of flesh on the table was not actually me at all. The real Ada was at home, holding up the little fiddle and walking strong fingers up the fingerboard. The first exercise in the Wohlfahrt book began in my head and played like a rondo that had no beginning and no end.

The doctor found a small pink scar at the lower edge of my rib cage. "Did she have pneumonia?"

"As an infant." Grace studied my stringy body as intently as the doctor, as if she might have overlooked something up to now, but nothing else of interest was found.

"The fact that the dysfunction is identical in both hands suggests the problem is with a nerve in her back governing both sides of the body," the doctor said.

I began to chill in the bare, metallic room. I lay on my back and pictured the nerve, a slender steel wire like the E string of a violin, saw it snap suddenly, the two ends curling into serpentine coils. In a moment, the doctor would open my body at the point of the pink scar, insert his hand, search through the goo of my insides for the small, sharp broken ends of the nerve, and reconnect them.

My purpling skin, sharp elbows, blunt toes, protruding ears, gleaming horse teeth, skinny buttocks, and crinkled navel were wrapped into a paper gown. I was rolled down the hall on a cart to the X-ray department and photographed in every conceivable position. I suspect this array of pictures still molders in some subterranean record room of Children's Hospital in Indianapolis, in the company of broken legs, cracked vertebrae, and fractured jaws—the orthopedic disasters of the state of Indiana.

We sat in a waiting room while the X rays were developed. A nurse came and wrapped a blue blanket around me. The room had no windows but yellow light fell in circles from three tall floor lamps. Grace searched through the folds of the blanket, found my hand, and we sat in warm silence. The lamplight caught the color of her dress and turned our skin an ominous black-red. Her face was flushed, tightly drawn.

Across the room from us a small boy sat morosely with his father, holding a towel wrapped about an injured wrist. They waited, endlessly it seemed, for help that never came. The towel was spotted with darkened bloodstains that appeared a sickly green in the lamplight. Grace smoked a cigarette and dropped the ashes on the tile floor. The father of the boy rose and handed her an ashtray. "It's tough," he said, making the ashtray a small gift of friendship. In return, Grace smiled at his son.

An elderly nurse with a soft gray voice brought trays of food, orange Jell-O in a saucer, a sandwich with a mushy brown filling. Grace lifted a spoonful of Jell-O to my lips.

The quivering mass looked ominous and I felt sudden nausea. "I can't," I whispered, and Grace took the trays away. Across from me, the boy held his sandwich in his good hand and took a large bite.

Disembodied sounds drifted into the room: the sharp click of heels in the corridor, a splash of running water, the opening and closing of doors. The boy finished his sandwich, looked at me with solemn, steady eyes, and said, "This is the place you come to and they tell you what they're going to do."

"I know," I replied.

Eventually, a doctor appeared and called Grace away for a private consultation. I suspect he told her my disability was irreversible and untreatable. I am sure he told her I was very lucky, that many people had misfortunes greater than mine, because these are the things every doctor since has told me. They have also said my dysfunction was unlikely to become worse, and this has been true.

When Grace reappeared in the waiting room, it was like the sun rising. She had shed every trace of fear and uncertainty. She smiled, and even laughed, and I felt my own fear drop away. I suspect now that the doctor had made her angry. In battle, Grace was never bested. Any sort of contention stimulated her, brought out all of her strength. "Everything's fine!" she announced and, to the father of the boy, "Isn't that marvelous?" She scooped me up in her arms and threw the blanket to the floor as if it were a hateful, diseased object. "They don't need to do one thing to you, my darling! Not one single thing!" We swept grandly from the room. The father and the boy, still waiting, looked after us with giddy, uncertain smiles. Then the boy raised his good hand in a happy little salute.

Grace found my clothes, hurriedly dressed me, and we set off for the finest tearoom in Indianapolis, where we ate tiny, delicious sandwiches and pink ice cream with chocolate sauce.

By the time we drove into our own street, we were in a holiday mood. "It's nothing at all!" Grace called merrily to Reynard through the open window of the car. "The doctors say we must start the music lessons again, right away!"

My father looked perplexed, but he prepared a victory celebration for us. He spread the table with several kinds of cheese, sliced rosy ham paper thin, peeled a large Bermuda onion, set out Italian bread and French mustard, rushed out to the market and found fresh peaches. What I remember most now about that day is how much I ate, first at the tearoom and later at our kitchen table. I was ravenously hungry and I ate until my sides ached. That night I tossed restlessly in bed, understanding quite well that nothing at all had changed. Raising my hands, I made shadow pictures on the wall with my fingers.

I do not know what words passed between my parents, but when Reynard resumed my music lessons he never again questioned my fingering. He continued to teach me theory and harmony. He provided ear training exercises. He moved me rapidly through a comprehensive repertoire on both violin and piano. But he permitted me to finger in my own manner. An atmosphere of conspiracy hung over the lessons. I understood quite clearly that there were certain issues that must never be raised.

But by this time our lives were laced with many kinds

of conspiracy. More and more of my mother's time was required to control my father's increasingly erratic behavior. When she failed to intervene in time, she covered for him with remarkable resourcefulness.

One day Grace made the comment that she would like to have a pair of red shoes. Reynard rose in the middle of the night, took all of her shoes from her closet, and painted them with bright red porch paint. We found them drying on the kitchen table the next morning. Grace treated it as a prank. Later in the day, she drove to a city park and deposited all of the shoes in a trash basket. The garbage man never found anything out of the ordinary at our house.

Grace now began to sleep with me, saying simply that the mattress on my bed was firmer and better for her back. In fact, she seldom let me out of her sight. Reynard had begun to roam aimlessly through the house at night, never turning on a light, sometimes singing or whistling.

I now accompanied Grace when she went in to her office at the newspaper. I appeared there so regularly that she wrote a column about it, anticipating I believe, curious questioners. The column said, "Important learning occurs when children share in parents' day-to-day activities." Another Ada column. It was well received and the staff at the newspaper made me welcome, but more and more, Grace worked at home, with a watchful eye on my father. Despite all of this, Reynard continued to teach me, and in the music studio his reason never faltered.

Reynard's displays of lunacy were occasionally public. Even then, Grace could sometimes explain them away. The memory of one such incident is vivid. Reynard was scheduled to play a recital in a nearby town. It was a benefit to raise money for the local hospital. Grace had arranged it, perhaps to dispel rumors that he was ill. She insisted that he play a program of Fritz Kreisler selections, followed by Stephen Foster songs. "This audience simply isn't sophisticated enough for anything more demanding," she argued. "You don't want to alienate them." Even I knew that the music was simple, a program my father could play without worry or strain. To prevent all possible problems, it was arranged for Reynard to play unaccompanied, since he sometimes flew into a rage at accompanists.

In spite of all Grace's careful planning, she had miscalculated. Reynard could no longer perform any task without worry and strain. He fretted for days about the recital, was unable to sleep, threatened to cancel, refused to practice. But in the end he performed, while Grace and I sat in the audience holding our breath. The program went well enough, but when he was called back for an encore he suddenly launched into Sarasate's *Zapateado*, a showpiece with incredible technical demands, rapid double-stops, pizzicato, and wrist-wrenching harmonics. Amazingly, as if summoning some memory of his former self, he played it brilliantly and completed it. Applause exploded in the auditorium. Reynard bowed graciously. Then, instead of leaving the stage, he raised his eyes to the ceiling and stood still as if frozen to the spot.

Grace was on her feet in an instant. Her reaction was so swift I believe she had prepared in advance for just such an emergency. She spoke to an usher in an urgent whisper. Yet, her voice was loud enough to carry, as I'm sure she intended it to be. Her words were: "He smells smoke."

Within seconds, people were pushing frantically to reach the exits. In the confusion, we took Reynard home. Fortunately, no one was hurt, nor was any sign of fire discovered. Yet my parents were credited with a human-itarian act. The story was told in different ways: that my father had passed a silent signal to my mother, that the usher had signaled Reynard to remain where he was to avoid panic, that Reynard had planned to continue play-ing heroically through the fire to calm the audience. If individuals here and there believed otherwise, they did not speak out. Young as I was, I realized that my mother had broken the law.

For weeks afterward, Reynard slept with the light on in his bedroom. Along with his audience, he believed totally in the fire, and smelled smoke everywhere. He did not attempt to play a solo program again. He settled into a routine of teaching his students and playing with the orchestra; he had been doing these things for so long he performed them almost automatically.

When my mother died, I retreated into confusion. Like all children raised with an unreliable parent, I had become wary and wise beyond my years. I knew how to handle my father and how best to help my mother. I had been a model child. But with my mother's death I lost all of these skills for a time. Our house filled with neighbors and friends, my parents' associates from the college, the orchestra, and the newspaper. I became totally depen-dent upon them. My clothing had to be found for me. I tried to dial the telephone and found I could not. My first

memory of my aunt Edlyn's arrival for the funeral is her
leading me to the table and attempting to feed me with a
spoon. "Ada, I'm your aunt. Don't you remember me?"
Grace's sister, she was our only relative.

Edlyn, of course, remembered all of this. Later she was
to say, "Even when the child was eight her coordination
was so poor I had to feed her, and her behavior was
already showing signs of deterioration."

Edlyn and my mother were very similar in appearance. Like Grace, she was plump and fair. There were
subtle resemblances as well. She was intense, an indefati-
gable worker. This was evident in her persistence with
the spoon. When Edlyn launched her campaign against
Reynard and me, it was much like having Grace's skills,
used so long to protect us, suddenly turned against us.

The cluster of people in our house whispered about
Edlyn. This surreptitious side play seemed important to
me, perhaps because it involved a mystery, and my
mother's death had confronted me with mystery. These
adults were set on solving a puzzle. If they succeeded,
everything might still be set to rights. Their whisperings
are now the only events of the week I remember clearly.

No one understood the dispute that had turned sisters
against each other, but at the time of my mother's death
it was common knowledge that she and Edlyn had been
estranged for several years. It made delicious gossip and
many speculations were offered. Reynard's explanation
was considered and rejected as outlandish. When he saw
the spoon in Edlyn's hand, he grabbed her wrist viciously
and snarled, "Don't touch my daughter, you criminal!"

Edlyn looked up in mute, horrified embarrassment,
her frantic eyes appealing to the assemblage for under-

standing. She received it at once, knowing nods, conciliatory pats to both her shoulder and Reynard's. The whisperers decided Reynard was merely distraught. With his sensitive, eccentric nature, he had invented a fantasy. They forgave him. The only fact that could be established, it seemed, was that Edlyn sold real estate in Chicago and that she sold it uncommonly well. I don't know if this conclusion was based simply on the evidence of her expensive white car and beautifully tailored clothes or on more solid knowledge. Shortly after the episode with the spoon, I heard my father, recovered from his outburst, ask Edlyn for money, and I believe she gave it to him. The whisperers eventually departed, and I had to concede that no mystery would be solved.

My mother was laid in state in the chapel of a funeral home on D Street. Someone dressed me in a pale yellow dress and led me to the casket, then settled me in an overstuffed chair nearby. I believe I was then more or less abandoned and that I sat on in the chair for several hours. At this time, I was in the third grade at school. I remember vaguely that my teacher came and knelt briefly by the chair. When she spoke to me, I was unable to answer.

On the day of the funeral, I was put into a limousine between my father and my aunt. The upholstery was gray, soft, and puffy, and the interior of the car smelled, oddly, of talcum powder. At the cemetery, I stood beside a bank of yellow chrysanthemums with a sour, bitter smell. When we returned to the house after the funeral I went and sat on Grace's vanity bench in what was now my father's bedroom, opened the drawers of the dresser, and looked at my mother's jewelry.

That night I woke in my bed and heard noises in the living room where Edlyn was sleeping on a couch. I seem to have known she was sorting through my mother's papers. At this time, the thought did not disturb me. The following morning she left, and Reynard and I were both glad to see her go.

4

BECAUSE GRACE had protected my father so carefully, no one really knew his true mental state. To outsiders, his eccentricities seemed rather charming. Weren't all musicians temperamental, a bit difficult? And if he occasionally seemed peculiar, he had, after all, just lost his wife. As a result of this, when Reynard declared he would stay on in the house and raise his daughter alone, no protest was raised. The two of us settled into a comfortable, if unusual, routine. My father continued to be fairly stable for some time. The next years were not the worst period of my life.

Although my formal music lessons stopped, Reynard and I played music a great deal. For the most part, I played his accompaniments at the piano. We undertook many projects with great diligence. We played all of the Beethoven sonatas, all we could find of Bartók, quite a lot of Robert Schumann. One winter we systematically worked our way through Scarlatti and Boccherini, and Reynard made elaborate plans I knew could never be carried out. "We'll make a little tour next summer," he said, "go to all the mountain resorts. We need only a soprano. Write to Elise Krause in Chicago and tell her she must come with us. Then write to my old booking agent. He'll remember me. You know Elise. You already know the accompaniments for all of her arrangements."

I dutifully wrote the letters. After Reynard had studied them scrupulously, I carried them to school, ripped them to pieces, and disposed of them in a wastebasket. I had never met Elise Krause, a singer my father had once worked with, and the agent was dead. One month there were forty-two letters, to nearly every colleague my father had had in a long career. This was his first letter-writing campaign.

I now played several roles. Often, to my father, I was my mother. "Look Grace, I've made shampoo. I cooked up the little ends from bars of soap and scented it with rose water."

"It smells good." Reynard loved scent. After he cleaned the house he touched each light bulb with perfume to freshen the rooms.

Sometimes I was Elise Krause, the ill-tempered soprano. "Elise, dear Elise, you cannot walk out on a booking. We will transpose the music up, down, or sideways, whatever you like, but come and get in the car."

"Let's work it out on the piano first, Reynard. Show me exactly what you mean. Now turn off the ignition and give me the keys. Hand them out the window."

"If we don't start now, we'll never make St. Louis in time."

"We can fly, Reynard."

One day when I was eleven or twelve my father disappeared for several days. When he returned, he lifted a cello out of the back seat of the car.

"Where did that come from?"

"I found it in a pawnshop in Fort Wayne, twenty-five dollars." A bill of sale from the pawnshop confirmed this. I was relieved he had not stolen it. "It's a present for you. Next year we'll get you a viola." He planned vaguely that I would someday play in the string section of the orchestra, and never fully accepted the fact that I was only a mediocre string player.

"Thank you."

"Where is Grace?"

"I haven't seen her."

"She must be in the tub. I believe I hear the water."

I never became a proficient cellist because the span of my hand was far too short for the long neck, but I loved the instrument, the growl of melody in the lower registers, the melancholy plaint in the minor keys.

An ancient cello method book had come with the instrument. "Reynard, the instructions are all in German."

"Say the words aloud, very slowly, and it will all come clear."

I went to the attic where my father had stored all of my mother's books and papers to search for a German dictionary. After about ten minutes Reynard, suddenly solicitous, called up the stairs, "Any luck?"

"None!"

"Look in that dead space behind the chimney, where

it goes out through the roof. Those were the things I didn't want Edlyn to see."

It was the first time I knew anything had been hidden and I thought little of it. Compared to other things my father had done, hiding books behind a chimney seemed a matter of no consequence. "Why would you hide a dictionary from Aunt Edlyn?"

"Your mother wrote things on the endpapers of books. I don't remember anymore. Just look behind the chimney!"

What I found behind the chimney was the first draft of my mother's history of Indiana and a volume of Whittier's poetry. I found the German dictionary in one of the cardboard boxes Reynard had left in plain view.

"Is anything written in it?" he asked when I reappeared downstairs.

"No. Why did you hide those things?"

"It's all the Chicago business. Your mother had the goods on her. Are you sure there's nothing in the book?"

"Nothing. Whom did she have the goods on?"

"It's all written down. Someday I'll pull it out and clean up on her."

I could get nothing sensible out of him on the matter. Since there was nothing menacing in my mother's first draft, nor in Whittier, I could only conclude that my father had become confused and hidden the wrong books—if any had existed at all. "I guess I'll go back up in the attic and read this. It's cozy. Why don't you make lunch."

"Good idea."

I began a methodical search of the attic that eventually consumed nearly two weeks. I found a scrapbook of the

Ada columns that Reynard had hidden under a loose
floorboard, and I opened several books he had sealed
with masking tape, but all of the material was completely
innocent. My mother had never been an investigative
journalist and it seemed unlikely to me that she had been
preparing any sort of exposé. I strongly suspected my
father had invented the whole idea, that his dislike of
Edlyn had expanded into some fantasy about her engaging in criminal activity. I put the matter out of my mind.

After Grace died, we saw few people except students.
Neither Reynard nor I were social by nature. I suspect
the few visitors who did call did not feel encouraged to
return.

I thought it would go on forever. In the eyes of our
neighbors we continued to live for some time under the
umbrella of Grace's fantasies; the charming if eccentric
violinist and his prodigy daughter. Opportunities—jobs
for pay—that would never have been offered to a child,
came to me. By the time I was thirteen, I was playing the
organ at a local church and directing the choir. The aura
of the clever Ada of the columns hung over me like
scent. "She's in gangly adolescence," people said with
enormous charity when confronted by my gawky, imperfect presence. The church work was simple enough
and—an important point—I was reliable. I never failed
to appear for choir practice, weddings and funerals, early
services. No second organist was required. Without
Grace's salary, we needed the money, but my regularity
was viewed as dedication, even a mark of talent. With
the sweetest tenderness I was asked, "How long can we
keep you here? Will you be off pursuing your own career
soon?"

I did not, of course, suggest that my father required constant care, nor that my performance skills were too limited to give me entrance to a concert career or even a mediocre conservatory. "My real interests are music history and composition. I can work anywhere. The rich legacy of church music has never been fully examined. I see new compositions arising from that heritage."

"Our very own Lutheran music. Imagine!"

Methodist, Episcopalian, United Brethren . . . Presbyterians consistently paid their music director the highest salary. At fourteen, I was given that job.

I played occasional programs at civic functions, lodges, and political rallies. I began to help Reynard repair instruments. Most of all, I managed my father, with nearly as much resourcefulness as my mother had.

In the same month that I took the job at the Presbyterian church, I began teaching my father's students. It was the beginning of the end. Reynard had begun to complain of pains in his abdomen and chest. He saw a doctor, who diagnosed his condition as nerves, but this explanation did not satisfy him. He carried anatomy books home from the library and studied them furiously. He took his pulse and respiration rate and began to chart them. He bought a device to check his blood pressure. He concluded that a major blood vessel in his chest had dropped into his abdomen, and that it lay perilously close to an upper bend of his intestine. "The closeness causes the pain," he said. "It's unnatural, and if they come into contact, matter from the intestine could seep into the bloodstream and cause blood poisoning." Reynard trusted his highly trained ear above all other senses. "I have it now," he declared a short time later. "I know the precise location of the two, and if I listen carefully I can hear their movement each time they shift."

This situation created serious problems in our daily routine. "Now!" Reynard would cry out suddenly when he believed the intestine and the blood vessel were approaching each other. He would instantly throw himself down on his back—on a couch or bed, in the yard, and on one occasion, in the street. In a prone position, he believed, the force of gravity would be exerted on both the blood vessel and the intestine, pulling them earthward and away from each other. This fetish disappeared in a few months, to be replaced by others, but not before it had done us damage.

Eventually Reynard had such a seizure during a lesson. "Now!" he cried in panic, rushing from the studio to his bedroom. "Ada!" he cried. "Finish the lesson!"

The student was a huge beefy boy of sixteen or seventeen, with wild hair and hard, bright eyes. The violin looked like a toy dangling from his large clumsy hands. He was waiting for me on the sun porch with a broad, knowing grin. "He's really nuts, isn't he?"

"Certainly not," I replied. "He isn't feeling well."

"Why don't you admit it? Everybody in town knows he's crazy." He lifted his chin suddenly and laughed, a short, mocking burst of sound. The laugh made his face wrinkle deeply and he looked like a fat old man. "I only come because my folks make me. My dad feels sorry for him and my mom says if I don't learn to play the violin I can't drive the car."

"I see." Was I really surprised? Perhaps I had lived with my father so long that nothing surprised me, even the prospect of a circle of town gossip closing in upon us.

Probably, I already knew what people were saying. Perhaps, like my mother, I didn't have a high regard for facts. The truth was what you made of it. Only the boy's boldness truly surprised me. His daring to speak so frankly was surely a measure of the intensity of the gossip. I had seen Grace in action dozens of times. Like her, I now warmed to the battle. "So tell me, *are* you learning to play the violin?"

"I hate it."

"Isn't it true that you find it easier to spread vicious stories about Mr. Cunningham than to practice and prepare your lesson properly?"

"Everybody knows about him."

"Do you want me to call your mother and tell her what you've said?"

He grinned. "You wouldn't dare. Then I'd tell how he ran out of here, crazy."

I saw that he was essentially a dullard and pressed harder. "Because he became ill and left the room? There are at least one hundred people associated with the symphony who would say you are wrong. Do you realize you and your parents could be sued and taken to court for slander for the things you have said, and fined a great deal of money?" He wavered. Seeing his ignorance, I plunged on recklessly. "You could find yourself with a criminal record. *Ex abrupto, hic et ubique, aurea mediocritas, sine qua non.*" An eclectic bouquet of Latin. "You could be denied a driver's license." All of the fight went out of him; he looked like a frightened sheep. "But I have decided to overlook it this time," I concluded triumphantly. After this event, I remained nearby when-

ever Reynard was teaching and intervened when necessary.

"You're a fine teacher!" Reynard decided.

The teaching was no more challenging than the
church work. Most students were awkward beginners.
Here and there one advanced to an intermediate level.
The violin was simply too difficult for most children. I
believed our lives were going well enough. I had discovered that a small town, despite its gossip, was mercifully
slow to take action against eccentrics.

At school I was quiet and competent. I lived a double
life, a triple life, did elaborate bookkeeping in my head to
separate the roles I played. I was like an actor in reper-
tory who can turn from Thursday's Shakespeare to Friday's Chekhov without missing a line. All of the while I
thought, I'm good at this, I have a gift for deception, I run
the world. I was like a pianist making blind leaps from
the middle range for low Ds. Never looking. Hitting it
right every time. Even now it sometimes seems to me I
could have kept Reynard under control if I had been
clever enough to foresee the business with the newspapers, and where it would lead us.

"Look at this!" Reynard declared one day, shoving the
morning paper under my nose. "This is the work of Communists!" African tribesmen in a remote village had been
found to possess Russian-made rifles. He ripped the offending piece from the paper, wadded it into a ball, and
carried it out into the yard. There he set fire to it, crossed
his arms, and watched it burn, making a small strawlike
patch of brown on the green grass.

My father had always fancied himself to be a keen
political observer. He read the newspaper with enthusi-

asm every day. "Democratic institutions rest on a free press." From my mother's work, he had a peripheral understanding of journalism. But his political stances were shallow and often naive. Most of all, they were ambivalent. His early years had made him aware of the tribulations of the poor, yet his profession cast him on the side of the rich. "Nothing has changed in two hundred years," he liked to say. "Esterhazy supported Haydn. Eli Lilly underwrites the symphony." He found this idea comforting and troubling, by turns. For evidence, I had not only my own experiences with him, but both of my mother's biographical manuscripts.

Reynard's peculiar politicalization had begun when he was ten or twelve, fiddling for nickels on street corners, in barber shops, and in bars, with his brother Donald, who was a year younger. They were artful dodgers, evading police officers who often could not decide whether to arrest them or turn them over to social welfare officers. Either way, they always escaped, to another street corner in another town, and then another.

"How old are you boy?"

"Sixteen."

"You don't look sixteen. You got a permit?"

"Pa went to get it. He'll be right back. I'm short for my age, from disease."

"And you there?" To Donald.

"What he said." Donald was only a fair musician. He played violin chords to Reynard's melodies, was less inventive and probably more sane. Donald followed Reynard, whom he took to be clever and a natural leader. He followed him into bedbug-ridden hotels and into bus stations. When they hitchhiked, Reynard decided which rides to refuse. When they played, Reynard always knew when to change keys, would call out all of the chords. Even in fistfights, he called out instructions to Donald.

My mother transformed this, writing, "As a youth, Reynard Cunningham traveled widely, studying, learning. For the most part, he stayed in America. He realized early that the center of the artistic world had shifted to the United States, and rarely went abroad."

The fact was that once Reynard and Donald had crossed from Detroit to Windsor. "This is another country," Reynard told his little brother. "The money's different, see?"

Donald said it looked like play money. "Let's go back, Reynard. The jails here might be bad. Awful."

Reynard said he had to get a stamp. The boys sent half of their money to their father, put half of their cash in envelopes and mailed it home. Sometimes there was a great deal of money.

I asked Reynard many times, "Tell me about your parents, my grandparents."

"They died," was all he would say. "My father bled us dry. We were foolish to send the money home."

Grace met Reynard's parents once, and had difficulty comprehending them. The second manuscript dismissed them with a single breezy sentence. In the first manuscript, the account had been scratched out and rewritten several times. The family lived in that section of southern Indiana that belonged culturally to Kentucky. Three sons had been born. The words Grace had crossed out were "enervated hillbilly English." Growing up, I sometimes saw such people drifting north through Richmount, men and women with angular bodies and pinched expressions who looked out at the world through suspicious eyes. Most often the men were silent or rowdy, as if unable to find a middle ground between the two extremes of behavior. The women were obedient. I always recognized such men and women, seeing in their faces my father's face, and my own.

Reynard's father offended Grace's humanity. Her crossed-out words revealed her frustration and her desire to soften the man, to rewrite his history—neurasthenic, hypochondriacal, powerless. He tended a small, hilly acreage without enthusiasm and played music— fiddle, banjo, and harmonica. He felt he had done well by his sons; sending them out to beg had freed them from the farm labor he himself loathed. Reynard's mother was a quiet woman. She did not inspire my own mother to eloquence. "She smiles furtively," was the best Grace could offer.

Standing on a street corner in Windsor, Ontario, both boys realized at once that their father would not trust the strange, colored Canadian bills. They changed the money, went back, and mailed it from Detroit. And kept moving.

"Officer, our mother's sick. We have to fiddle to make a little money to buy her medicine."

"You boys expect me to believe that?" Sometimes they did believe it.

"Officer, that dog's foaming at the mouth." That woman's bleeding, the drunk is vomiting, pulling a knife, going for a gun.

"Where?"

"Run, Donald!" But Donald was already on his way. They split, went in opposite directions, came together again by plan or perhaps by instinct. "Donald, let's get a cup of coffee and a piece of pie."

My mother wrote, "Traveling provided him with diverse experiences and broad understanding. These are evident in the depth he brings to his interpretation of music."

By the time he was fourteen, Reynard had taught himself and Donald to read, from newspapers, billboards, and bus schedules. "Sound it out, Donald, L-U-C-K-Y Strikes." To hone their reading skills they sometimes ordered unusual items from restaurant menus. "Give my brother and me two orders of French dressing."

"Reynard, what are we supposed to do with it?"

"Leave it. Let's go, Donald."

But my father never completely overcame his lack of education. It persisted in his poor spelling. When he launched his next letter-writing campaign, letters he wrote himself, they began, "To the Editer . . . Dere sir . . . It has come to my atention . . . connsidering events." They ended, "Yours truely."

Until he set the first fire in our backyard, my father's political enthusiasms, though keen, had seldom lasted more than a day. When he remembered his own poverty, he was a liberal. When the orchestra was applying for foundation grants, he was a conservative. He could despise minorities one day and give his support to them the next, curse the Democrats and praise the Republicans, then reverse the order. In the end, his good nature and his sweetness always returned. It was only dogs and cats that really troubled him.

"Russian guns in Africa," he growled, rubbing the small pile of ash into the ground with the toe of his shoe.

I was certain he would forget the incident within an hour. "Shouldn't you save the evidence, Reynard?" I spoke out of a memory of my mother. It always hurt Grace to dispose of newspapers and magazines. She treasured them, collected them in enormous piles, and gave them up with great reluctance.

"I burned it as an act of peaceful protest against the militarization of innocent people in Africa."

"But it has a bad feel to it. It's a little like burning books."

"No, it isn't," he said. "It isn't anything like that. Not at all." He knelt and peered at the earth as if he expected some mischief to sprout from it.

At heart, I think my father believed in magic. His early years had taught him that he had little control over his own fate. Except for his skill in evading police officers—and this was a game he and Donald frequently lost—he had no power to order his own life. The world ran according to inscrutable principles. Perhaps from boyhood he had sensed that the dark pressures in his own mind would eventually overtake him. People might play at the game of running the world, but in the end, magic prevailed.

The event that changed his life, in Toledo, when he was sixteen, had seemed magical. Afterward, even years later, he could not conceive that his life might have gone in any other direction.

"You, boy, where did you learn the Bach-Gounod Ave Maria?"

"What, mister?"

"The music you're playing. Move over here by the curb. Let the people pass."

"I heard it, mister."

"Where?"

"I don't know."

"You can hardly follow it," said Donald. "The melody doesn't move. I can hardly make a second to it."

"I hear things sometimes," said Reynard.

"What else do you play?"

"This." He knew immediately that the man meant classical music.

"That's 'Minuet in G.' Beethoven's."

"If you say so, mister."

They had begun their odyssey on foot, hitchhiking. Then they began riding buses. One sunny day in Harrisburg, they bought their first motorcycle. Eventually there were twenty-two motorcycles, but always one at a time, two boys on one motorcycle, for frugality, for compactness.

They also had a trump card, a real crowd pleaser, in the canvas bag of clothing they carried along with their instrument cases. It was a torn shirt, child-size. Usually Reynard saved it for crowds and did not waste it on a singleton, but this man seemed special. After he finished the Beethoven, Reynard rummaged through the bag of clothing strapped to the motorcycle and swept the shirt out for display. "Here, mister, see this shirt? Our brother was killed by lightning, struck down haying in the field, trying to get the hay in before the rain. Then it came, knifing out of the black sky like God's own judgment. Struck down our brother Frankie. The shape of the lightning is etched into the very fabric, a monogram of death, sir. Frankie was only twelve years old. My brother and I are trying to raise a little money to buy our brother a marker, a monument, sir; a simple tombstone, a remembrance, a memorial to our beloved brother, sir. We're a poor family. Our father is crippled and our mother takes in sewing. We use the gift of music the Lord put into our fingers, sir, and into our hearts."

The man was tall, bushy-haired, bearlike, but well turned out in a white shirt and shined shoes. He studied the shirt, the boys, the violins. "Who taught you to play?"

"We're all natural musicians, sir, by the Lord's grace. See the burns in the fabric? Smell the char of cloth and young skin?" Enough of it was true to give Reynard inspiration for these speeches, to let him feel lifted up into the oratory. A brother had died, killed by lightning. That the money was never used to purchase a tombstone was incidental. Their father had invented the act for them in the beginning. Reynard improved it with years of practice.

"You boys come with me," the man said. "There are some people I want you to meet."

"Don't go, Reynard." Donald had decided the man was a deadbeat. He had not reached for his wallet. Donald whispered, "They're probably queers."

"We'll go," Reynard told his brother. "We're not making anything here." The open violin case set out for tips was empty. "You having a party, mister? You want us to play?" Sometimes people did invite them in off the street to play for private gatherings. "You having a party, mister?"

"Don't go, Reynard."

"You running out on me, Donald?"

Donald went along, wheeling the motorcycle in the gutter beside the two figures on the sidewalk.

The man took them to a suite in a downtown hotel and presented them to the Amati String Quartet, four Italians on tour, playing Toledo. The man was their manager. He must have said, "Look what I found on the street." Everyone now spoke Italian.

The rooms seemed a wonderland to Reynard. There were instruments, music stands, the leftovers of lunch on a room service cart. These were wine sippers with large moustaches. Shiny black patent leather dress shoes were kicked about carelessly. Tailcoats waited on hangers.

Only the manager spoke English. When he had finished his preliminary remarks in Italian, he said to Reynard. "Play the Bach-Gounod." And, finally catching on, he withdrew a five-dollar bill from his wallet.

At the sight of the money, the Italians roared with laughter and took bills from their own pockets. Years later, my father enlarged on this scene: "The beggar is a universal figure, no translation is needed, and all musicians are beggars. Who, after all, requires music? It fills no basic need and so it is a beggary, even below craft and those arts that put something in the hand—a silver bowl or a rug with your initial cleverly worked in, the Lord's Prayer in needlepoint to hang on your wall. The Italians understood. They weren't looking down on us. It was just enormously funny, the juxtaposition, pulling out the money in those rooms, and in the presence of two Guadagnini violins."

Reynard played on and on for the Italians.

"Who taught you to play?" they asked, with the manager translating.

"Our father. He fiddles for barn dances, in the back country."

The Italians laughed and chattered. "They say you are another Mozart," the manager explained, "exploited by a heartless father."

The Italians played too. They put music in front of Reynard and discovered that he could not read it, but that he learned quickly by rote. They passed him one of the Guadagninis to try. As he drew the first notes from the magnificent instrument, tears leapt to Reynard's eyes, and the Italians laughed again. The first violinist rummaged through scores and found the "Ave Maria" Reynard had played.

"I recognized it at once," Reynard said later, probably exaggerating only a little. "I saw the row of measures like inches on a ruler, the beauty of the system, quarter notes beamed down into eighths, swollen to halves and wholes. I heard the silence of rests, perceived the authority of the double bar. I learned to read music in one afternoon. I could not believe how simple and logical it was!"

What did all of it mean to Donald? Perhaps he had already been polishing his own star, seeing the fruitlessness of a life spent playing violin chords. Perhaps, being more sane, he understood better than Reynard that their lives had changed and would never be the same again. When he was able to break into the rapid flow of Italian, he said, "So long, Reynard, I'm going to Omaha and get a job in the stockyards. They're hiring. I've been hearing it all over. You keep the fiddle. You can use two. I'll still send the old man some money, soon as I'm settled."

And Reynard, in flux, said, "No, we did enough. Don't send him any more money. That's over."

"I guess you're right, Reynard."

They were saying good-bye, but boys' business did not

have great importance when men were present. "So long . . . so long." It did not occur to them to say, write. Neither had ever written a letter, hadn't had a permanent address in years. They just put the money in the envelopes and addressed it home. "You take the motorcycle," said Reynard.

That evening Reynard attended the quartet's performance, standing in the wings. Afterward at the hotel, they played most of the night, in twos and threes, until it was time to catch an early train for Columbus. Reynard went along, moving in with them. He still spoke no Italian but began receiving music lessons administered through the manager's translations and by demonstrations that included explosive vocals of disapproval, hmms and ahhs when he got things right, and many gestures. He received regular food of a quality he had not known existed. This began his interest in fine food exquisitely prepared. He learned to disappear when women were brought to the rooms. He learned to be helpful in small ways, handling matters with bellboys, and to sleep in beds that had no bugs. He began to wash his hands, frequently and then compulsively, as if to wash off his disreputable past.

Sometimes the Italians took him to symphony concerts. Once they took him to the zoo. They introduced him to opera. After attending *La Traviata* or *Madame Butterfly*, the Italians sometimes spent the rest of the night singing the music in their hotel rooms, often to irate wall-pounding from other guests. Bellini's *Norma* was a great favorite. The Italians fumed because American companies presented it so rarely. When they happened on to a performance in San Francisco, it was an occasion for great celebration.

Reynard sang along. He discovered that if words were associated with music he learned them easily, memorized them automatically, it seemed. Because of this, my father could sing long passages of operas perfectly, even though he could not speak the languages in which the librettos were written. Years later, hearing him sing, I was sometimes curious enough to look up the foreign words.

"Reynard," I told him once, "that section you're singing so cheerfully actually says, 'Without my love I cannot live. I die in anguish and great pain.'"

"Really!" he exclaimed, and continued singing joyously.

The Italians introduced him to a wide spectrum of classical music. They bought him clothes, lectured him on ethics through the manager's translations, advised him to remain chaste until he was twenty-one, refused to share vulgar stories with him, had his hair cut regularly.

Into the third week, he began to miss Donald. The Italians commiserated with him. Reynard said, "I want to go to Omaha and work in the stockyards. I've always wanted to kill animals and cut them up. I'm done with the fiddle. I miss the motorcycle."

The Italians promised, without meaning it, that they would book into Omaha. "We will travel from town to town and find your brother!" they declared. "Aren't we looking every day? What else are we doing but looking for your brother? Just for your brother! He will come back."

The manager said, "You have become their mascot.

You remind them of their own children in Italy. They say their own children are lazy bums who won't practice."

The sound of Italian was beginning to grate on Reynard's nerves. "Donald won't come back," he said. "He couldn't find us."

"It is better for Donald to look for you," said the first violinist. "He has only to read the paper, learn where the quartet is playing, and come and knock on the door!" He made a fist and knocked exuberantly on a door to demonstrate what a perfect solution this was. "Your vibrato is excellent but you must work on your trill." All of his children were girls, he explained. He longed for a son.

With the delay caused by the translation, Reynard believed the knock on the door was meant as a demonstration of trilling, and that he was being told he played like a girl, an insult from an Italian.

When the matter had been fully explained, Reynard said only, "Donald won't come back."

They traveled on, Reynard looking for his brother and plunging into Wieniafski, then Sarasate, and finally Paganini. Perhaps the Italians thought this was the way Americans raised children, leaving them on street corners to be picked up by strangers. How old was this boy? Who had guardianship? Perhaps the manager, an Italian-American, invented a tale for the musicians. He was grooming Reynard for the stage and had not yet decided what to do with him.

After seven months of touring, everyone tired of the arrangement. The Italians finished their tour and wanted to go home to their own families. The manager could not find capital to finance an unknown violinist. They dropped Reynard off in Hartford, Connecticut, giving him to a violin teacher as one gives gifts at Christmas, remembrances to old friends.

"Who does this boy belong to?" the teacher asked. He was the first to raise that question. "Should I make some arrangement with the family?" He was an elderly Englishman transplanted from London to Connecticut, a Quaker with a pious but pleasant wife. A paradox, a musical Quaker. Shortly after George Fox founded the Society of Friends he banned music as frivolity. His followers were to live simply and keep silent, to worship without distraction.

My mother's scholarship, from an essay she wrote on early Quakers in Indiana, is enlightening: "Fox's distrust of music easily and quickly drew in centuries of myth holding that music, and especially the violin, was the voice of the devil. William Penn had written, 'True silence is the rest of the mind and is to the spirit what sleep is to the body, nourishment and refreshment.' Because Fox was a student of the Bible, and little else, he did not perceive that he had unwittingly annexed a form of mind control to an otherwise liberal religion. Many denominations had banned music, always with a view toward controlling the emotional life of members. Fox certainly never realized he had thrust his people into a strange and unsympathetic company. Later the Quaker interdiction, which had been against all of the arts, was lifted. Art was held to be a true expression of the Inward Light. Certain art at least—good art, better art, some art. Yet devout Quakers hedged, reluctant to make Fox uneasy in his grave. Admitting art brought with it the necessity of making judgments about it. The doctrine of silence was infinitely more comfortable. It honored Fox and also evaded the troublesome mythology, the figure of Satan with a fiddle. Only in modern times has the dilemma been resolved."

The dilemma was resolved only in my mother's essay. The teacher in Connecticut, who taught violin lessons in his living room, associated himself with no organizations nor institutions other than the local Friends Meeting, fearing that an orchestra or even a music school might draw him into the company of sinners. He was a divided and uneasy man. The thought that he might love music more than he loved God tormented him.

The quartet's manager told him, "The boy doesn't seem to have any family."

"I have a brother," said Reynard.

"Very well, then," said the teacher, who had heard Reynard play by now and probably did not wish to surrender him in any case. "My wife and I shall take him into our family." There was no other family. They became three.

They did not put him into school, perhaps for fear of raising the issue of formal guardianship with local officials, but the teacher's wife gave him books to read. When the professor was not teaching him formal harmony, his wife taught Reynard the names of birds. She taught him how to fish for shad in the Connecticut River. It was she who taught him cooking and housekeeping, the two crafts that eventually gave him greatest pleasure.

Reynard began to attend Friends Meetings. For the first time, he heard the discussions meant to solve and resolve music's joy and its beggary, its superfluity. Were they merely verbalizations of questions already in his mind, in every musician's mind? Were there circuitous connections to a father who loathed manual labor? To a beloved brother who had rejected music? In these discussions, he heard compromises proposed. Music with a solemn theme might be acceptable to God, music of an uplifting nature. Perhaps music sung without instrumental accompaniment was purer, God having made the human voice. Soft music might be better than loud, slow better than fast. Reynard, recalling this period of his life, said, "If I am unstable [from my mother's first biographical manuscript] it is because those people tormented me with religion. With their doctrine of silence, they were anything but silent. They pierced my heart, filled me with alarms. I could better deal with police on the streets, with cuffs and chases, jails and homosexuals. I never had the constitution for religion."

When Reynard was eighteen he left Connecticut. He tried a concert career, making several tours. In many cases, he returned to cities where he had played as a boy, in bars and on street corners. "And the same people were in the audiences." (The first manuscript.) "I always seemed to recognize them, always imagined they recognized me. 'There's that bum of a kid. Who does he think he is, standing up on a stage? We should ask for our money back.'" When torments like these became unbearable, he turned to teaching. Nervous instability hounded him. He slipped into symphony playing like a shy squirrel into its dark nest. My mother, a Quaker covering music for her paper (untroubled by this task, not divided as the teacher had been, but unified always in purpose and determination), found him there and married him. Because she believed a musician to be a prestigious person? In order to make him over? Simply from love? The answer does not appear in her manuscripts.

Reynard bought a car and took Grace to Niagara Falls for a honeymoon. When he stopped at gas stations to ask directions, he locked her in the car. "To keep you safe!" When they drove through rainstorms, he abandoned her in the car and sought shelter at farmhouses. "Grace, please come inside! My brother was killed by lightning!" I think my mother believed she would always be able to handle it.

When Reynard set the first fire in our back yard, the event had been years in the making.

My father had always been an enthusiastic newspaper reader. Now he became obsessed with newspapers. He ordered two additional daily papers and spent hours poring over them, ripping out offending articles and burning them. "The Communist conspiracy now controls the papers. Journalism has sold out."

"You know that isn't true," I argued. "Grace worked for a newspaper."

"Yes, it was she who kept things in balance. Without her, the others took over."

Reynard was angry—enraged—over my mother's death. Grace had been a newspaper writer. By some convolution of spirit, newspapers became the target for his rage.

I believed it would run its course. "Reynard, just put the papers in the wastebasket."

"No! They must be burned. Your mother cannot rest without it."

"But it's like censorship." Sometimes I could reason with him.

"It's limited censorship to control terrorism," he replied. The terrorists were only in his mind, the dark pressures that each day threatened his sanity with greater and greater intensity.

It was July of a hot, dry summer; one day Reynard managed to set the grass on fire. "Get the garden hose!" I cried, but he stood transfixed, watching the flames. I put out the fire easily, and that afternoon I bought a trash burner for the yard, but it solved nothing. He had begun to delight in the fire itself and began simply to burn wads of newspaper. "The whole paper is trash anyway," he declared.

Eventually, perhaps inevitably, he started a fire that spread to a neighbor's house. It was not a serious fire, but it was the end. I suspect the authorities had been quietly watching and waiting. The police arrived with the firemen. Reynard was taken across town to the state mental hospital for an evaluation, under suspicion of arson. Following the evaluation, he was not released. Until his commitment—it seems incredible to me now—Reynard had never missed an orchestra rehearsal or a performance.

When the fire truck had gone I packed a bag, taking Reynard's violin and my own. I walked out of the house on the National Road and locked the door. The police drove me to the home of a young couple who had volunteered to take me in. The following day, Edlyn was summoned. My father was declared a public charge.

5

IN THE circus, timing is crucial. The truck bearing Joe, Belle, and the butchering equipment has barely rattled out of sight when the figure of Alexander Sandler appears in the road. Working beside the window to make the most of the dim winter light, I see him step from behind a tree in the nearby orchard, heaving into view like a ship that has lain in wait. This nautical image is enforced by his sailor's coat, the cast-off garment of some Indiana naval recruit, dark serviceable wool to protect his mighty chest. Above it, he wears a fisherman's cap. He is unwilling to cover his ears, winter or summer, as if fearing some propitious sound might pass him undetected.

From a distance, the tall, sturdy figure does not look seventy. By his own account, Alexander's robust health comes from good lungs acquired through playing the trumpet and a careful diet. Selecting food with discrimination is not an easy task for a poor man, but Alexander persists with Jewish determination, and does not complain. He walks with a measured gait, as if counting something, giving me time to set his tea brewing before he reaches our drive.

"Good morning," says Alexander, looking past me to appraise the empty room. "You are alone?"

When two fine minds contend, strategies are complex and circuitous. Alexander knows quite well that Belle has gone, the purpose of her trip, and approximately how long she will be away. "All alone, and glad for your company," I offer. He removes his coat and studies the polished glass as I pour out his tea. "You shouldn't have waited in the cold. You'll get sick."

"I never get sick." He seats himself at the table and tests the scalding tea with tentative lips. "Please, continue."

I return to the fiddle neck. "What did Belle say to you?"

"What could she say that she has not already said in fifty years?"

"Something that made you wait outside until she had gone."

"When the fire is too hot, it is better to step back from the flame."

I am never sure if Alexander's solemn utterances are Jewish proverbs, Russian proverbs, or creatures of his own invention. He is our band director, a seasoned hornist who can improvise at the instant any music or rhythm a circus might require. He can match the hoofbeats of accelerating ponies or the lagging pace of reluctant elephants. He can showcase a master performer with music so modest it directs attention away from itself. He can also cover a bumbling beginner with the rich flourishes that soften a crowd's condemnation. He does not read music ("Why should I?" asks Alexander, with level, untroubled eyes), yet when his horn falls silent, his speech is pointed and unswerving. I do not think Alexander invents his proverbs. "Belle said to tell you the new flyers are Italian."

"Italian. I see." He accepts the insult—Belle's suggestion that he will require months to prepare the music for this act—with equanimity, and continues to sip his tea, a man who has seen and heard everything. Alexander was only thirteen when he came through Ellis Island, but he was tall for his age and already an experienced musician. In New York, the sounds of jazz and ragtime enticed him. Tin Pan Alley beckoned. He exchanged his old-country fiddle for a trumpet. Was it possible? A land where brass horns could be had in pawnshops for four dollars? His Yiddish melodies, garnering the music of Eastern Europe, flowed into the horn as easily as his mother's sweet butter flowed across warm bread. To these were quickly joined the new American music. He was a youthful Louis Armstrong in a round black hat, a shy Bix Beiderbecke turning down Friday gigs, a jazz trumpeter who favored minor keys.

He worked as he could, sometimes in clubs; at festivals, parties, and weddings; in cafés. Covering his inability to read music with a prodigious memory and solid improvisational skills, he sometimes found spots in pit orchestras ranging from burlesque to Broadway. Once, improbably, he was hired to play on the soundtrack of an animated cartoon. But times were not good. One day, by accident, he joined the circus. Looking for work in a snowstorm, Alexander saw a man carrying a trombone case. The man's skin was pale, his hair black as soot. Alexander took him for a Jew and followed him into the winter offices of a circus. By the time he discovered the man was an Irish Catholic who carried a missal in his trombone case, Alexander had auditioned and been hired by the circus.

He left the job in New Orleans, staying on in the city for a year. Another circus carried him as far as St. Louis. After a stint on a Mississippi cruise boat, he tried Kansas City, then Chicago. Several times, he returned to New York. Eventually, he dedicated himself to the circus. (For the mobility, he explains. For the friendship, he says with a warm smile.)

I replenish Alexander's tea and he decides that he will, after all, confide in me. "Belle says there was a stationary calliope at the Medrano circus in Paris." He looks into his glass with solemn eyes.

This, then, is the subject of the debate Belle was prepared to continue when a dead horse intervened. "And was there?"

"I wouldn't know about the Medrano." The question vexes Alexander and he dismisses it. "She has no need to imagine the past," he says, growing heated. "The facts are enough. The true past. The first time I saw her in New York, I thought an angel had flown out of heaven! I was barely twenty, a stupid boy from Russia. What did I know? But I knew rhythm. She always went a little too long, a little too far, because it pulled the crowd to her. Oh, she was vain! She sent a terrible fear into them! Then, when her hands found the catcher, she took back the fear. She gave the people back their hearts!" He pauses to remember it, smiling out into the room at a picture only he can see. "And they loved her for it! She swept them all to the brink of the abyss and then, with those little hands, saved them from hell! She owned every crowd she ever played. Later, I would know she did it every time."

He pauses while I add wood to the waning coals in the stove.

"But that first time! I knew only that she was not on her beat. I had been in many circus bands already. I had seen flyers, many flyers. They must fall into the net first on their backs. But at the angle her body took, and at her speed! She would have torn through the net like a knife. I saw her dead on the ground! It was as real as that fiddle in your hands. Do not cut away any more wood. The neck will be too loose."

"I can shim it if I have to."

"A shim might not hold when you pull up the strings," says Alexander.

"See? It fits."

"My mouth went dry," he continues, "I could not play. I laid down the horn. Afterward, I went to her dressing room. I wanted to touch her, to know that she was still alive."

I paint the stub of the neck with warm glue and set it in place. "Will you hold this while I put on the clamps?"

"She was as beautiful standing on the ground as flying! All flyers are beautiful in the air, but Belle was beautiful standing on solid ground. I only touched her hands." He studies the fiddle he is holding with a rueful smile.

I tighten the clamps thoughtfully. We have reached

the part of the story that is never told, neither by Belle nor Alexander. There are two possible scenarios, both plausible. Belle had four powerfully built brothers who drove off suitors. Indeed, it was often a brother, hanging from a swing, who caught her. I know from the accounts of other circus veterans that the brothers turned away men in every major city in Europe and America. Included in this number were noblemen and sons of wealthy families. Flowers and even jewelry were thrown into the faces of these presumptuous suitors. In addition to being protective, the brothers were devout. They prayed with rosaries before each performance. It is not difficult to imagine their scorn for an infidel, a Jew, a trumpet player.

But living with the circus, with its tricks and illusions, has taught me to be cautious of all easy answers. It is just as plausible to picture the Belle of the faded posters, fearless before heights and crowds, standing tentative and afraid before this son of Israel, who will transgress no law, make no league with the inhabitants of strange lands. Were the hands that touched her with such wonder the only hands ever to turn her away? "Thank you, Alexander. I'll take it now."

He wipes traces of glue from his fingers with a scrap of newspaper. Then, as if to confirm my speculations, he steps to the sink and scrubs his hands vigorously with soap. This glue is made from dead horses.

Neither Belle nor Alexander ever married. All that remains of their past is this shifting debate that cannot be won, this question that can never be answered. They are completely devoted to each other, and to contention. They will spend their last days together. With his skills,

Alexander might yet work in clubs, cozy in a warm city apartment free of animal smells, but he will not leave Belle.

"I doubt the Medrano in Paris had a calliope," he resumes. "The Medrano, although I never saw it, was a foolish concept. A circus in a building, with carpets on the floor, ladies in gowns and men in evening wear. Is that a circus? I think a calliope would have been too rowdy for their taste."

In the traditional American circus, the calliope was pulled at the end of street parades. It was also played outside the tent to warm up crowds and draw in customers. Inside the tent, the concert band played. The calliope was too loud to be played in combination with other instruments.

To enhance the display barn, the founders of our circus museum wrenched our vintage calliope from its aging wheels and gave it its gilded, baroque mounting, making it an artifact among artifacts. Alexander favors returning it to its mobile mode so it can be pulled from the barn to sit before the tent at showtime. His arguments are authenticity and pageantry. "No real circus," he tells me now, "would hang a calliope on a wall. And the sight of a circus wagon always brings excitement."

This polemic of Alexander's is emblematic. He is a traveling man who finds motion superior to stasis. This is an article of his faith that functions in every situation and on any scale, even to sending our calliope rolling the fifty yards from the barn to the tent and back again. "Consider this," I challenge, "the calliope is nearly a hundred years old. It might not survive another carpentry job. The last workmen virtually enclosed the mechanism. We have no idea how fragile the guts of the instrument may be."

Alexander's laughter booms like a shot in the small room. "Look at this girl who is talking!" he cries, his voice blending felicity and triumph, reprimanding me with a velvet touch. "Norma, what do you have in your hands? What do you do all day but make old instruments new again?"

"This is a wooden fiddle. The rust and corrosion of metal are something else entirely."

"I can tell you were never a poor child in Russia," he declares, undeterred. "Americans do not understand real poverty, where everything must be made over and used again, sometimes for generations."

"Alexander, whenever you think you are in danger of losing an argument, you cry poverty and fall back on Russia. That isn't fair."

But my petulance only evokes more laughter. Clearly, Alexander does not believe he is in danger of losing anything. In fact, I am not his chief adversary in the calliope debate. That honor belongs to Belle. She favors permanence. She has had enough wheels beneath her. Her nesting impulse, so long deferred, has reached its full flower in this setting: in this house, in Monumenta's shed, in the great hall of the museum barn. The hall is her drawing room, her royal court. It features, like a throne, the stationary calliope. With consummate generosity, she has made me her royal princess.

"Will you have more tea?"

"Thank you, no." I discover now that Alexander has not come about the calliope at all, but with European courtesy he has saved his business until my work is finished. "Norma, I want you to come and hear a young man I am thinking of hiring for the band. His name is Rick Ross and he lives here in town. Daviso and Mike will be here soon. We want you to come with us."

Our concert band consists of Alexander leading on trumpet, Danny Brundage, our eighty-one-year-old drummer, and the Calabria brothers, Daviso and Mike, who play all brasses. "What instrument does he play?"

"Most of them. He is very bright. He would give us a little new blood."

"If he suits you, he will certainly suit me."

"But I am an old man," Alexander pleads. "The boy is nineteen, about your age. Will you not speak as my representative?"

Alexander is a seasoned performer. I do not suspect for a moment how carefully he has phrased this entreaty. "Of course. I'll be glad to come along."

By the time I have put away my tools and banked the fire, Daviso and Mike Calabria have arrived in their ancient station wagon, its back loaded with instruments. Daviso, seventy-two and the eldest by a year, blows the car horn urgently and waves to us. Beneath his huge head of white hair, his smile is merry. Before we are in the car, he is already telling us how much he won playing poker the previous night, in the back room of a local tavern. "Fourteen dollars on a two-dollar bet!" he cries.

"And most of it honest!" says Mike beside him, an only slightly smaller and younger version of all this Italian animation.

"Honest!" scoffs Daviso. "Of course it was honest! What need have I to cheat with such simpletons?"

"He has a rubber face!" says Mike, who is really delighted with his brother's success. "Do you call a rubber face honest?"

The station wagon coughs twice and then leaps backward, carrying us swiftly into the road and beyond it. "Christ in a manger!" cries Mike to his brother. "You are a blind old man! Let me drive." But they are both thrilled with all this speed. Daviso shifts, turns, and sends us hurtling down the road in great ragged lunges.

The Calabrias worked their way into the circus gradually, beginning at the periphery. As young men in Italy, they ran a shell game, taking turns playing the shill, at the edges of circuses. When their trusting customers could not put up money, Daviso and Mike encouraged barter. They amassed piles of pocketknives, watches, and finger rings. One day, improbably, a customer handed over a cornet. ("I played it at once!" Daviso boasts. "On the first blow!" "But I played it *before* you!" his brother insists.) It seems safe to assume that brotherly competition drove them to practice, that their already clever fingers put them ahead of the game. Their observant eyes did the rest. ("We saw the men in circus bands getting drunk on the bandstand," explains Mike. "So," adds Daviso, "we got jobs by betting. We said, 'If we play well and stay sober, you pay us double. If we play bad or get drunk, we pay *you* the same amount!'") Sobriety during working hours and growing musical skills carried the brothers out of Italy to Germany, to France, and eventually to England, where they joined a touring American circus. ("You paid good money for a boat ticket!" they chide Alexander."We rode free! Guests of the circus!") The years have taken their toll on the Calabrias' blowing lips. They acknowledge they cannot match Alexander's playing. But their agile fingers have lost none of their dexterity. Only the state's gambling laws prevent them from practicing their original trade. In their pasts are wives and children, seemingly prodigious numbers of both, but they are rarely mentioned. The brothers began together and they remain together.

Rick Ross opens his door to us with a smile. He is a slight, quick youth, with dark hair and splendid forceful eyes. His size makes him appear younger than his age. When he has turned away to lead us down his basement stairs, I find myself remembering his pliant mouth. His lips do not have the subtle muscularity of a horn player's. Something is wrong here. Then understanding comes in a rush, from all directions: Alexander is chatting easily with this boy, he requires no spokesman; Danny Brundage, our drummer, has not accompanied us; and at the foot of the stairs, prominently displayed, is a set of drums.

Alexander moves swiftly into the breach. "Rick plays many instruments," he declares. He sweeps one arm to draw my attention to a dusty clarinet lying on a shelf, a saxophone abandoned on a far chair. "Even this piano!" He offers a hopeful smile and two gesturing arms, as if the sight of the piano will buy my goodwill.

"But he is mostly a drummer," I murmur. "You deliberately misled me. You and the Calabrias . . . you're planning to fire Danny."

"Only to retire him," Alexander says quietly, eyes pleading for understanding. "Norma, he is eighty-one. He can barely hear."

"Belle will be furious. Danny Brundage has been Belle's friend and colleague for years."

"That is why you must speak to her. First, listen to Rick play. You will see what I mean. Then you must make Belle understand. You are a musician and a woman."

"And that is the sort of representative I am to be?"

But Alexander can scarcely give me his attention now. The Calabrias are carrying in instruments. Rick has seated himself behind his drums. A rock rhythm ignites all of the space around us: a hot hiss on the ride cymbal; the tight rattle of the backbeat on the snare; *pop, pop, pop,* on the tom.

"Listen, Norma!" Alexander commands, joy creeping into his voice and across his face as he takes out his horn. He loves this rustle of preparation, the snapping of latches on instrument cases, the way Daviso frowns and wets his lips before raising a trombone to his mouth, the blast of the single note Mike blows and then overblows on a cornet.

"Give me the phrase again!" Alexander calls to the drummer, and I am forgotten. Rick turns to the piano and plays four tones, pitches without tempo. Alexander acknowledges his cue with a quick nod. He raises his trumpet with his right hand; with his left, he salutes the drummer with three curt tempo sweeps. Then out of his horn lurch the syncopations of rock and roll, complete with ornaments to fill the long, sensuous ties. Rick leans to the tom, sets the full-throated bass pulsing, working beat for beat with total accuracy.

Daviso ventures tentative notes, then finds his confidence in time to solo off on the chorus. In the respite provided by the trombone, Alexander drops his horn from his lips and calls to Rick, "Stay with four! I will be back!" The trumpet tails in on the last notes of Daviso's solo and the melody is carried off to Russia in a cascading minor wail. The tempo is violated, ravished, pummeled to the point of extinction.

"Still four!" cries Mike to the drummer with a reassuring smile. He is dropping oil into a recalcitrant cornet valve.

Alexander, as promised, returns to four, but the drummer is troubled. "Again!" Rick orders. The boy's voice is that of a full participant. How long has this been going on?

Alexander complies, but cannot resist pulling the music south into Rumania. Mike's cornet enters in counterpoint. Recognizing Gypsies, Daviso finds a Romany air. But, argues the trumpet, these are not Gypsies after all. They are Yiddish folk in bangled trappings, slipping past in disguise. Daviso's molto rubato is hurried into a hora. But Mike spots a countryman in this melange; the cornet offers a gloss on Verdi, urging the travelers westward to Italy, offering sunny delights. The drums hold now to a confident four. Then the trumpet screams in triumph and the rock tune is brought safely home, intact and unharmed.

When they have fallen silent, Alexander turns to me with an exuberant smile. "So?"

But it is only a courtesy question, old-world good manners. He knows he has won. The boy is quick as lightning to learn, a strong talent with keen intelligence. I have never heard our band sound this fine. "Belle will never forgive you."

"I know," he sighs. "I know."

"Danny Brundage was drumming for her when her

brother fell, when he died. She has always said except for Danny's encouragement she would have quit for good."

"Yes, Norma. I was there." But he has already finished with this conversation. His eyes dart from me back to the young man who has enthralled him.

"Alexander?" the boy calls impatiently. "Here is the other one!" At the piano, he produces a darker, more complex pattern of tones.

"Yes!" Alexander calls back. "Again, Rick. Again, please!"

The deed has been done beyond recall. It is plainly Alexander's work, yet it occurs to me this is really a Calabria-style enterprise. Two for one. Alexander has secured a first-class drummer and also found entrée into the world of rock music. His efficiency is impressive. "I'll walk back, Alexander."

"And you'll speak to Belle for me?"

"I don't know. I really don't know."

As I climb the stairs, I hear the trumpet following the piano, searching out the shadowy path. Then comes a burst of sunshine, of confidence, as the broad highway is discovered. Alexander's wheels are rolling. "Again!" he commands. The piano fades out and the drums begin.

6

MY FOSTER parents were Michael December, whom everyone called Mitch, and his Japanese wife Schutzie; a young couple with no children of their own. Mitch was an attorney known for his willingness to accept indigent clients without pay. Grace, looking for colorful and eccentric subjects for her column, had found herself involved with Mitch's clients more than once. He also worked without charge for peace groups. From time to time, Pendle students organized and demonstrated. Then Grace and Mitch had found themselves standing side by side, looking on. They were casual friends.

"Your aunt Edlyn will be here soon," Mitch said, greeting me at the door of his small house on D Street. The police officer set my suitcase on the porch, touched his cap, and departed. "But you're welcome to stay with us as long as you like."

"You're very generous," I replied, but I entered the December home with a divided mind. I resisted becoming one of Mitch's causes. In the past year he had defended in court an American Indian family living in a tent and a welfare mother with two sickly babies. I wondered what had ultimately become of these people, and how Mitch saw me in relation to them. I wanted only to get Reynard out of the hospital and go home. Until now, I had escaped pity, and I did not want Mitch's. At the same time, I was fascinated at the prospect of living in a conventional home.

"Put everything in the little bedroom," Schutzie said. "It is all ready, everything." She smiled at me and tugged at Mitch's sleeve to hurry him, a gesture of hospitality.

"We hope you'll be comfortable," Mitch said. He was a thick blond young man. In spite of this there was a lightness about him, as if, put on a scale, he would weigh surprisingly little. "Call us Mitch and Schutzie."

"Thank you," I said.

A baby would have been the proper age for a child in this home. A teenager probably seemed an adult to them, and they treated me as one. Still Schutzie and Mitch were good custodians for me, fair-minded, courteous, and gentle.

Schutzie was only a little older than me, perhaps nineteen. She was small, pretty, and always pleased. She liked the way her clothes fit around her small body and glanced up at herself whenever she passed a mirror. She liked the way peelings came off apples, the way bread fell apart when she sliced it. She clucked small sounds of approval at the food as she cooked. She liked the way fresh towels fell across towel bars and sometimes stood stroking them into perfect alignment, murmuring gently.

"Here is dinner," Schutzie said that first evening. Awkward phrases and traces of an accent lingered in her speech. Sometimes her word combinations were nearly unintelligible. At other times, inexplicably and without warning, perfect and precise sentences rippled from her lips without apparent effort. She seemed to have no control at all over this phenomenon, and the subject of correct English usage did not interest her at all. "Here is broccoli."

"Would you like some broccoli, Ada?" Mitch asked, as if translating.

"Here is meat loaf."

"Would you like some meat loaf, Ada? I'm sure we'll get a call from your aunt this evening."

"Or you can stay here," said Schutzie.

Neither alternative appealed to me. "I think my father will be well soon, and I'll just be going back home."

Edlyn was really little more than a vague memory to me. She had not visited us since my mother's funeral. At Christmas she sent me gifts. Otherwise, Reynard and I had not heard from her. The idea of her sweeping into our lives and perhaps carrying me off to live with her in Chicago held no appeal for me. As the days passed without word from her, I felt relief. Each day, I believed, provided a little more time for my father to recover. Two years later, when Edlyn filed her custody suit, Mitch was to say, "If this woman really cared about the child, why did she not appear when Reynard Cunningham was hospitalized and his daughter was without home or family?" But, at the beginning, such thoughts did not occur to us.

"Here is pie," said Schutzie.

"Do you think I could take Reynard his violin?" I asked.

Mitch looked dubious. "A hospital might not be the safest place for a valuable instrument."

"It's not valuable," I replied. "We've never been able to afford good fiddles. Only gourds."

"Gourds?" Schutzie asked.

"Inexpensive instruments," Mitch translated.

"Junk," I said.

Dutifully, Mitch delivered Reynard's violin to the hospital the following morning.

I settled in, and except for Edlyn, I would probably still be in the Decembers' small house; shabby stucco, roof gabled like a fairy cottage, tiny yard strewn with prickly yews, one gently rising cedar where a brave cardinal sat all winter, alert and patient, keeping watch over the house. I still think of the bird, whistling in the cedar like some disembodied oboe. Across D Street was Pendle College, aging but, to me, lovely and enduring, with its wide winding walks, stone and brick, and splashes of white clapboard. But the cardinal never looked in that direction. He belonged to the little house.

In the two years I lived with the Decembers, I never learned to pronounce Schutzie's name properly. She would say it for me over and over again with a wide, hopeful smile, but I never mastered the elusive, melodic syllables.

Equally unclear was the story of how Mitch and Schutzie had met. Mitch, a pacifist, had spent a year working on a project called the Politics of Peace. During this period he met and married Schutzie. There were refugees in the account, and all of it had happened in Minneapolis. Mitch preferred not to speak of this period. His efforts had come to nothing, and he had lost a year's income into the bargain. The account Schutzie gave was all but incomprehensible.

So I had a place to live. "Have a pleasant stay with these people," Reynard said when I began to visit him at the hospital. "I'll soon be able to come home and look after you."

"Yes," I said, "I will." I told him nothing about Edlyn and he did not mention her.

Schutzie liked me in the same way she liked the plaid woolen vest that nipped down over her flared skirts, as she liked the bright ivy that spilled over its pot in the dining room window and glimmered silver and white in the morning sun. We were comfortable together.

And Mitch was agreeable. I was not the only rare object in his collection. He owned an elaborate chess set carved from jade. It may have come to him through Schutzie's family because all of the pieces were designed as oriental warriors, ornate and highly detailed. Mitch and I played chess sitting on the floor before the fireplace. He played keenly, ferociously. In broad daylight, he was a plump, pleasant man, but in the firelight he was a solemn warlord despoiling the East with bloodthirsty cunning.

There was yet another Mitch. Besides our interest in chess, the two of us had another quality in common. Neither of us slept well. My weak leg had begun to trouble me more and more, especially at night. The only remedy for the ache was to get up and walk. Many times, Mitch was up too. On these occasions, we rarely spoke. I walked back and forth in the upstairs hall in the dark, and Mitch slumped on a small cane chair by the hall window, gazing out at the sky above the rooftops. The little window was round and set at the edges with small pieces of colored glass. Schutzie had placed a lacquered table beside it and set a crystal vase of silk flowers on it. The result of all this—vase, table, and flowers—was that she had created a small altar.

The window was magical. In the dark hallway, as I watched Mitch half crouched in the chair, with moonlight spilling over his head, his pajamas, and his big white bare feet, waiting for something that was not quite part of him to carry out some transformation, I too could believe in magic.

But in the morning, all of the magic would be undone. Schutzie would be smiling, eternally smiling, everywhere spilling smiles like orange shellac, and Mitch would lather up his face and shave off all of the little prickles of moonlight. Then he would kiss Schutzie and go off to his office.

I loved the little house on D Street. When Mitch and Schutzie married, they bought and restored it, but Mitch's projects seldom worked out well. He lined one wall of the living room with bookshelves, using fir instead of pine lumber, or something better. This meant the shelves did not finish off well. They splintered out when Schutzie tried to dust them and eventually warped. Even the good fiddle varnish I put on them when I lived in the house did not help. The lines of books appeared to march up and down little hills.

None of this alarmed Schutzie. Although she read little herself, she had arranged all of the books in alphabetical

order by author. On warm summer afternoons she sometimes sat on the couch opposite the books, smiling, sipping lemonade, and watching Faulkner titles march up a
little hill to meet Flaubert titles.

The old Victorian staircase had been painted white.
Mitch restored it by removing the paint, but he did not
clean out the tough old pigment at the base of each
banister dowel. Each still carried a little collar of ancient
white peeping through the varnish.

In the bedrooms he painted over the old wallpaper,
which soon loosened and billowed out from the walls in
large, pastel bubbles. As I lay in bed, islands and peninsu-
las swelled out at me from the walls and ceiling like
Atlantis rising from the sea.

Mitch had seeded the small yard with prairie grass, but
the old yews shaded out most of it. Still, bromegrass and
barley persisted in clumps here and there. The entire
place had the character of a tree house.

I was not surprised when Edlyn failed to appear, since
her interest in us had been so slight in the past, but this
situation disturbed Mitch and Schutzie. The house was
small, and one morning, standing in the upper hall, I
overheard them talking.

"What kind of person can she be?" Mitch asked his
wife. "She won't even make a trip down to see the girl.
She won't return my phone calls. A letter from her secretary says she assumes financial responsibility."

"Here is a home for Ada," said Schutzie. "If the woman
does not want her, then she should not go there. It is not
good to live with someone who does not want you. And
here she can visit her father. You sent the woman's

money back. We keep that up. Better not to take her money."

"It's an act of outright rejection," Mitch said, "and the girl's been through so much already. We need to do something to let her know we care about her, that *somebody* cares."

"We do it every day," said Schutzie. "We can do more things. We will do a lot of things for her."

"I mean something concrete. Right now she's a ward of the court. I'm going to ask for permanent custody."

What interested me most about the exchange was learning I had been made a ward of the court. No one had told me.

That evening, painfully, Mitch explained it to me. "Your aunt Edlyn isn't able to come. She's very concerned about you, but she isn't able to come down here right now. She wants you to know that if there's anything you want . . . financially . . . she'll provide it."

I felt relief. "There isn't anything I want."

Mitch and Schutzie were granted custody of me. Edlyn was formally notified and made no objection. Our house on the National Road, which had been standing empty, was rented out to Pendle students, and the Decembers agreed to accept the rent as a support payment. They made space in their small living room and our piano was moved to the house on D Street. "We'll just have to move it back again," I said. I still believed Reynard would recover and we would be able to return home.

But Reynard showed little interest in coming home.

"Jesus is a patient here," he said to me when I visited

him one afternoon. "He sees the problem with the newspapers."

We were in the dayroom, a large, elongated hall where patients received visitors and carried out a variety of activities—card and checker playing, knitting, television viewing. Tables and chairs, sofas and footstools were set in conversational groupings. The walls had been painted bright yellow. Despite these attempts at cheerfulness, the room was grim. There were always patients roaming aimlessly. While many were fully dressed, others were in bathrobes. Some appeared catatonic and sat staring into space. There was a variety of odors, sometimes faint but other times pervasive; cleaners and disinfectants, stale food, urine. Somehow, Reynard still managed to wear a suit and white shirt. He was also permitted a belt and necktie. I wondered if these were rewards for good behavior. He said, "We call him Jay here."

"Who?"

"Jesus. He's helping me with the Communist thing. He doesn't like the godless aspect."

"You have to get well so we can move back home."

"Yes, I'll leave just as soon as my work here is finished. With Jay's help, it's progressing nicely. Very nicely. He has explained to me that vengeance is sometimes necessary. He's much more pragmatic than most people realize. Take the cleanliness here, for example, or the lack of it. Jay says we must tolerate it for the good of the cause. He gets right into things."

"What do you have there, Reynard?"

"It's nothing," he said, "just a scrap of cloth."

I soon learned that patient networks could produce almost anything that was wanted. I never understood where the things came from. What Reynard had was a piece of black velvet a yard square. He also had a large box full of marbles. He spread the cloth on a table and laid the marbles out on it carefully. "This is Beethoven," he said.

Beethoven was a large, perfectly transparent amber marble. All of the marbles were named for composers. Sarasate was smaller, bright blue with a smoky trail of white running through it. Schubert was bright red for melody, Wagner a deeper red for fire. Mozart was royal purple. The marbles and the black velvet were a complex game requiring clever strategy. Principles of astronomy were involved. The arrangement of the marbles influenced events in the outside world. "You know Jesus isn't here," I said.

"But of course he is!"

"Where?"

"He's just gone down the hall to go to the bathroom."

"You have to get well so we can go home."

"Of course. Grace, the next time you come, bring me my gray necktie with the little flecks of red in it."

"Why?"

"I'm going to give a recital next week, all Bach. But informal dress. I'll tell them at the box office to let you in without a ticket."

"What does Jesus talk about?"

"He likes music. He's keen on Mendelssohn, especially the second movement of the violin concerto." Reynard was permitted to have his violin. He now took it up and played a bit of the Mendelssohn. A few patients looked on curiously. Most continued to roam and stare. A tiny woman with white hair clapped her hands rhythmically until the music ended.

"Ada," Reynard whispered. He laid down the violin and drew me close. "You know I haven't always been a deeply religious man. Until I got into this work I thought . . . Well, if you see Jay, just don't mention that part of it."

"All right. Why does Jesus spend so much time in the bathroom?"

"I don't ask," Reynard replied.

In the fall, I returned to school. I had never had a real place there. My mother had always made it clear that my school attendance was a mere formality, that I was being educated at home. Teachers treated me with deference. Other students, unimpressed with my reputation as a prodigy, perhaps seeing this fraud for what it actually was, did not seek my friendship. Despite Grace's death, I gained little sympathy from my peers. My lame leg, the coarse plain features of my face—its natural expression in repose a crimped gawk, the glare of the spy, the peer of the eccentric—were enough to continue my isolation. Stories of my insane father now completed the picture. I did not care. Grace had been my friend. In many ways, Schutzie had taken her place. I did not feel lonely.

I continued my job at the Presbyterian church, giving most of my pay to Schutzie.

"We don't expect you to pay anything," Mitch assured me.

But living in the December home, I had quickly discovered that Mitch's law practice was not lucrative.

"Contributing a bit makes me feel like part of the family." Mitch smiled uneasily, and at last nodded.

But after this conversation, I gave the money to Schutzie quietly and on the side.

Reynard's old repair customers drifted back. "My father isn't here but he can certainly set a sound post. You can leave the violin with me."

"I'd be very grateful. When I went to the house, your tenants said to try here, that you might know. I did hate the thought of driving to Indianapolis just to have a sound post set." Loose pegs, opening joints, new bridges, bows requiring new hair.

It seemed to me that repairing instruments would be the perfect occupation for Reynard in the hospital. He was a fine craftsman, an artist with his micrometer, his tiny chisels, his doll-like glue spatulas. "Come back on Tuesday."

I went back to the house on the National Road, where our personal belongings had been shoved into the attic. "I'd like to get my father's tools." The students renting our house were a young married couple with a baby. They had conscientiously covered our worn upholstery with sheets of transparent plastic. Our own slipcovers—Grace's old drapes faded nearly white—showed through this crackly gift wrap like antique weavings preserved under glass, shabby discards that had been assigned new value. Seeing another family in our house was unsettling; looking at our old couch made me a little dizzy.

"We never expected to find a completely furnished house," said the wife, "and it's such a pleasant place." They were at Pendle College, preparing to be missionaries in Southeast Asia. Books and tapes of Asiatic languages were stacked on every available surface and in mounds on the floor. These reminded me of Grace's piles of books. The baby crawled on the bright linoleum of the sun porch, drooling and chuckling, a perfect white and silver child in the slanting sunlight. A rocking horse occupied the spot where our piano had stood. I watched the child crawl to it and pull himself up with his perfect arms and legs. "I'm reading the books your mother wrote," the woman said, "and enjoying them." She offered this like a gift. The little boy's eyes found my face and lingered for a moment. We exchanged some silent acknowledgment about the weather in this house. But this baby was filled with platitudes, drool and shimmer. There was nothing useful I could pass on to him. Not to a child like this. I took the tools and fled.

But the hospital would not permit Reynard to have his tools. A nurse examined the little chisels and shook her head, ran her finger along the slender sound-post-setting tool with real anxiety. "It's almost like an ice pick."

"No, it isn't. It isn't anything like an ice pick."

I set the sound post myself, charged the man four dollars, and shoved the box of tools and Reynard's blueprints under my bed. The next day I returned to the old house and collected the rest of my father's workshop— the box of wood sheets, the fiddle necks and bridges, the hanks of bow hair, the gluing clamps, his small library of repair manuals, even the tiny bag of spruce sawdust he used as filler. I set up a card table in my bedroom, and Mitch provided me with a heavy sheet of plywood to use as a cutting board.

My income was not impressive but there were now

extra dollars flowing through the household. Schutzie accepted the money with undisguised gratitude.

"Here is seafood casserole," she said shortly. "Lobster, crab, the works."

"We haven't had this in months!" Mitch declared. He ate happily, and if he really grasped what was happening, he chose not to comment.

"Here is roast beef! Good cut!"

That winter, four of Reynard's students asked me to continue their lessons. A mother said, "I believe you were doing quite a bit of the teaching anyway."

Whether they came out of charity to me or from a sincere desire to learn the violin, I could not tell. I accepted them, and their money. "It's nice to see you again. Please bring to the first lesson the last music you were playing." My earnings became almost respectable.

Schutzie bought a replacement for her ancient electric mixer. It included a complete set of modern attachments. "Chop and grind!" she exclaimed. "Knead bread dough! Milk shaker!" She examined each attachment with deep satisfaction. "For this, Ada, I sew you dresses. Fair trade!"

Under Schutzie's clever and thrifty needle, my wardrobe blossomed. Schoolmates who had never envied me my looks, my crippled limbs, my eccentric family, suddenly envied me my clothes. "Stop, Schutzie," I pleaded. "You're overwhelming my natural beauty. I'm a very simple person."

"What is 'overwhelm'? Too big?"

"No, too many!" My closet bulged, bristled, bellied. Dresses elbowed slacks, skirts crushed blazers and topped stacks of blouses. Schutzie even sewed fancy underwear. "Mercy!" I cried.

Schutzie burst into frantic laughter. She shook and shimmied until tears coursed down her cheeks. Then, sniffling and wiping her nose, she said, "Kiddo, don't worry. Because no waste, no extravagance. Most stuff come from Goodwill. I start with that, take apart, cut over. I got maybe a hundred dollars in the whole shebang. Shebang?"

"Yes, shebang."

"You play fiddle, I fiddle with needle. You just gotta know how. We both know our stuff. Stuff?"

"Stuff."

"We partners. We businessmen. You like lamb chop for supper?"

One day a musician from a country band appeared at the door carrying the pieces of a bass viol in a large, galvanized tub. "I rolled my Volkswagen and the bass was strapped on top. It's a valuable instrument."

"Two hundred dollars," I told him, "and three weeks. All work guaranteed."

Before the man was off the porch, Schutzie was dancing a jig in the kitchen, lifting her skirt and clicking her heels. "We rich, kiddo! Helluva thing, we rich! 'Scuse my French!"

The Decembers had become my closest friends. They gave me sanctuary, and it was more than just room and board. They went out of their way to avoid the pity I had feared.

7

MITCH AND Schutzie respected my fantasies about my father. "Here is Ada! Back from the hospital! Is your father better today?"

"Much better! I think we'll both be back home soon."

"Mitch, did you hear? Ada will be going home with her father soon."

"Yes! Schutzie and I are certainly going to miss you."

The state hospital where Reynard was confined was an enlightened institution. Patient mail, both incoming and outgoing, was not censored. When I had been with Mitch and Schutzie almost two years, Reynard began writing letters. At first, they were harmless, letters to editors of newspapers and magazines. Often the letters were completely rational. Occasionally, one was published in the local paper. Then they became an embarrassment, threatening letters to former students, political tirades sent to local citizens. Mitch, who watched over all of us, asked that Reynard not be permitted to buy stamps. I had been giving my father spending money. I gave it now to a nurse, to parcel out only for approved purchases. But both Mitch's efforts and mine were futile. The patient underground could supply Reynard with everything he wanted. It was at this time that he began writing to Edlyn. Sometimes I saw the letters and was able to intercept them. Many others got through. Reynard accused her of all sorts of criminal activity, but especially of dishonest dealings in real estate. His campaign against newspapers and Communists virtually ceased. Edlyn became his target.

The first I knew of the letters was when I visited him in October. "I want a subscription to a Chicago newspaper," he announced. "I can't always get it here, not every day. The patient who had the subscription died. That's significant, isn't it? Sinister."

"Why do you want a Chicago paper? You hate newspapers."

"Nonsense. Democratic institutions rest on a free press. And, it's all coming to a head, the Chicago business."

"What Chicago business?"

"Real estate. It's time to pull the rug out from under Edlyn."

"Why Edlyn?"

"Because she's the one who put me in here, to shut me up. It's all in the papers hidden at home in the attic, but I remember most of it. I remember enough. All of her dishonest deals. She and her unscrupulous friends."

"There's nothing hidden in the attic, Reynard."

"I've been writing to her. You'll see. Just get the Chicago paper. I don't want to miss any of it when it starts. There are hints already, in the back pages, but soon it will be front page news. I only wish your mother were alive to see it happen."

I ignored Reynard's request, but somehow he managed to get daily delivery of a Chicago newspaper.

Actually, I was glad he had chosen to write to Edlyn rather than to outsiders. She, of all people, knew his condition and would disregard the letters. It would keep the problem in the family.

Mitch agreed. I heard him tell Shutzie, "Miss Simmons has ignored everything else. She will ignore this."

So it came as a complete surprise when Edlyn telephoned a few days before Thanksgiving. "Everything is arranged," she said to me—and to Mitch, who had picked up the telephone extension. "I'm coming to spend Thanksgiving with you, Ada. Your father is better, and they tell me he can have a furlough from the hospital if he is supervised. The students in your house are going away for the holiday, so it will be empty. The three of us can spend Thanksgiving together, in your old home."

We were all delighted, Mitch and Schutzie because Edlyn's appearance would, they were certain, restore some of my family feeling; I because I was going home with my father.

"But we should have thought of a furlough," Mitch said.

"Mitch," said Schutzie, "you should have thought of that. Mr. Cunningham could have come here."

Later, we learned that the granting of the furlough

had not been an easy matter. Edlyn had pressured, even threatened hospital personnel.

"Tell me about your aunt," said Schutzie. She was rubbing lemon oil on the piano. This was a vigorous, juicy, drippy enterprise. I believe her overzealous care of my piano was part of her effort to make me feel welcome in her home. Schutzie was enormously generous. If she could have polished *me* with lemon oil to demonstrate her hospitality she would have done so, like giving earnest money. "Your aunt tall, short, fat, thin? Your mother good-looking. Like you!" Schutzie could say this with a completely straight face. "Only difference your mother light hair. So she sister also?"

"Not the keyboard, Schutzie. Just the wood, not the ivories. I'll do the keys with a damp cloth. You don't put oil on the keys. Besides, the keys aren't dirty. Nothing is. Stop, Schutzie. Everything's beautiful already."

"I know. We gotta save the elephants. We probably gonna go to jail but we don't care."

We had been over it again and again. Schutzie liked stories, asked to have jokes told over again, plotted to trap people into endless repetitions.

"It is now illegal to put real ivory on piano keys," I began.

"Sure! How you like it hunters cut off *your* trunks?"

"Tusks. But if the ivory is already there from years ago, it's all right. Perfectly legal. It's an old piano."

"But we move it here. Like a new owner. You sell a car, you may lose warranty. Mitch told me that. They probably gonna arrest us anyway, so I clean the keys. You wanna take all the burden on yourself. We share. Your aunt good-looking?"

Schutzie was not as confused as she pretended to be. She was baiting me. To her, ivory was either right or wrong. She could not abide equivocation. Her moral world was as black and white as the keys of my piano. I always thought Schutzie, not Mitch, should have gone to law school. Her grasp of the law was much keener. "Ada, you fix instruments all the time. Easy to fix this. Take this stuff off, put on plastic." Her sympathies were entirely with the elephants. "You think I won't go to jail with you, but I will. You want to see me in jail?" This was Schutzie's idea of subtle leverage. She put away the lemon oil and brought out a pail of water.

"I'll think about it," I said. I liked the old ivories. They were the keys on which I had first played music. "I hardly remember Edlyn," I told Schutzie. "She looks a lot like Grace. Squeeze out the towel."

"It's only water."

I took the dripping cloth from her and wrung it out into the pail. "Edlyn is round, not quite fat, not skinny like me."

"You skinny? Look at me! Nothing wrong with thin, Ada."

"And she sells real estate, a lot of it, I guess. She and Grace were both raised Quakers but I don't think Edlyn has lived as a Quaker for a long time."

Endlessly optimistic, Schutzie smiled. "Your aunt sounds like a lovely, delightful woman."

The sentence came out in perfect, unaccented English. Tenses, endings, and prefixes had fallen into place flawlessly. When this happened, it always took me by surprise. "My aunt is . . . turbulent," I said, and then wondered where the word had come from.

Edlyn arrived the day before Thanksgiving, driving a sparkling white Lincoln sedan filled with gifts and groceries. There were stylish dresses for me, a new suit for Reynard, flowers in a silver bowl for the Decembers. There was turkey, sweet potatoes, fresh asparagus, and strawberries. Mitch, Schutzie, and I went out to the curb to meet her. She emerged from the car wearing a fur coat and elegant kid gloves. Her hair was now platinum, drawn into a stylish chignon. Even so, her resemblance to my mother startled me. She offered us a tight smile. It was as if Grace's face had been caught up momentarily in some troublesome business. I expected that at any moment the features would relax into my mother's pleasant, warm expression. Schutzie stared at her with undisguised admiration.

Mitch and Schutzie forgave Edlyn everything. "This means so much to Ada," Mitch said, pumping her hand, "but you would both be welcome to celebrate Thanksgiving here with us, more than welcome."

"If you don't mind too much, Mr. December . . ."

"I understand perfectly!" Mitch replied, nodding his head earnestly. "A private reunion! A family gathering!" He stood on the sidewalk holding the bowl of flowers Edlyn had given him, coatless, fawning, turning blue and white in the chilly November air.

Schutzie moved me into Edlyn's car and handed me my violin case. "You need anything, Ada, you call. You telephone! Paprika, lemons, pillowcases, toothpaste!" And to Edlyn, "You gotta wash this car all the time I bet."

* * *

Reynard's attitude toward his confinement had become ambivalent. At times he praised the hospital as the finest home he had ever had; frequently he believed it was a hotel. But at other times, he complained bitterly of the constraints on his freedom. Edlyn had caught him in one of his negative phases. At the prospect of freedom, he relinquished all his hostility toward her. "I like your hair, Grace," he said to her when we picked him up at the hospital. His violin case was tucked under his arm.

"The house," said Edlyn as we drove, "was never properly closed. I was against your renting it out to strangers with all of your belongings still in it. All of Grace's manuscripts are there."

"Aunt Edlyn," I said, "it's only temporary. Reynard is getting better. We'll be moving back soon."

"But we're going to get everything properly into storage," she insisted.

Reynard carried Edlyn's bags of groceries into the house and joyously commenced to cook our Thanksgiving dinner. Our tenants had left the house scrupulously clean. They had generously provided clean sheets, fresh towels, milk, butter, eggs, even a plate of homemade cookies. I took the plastic covers off the furniture and folded them, then I walked through the house touching familiar objects. The sharp odors of onion, mustard, and sage wafted through the rooms; the first of Reynard's sauces was under way.

Edlyn went at once to the attic. "You can never predict what strangers will do in your house," she called to me over her shoulder, I took my fiddle out on the sun porch, where Reynard's acoustics remained excellent, but after

I had improvised a little, I could think of nothing to play. Finally I played "Pony Boy" for the rocking horse sitting in the pale November sun edging through the broad windows. Then I put the fiddle away and went out to the kitchen to help my father.

Reynard stuffed the turkey expertly, mincing oysters and celery into the dressing. He made a cinnamon sauce for the sweet potatoes. He baked a pumpkin chiffon pie. But his seeming competence was only superficial. After a couple of hours in the kitchen, he walked to the attic stairs and called up absentmindedly, "Ada, look in the space behind the chimney! That's where I hid everything on the Chicago business!"

I climbed the stairs and found Edlyn on her knees leafing through the *Poetic Works of Whittier*. "There's nothing hidden here, Aunt Edlyn. Please try to understand. He just writes a lot of letters."

"I understand perfectly." She put forth a small, hard smile. "It's only your mother's manuscripts I'm concerned about. They must be preserved, not left for renters to rummage through."

"They're wonderful people," I said. "They'd never bother a thing. I'm certain of it."

"You can never be certain."

"Aunt Edlyn, Reynard is often perfectly rational. He's getting better all the time."

"I'm sure he is," she replied. "The letter writing is probably therapeutic." But all pretense of comradeship was gone. Her fretful, rising tone had a hostile edge.

Eventually Reynard remembered to make us a little supper. He found a candle for the center of the table and served us a soup made from turkey stock and dotted with golden dumplings. In the shadowy flickering of the candle, Edlyn's tense face and brassy hair appeared coarse, almost ugly. Reynard no longer confused her with my mother. He turned melancholy, remembering Grace, and we ate almost in silence.

Then he put the turkey in the oven on low. We all went to bed, but it was not to be a peaceful night. Soon, I could hear my father up walking, moving through the dark rooms, singing hymns in a mournful tenor: "There is a Fountain Filled With Blood," "Rock of Ages," "Jesus Calls Us," and then, inexplicably, "Casey Jones." Edlyn, who had been trying to sleep on a couch in the living room, rose and turned on a light. I finally fell asleep hearing the low hum of their voices and the occasional rasp of the oven door as Reynard checked the roasting turkey.

Just before dawn I awoke to the smell of incinerated food carried on hot, heavy air. I realized my father was calling me. "Don't open your door, Ada!" I came fully awake and saw the yellow glow of flames beneath my closed door. Reynard was at the window. He reached in and pulled me to safety. A few moments later, our house was an orange ball, an exotic shape and color in the night like a fallen star or a gigantic ball of burning newspaper.

Edlyn ran about the yard in a bathrobe screaming hysterically. Neighbors appeared, fire trucks arrived, the Decembers were summoned.

My father and I held each other tightly. "My little girl," he murmured, stroking my hair, "my dear little girl." Then, "Edlyn set fire to the house to destroy Grace's manuscript. She set the oven on five hundred degrees. I saw it as I came out through the kitchen. Since

I am a famous cook and a famous arsonist, they will blame it all on me, of course."

"Reynard, try and tell the truth!" I pleaded.

"Surely you know I would never attempt to cook a turkey at five hundred degrees," he said. "Besides, I outwitted her. The manuscript was not in the house."

It occurred to me that in a crisis, Reynard's poor mind might be jogged into recalling the facts. "Is there really a manuscript?"

"Of course!" he replied confidently.

"Then where is it?"

"I can't tell you. Your knowing might put your life in jeopardy. Edlyn already fears that Grace may have told you the whole story. But look here!" He was suddenly jubilant. "I saved both the fiddles!" They were lying on the ground under the mock orange.

The police took Reynard back to the hospital. Edlyn declined the Decembers' offer of hospitality and went to a motel. Mitch, Schutzie and I walked to the Decembers' car in silence.

"Mitch," I asked as we drove, "is it true the oven was set at five hundred degrees?"

He had difficulty answering me. He made a show of busying himself checking traffic—there was none—and finally, trying to sound casual, said, "I guess someone did say that. It doesn't matter anyway."

Schutzie tried to help. "What's done is done."

"I see," I said. "You're telling me there will be no investigation of this fire, that Reynard's record will speak for itself."

Mitch hedged. "Ada, it's the middle of the night. I don't think anyone knows a great deal at this point."

"It's seven o'clock in the morning," I countered, and then could not continue. Despite my parents' eccentricities, I had been raised in a reasonably civilized world, not one in which well-dressed women with white Lincolns set fires. I could not bring myself to repeat Reynard's accusation of Edlyn. The Decembers would have considered it an invention to shield my father in any case. Yet, I could not erase the memory of Edlyn's hostility toward me in the attic, the concern with which she had flipped the pages of my mother's books. "My aunt Edlyn," I began carefully, "was not especially . . . friendly toward me yesterday." I'm not sure precisely what else I had intended to say.

Mitch interrupted. "You're afraid of your aunt, aren't you? I can understand why you would feel that way. She represents a threat to your loyalty toward your father."

"What?" Schutzie asked.

"Mr. Cunningham was writing letters to Miss Simmons," Mitch told Schutzie, "making accusations. Ada knows the accusations are not true, but to deny them would be a show of disloyalty to her father."

Mitch's statement startled me. For a moment, I wondered if he had meant it as a joke, all of the circumlocutions, the psychology. But he was completely serious, and I saw how difficult it was for him to accuse people. I think Mitch believed evil lay in institutions, in repressive laws and insensitive governments. He liked people and felt everyone had a story to tell, a point of view to be considered.

He had pulled into his own driveway; we were still sitting in the car. "That's too bad," Schutzie said with quick sympathy.

"But," Mitch continued, "this fear is something we can deal with. Absolutely. Schutzie and I have your custody. The legal system is behind us. You are going to stay right here, in a comfortable home, and we are going to protect you. You have nothing to fear."

"Good," said Schutzie.

Mitch took her remark as a question. "Because it doesn't matter whether Ada's fear is rational or irrational. She perceives it as being real."

It occurred to me I had never seen Mitch work in court, and knew virtually nothing of his skills as an attorney. "Let's go inside," I said. "It's getting cold."

Just before noon, Mitch announced he was going to a meeting with the superintendent of the hospital. He insisted that I accompany him. When we arrived, Edlyn and Reynard were already present. Edlyn, perfectly coiffed and in a neat gray suit, opened the discussion by lecturing the superintendent. "You must understand this man can never be released again, under any circumstances." It was she who had persuaded the superintendent to come in to the office on Thanksgiving Day, perhaps for effect. The holiday dramatized the fire, made us all seem a little bigger than life. I think now it was Mitch who had arranged for Reynard and me to be present. To protect Reynard's rights? He really had none. He would simply be taken back into the hospital, ruled too ill to face charges of arson. I suspect it was all for my benefit. Mitch wanted me to see my father in a realistic light—a broken man, incurably ill—against the backdrop of the superintendent's shiny walnut desk. The thin, white hair on the man's official-looking head, his blue-iron jaw and ferocious eyes would come across to me, show me it was all over for Reynard. I would see, as well, Edlyn at her best, not a figure to be feared but a businesswoman accustomed to serious meetings and shiny walnut desks. Mitch still clung to the notion that Edlyn could be a loving relative for me. The bright noon sun streaming through the room's tall, old-fashioned windows would show me who was who. It was all there in Mitch's comfortable, confident smile.

"My sister's manuscripts have been destroyed," Edlyn said, rising from her chair for emphasis. "They are irreplaceable."

Then the superintendent, who probably wished to settle matters quickly and return to his Thanksgiving dinner, gave her away. "Please consider, Miss Simmons, that you were the one who insisted on this furlough, against my better judgment." I glanced at Mitch, but it had gone past him too quickly.

"Only because you led me to believe it was a reasonable thing to do," Edlyn said heatedly. "You misled me, sir!"

"Indeed, no! You practically—" The superintendent changed his mind and did not complete the sentence. Instead, he raised his hands, as if to protect himself from Edlyn's assault. "We will place him in our most secure unit," he said simply.

This move, putting Reynard in solitary confinement, was really pointless. He had been a model patient. I found the act unspeakably cruel and discovered I disliked the superintendent intensely. I wondered how many times this man, the seasoned administrator and bureaucrat, had dealt with human life in such cavalier fashion. I was heartened only by the thought that the patients themselves managed to undo many of his regulations. If a certain spirit of humanity survived in the hospital, it was in spite of the superintendent, not because of him. In their brighter moments, the patients had a better understanding of human organization than either the superintendent with his edicts or Mitch with his psychology.

Mitch listened courteously and occasionally made notes on a pad of yellow paper. Reynard took no interest at all in the conversation but sat half smiling, examining his nails. He had been issued hospital pajamas and a robe. He was rumpled and unshaven, but he seemed oblivious of his condition and sat with his customary poise, shoulders squared. "Grace?" He gestured to me and leaned close to whisper. "Since the fire, I have developed the gift of second sight. I can tell you the exact layout of this place, where every room, door, and hallway is placed, even though I have never been here before."

He seemed to have confused the two fires. He believed he was in the hospital for the first time. Still, he moved back and forth, from past to present, from fancy to reality. A bit later—the meeting lasted almost an hour—he gestured to me again. "Ada," he whispered, "it's a shame they have to put Edlyn in a place like this, but it's all for the best. She's had a try at me. Her next target would have been you." And he reached over to pat my hand. "Did we lose the fiddles in the fire?"

"No, you saved both of them," I whispered. "I'll bring yours the next time I come. But if Edlyn did this, weren't we both targets? I was in the house, too, you know."

"Of course. Don't fret. She'll be locked away now."

Then, moving close to my ear and cupping his hands he whispered, "Last night she was pumping me about how much you knew."

Despite his confusion, Reynard was completely correct about one thing; I was Edlyn's next target. As she concluded her denunciation of the superintendent and my father, she turned her attention to me. "Can you conceive of what this child has endured?" she asked of Mitch and the superintendent. Then she looked narrowly at me, as if I were a distasteful object, perhaps a bug held up between her fingers for display. "She was born with marked disability, which has never been competently treated. She has lost her mother and seen her father become insane. And now she has endured the trauma of near-death in a fire." With this, she glanced at Mitch with open hostility.

The first flicker of doubt crossed his eyes. He wrote hastily on his legal pad and passed it to me: *Don't worry! We have custody!* He did not seem to feel any other issues were at stake, but a grim thought had entered my mind. Why would Edlyn say these things to the superintendent of a mental hospital, unless she wished to imply that I, like my father, was mentally incompetent?

Confirming my suspicion, Edlyn now launched into her account of my behavior at the time of my mother's death. "The girl was eight years old and she could not dial the telephone. She was unable to feed herself." She sketched a quick but sure portrait of a mentally retarded child. Mitch looked pained but chose not to answer. "Oh, I admit my share of the blame," Edlyn concluded. She had orchestrated the entire meeting and now was drawing it to a close. "As next of kin, I was remiss, and I'm grateful to the Decembers for the temporary care they have given my niece, but the time has come to get matters in hand."

After the meeting, Mitch asked Edlyn what her plans were. "To see that Ada has appropriate care," she replied.

"I believe she is receiving that care now," Mitch said. He had been surprised by Edlyn, perhaps hurt, but he was still not really angry. "Miss Simmons, you have been through a great deal in the last twenty-four hours. You are understandably distraught, but some of your comments about Ada were really quite hurtful. When you've had a chance to calm down, I'm sure you'll want to explain to her that you really didn't mean the things you said." He was carrying a thimbleful of water to a blazing inferno.

"All of those things will have to be evaluated," Edlyn answered in a level voice. She was not interested in compromise. Then she drove off in the white Lincoln. In the back seat I could see the belongings she had salvaged from the fire. These appeared to include all of her luggage and the fur coat. To me, her leaving seemed a curious act for someone interested in our family affairs. There was, after all, the burned-out house to cope with.

But Mitch showed no suspicion. He seemed only to feel relief that she was gone. "Guilt," he said to me when we were in the car. "She realizes she has neglected you. Now she feels she must make some show of concern, carry out some grand plan. But I don't think the woman is capable of real affection. It's too bad she doesn't see what a delightful friendship she could have with you. Ada, when she gets back to Chicago, I think she'll forget all about us. She'll get caught up in her own affairs. There's nothing to be concerned about, in any case. Schutzie and I have your custody. I think you are going to have to be the mature person in this situation and take your aunt in stride. All of her remarks . . . That was hysteria talking. You know that, don't you?"

"My mother was never hysterical," I replied, "even when she wanted people to think she was."

Mitch and I drove home past the remains of our house. "I want to stop," I said. He parked the car and followed me up the walk. No one had remembered to keep up the insurance on our house and its furnishings, and everything was gone. The tenants, also without insurance, had been notified and took their loss stoically. I was the owner of a charred shell on a small city lot. "Sell it, Mitch," I said. "Give half of the money to the renters; you keep the other half." We stood on the sidewalk and surveyed the dead, black hulk, a winter wind stinging our faces.

"Schutzie and I want nothing from you," Mitch said gently.

"Then give the money to the tenants. It's all I have to give them."

"I'm sorry, Ada," he said.

"They're very nice people." I found I had a keen interest in the little boy who had crawled about on our sun porch. My thoughts returned to him again and again and I could not take my eyes off the black, twisted skeleton of the rocking horse. The stream of water from the fire hose had carried it through the house and into the backyard. It sat upended beneath the apple tree, in the spot where my swing had once hung. "Mitch, they're going to take that child to Southeast Asia," I said. "He could catch some awful disease." I wanted him safe somewhere, encased in joy and sunshine, like an investment, a secret bank account that keeps on drawing interest.

"Let's go home," said Mitch. "You're chilled."

We went home and tried to eat the Thanksgiving dinner Schutzie had kept warm for us.

"Ada," Mitch said, staring at his plate, "the things your aunt said about you are not true."

"None of my relatives are noted for their ability to tell the truth," I said. "It runs in the family."

"That's just the kind of thinking you must not do!" he said, suddenly animated. "You are a unique individual."

Schutzie tried to help. "You are separate, Ada. Not connected. Nothing is in the blood."

Until now, I had played a role in the December home, that of the agreeable guest, but my control had been worn thin by the day's events. Without warning, my true feelings surfaced. "Look," I said, "there's no point in reviewing my heredity. My home has been burned to the ground and all you're concerned about is that it shouldn't give me an inferiority complex! What if Reynard didn't start the fire? What if Edlyn started it? Reynard had convinced her something damaging to her was hidden in the house. And there was nothing! I'm sure of it. I searched the house over and over! But now I'm convinced there is something, somewhere! Edlyn and my mother fell out years ago. I don't know why. Reynard thinks Edlyn is involved in criminal activity. Mitch, I don't know what's going on, but I think we have to start taking Edlyn seriously. I'm sorry—so dreadfully sorry—that I am a minor and must bring this down on your heads! I'm sorry I'm shouting! I'm sorry, sorry, sorry!" It was at this moment that it occurred to me for the first time that I could run away.

My protestations did not move Mitch and Schutzie. They believed I was attacking Edlyn to shield Reynard from blame for the fire. Pathetically, Schutzie stumbled on. "Setting fires is not the worst thing. It does not make your father a bad person. He can get well. You are like your mother, Ada. You can tell wonderful stories. Do you see how you are making a story?" Struck by the wonder of this, Schutzie smiled and clapped her hands. Then she made a little shape in the air with her fingers and studied it. Presumably, it was my fertile imagination. "You could write all those things down, Ada. An exciting story!"

I tried once more. "Edlyn could have started the fire and covered it up by setting the oven control on five hundred degrees. My father, even in his worst delusions, would never have attempted to cook a turkey at that temperature. In two areas, he is totally sane; music and cooking." Predictably, this did not impress them. I only half believed these statements myself.

"Let's go at it from a different angle," Mitch said, trying to calm me. "First of all, you have nothing to worry about. We have your custody and your father is receiving good treatment. There is nothing your aunt can do to harm or endanger either of you. She was unpleasant, but perhaps that wasn't too surprising, under the circumstances."

I felt sick; I had brought all of my problems into the December home. Without me, they would have been enjoying a pleasant Thanksgiving dinner. I realized fully what a burden I had become to them.

"That's the first thing," Mitch continued. I believe there was going to be a second point, but the ringing of the telephone interrupted our conversation. Mitch went into the hall to answer it and returned with a puzzled expression on his face. "Someone named Ezra Cantor wants to talk to you, Ada," he said.

8

BELLE AND Popcorn Joe are back by noon, their faces earnest and weary. Watching their arrival from the window, I decide that Alexander can carry his own hurtful news about drummers. Our lion must be provided for.

The horse meat, dressed down, makes a surprisingly small cargo. Joe can carry it all from the truck to the barn in two galvanized tubs. "Shall I bring newspapers?" I call out the door to Belle.

"From the stack by the window!" she directs. Her voice carries over the frozen air with vigor, authority. Was this the voice she used to call down to riggers, roustabouts who held her life in their grimy hands? Everything is still under control. A certain stack of newspapers, already scanned and clipped, sits under a window, set aside for wrapping meat.

The aroma of dead horse intoxicates Monumenta. She

throws her powerful shoulders against her cage with threatening blows that shake the entire barn. Her bellow is fierce and ragged; hoarse, voracious, desperate. We can scarcely hear ourselves above it.

"It's the blood!" Joe shouts. "That's what she smells!" He gives a choice morsel to the lioness to calm her, and moves the tubs into the barn's farthest room. Belle closes two sets of doors, but Monumenta is not appeased. Her nose could smell through twenty doors. The taste of horse only increases her appetite. She is coming for us, she will have it all, only one more lunge will do it. There is a hint of victory already in the roar. She does not remember the other times she has tried and failed to break out. The smell of bloody meat erases all recollections.

We roll up our sleeves and begin, Belle deftly cutting the meat, Joe and I wrapping, stacking the packages in neat piles. It is like working next to a roaring, vibrating locomotive.

"Once when I was with Pogey O'Brien's show," Joe begins, shouting to be heard, "we had a lion get loose in the dead of night. We were loading up, and something fell on the cage and split it open. That lion slipped off like a stone dropped in dark water. We took lights and searched and finally found her. She'd smelled cow and tracked it to a farmer's backyard. When we got there, she'd jumped the fence and got the cow down by its nose, killed it in two slashes of her teeth. We got her into a cage and paid the farmer. Then he said, 'And you take the cow along. I don't want any meat's been chewed by a lion.' I rode back in the truck with the dead cow and, do you know, there was scarcely a mark on it? But when we dressed it out for the animals to eat, there was hardly a trace of blood. That lion had sucked it dry."

I am an experienced meat wrapper. Under Belle's direction, I have learned to square off the ends of packages and fold them under so that each package stays securely wrapped without any sort of binding. The blood on my hands no longer bothers me. The faintly putrid smell of the meat, the surprising toughness of its sinews, the soft, light feel of veined fat—all of these are familiar now. I have wrapped fox, dog, skunk, sheep, cow. I have wrapped possum and woodchuck. I have wrapped goat. Once, incredibly, we butchered and dressed a small gray timber wolf, an animal of unknown origin.

Finished with the cutting, Belle wipes her hands on dry hay and opens her food lockers, rusting metal boxes salvaged from somewhere long ago. The packages of meat are piled neatly inside. Even in the cold, they will not freeze immediately and some of the meat will spoil, but there is no help for it. We have tried laying packages about for quick-freezing before packing them away, but the smell draws rats. The meat must be safely put down at once. In summer, space is sometimes found for the meat in refrigerators and freezers of friends. In summer, much of the food fed to Monumenta is simply spoiled.

Joe is left now with a third tub of useless scrap which he and Belle have conscientiously brought back with them, hooves, ears, hide, entrails, still sitting on the truck. Joe will carry it off to an unknown spot for burial. I am not certain how he will manage to break the frozen ground but it will be done. This is partly to keep marauding animals from our door, and partly from circus tradition. Animal remains are always buried, and the burial place is kept secret. Any animal buried openly, and buried whole, might be taken up again and stuffed. Circus people do not like stuffed animals. They do not like grave robbers. An animal, or a human being, may serve any useful purpose until it goes into the ground. It then becomes a sacred thing. It seems unlikely anyone would rob a grave for the entrails of a horse, but the tradition will be observed.

In the kitchen, Belle and I scrub up, as satisfied as surgeons over our work. "Now!" Belle declares when she has finished, her face lighting with pleasure. "I've brought a surprise!" She points out the window and I see for the first time a small monkey sitting in the cab of Joe's truck, waiting for Belle to finish with the meat. She fetches the monkey, cradling it in her arms like an infant. "He's a spider and I've named him Scaddegood," she says, proud as a new mother, and even spells the name for me. "S-C-A-D-D-E-G-O-O-D. Homer Scaddegood was a watchman for the Mabie Shows, a little fellow with a pin head as small as this monkey's. He's lovely, isn't he?" She holds the animal out to me, insisting, and I reach cautiously for him. But the monkey lunges suddenly and sinks his teeth into the back of my hand.

"Bad boy!" Belle cries, hauling him in, but she is clearly delighted by his high spirits. "He knows a lion is here," she says. "It's made him grouchy. That means he is a circus monkey after all. The big cats make them nervous; then they settle down."

Animals, like people, come to this community in mysterious ways. Often, they are surreptitiously delivered and dumped by owners who can no longer care for them. In the nearby village people say, "Those circus folks will take in any animal." Perhaps somewhere someone is into monkey hating, as vigorously as my father was into cat hating. Perhaps Scaddegood traveled in the trunk of a car.

"Belle, he probably came from a roadside zoo," I say, "or someone brought him back from Florida and then got tired of him." These are demeaning notions, meant to insult this little brown beast. They are revenge for my injured hand.

Belle caresses the monkey with her cheek. "He'll calm down. He'll get used to lion smell. He'll settle in."

By the grapevine of gossip, everyone knew Belle would go for the dead horse. The monkey was at the farm waiting for her when she arrived, sitting and shivering on the farmer's mailbox.

The animal reaches around Belle's shoulder with one stealthy hand, picks up an empty coffee mug from the table, and suddenly hurls it at me with wicked delight. The mug sails past, inches from my head, and shatters against the wall.

"He doesn't like me, Belle."

"Of course he does," she croons, jiggling her furry bundle. Scaddegood touches Belle's cheek with the same leathery hand that hurled the cup, and pats it gently, but his watchful eyes do not leave my face.

This house has not sheltered many stray animals. Despite Belle's love for all creatures, she saves her energy and substance for Monumenta. Many of the animals who come to this farm are already dead. The others are quickly put to death. (Do the villagers suspect what happens to their stray pets? I think they do. I think it is an open secret, and Belle serves a useful function in this community, without pay.) But a monkey is different.

Like Belle, this monkey is an aerialist. He leaps now from her arms and, all skinny limbs, swings to the top of a cupboard in one graceful movement. Belle smiles up at him with admiration. "The spider is the most acrobatic of all monkeys," she says.

I wash my punctured hand at the sink. Belle insists the mouths of animals are not dirty—"That is a myth!"—but like all of the animal handlers in a circus, she keeps a bar of strong lye soap beside the water tap for bites and scratches. The soap stings viciously. "Belle, how did he throw the cup? He doesn't have thumbs."

"No, spiders have no thumbs," she says indulgently, still watching Scaddegood, making it clear that this monkey has so many other virtues that the lack of thumbs is a matter of no consequence.

The monkey, with his small, dark, pin head and large round eyes, glares down at me malevolently. Perhaps the boring eyes see the ghosts of all the animals who have passed this way, en route to Monumenta's cage.

Joe comes in to wash up. He glances at Scaddegood with concern. "Belle, you shouldn't have left the monkey sitting in that cold truck so long. He'll surely take a chill. You watch, by tonight he'll have pneumonia."

But Joe's complaint is only perfunctory. He knows Belle puts Monumenta's welfare above all else. Monkeys, even an acrobat as adorable as Scaddegood, must wait, third in line behind a hungry lion and a dead horse. "Once we had a monkey get loose in Canton, Ohio," says Joe, "a big mandrill. He went up a tree and drove off everyone that came up after him. We finally had to saw the limb off the tree."

My hand has not stopped stinging. "Joe, he threw a cup at me. How did he pick it up with no thumbs?"

"They're quick," Joe says for explanation, "quick as lightning."

"I'll keep him," says Belle, "and we'll see about him."

The circus has no monkeys. They are tropical animals, fragile, subject to ills. Two or three times in the past two years, monkeys have arrived, single vagabonds. Each time they have died in the Indiana winter. Perhaps they were ill before they came, poorly cared for, not inoculated. But the appearance of a monkey is always greeted with joy and great hope.

Joe shakes his head. "If you make a pet of him, he'll never be worth a pittance in an act. You know that, Belle."

"We'll see," says Belle, raising her arms, wiggling her fingers, trying to lure the monkey down from the cupboard. "We could just display him."

But Joe leans toward acts. "Best monkeys for an act are chacmas. They're too mean to tame. They're all business."

Scaddegood purses his lips, extends one arm, and wiggles his fingers in imitation of Belle.

Now, when the day is more than half gone, Joe remembers his carpentry job on the grounds.

"I'll ride along and practice awhile," I say.

Belle's brows fly up in alarm. "And walk back? You'll be frozen, Norma!" Here, it is everyone's pastime to complain of the cold, to exaggerate it, exploit it, make it a personal enemy. Nearly every disappointment and most misfortunes are attributed to the winter. Without the cold, these people would flourish. Their successes would stagger the imagination.

The half mile is actually an easy walk. "I've walked farther, Belle, and in colder weather. Worry about your monkey."

Belle sighs. "At least the building provides shelter. If the calliope were on a wagon, you would perish from exposure." She casts one quick, disapproving glance at the tea glass Alexander has carefully rinsed and left in our sink.

"I told him the flyers were Italian," I offer.

Belle sniffs, then sends the monkey a bright, supercilious smile. She is paring an apple, laying the slices on the kitchen table to lure Scaddegood down. Watchful, he bides his time, then sweeps down suddenly and back up again. The ends of two apple slices can be seen in one of his wrinkled hands. Belle is delighted.

"It's a game, Belle," Joe warns. "You'll tame him."

"I think he's already tame," she says happily. "It's too late."

"How does he do that?" I ask again. "How does he pick things up without thumbs?"

In winter the museum barn, stripped of its summer life, is solemn and silent. Joe produces a master key and unlocks the door. "You want me to lock you in, Norma?" he asks.

"No, Joe. Don't fret. Leave it. I'll lock up when I go."

"One girl alone in this big place? There could be a prowler."

There are no prowlers. I believe Joe's preoccupation with crime dates from his early years, before he became an honest man. "Thanks for the ride, Joe."

I close the door behind me and climb to the calliope loft. The hall is warmed by sun gathered in the building's high windows. The air is warmer with each step. Near the roof, I am able to shed my coat and massage my cold fingers back to life.

My calliope runs on steam. Originally, its boiler was fired by coal. It has now been converted to gas. I cannot justify the expense of starting it up when there is no audience, and the calamitous noise of my practicing would be an assault on community ears. The keyboard I play on is mute. I could manage as well practicing on Belle's kitchen table or picking out notes on my fiddle, but it is reassuring to see the small array of black and white keys before me. Built onto the machine is an old carousel sleigh. I like this cozy little cockpit.

In the music shelf under the keyboard are the house copies of "Red Wing," "You Are My Sunshine," "Columbia, the Gem of the Ocean," "In the Good Old Summertime," "Oh, Susanna," "Daisy," "Camptown Races" —all of the classic repertoire of the calliope. Beneath these are my staff paper, a folder with a pile of scruffy sheets several inches thick. The first sheet is a title page boldly lettered in red crayon: *Suite for Calliope.* It is a sham to divert the attention of casual browsers, a sideshow pitch, a circus con. Beneath it is a second page, modestly lettered in black: *Suite for the Dead, an Orhestra Suite in Six Parts.* Only the name of the composer is missing.

I am writing this composition for the second time. When Belle took me in and provided me with those superb luxuries, shelter, food, and time, I intended to rewrite my lost manuscript from memory, but that was not possible. My memory was keen enough. Like my father, I can carry long musical passages in my head with more than fair accuracy, but I found it impossible to copy out the notes without altering and embellishing them. Perhaps a thing can never be the same way twice.

In one of Reynard's worst deliriums he believed that all of the notes he had ever played still existed, hung over him and were crushing the life from his body. Frantic to calm him, I finally said, "Reynard, I've shoveled up all the notes, put them in garbage bags, and burned them. They're burning. Smell, Reynard! You can smell the smoke!"

This tactic failed. Clutching his chest and struggling to breathe, he cried out, "I still hear them! It's no use. They can never be destroyed."

What intrigues me about this story is the question of whether the notes were orderly patterns of music remembered or random sounds, mere raw goods. In the heat of the moment, I never asked.

I am working today on a scherzo, a rapid and complex pattern that has no key center but depends on a tone row. *Scherzo* originally meant a humorous passage, a musical joke, with lively tempo and jesting style. But with time and usage it has come to mean almost any sort of passage work that is played very rapidly. My score holds to the original sense of the word. It is whimsical, filled with sudden starts and stops, designed to reverse the listener's expectations.

The subject of my scherzo is Ezra Cantor. Like the music, he moved through life rapidly; like the music, he had no center. His story was one of my mother's favorites. She wrote it again and again, a single theme with a dozen variations. In her columns, stories, articles, and chapters she presented Ezra as allegory. Many allegories. He was, variously, Virtue disguised to mislead the proud; Perseverance; Simplicity that speaks truth to power; The Prince disguised as a lame beggar; The Little Match Girl. For Grace, his names were legion, his sex interchangeable, his age and place of residence negotiable.

Ezra was born to a thirteen-year-old white prostitute in Philadelphia. His mother's intelligence appeared to be at the level of a moron. She was picked up from the streets by police, who found her crouched in a doorway, in labor. She did not appear to understand that she was about to bear a child, but seemed to believe her pain was the result of a beating. At Temple University Hospital, where she was taken by the officers, a doctor discovered that she had an undersized heart and several other deformities associated with her syndrome of retardation. These included an underdeveloped pelvic structure. This presented a medical dilemma. Her overburdened heart could not endure the stress of the anesthesia required for a Caesarian birth, and her frail, childlike body could not deliver the child in a normal fashion. The doctor chose to administer the anesthesia and the girl died on the operating table.

Ezra emerged bruised and bloody from the protracted labor. He had suffered oxygen deprivation, the most common cause of brain damage in infants. The doctor laid his frail body under a warming light and turned his attention to other tasks for a moment, the standard procedure for allowing a damaged newborn to die peacefully. But Ezra did not die. After a few minutes, a nurse noticed that his pale blue skin was growing pink and that his thin, labored breathing had stabilized. A small, high wail broke from his lips and his battered limbs twitched to life. His broken bones began to mend and except for his peculiar appearance—Ezra was never handsome— he seemed normal.

The doctor had a sporting disposition. Rarely had he seen the odds against survival reverse themselves in such a startling manner. He discovered he had an ardent interest in this child he had delivered.

Ezra lay in the hospital nursery, already a ward of the welfare system. The doctor could see this ugly baby moving into the world of institutions, foster homes; the ranks of the unwanted, the abused, and the exploited. When Ezra was strong enough to leave the hospital, the doctor intervened.

Busy with the demands of his patients, he was not really familiar with hospital affairs beyond obstetrics and pediatrics. He rode the elevator down to the first floor, his goal a door he had often passed, bearing the legend VOLUNTEER SERVICES. He believed this to be the office of the women who donated their time to the hospital. He had seen them often, reading stories to small patients, watering plants, running errands for new mothers. It was his impression they were all wealthy matrons, women of influence. He planned to lay before them the story of the remarkable baby. Surely such ladies would know what to do. He saw the child becoming the *cause célèbre* of some genteel and prestigious organization, a women's club, perhaps a private foundation.

In fact, this office was occupied by the clergy—a priest,

a minister, and a rabbi—who served the hospital's un-churched patients in times of stress on a rotating basis. When the doctor opened the door, he found himself facing an elderly rabbi. The man did not look at all wealthy or influential.

When the rabbi asked, "Can I help you?" the doctor decided he would ask directions to the headquarters of the women volunteers.

But he had been rehearsing his story all morning and the old man's face invited confidence. "I have in my care a most unusual child . . ." he said instead.

The story itself did not amaze the rabbi. He had been listening to tales of distress for most of his life. What startled him was the teller of the tale. In addition to serving his regular congregation he had ministered in hospitals for many years. He seldom encountered a phy-sician who expressed such personal interest in a patient. He wondered briefly if this whole affair might be a charge from God.

He opened his mouth, intending to say, as he always did, I will see what I can do—and was astonished to hear his own voice announce, "I will take responsibility for this child."

The doctor was equally surprised to hear himself say, "Thank you. Everything is settled, then."

When the door closed behind the doctor, the rabbi found himself quite shaken. It occurred to him he really had no greater ability than the physician to send one infant to the head of the line of human beings needing succor. But that night he had a curious dream. The solu-tion it proposed did not seem plausible, but no better idea presented itself.

Following the suggestion of the dream, he went the next day to call on Gabriel and Preva Cantor. The visit required courage. The Cantors, a couple living quietly in Ridley Park, had recently lost their only child in an automobile accident. At twenty, the boy had already been an instructor at Swarthmore, a brilliant scholar in mathematics. At the same school, his father held a professorship in history. The Cantor home was serene and bookish, a setting where fine minds undertook serious conversation. The rabbi had always enjoyed visits there, but this time, seated in Gabriel Cantor's leather chair, sipping Preva's decorous tea, his voice caught in his throat. "The child," he said, barely above a whisper, "is probably retarded."

Preva, almost fifty, thin and pale from grief, rejected the idea at once. "That portion of our life has ended," she said quietly, looking through the window at well-tended lawns. "The Lord has taken a great interest in us, Rabbi." It was said without rancor, without cynicism. "He brought us from Lipkany to Philadelphia. He raised us up to such happiness in order to show us sorrow. We have accepted his will. Would you have us do more?"

"Sorrow is not God's will," said the Rabbi, "not for you nor for this child. I only ask you to come to the hospital."

Gabriel Cantor was desperate to help his wife. She refused to eat, to see friends. She rarely left the house. The loss of his son had been a crushing blow. Now he saw his wife slipping from him as well. "We will come to the hospital," he told the rabbi.

At the hospital, it was Gabriel who accepted the wrapped bundle the nurse offered. A scholarly man with graying hair, he looked odd holding an infant in his arms.

With two gentle fingers, he found a tiny hand and raised it to view. Startled by the touch, the baby opened his eyes and then his mouth. He uttered one small, melodic sound.

"He called to me," Preva would say ever after, "a single perfect note."

With the doctor's help, the Cantors cut through the red tape of the welfare bureaucracy and assumed responsibility for the baby. Eventually, they adopted him, naming him Ezra: He who has prepared his heart to seek the Law.

The baby was a year old when Grace appeared as a freshman on the Swarthmore campus, mad for the East, mad for culture, mad for history.

"You have red hair," said the head of the history department to his new typist, "like my son." Rarely had he seen such energy in a student assistant.

He did not immediately know that Grace already had two hundred pages of manuscript she wanted him to read. "Perhaps fifty pages," she lied. "I could bring the manuscript to your home."

"We'll see," said Professor Cantor, stalling.

Grace brought the manuscript anyway. The man was trapped. By the end of the semester, the two hundred pages had commandeered the Cantor dining room table. The manuscript would become my mother's history of Indiana.

Ezra was not brilliant but his parents were thrilled with his status as a normal child. Preva kissed his flaming hair and told him he was beautiful.

Grace was fascinated by Ezra. While Gabriel Cantor labored over the two hundred pages, Grace wrote nearly as many more, gathering and recording every detail of Ezra's marvelous story. These pages, her Swarthmore journals, would be the source material for stories and articles years in the future.

I saw Ezra for the first time when he came to Richmount to call on Reynard. I was five or six; Ezra was perhaps eighteen. He had just graduated from high school. He arrived on a motorcycle with a guitar and a knapsack strapped to the back. The purpose of his visit was to ask Reynard how the harmonies of the guitar would function with a capo he had designed.

"Ezra Cantor!" My mother greeted him with unabashed love, such was her delight at seeing her favorite living literary subject, after so many years.

Although I had heard the Ezra stories again and again, I was not prepared for his exotic appearance. I crept off and hid behind a chair, peeking out at him with apprehension. Ezra was short and stocky. His body was turgid. He looked vaguely as if he had been compressed from some larger unit. His hair was yellow-red, wild and abundant, but by some fluke of heredity he did not have the pale skin and light eyes to match it. At eighteen, his complexion was already shadowy with the blue highlights of a coarse, heavy beard. His eyes were nearly black. His round arms and legs were finished off with slender, womanly hands and slim feet. He looked like a wild man, or someone done up for Halloween.

He delivered greetings from his mother and father, and declared he virtually knew us from Grace's engaging letters. "I promised my parents and myself that if I ever came to Richmount, I would stop in." While I watched from behind a chair, he told Grace, "I've decided not to go to college." His voice, amazingly, was a rich, sonorous bass baritone, a singer's voice; a perfect thing placed in a ludicrous setting, a clown's body. "I'm keen on reality, the nuts and bolts of real life," he continued. He gestured, indicating the motorcycle outside, as if its nuts and bolts played some role in this explanation. "My problem is connecting the real world with the fancy dances in my head. The space between the two is like the distance between stars." Volumes of sound filled the room. He could have been reciting poetry or preaching a spirited sermon.

"Are you a musician now?" Grace asked.

Reynard wandered into the room to see who had arrived. "I have designed this capo," Ezra said without preamble, presenting the object on his open palm.

I had never seen such a device. Nor, it seemed, had Grace. "What is a capo?" she asked brightly, ready to offer admiration.

But Reynard sniffed his disapproval. "A clamp for a guitar neck, to let simpletons play difficult chords with easy fingering." My father permitted no musical shortcuts. His expression suggested that his household had been violated. "You must learn to finger all of the chords," he told Ezra, "even the difficult ones. What is your name?"

"Cantor," Ezra began.

But at that moment Reynard glanced out of the window and everything came together at once. "You have a motorcycle! From Philadelphia! Sit down! How long have you had the motorcycle? I had twenty-two motorcycles when I was a boy, one right after the other."

Ezra looked at my father with amazement and admiration, and dropped the capo back into his pocket.

"Welcome!" Reynard cried. "Once my brother Donald and I were coming back from Cincinnati to Indianapolis, after a heavy rain, and the road was rutted so badly we rode in the ditch."

"On one cycle?" Ezra sat down on the edge of our worn sofa and scarcely moved for the next hour and a half.

"One cycle. There were still quite a few gravel roads back then."

"Twenty-two motorcycles?"

Grace brought coffee. I overcame my fright and helped her prepare a supper for all of us.

"By the river," said Reynard.

"The Ohio River?"

"Yes, flowing."

"In the ditch?"

"No, the road."

"Yes."

"Cylinder . . . ignition . . . generating. My brother on the back . . . my little brother."

Reynard's brother was a page out of the past, a scene from an old movie. The scene appeared, disappeared, reappeared. When Reynard recalled his lost brother, it was with great joy. Then, he could not understand why he had forgotten him all this while, and could only be grateful that he had come to mind now. He could have been thinking about his brother every day, savoring all of the pleasure of those memories.

Ezra looked on in wonder.

Reynard relived their adventures, the motorcycle plowing gallantly through the flooded side ditch, the police chases, a cheap hotel in Lexington that had provided —could it be believed!—down comforters, a man in a barbershop in Memphis who had paid them a hundred dollars to play "My Old Kentucky Home" one hundred times in a row, a jail cell in Peoria shared with a drunk who kept a live snake in his mouth, an account of Frankie's burned shirt extracting two hundred and fifty-seven dollars from a single, teary-eyed street crowd in Gary.

Ezra was mesmerized. He fell in love with my father. Later, he told Grace and me what finding Reynard had meant to him. "Until then I had seen myself as a cluster of vagaries that might at any moment come to something. I wondered, watching Reynard, if this might be the moment. Was he *myself*? Suddenly carried to a logical conclusion? I was momentarily uncertain about *things.*"

Eventually, Ezra brought in his guitar. Reynard picked up the instrument and peered inside of it earnestly. This act left an indelible impression on Ezra. "The point was," he said later, "my guitar looked different in Reynard's hands. It glowed with . . . mystery, maybe, and I wondered what he was seeing when he looked inside of it."

Ezra longed to know how the world had looked so many years ago, felt pain that he could not experience it directly, feared that everything wonderful had already happened. What was most apparent to him, he told us, was Reynard's integrity.

To support himself, Ezra was writing and singing

moody songs in bars, telling his audiences only love could save them in an absurd world, and trying to get around rhyming on *absurd* so often. But he told us he could not directly experience love. "I think the circuits in my brain might be crossed," he said.

Following his first visit, Ezra came often, stopping off on his journeys from Detroit to Birmingham, Little Rock to Pittsburgh, Denver to Columbus, dropping by between Charleston and Des Moines, catching us en route to Tampa, New Orleans, and Nashville. He emulated my father and tried to appear even more eccentric than he already was.

"You must branch out beyond the tonic and the dominant chords," Reynard advised, and began teaching Ezra harmony. He proved a bright and dedicated student. Sometimes he spent days with us, sometimes he disappeared for months.

"Ada," Ezra said to me once, sheepishly and on the side, "you seem to know things, even if you are a little kid. I can't understand additive rhythm."

"Ask Reynard," I said.

"I can't understand his explanation."

"It's like 'Old MacDonald Had a Farm,' " I told him. "You can keep adding in things. Like 'a chick-chick here,' and 'a moo-moo there.' "

"Whenever you like?"

"Just about. I think the Hungarians thought it up. Maybe it was the Gypsies."

"How do you know these things, Ada?"

"They make me learn them," I said. "That's all they do."

* * *

Ezra began writing songs with additive rhythms about love, syncopation, hemiola, pentatonic scales, major seventh chords.

"A little like Bartók," Reynard observed.

Ezra's drunken audiences woke up, began to listen. Ezra went to the library and read about Bartók, played Bartók records.

Ezra got a Chicago agent, then a recording contract. Somewhere along the line, he finished the capo, and that worked out, too, because everything was working out for Ezra. He was on a winning streak. He appeared on television, went on tour.

Suddenly, things turned wrong for Ezra. While he was singing at a bar in Fort Wayne, a brawl broke out. A man was stabbed to death. While Grace was dying and Reynard was losing his battle to remain sane, Ezra was being sentenced to prison.

In the calliope loft, time passes swiftly. I read the hour by the angle of the sun's rays through the mullioned windows, knowing I must stop at dusk. On the page, my sixteenth notes march like small black bugs.

At a little past four, a mouse stirs to life somewhere in the depths beneath me and scrambles off with unusual urgency. Its scratching is followed by a distinct thud, as if an object had been knocked to the floor, and I realize that something more than a mouse is in the building with me. Joe's prowler? A marauding cat? But before I have time to consider and become frightened, a small, dark body hurtles down from the girders overhead and lands solidly in my lap. It is the spider monkey. "So, you can also open doors without thumbs!" I say.

He stares hard, directly into my eyes. One black fist flies up and then down, striking the mute keyboard. Then he claps his small hands over his ears. His face wrinkles into a grimace, as if he were in pain, and a low whistle escapes from his lips. "Ah, little monkey man," I say, "it's the music you don't like."

Scaddegood considers. Then, a black hand reaches out tentatively and points to the line of sixteenth notes.

9

MITCH HELD the telephone receiver at arm's length, beyond my reach, and covered the mouthpiece with his hand. "Ada, is this the Ezra Cantor who . . . ?" His face displayed both curiosity and apprehension.

"That's the one," I said, reaching for the receiver. "Ezra was a good friend of my parents."

Mitch was wary. "Then he's the one . . . ?"

"Who made the records and appeared on television and went to prison. Yes. May I have the phone please?"

Reluctantly, Mitch surrendered the telephone.

"Ada!" Ezra cried. The dark, resonant voice sounded older but still familiar. "You're the only one left. I go to prison and everything falls apart."

"You're out of prison?"

"On parole. I'm in Indianapolis. I've been here almost a year. I was trying to work up the courage to come to

Richmount and see all of you. I know how badly I disappointed your parents." The words rolled out, voluminous, like a song or a recitation.

I was more touched by the sound than I would have imagined possible. Ezra was a part of our happy past—Grace's, Reynard's, and mine. That he was volatile and unreliable mattered to me less than the simple fact that his voice was familiar. "How did you find me?"

"I read about the fire in the morning paper. Then I started phoning around to find where you had gone . . ."

"And you heard the rest of the story."

"Yes. Ada, I'm so sorry about your mother, so awfully sorry."

"Thank you, Ezra."

"We should have kept in touch."

"Yes, I suppose we should have."

"And they've locked Reynard up?"

"They say he sets fires."

"Ada, it's a terrible thing, being locked up."

"He didn't set the fire," I felt compelled to say.

"I believe you." His voice was laden with emotion, love for my father, loyalty, concern. "I'd like to go and see him first thing in the morning, if they'll let me in. Do you want to come along?"

"Yes," I said. "They've put him in solitary confinement. We'll have to see if we can get him out, and I want to take him his violin." I gave directions to the house on D Street. "Will you pick me up on your way?"

"I'll be there by ten."

"And Ezra?"

"Yes?"

"It's very good to hear your voice."

When I returned to the table, both Mitch and Schutzie raised apprehensive faces. "Don't be afraid of Ezra," I told them. I related the story of our friendship with him.

"He was almost family, then," said Mitch, softening. "Your mother admired him and wrote about him."

"Welcome here," said Schutzie. "I can tell you gonna be glad to see him. You gotta happy face."

I saw where the conversation was leading. The Decembers had held my mother in high esteem. They would accept her affection for Ezra as a character reference.

"I remember his trial," Mitch went on. "The defense was clumsy. The charge . . . did not seem appropriate." The words Mitch preferred not to say were *charge of first degree murder.*

Edlyn hadn't worked out as a loving relative. Now Mitch and Schutzie were willing to try Ezra in that role. "I don't want to mislead you," I said. "Ezra was always a drifter. He was never a pillar-of-the-community sort of man."

"He was a vagabond musician," said Mitch, "but there's nothing illegal in that."

"Maybe you'd better wait until you meet him," I suggested, "before drawing a lot of conclusions."

When the dishes were done, Schutzie said, "Play a little music, Ada, for Thanksgiving. Play away all this bad air."

I accepted the offer without prompting. I sat down at the piano and quickly lost myself in Schumann's songs, grateful for their power to soothe and to strengthen. If music was difficult enough, its technical demands drove everything else from the mind. But even when it was easy, music's patterning shaped the emotions, pushed uncertainty and apprehension into the formal order of theme development, reprise, dissonance and resolution. Even sad passages were optimistic, reassuring. Music proclaimed an orderly universe, promised a better place. I moved from Schumann to folk songs, then to hymns.

When I had been playing for almost an hour, Mitch said, "You very rarely use the music. You have a remarkable memory."

"Not really," I replied. "I don't have all of this memorized. Musicians fool you. They do a lot of improvising, playing by ear, chord playing. Then, the things you memorize as a small child stay with you forever. It's in the fingers. Finger memory."

"Perhaps," he said, "but your mother wrote that you had almost total recall."

I had to smile. "Mitch, my mother was a wonderful person and I loved her, but she didn't always tell the truth. The necessities of whatever piece she was writing came first. She'd say almost anything to make a good story, especially about me."

"Perhaps," he said. "What do you remember about your mother and your Aunt Edlyn?"

"Apparently that's what Edlyn wants to know, too," I said.

"But your mother must have said something," he insisted. "She must have given you some explanation for the disagreement between them. After all, her sister was her only relative."

"I don't think the subject ever came up. It was a fact of life I accepted, like Reynard's having a sink in his studio.

It was years before I realized how peculiar that sink must have seemed to people."

He nodded, still unconvinced. "Will you play 'Clair de Lune'?"

"Of course."

But this strange day which had begun with the fire before dawn was not over yet. Before I had finished the Debussy, Edlyn appeared at the door. She was carrying an old photograph album from our attic, and she had been drinking. "I want to tell Ada about her mother," she said to Mitch. She was smiling, puffed up with some enthusiasm. Her pink, bleary eyes were merry.

Mitch, Schutzie, and I gathered in the doorway, a defensive trio. Edlyn was wearing her fur coat, but her hair was disheveled, tied down with a scarf that pressed her face into deep lines. Her breath was odorous. The contrast with her appearance earlier in the day was striking. However she had spent the hours since our meeting, they had been difficult for her. I wondered if her drinking was a response to the day's events or a habit of long standing, and it came to me how little we really knew about her. Mitch looked at her with frank astonishment. "Come in, Miss Simmons," he said guardedly.

But Edlyn was already in. She seated herself on the couch without removing her coat and drew me down beside her. "This wasn't Thanksgiving, you understand, but Halloween." She was giving me the ground rules for some game. She held the album closed on her lap and looked at it with anticipation. "You'd have fit right in, Ada." Warmth had crept into her voice. She reached out and squeezed my hand with real affection.

"You gonna show us those pictures or not?" Schutzie asked, wary and unsmiling.

Edlyn raised a hand as if to restrain us. "Of course! But I have to set the stage. Ada, your mother loved costumes. She had that touch. Magic. Or bewitchery." I had seen the old album often. I could think of no reason why it would assume significance for Edlyn. She had obviously taken it from the attic, really an act of thievery. "Bewitchery," she said again. "Even when we were very small. I was two years older but your mother was the leader. Do you understand what I'm saying?"

"Not really," I replied.

She grew impatient. "Then let me go back to the very beginning. Your mother gave names to things. We had two cats, and she named them Suzabelle and Opal."

"I never knew Grace had a cat," I said. "My father doesn't like animals."

"She would say, 'You never give a name to a cat without asking,'" Edlyn continued. "She would whisper to the cat and it would tell her its name."

Schutzie said, "I don't believe a thing like that. I'm gonna get you a cup of coffee."

Edlyn ignored her. "And dolls," she continued. "Once Grace said a doll was going to die, and it did."

Schutzie had started for the kitchen but now turned back. "You gonna tell us a doll died?"

"But it did!" Edlyn declared. "You could see it! Every bit of life went out of it. Grace and I got up in the middle of the night and buried it in the garden without telling anybody. I was eight years old that summer and Grace was six. And we cried! Oh, we cried for days. It was a touch she had." At last, Edlyn opened the album and pointed to a photograph. In it, several girls, fifteen or sixteen years old, were costumed for Halloween, but the masks had been removed to reveal bright faces. Below the faces were ghosts, hoboes, ballet dancers. I recognized Grace, dressed as a clown. Standing a bit apart from the others was a single figure, neatly and incongruously dressed in a belted coat, a cloche, and high-heeled sandals. "She made me a twenties flapper," Edlyn said with delight, pointing at this figure. "Oh, Grace always liked to dress me up!" The face of this youthful Edlyn was shy and hopeful. The head was cocked a little to one side, full of trust.

Mitch had come over to look at the picture. "You were a very pretty girl," he said.

This pleased Edlyn. "Grace always told me so!" she said with animation. "But it wasn't easy for me. You see that, don't you?" The question was directed at Mitch, and when he did not respond, Edlyn's smile changed direction and shrank into petulance. "I was never extended the privileges Ada's parents received. I have always had to earn a living in the real world." Angry patches of red appeared in her cheeks.

So there it was, injury going deep, things stretching back before my time, aggrievement seeking redress. She was drawing us into the middle of some old argument, private, hard, and cruel. I said, "People think musicians and writers get a free ride, that they're paid money for doing nothing. They think it's all bewitchery. Magic. If you believe it, you believe it."

Schutzie returned with a cup of black coffee. "Ada, we don't think that," she said. "Mitch and I never said that."

Everything had gone out of control. "Families!" Mitch

said with false cheer, attempting a lame smile. "We all have our grievances, but consider, Miss Simmons, you and your sister both succeeded. You simply chose different paths."

But Edlyn shook her head, closed the book, and rose to go. "Everyone at home is dead," she announced. "There's nothing left but the cemetery. I just wanted to explain these things. That's why it was necessary to come tonight." Then, considering, she smiled.

"Wait," said Schutzie, "what you mean about the cemetery?"

Mitch looked alarmed. "Wherever you're going, I'll drive you." Clearly, the prospect of Edlyn driving drunk appalled him. But she waved the offer aside and slipped out of the door.

"Can you believe it!" Mitch cried when she was gone. "She came here seeking compassion."

"It's probably too late for that," I said. "She just wanted to tell us Grace got the best of her, and now Reynard and I are going to pay for it. I can believe the things she described. Grace could do things like that without batting an eye."

"No!" Schutzie said stoutly, still holding the cup of coffee. "Cats not gonna tell people their names. Dolls not gonna die."

Ezra arrived on a motorcycle the following morning. I was waiting at the window with Reynard's violin case. "He gotta guitar there, on the back," Schutzie said, following me out to meet him. "I know the shape of that box."

Ezra looked startlingly different. He was wearing a full

and luxuriant black beard. "Ada!" He drew me into his arms and suddenly he was shaking with soft, silent sobs.

I held his head against me. "It's wonderful to see you!" I forgave him everything, large crimes and small, real or imagined. "This is Schutzie December."

"You sure gotta lotta red hair!" said Schutzie, smiling hugely. She liked Ezra immediately. Perhaps it was because of the guitar. "You come back from the hospital, you come in and play that thing," she said to him. "I make something good to eat. Ada, you hold on. You don't let that motorcycle fall over on you."

Ezra dried his tears and smiled at the diminutive Schutzie. "You know any Japanese songs?" he asked.

"No," she replied. "You know 'On the Road Again'?"

At the hospital, we confronted a nurse and an orderly. They were apologetic. "I'm so sorry about this," the nurse said. "Your father has never caused us any trouble. Isolating him is very unfair."

"And the other patients miss him," said the orderly. "He was their in-house priest."

"This man is an old friend of Reynard's," I said. "He's come a long way to visit."

"It's against the rules," the nurse said, and then reconsidered. "Bring Mr. Cunningham into the dayroom," she told the orderly.

Reynard recognized Ezra at once. "Come in!" he cried, even though he was the one entering the room. "They have finally given me private quarters. It's much better, much quieter." The two embraced.

"I'm sorry about Grace," Ezra said. "I can't tell you how sorry I am."

"She'll be sorry, too," Reynard replied, "sorry she missed you."

"We'll get you out of solitary," Ezra said, "and we'll get you out of this place, too. Don't worry."

"I'm not worried!" Reynard replied. "I haven't a worry in the world. Except for the acoustics. I much prefer bare walls, and the walls in my new room are padded. But I'm just settling in. I'll speak to them about it. And, next time you come everything will be set to rights. You'll see!"

"We'll get you out," Ezra said again.

"Don't," I said to Ezra. "Don't promise him that."

"Ada, you know nothing about being locked up." Ezra smiled. It was a wry, peevish grin.

"Here's your fiddle, Reynard," I said.

"Thank you!" He grinned, sly as a fox. "Fiddle while Rome burns, eh?" He understood and he didn't understand. It was always the same with Reynard. "Tell me about your music," he said to Ezra.

"It's different now," Ezra replied. "Give me a D-minor obligato." He sat back in his chair and began to sing. Reynard followed with a descant on the violin:

> " 'I have no name,
> I am but two days old.'
> What shall I call thee?
> 'I happy am,
> Joy is my name.'
> Sweet joy befall thee!
>
> Pretty joy!
> Sweet joy but two days old,
> Sweet joy I call thee.

Thou dost smile,
I sing the while,
Sweet joy befall thee!"

He had been setting the poetry of William Blake to
music. He sang on. Here and there a patient looked up
with mild interest. The melodies were baroque, flat runs
with biting, bitter dissonances. In many cases, they were
totally at odds with the sweetness of the lyrics. The juxtaposition of the two created powerful irony.

"I can't stand my own lyrics anymore," Ezra said when
he had finished. "I guess I got out of that anyway, got out
of myself."

"You've become a scholar," Reynard said.

"That's true in a way," Ezra replied. "I've read a lot of
books since the last time I saw you."

I asked, "Do you have a job?"

"I pick up work in bars on weekends. Enough to keep
going. But I have plans. No one wants the old Ezra. I'm
going to be Larry Lederman now."

It took me a moment to place the name, and then I
remembered it. In her journals, Grace had recorded the
name of the Cantor's natural son. The mathematics
scholar at Swarthmore had been Laurence Lederman
Cantor. As a child, curious about the eccentric Ezra who
visited our home, I had read most of the journals.

It was an area too sensitive to probe, but the name
spoke for itself, for resolve and restitution. Eventually,
Ezra would tell us that his father was dead and his
mother in a nursing home. When he visited, she recalled
only a younger Ezra, the child who had filled her home
with singing.

"I've already talked to a couple of agents in Chicago," Ezra continued. "They let me call them before I left prison. You see, there seem to have been improprieties in my trial, defense issues that weren't raised. After the fact, I think the authorities decided the trial might not have been completely legal. At the end, everyone was pretty nice. I think they were trying to make it up to me." He looked away for a moment. His appeal for understanding was touching.

"And the agents?" Reynard asked.

"They may be interested. They said they might send me to Europe, and even the parole board agreed to that. After a while, maybe I could perform here again. The public is fickle, they forget. My following was never really that large anyway."

"Now Ezra," Reynard began. It was as if our conversation up to now had been only small talk and the time had come to get down to more serious concerns. "I knew you were coming. You probably wondered why I did not appear more surprised when you walked in. You see, I have second sight now, since the fire. I also know the purpose of your coming. You are to continue where I left off, getting the truth out, and to the proper authorities. Most of all, I must depend on you for Ada's safety."

"Do you want to explain that?" Ezra asked gently. His eyes registered surprise, but he did not appear alarmed —a measure, I felt, of his trust in my father.

"Ezra," Reynard began, "Grace's sister Edlyn is a real estate agent in Chicago. She's very prosperous today, but that success was built on unscrupulous dealings that she transacted years ago. Grace and I were aware of these deeds. Grace recorded everything fully in a manuscript.

Every kind of mischief was involved—buildings that weren't up to code, mortgages called in, arson. Once a child died. It was Edlyn who had me committed to shut me up. Then she set fire to our house to destroy the manuscript. Her next target is Ada."

Ezra asked only one question. "Why did Grace remain silent all of these years?"

"Strategy," said Reynard, giving the word an ominous tone. Then he began his story again. This time the buildings are warehouses and Chicago politicians were involved. Grace had learned of it all only a few days before her death.

"That's how it is," I said when Reynard had finished. I waited, giving Ezra an opportunity to bow out, to bid us farewell, perhaps to bolt and run from the room, but he sat on quietly, unjarred, unhorrified.

Eventually, he turned to me. "And can you confirm any of this?"

"There are only two things I feel certain of," I replied. "Edlyn and my mother fell out and were never reconciled, and I'm convinced Edlyn believed something incriminating to her was hidden in our house. I know how preposterous that sounds."

Ezra nodded. "I suppose it does."

Reynard picked up the violin and began playing a Strauss waltz. Ezra and I listened in silence. A patient, a man in blue jeans, wandered by and stroked Reynard's head as he played. Somewhere a buzzer sounded. The orderly glanced over at us as if surprised by the time, and approached with a reluctant smile. "I'm going to have to take your father back now. Shall I put the violin in a cupboard? I promise you I'll look after it."

"Let him take it with him," Ezra said.

"I'm afraid I can't do that."

"Yes, put it away," I said. "Thank you. We're going to talk to someone about getting him out of that room."

"Of course," the orderly replied. He took the violin and led Reynard away.

Ezra and I sat on in the grim, odorous room. "You think I should be shocked?" he asked. "I'm not, you see. Part of that comes from being in prison. You wouldn't believe the things I saw there, the full spectrum of human behavior. When you cut people off from the world, it's amazing what strange potentials surface and grow in them. Not only the vicious, although there's plenty of that, but the strange and the beautiful, too. Things you never noticed before." He paused, and the peevish smile returned. "That doesn't mean I think prisons and hospitals are good for people. They are not."

"I think you're moving in the wrong direction, Ezra." He was almost thirty now. There were fine lines around the dark eyes. Despite the mass of red hair that remained, there was thinning at the temples. I wondered if I knew him at all anymore. Glad as I was to see him, the memory of Edlyn's drunken scene made me cautious of people who suddenly reappear after years of absence. "Reynard was sick before he came here," I said. "The hospital didn't cause his delusions."

"I understand, Ada, but he says he has second sight now. Don't you think that's a response to being hospitalized?"

"He's had one fetish after another, regardless of where he's been."

"I see." Ezra paused and ran his hands through the

wild hair. They were the slender, delicate hands I re-membered. The sight of them seemed reassuring. "It's more than that, anyway," he continued. "I've always had flights of fancy myself. I guess I don't find other people's fancies all that odd. This is a little strange, isn't it?"

"Strange?"

"As his daughter, shouldn't you be the one defending him rather than me?"

"Perhaps you are his true child, Ezra," I said. I suppose an observer would have found my behavior curious. I had urged Mitch to give full consideration to Reynard's notions. But Ezra was different. He was always more than anyone bargained for—wilder, more intense, ad-versarial. "I love Reynard," I told Ezra now. "I'd do al-most anything to help him get well. I even think the truth about Edlyn may be buried in his mind some-where."

"But you aren't really ready to trust him," said Ezra. "Ada, who burned your house down? What if you are in danger?"

"Michael December is looking after us. He's a lawyer."

"Shall I tell you what lawyers did to me? Look, Rey-nard has asked my help and I intend to give it. I owe a great deal to Reynard."

"What about touring Europe?"

"There's nothing firm on that anyway. They've al-ready kept me waiting for months."

"And you're willing to take direction from Reynard?"

"They called Blake mad. You know that, Ada. Once when I came to your house, your mother was reading to you from *The Four Zoas*."

"Blake anticipated Freud in every significant way." I

immediately wished I had not said this. Ezra would believe he had won me over. Conversations with Ezra always lost their center. "I don't think this is going to
work," I told him.

"What other choice do you have?" he shot back.

In argument with Ezra, I leaned toward protective
coloration. "Edlyn's gone. Things will calm down. They
always do. You might stir up trouble and make everything worse."

"How could it be worse? You lost everything in the fire
and Reynard's in a padded cell."

Ezra's fervor backed people into corners, provoked
responses. "Maybe the issue here is prison," I said, bolder
than I'd meant to be. "I'm not sure you can fight your
own battle on our turf."

But he changed the subject. "Ada, what do you want to
do with your life? Your own life?"

"I don't think about it."

"Maybe it's time you did."

This effort to distract me was manipulation and I didn't
like it, but argument was futile. Ezra would do as he
pleased, with or without my blessing, and my father
didn't have many fans left. "You and I are the only people
left in the world who love Reynard," I said.

"I'll work with him every day," said Ezra, "or as often
as they'll let me see him."

"Let's get out of here. I want to talk to the superintendent." As we rose to leave, an old woman in a bathrobe
paused before us and curtsied. "I'm glad you're here,
Ezra," I said, "enormously glad. But I think you're going
to end up . . . writing a song."

He laughed, a sudden, booming explosion. "I admit it! This is all a song. A marvelous, intricate song!"

The superintendent's secretary told us he was not in, a situation that would remain the same through repeated visits and phone calls. We went home and ate Schutzie's French onion soup.

In the afternoon, we returned to the hospital; this time Ezra brought his guitar in. He persuaded the orderly to bring Reynard in again. We settled back in our seats with Ezra strumming idly on the guitar. "Begin at the beginning," he said to Reynard.

Reynard plunged in at the middle, of course. "After Edlyn signed the contract to put up the first building in Chicago—"

"Wait," Ezra said, "tell me about the building. Did you ever see it?"

"Of course! She took your mother and me through it." Reynard now seemed to believe Ezra was his son.

"Think about the building," Ezra said. "Was it tall? Several stories?"

"There was a Chinese restaurant across the street. Do you know Chicago's Chinatown?"

"Did you eat in the Chinese restaurant?" Ezra asked. He was Freud going after William Blake. If the facts were buried, scattered through the dross of Reynard's fantasies, Ezra was determined to find them.

Reynard led him a circuitous course. At the center of my father's confusion, there was always the figure of my mother. He often spoke of her as a living person. He called me by her name perhaps half the time. Yet, on other occasions, the events surrounding her death seemed perfectly clear in his mind. When Ezra tried to pin down the details of Edlyn's building in Chicago, Reynard's mind jumped to Grace's funeral.

"Ezra, we should all make complete funeral plans in advance," he said. "I can look back on these things quite calmly now, but when Grace died, I was so distraught that the smallest decision was almost impossible for me to make. Everyone is like that, naturally. We should prepare, all of us. The problem is, you really dare not write anything down. Never put anything in writing, Ezra! It will fall into the wrong hands. It will come back to haunt you. So there's the dilemma, don't you see? Ada, you remember the rings, what a dreadful time I had with the rings?"

"No," I said.

"Of course you do," he continued. "When Grace was laid in state, her wedding band and diamond engagement ring were placed on her finger. The funeral director said to me, 'Before the casket is closed, we will remove the rings and place them in a box for you.' He even showed me the box. Ezra, I shall tell you what a funeral is like. It is a series of objects that appear, one after the other—floral pieces, lamps shielded to shine softly on the ceiling, a cream-colored satin blanket to cover the lower half of the body, a gold pen beside a registry book on a polished oak lectern—objects meant to give solace to the bereaved. The box for the rings was one of these. It wasn't a regular ring box, as one might have expected; not one of those little cubes with slits cut to hold the rings in an upright position. Not at all. It was a small flat box lined with black velvet—black, mind you, not blue or violet—with two impressions in the lining for the rings. That is, they lay flat in the box, just as a corpse lies flat in a coffin. Someone must have given some thought to that. I'd say quite a lot of planning went into that box, wouldn't you? Having the rings lie flat? Having them fit into those little impressions? They were really trying to give me a message, weren't they? Subtle perhaps, but a message nonetheless." Here Reynard smiled, a melancholy expression, and paused to study his own ringless hands. After a moment, he continued. "But that was not the point at all, Ezra. Forgive me for wandering. The funeral director should have removed the rings when I was not present, but he chose to make a little ceremony of it. You can't imagine how much ceremony is involved in a funeral! Did you attend Grace's funeral, Ezra?" Without waiting for an answer, he went on. "But there in front of me, at the end of the eulogy, the man stepped forward to remove the rings. It was unbearable! Like thievery! And so I whispered to him, 'No! Leave them. Don't take them from her!' And then, of course, a moment later, I wanted them. Back and forth! It was dreadful. How many times, Ada? Two or three?"

"I don't remember."

"Yes, two or three. So you see what I mean; all plans should be made well in advance. In the end, I kept them, of course. But what an experience!"

Ezra had followed the account with interest. "And Ada," he asked, "how much of this do you remember?"

"I remember the gold pen, people signing the book."

"It's a beginning," said Ezra. "We'll work to establish a valid body of knowledge—events that can be verified by others, such as you."

"How much can you make of a gold pen?" I asked.

Ezra was not discouraged. He smiled at me with infinite patience.

Reynard reached over and patted Ezra's arm. "It's wonderful to see you again," he said, "just wonderful."

I surrendered. "You've made my father very happy," I said to Ezra. "I'm glad you are here."

Ezra and I eventually went back to the house on D Street to eat Schutzie's dinner. When the Decembers offered their hospitality, Ezra accepted. He took up residence in Mitch's small den, sleeping on a folding cot. The following day, he found a job playing in a nearby bar. On Saturday, he borrowed Mitch's car and moved his meager belongings to the house on D Street. That evening, Ezra got out his electric guitar, plugged in the amplifier, and plunged the house into darkness. "It's only a fuse!" Mitch assured us, and a moment later light was restored. Nothing about Ezra had changed. Wherever he went, excitement followed.

10

A FEW days after our disjointed conversation about dolls and cats, Mitch received a personal check from Edlyn, sent registered mail from Chicago. Her note read, "You'll need this to replace belongings lost in the fire."

"She's talking to lawyers," Mitch said. "The first step in establishing your right to something is to demonstrate your financial tie to it, whether it's a person or property. I'm sure she wants this construed as a support check."

We were all in the kitchen; Schutzie was cooking something. She had Ezra grinding black pepper into our glasses of tomato juice. Real winter was moving in, gray, damp days with twilight by four in the afternoon. The small kitchen was warm and smelled sweet. A place of comfort, it seemed the ultimate sanctuary. Mitch's ominous tone was an intrusion not to be taken seriously.

Schutzie arranged lettuce on a plate. "She stay in Chicago, we get along fine."

Mitch said, "If you want to show you own a building, you bring in receipts that prove you've been paying the taxes. Judges like receipts and canceled checks. Pieces of paper. I can't think of anything they like better." We ate thoughtfully, almost silently. The next day Mitch returned the check to Edlyn, registered mail.

A week later he carried the second letter home from his office in the pocket of his overcoat. "Do you want to go to a doctor, Ada?" he asked. I read it while he hung his coat in the closet. The letter came from the office of a Chicago internist. An appointment had been made for me for a physical examination. Mitch telephoned the physician's office and canceled it. He informed the doctor that Edlyn had no authority to conduct my affairs. He followed this up with a letter on his office letterhead, confirming the phone call, and sent a copy of the letter to Edlyn. "We'll put everything in writing," he said when this had been done. Mitch had as much faith in pieces of paper as the judges he described.

The next letter came from a Chicago psychiatrist and included a medical history form. "Please fill out the enclosed pages completely prior to your first visit," the letter read. Again, Mitch canceled the appointment Edlyn had made.

He began his own campaign to collect pieces of paper, and brought a manila folder home from his office. "I see no way your aunt can get our custody set aside," he said, "but it's best to be prepared."

The next day I said to Ezra, "Mitch doesn't really think there are any vicious people in the world. He believes there are only unfortunates and extenuating circumstances. Most of all, he believes in the legal system."

Ezra replied, "I know. It's a form of mental laziness parading as virtue."

We were walking home from the hospital; the weather had grown too cold for the motorcycle. "Isn't that a rather uncharitable way of stating the case?" I asked. "Especially when you're a guest in the man's house?"

"Perhaps it is," Ezra replied, "but the time for niceties has passed. Mitch will have to face the facts soon."

Later, I would mark this conversation as the beginning of Ezra's domination of Mitch. It was all there, in the thrust of Ezra's body pushing against the wind. He had it in his heart to do great things at any cost.

Mitch decided I should see a local doctor. "I've already talked with him," he said to me one morning. "He'll give you a written evaluation . . . of everything."

Grace had protected me from doctors, treating my measles and chicken pox herself. My few visits to their offices had been brief affairs; my mother marched me in for routine inoculations, evaded questions about my crippled hands and lame leg, and marched me out again. In addition, she spread the visits around, never taking me to the same doctor twice. When Mitch's personal physician asked about my medical history, I told him, "I have none. I was never sick much."

He accepted my answer without comment. After a cursory examination and a few questions, he wrote: "Ada has congenital nerve dysfunction causing some disability to both hands and one leg. It was present at birth. It is permanent and untreatable. Her condition is stable. No deterioration is occurring. Both her physical and mental health are good." Then, ending in a blaze of glory, he listed my activities; playing organ at churches, teaching students, directing choirs, repairing instruments. "The disability is minor and does not interfere in any substantial way with daily activities."

It was obviously a put-up job, written to be presented as an adversary document in court. The doctor sent a copy of the report to Edlyn, and Mitch dropped his own copy into the manila folder. "Your mother took you to Indianapolis," he said, going for bigger game.

"Children's Hospital," I told him.

Mitch took an afternoon off and drove to Indianapolis. As my legal guardian, he had no trouble gaining access to hospital records, but the results were disappointing. The attending physician had written, "The child was not brought back for the second appointment. The evaluation was not completed." And the physical therapist had added, "Therapy was never begun."

That evening he asked me, "Why did your mother never take you back?"

"Because she wanted to pretend there was nothing wrong with me."

Schutzie plunged gallantly into the conversation. "And that is true!" she said. Then, addressing me in the third person, she declared. "Ada is fine! There is nothing wrong with Ada." I longed to take courage from her words, but Mitch's solemn expression prevented it.

Ezra was drawing a map of Chicago. He spent most of his days visiting Reynard, and his nights sleeping in Mitch's den. "I don't think I'll have to impose long on your hospitality," he told the Decembers. "Everything is coming together." In truth, he had turned up nothing substantial in his talks with Reynard.

"You are very welcome here," Schutzie told him. "Now, play a little on the guitar, sing something." She liked Ezra's music much better than mine. Not his new songs, which were nearly incomprehensible to anyone but a scholar of William Blake, but Schutzie soon discovered she could make requests and Ezra would cheerfully perform. She liked country and western songs best. "Willie Nelson!" she sometimes demanded, but she leaned toward Kenny Rogers. " 'You got to know when to hold 'em'," she sang along with Ezra, " 'Know when to fold 'em.' "

"Where did you learn those songs?" Ezra asked.

"Everybody knows them!" Schutzie insisted. Perhaps she had a secret radio tuned to a country station.

Ezra urged her to sing Japanese songs, but she seemed to know none. "The Japanese brain is organized differently," said Ezra, who apparently had read on every subject while in prison. "The Japanese process their native music on one side of the brain, and Western music on the other."

"I always liked western music," said Schutzie.

"Not western like Kenny Rogers," Ezra labored to explain, "Occidental."

" 'Know when to walk away,' " sang Schutzie, " 'Know when to run.' "

Ezra wanted to wire Schutzie up and see how her brain worked.

When the map of Chicago grew larger and more detailed and spilled over the edges of Ezra's sheets of paper, Schutzie supplied him with shelf paper. Chinatown was the district most prominently displayed. "Do you know any Chinese?" Ezra asked Schutzie one evening.

He speculated that fate might have sent him an ally in only slightly disguised form. Perhaps one Oriental was as good as another. Ezra believed that such things happened, almost daily, for people perceptive enough to recognize them and put them to use. Blake had taught him to seek hidden meanings everywhere.

But Schutzie shook her head. "No Chinese. A little Korean, a little German, and the French from cookbooks. A la mode. Café au lait. Cherries jubilee."

Mitch had accepted Ezra as a friend, almost as Reynard's son, but rebuffed Ezra's efforts to play the role of investigator. "I can't see any real value in the approach you're taking," Mitch told him. "If trouble comes, we'll work through the legal system." Still, as the days passed and the letters from Chicago made Edlyn's threat more and more real, Mitch found excuses to sit at the table drinking coffee, watching Ezra work on his map.

But if Mitch's interest in the project increased, mine diminished. I had lived too long with my father's fantasies to put great credence in them. "Quit, Ezra," I said one evening. He was trying to locate the building Reynard described again and again. Reynard felt certain a child had died there. Ezra now believed it had been built in violation of code, with shabby materials. "Give up," I said. "It's useless. You're hoping you'll find the only Chinese restaurant in Chicago that serves sukiyaki, and coast downhill from there."

"But sukiyaki is Japanese!" cried Schutzie. "Then, if it was the only restaurant, you would have the place! Pin point! On the nose! I am certain Mr. Cunningham knows sukiyaki. Everybody knows that, and Mr. Cunningham was always a cook Ada, quick! Does your father know sukiyaki?"

In his own fashion, Reynard tried to help. "The trouble is," he said when Ezra and I visited him in mid-December, "I don't think Grace gave me all of the precise details." They had refused to return his violin to him and he remained in solitary confinement except when we came to see him. "I'm centered on the late forties," he continued, "the period just after World War Two."

"That's logical," Ezra decided. "That was a period of housing shortages, of expansion and speculation for people who had money. Contractors were building with everything they could lay their hands on." This information, it developed, was based on Ezra's reading of a history of the American trade union movement. Fact and fancy met, merged, separated, and recombined. It struck me that Ezra's detective work was really a form of poetry, filled with subtle truths and nothing very specific.

"Edlyn was only an agent," Reynard said, "for other people, other interests. Most of her friends were dishonest. I'll get it. I'm sure I'll get it all if you don't press me. I was touring then with Elise Krause, the soprano—you remember her, Grace—and I believe she gave her money to Edlyn to invest. A good thing, too, because Elise could never handle money."

Ezra laid down the pad on which he had been scribbling notes.

"I'm sorry," Reynard said, "you know how my mind is. You'll have to indulge me. One thing leads to another, and then back again, off and on, back and forth."

But no one could have been more indulgent than Ezra.

Dutifully, he located Elise Krause and telephoned her. I believe he told her he was writing a history of music in America, because shortly after the phone call, she mailed him a large envelope of photographs, publicity pictures of herself that were at least twenty years old. Elise wanted to be sure she was properly represented in the phantom book. She also told Ezra she knew of no money invested by anyone. "Who had money?" asked Elise, incredulous.

Ezra and I brought the pictures to the hospital to show Reynard.

"She was a spinto," Reynard said, examining the photographs of his old friend.

"A spinto?" Ezra asked.

"A soprano with a strong dramatic quality to her voice, quite different from a lyric soprano. Elise belonged in opera, but she was too lazy to work hard. Is she old and fat now?"

"I really don't know," Ezra replied. "I only spoke with her on the phone."

"Perhaps she has dyed her hair," said Reynard, shuffling the photographs. "Something is wrong. These pictures don't have the right feel to them. They are not the proper sense of the situation."

"What do you mean by 'sense,' Reynard?" I asked.

"Dollars and cents!" he said with a chuckle. "I have made a mistake. There is money somewhere. That is very clear. But apparently the money does not lie with Elise."

We prepared for Christmas. Schutzie baked hundreds of cookies, perhaps thousands. The obliging Ezra was

given the task of delivering them, to the needy, the charitable organizations, to schools and Sunday schools, to the
local day-care center, to nursing homes. "Where else,
Ezra, think!" Schutzie commanded. "You still got that
whole shelf to get rid of!"

"Me!" cried Ezra, laughing. "How did this get to be *my*
project?"

We put up a small Christmas tree. The fourteen violins
from the high school arrived for their annual restringing,
in preparation for the Christmas concert. The house rang
with music as my students labored over "Silent Night,"
"Silver Bells," "Away in a Manger," "Up on the House-
top."

We all spent Christmas Eve at the hospital, Schutzie
distributing cookies to the patients gathered in the
dayroom, Ezra and I playing music for a sing-along. Reynard was spirited into the room quietly and kept in a
back row, because the supervisor of nursing was present.
I can't believe the woman did not see him, but she kept
her face averted. She did not turn, even when, between
carols, Reynard's voice carried clearly across the room.
"I'm not union," he said to Mitch who sat beside him.
"Only union musicians can play in this establishment."

With January, gloom descended. We had all been waiting for Edlyn to make some grand gesture—file a suit,
demand a hearing. Instead, she began to work quietly
behind the scenes. One evening an officer of the court
came to call, "To follow up on this custody," he said.

Mitch knew the man well and greeted him as a friend,
but it soon became clear he had come in the role of
adversary. "Blood relatives usually get priority in these
situations," he said. He was a colorless man, much older

than Mitch. He studied Schutzie with a rude, unblinking stare, seemed affronted by her Oriental eyes, her dark skin, her broken English. "You a citizen, ma'am?"

"Sure!" said Schutzie. "Somebody say I'm not?"

The man ignored her and turned to Mitch. "December, you never told the court you were married to a foreigner."

Mitch contained his irritation but the pitch of his voice rose. "My wife was present with me in court when custody was awarded. Look, I've received no notification of—"

"Hold on!" the man interrupted, raising one hand in annoyance. "You've been around long enough you should know how we do things. If you don't, I'll tell you. I've been in the courthouse thirty-five years. I was a court officer before you were born, long before the liberals and the Socialists started parading around here." In a few sentences, the man had really given a virtuoso performance. He had drawn a circle around the establishment in the courthouse and left Mitch outside of it. "And the way we do things," he continued, "is this: When minors are involved, we like to work quietly. We don't drag children into court if we don't have to."

"And you've had a complaint?" Mitch asked. "A *quiet* complaint?"

"An inquiry, December! That's all." He turned to me. "And you, Ada, your daddy's over at the hospital?"

"Yes," I said.

"And you work," he went on. "You work for pay. Do you know it's illegal to work in Indiana until you're sixteen?"

"I am sixteen."

"Just barely," he replied. "You were working before you were sixteen."

"They let people baby-sit," I ventured.

"Look here, young lady," he said, losing patience. "I followed this up. My grandson's a student over at the high school. You do the repair work on those instruments and the school pays you, makes out regular vouchers just like they do for any other vendor. That's not baby-sitting." And to Mitch, "If you're not able to support a child you have no business taking one into your home."

To this, Mitch made probably the worst possible reply. "Even young people need to do useful work to maintain their self-esteem. That was my major consideration in this case."

The man looked at him with undisguised scorn. Still, the court system was lethargic, blessedly slow to act. "Do you think you can straigthen out these violations, December?" the man asked. I sensed he had little real interest in my case, would take no initiatives, do no more than the situation required on a given day.

Clearly, Mitch realized he had angered the man. He sought now to repair the damage. "I'll see to everything," he promised, giving the words a mild, conciliatory tone. "You can tell your . . . informant that there will be no violations."

When the man had gone, Mitch said, "Ada, open a savings account in your own name tomorrow. Bank every penny of the money you earn from now on."

"All right," I said.

"We sell that mixer," Schutzie offered, "put the money in the bank. Son of a gun."

"Absolutely not, Schutzie," I said. "We'll say the mixer is my property and I'm letting you borrow it, okay?"

"Okay!" she said with relief.

"Mitch," I said, "who would have thought that man would find the vouchers at the high school?"

"He didn't," Mitch replied. "You can be sure of that. He doesn't have enough imagination to do something like that."

"Then it was Edlyn?"

"I'm sure it was," Mitch answered. "She—or one of her operatives—ferreted it out and brought it to the court's attention."

"Operative?" I asked. The word sounded ominous. "Mitch, what about Edlyn's drinking? Can we make something of that?"

He had already considered this angle. "I hope so," he said, "but we'll need more evidence than we have now, more than a single, isolated incident. We'll need objective witnesses to a consistent pattern of drunkenness."

A few days later, Mitch was notified he would be investigated by the Indiana Bar Association. Four years earlier, he had defended strikers in a labor dispute. "Labor unions have never been popular in Indiana," he said.

The investigation, which would drag on for nearly a month, eventually turned up no improprieties in Mitch's handling of the case, but the fact of it, the challenge to Mitch's integrity, would stand forever in the records. The first direct damage to the Decembers, on my account, had been done. "How did Edlyn do it?" I asked Mitch.

"We'll never know," he replied, "but starting an investigation isn't all that difficult. She may know a judge somewhere, or just a highly-placed attorney."

"I'm sorry, Mitch."

"For what? Having me proved an honest man?"

This display of cheerfulness, I knew, was only superficial. Mitch had been deeply wounded.

Futility was everywhere. It was time for me to leave. With my savings account, I even had a little money now. I no longer thought of "running away." It was a childish expression. Reynard had managed on his own long before he was sixteen; I could do as well. If I couldn't play on the street corners, I could probably play in bars. Ezra did it regularly, had done it for years. Still, I vacillated. The sun rose, I ate Schutzie's breakfasts, attended school, taught my students, rehaired violin bows. Could some act of Edlyn's really put an end to this routine? "It makes no sense," I said to Ezra one day as we walked home from the hospital. "If Edlyn wanted to keep me quiet, the best way would be to win my friendship, not to threaten me. If I had anything to tell, I would have spoken out by now. I would have defended myself. Why can't she see that?"

"You're right," he said. "It isn't logical. That's because we're not dealing with a reasonable person. What we're confronting is paranoia, pathological fear."

"You sound like Mitch."

"I'll tell you the difference between Mitch and me," he said. "Mitch believes we live in a civilized world with only an occasional aberration, here and there."

"And you believe the opposite."

"Exactly. Aberrations are the norm. Here and there you may find a civilized person—if you're lucky."

"When I sit in that dayroom, I can believe you. Then civilization seems far away."

"And outside of the walls, the prisons and the hospitals, things are only a little better," said Ezra.

"Did I tell you Edlyn described me to the hospital superintendent as a retarded child? A mental case?"

"You told me."

Edlyn gave us a period of peace; my apprehension subsided. Then one winter afternoon, as I was giving a little girl her violin lesson in the living room, I raised my bow to demonstrate a passage, and caught sight of my face reflected in the hall mirror. Adolescence had not been kind to me. My cheeks, always gaunt, had thinned almost to emaciation. My eyes in the dim shadows of the hall looked bright, wild, a little crazy. What I saw was a death's-head, an oval skull papered with sallow skin, fringed with thin, straight hair. Who would persuade the world I was not ill, not insane, not a monster, when all of the physical evidence showed clearly that I was? Not Mitch, surely not Ezra. A woman clever enough to invade the high school's files and instigate an investigation by the Bar Association would have no trouble at all having me committed along with my father. No patient in Reynard's dayroom had a physical appearance worse than mine. If Edlyn did not already see this simple solution to her problems, she soon would.

As I finished my student's lesson, Ezra was getting into his coat to go to the hospital. "Wait, I'll go with you," I said. One last time, I told myself, to say good-bye to my father.

"We're still working on the money," Ezra said as we set out.

I had not seen Reynard in a week. "The money?"

"You remember; he thought Elise Krause had given Edlyn money to invest."

"And you still believe him?"

Ezra looked pained and did not answer.

I don't think my father had missed me, or even realized I had been absent. He showed no surprise at seeing me and said, simply, "Tell me what you think about the letter *E*, Ada."

"What?"

"What are your associations with it?"

"E string," I replied. "Easter. How about Edlyn?"

"Yes, very good," he said, "but you are unfortunately wrong. I thought you might see what I see, which would confirm it in a way."

Erza asked, "What do you see?"

Reynard sat forward in his chair and lowered his voice. "You will recall that I initially thought of Elise Krause, but the money does not lie with Elise. Still, the letter *E* is unmistakable. It's so obvious that one of us should have recognized it immediately. The *E* is for Ezra."

"For me?" Ezra asked.

"Yes, you," Reynard replied. "You're going to come into some money."

This was too much, even for the indulgent Ezra. "There's no conceivable way that could happen," he said gently.

"Let me explain," said Reynard. He sat back, folded his hands thoughtfully. "At the beginning my . . . situation took the form of political fanaticism. I saw Communists everywhere. Then the problem redefined itself. I realized the threat was coming from Edlyn. Do you see how it all moved from the general to the specific? But the human mind is very complex; many things go on simultaneously. Polar compression is everywhere, the combination of opposites. The problem and the solution are always intertwined. All of that led up to the fire at Thanksgiving. But politics was only a defense, a psychic defense. Even my letters to Edlyn were defense. I was afraid to face the powers that lay beneath."

"Beneath?" Ezra asked.

"At the lower levels of my mind. I shut them out. Then, when the house caught fire, the strength of those powers became so great they broke through. I saw that Ada was in danger. Second sight led me to rescue her. Once the forces broke through, they were no longer frightening. The reason my behavior has stabilized is that the defenses are gone now, because I no longer fear what lies beneath them; second sight. Do you understand, Ezra?"

Ezra nodded with his customary courtesy. "Actually, I agree with a good bit of that."

I said, "I think I'll try again to see the superintendent."

"Don't bother," Reynard said, "in a day or two they will move me back to my old ward, without your doing anything."

"Did they tell you that?" I asked.

"They don't know it yet," Reynard replied. "They will say they are moving me because my health is deteriorating in that room, and because I have been a well-behaved patient. That will satisfy Edlyn if she happens to inquire. But the truth is, they will need the space for someone else, a violent patient."

The orderly appeared. "I'm sorry, I have to take you back," he said. "A doctor will be coming through here in a few minutes."

Reynard leaned forward and laid one hand on Ezra's head. "Money," he whispered, "and the move back to my old ward."

"Good-bye, Reynard," I said. "I love you. Good-bye."

But I did not leave Richmount. Before the week was out, both of Reynard's predictions had come true.

11

THE ARRIVAL of Popcorn Joe in the calliope hall alarms the monkey. He leaps suddenly from my lap onto the keyboard, then to my shoulder. He throws his scrawny arms about my neck and clutches me in terror, peers down the stairway to see the sudden menace, the dull, echoing shuffle of approaching footsteps.

"Is someone coming, Scaddegood?" I ask in a syrupy voice that astonishes me. Although I have lived with this circus and its menagerie for two years, I have formed no close bonds to animals. Traces of my father's dislike for cats and dogs linger in me. If Monumenta intrigues me, she also repels me; yet this monkey is different. His ability to communicate amazes me. "Who's coming?" I ask. At this moment, Scaddegood wrinkles his nose. He has caught the scent of a friend. He relaxes his grip, nearly smiles, and as if he has understood my question, moves his hands in the motions of turning a steering wheel. The purring hum of an automobile engine ripples from his lips. This performance deserves a reward. I stroke the fuzzy pin head with real admiration. "It's Joe, then! You're a clever little beast, aren't you?"

Shortly, Joe's face appears in the shadowed stairway. "Norma, Belle wants you!" he shouts up to me. "She says you should come. There's something for you, a package in the mail. She phoned me to come and bring you. I'll run you back." Reaching my secluded nest he discovers Scaddegood on my shoulder. "Belle thinks that monkey's lost!" he exclaims.

"He followed me, Joe. He can open doors. He came in after you left."

"She said she'd been searching for him, told me over the phone. She thinks he's hidden himself up in the roof of the house somewhere. Who'd send you a package?"

"Another package?"

"Yes, another one." Joe is alert with curiosity and a little breathless from the climb up the stairs.

"I ordered blue jeans from the catalog." This is a lie and Joe knows it. I am stalling. During my first year with Belle, my presence at the farm went undetected beyond our local community. At the beginning of the second year, Reynard started sending me packages. I do not know how he manages to mail them from the hospital, nor how long his curious method of addressing them will go unnoticed by others who may be looking for me. There is a package about every three months. With sinking heart, I wonder if I should put the score for the suite under my shirt, next to my belly, and start walking. If it is time for me to go, I do not wish to linger one day too long, one moment even. I have learned the lesson of not obeying that quick, hard grip at the heart, that signal to go without delay; but cold weather and the knowledge of Belle's warm kitchen make me reluctant. "Blue jeans," I say again.

"Naw," says Joe, "a big heavy package."

I try again. "I was kidding, Joe. It's old magazines for Belle. This man said they were free and I asked him to mail them to me for Belle."

The excitement slips from Joe's face. My guess, it develops, comes close to the truth. The mystery is mostly solved. "There's that writing all through them," says Joe. Belle, then, has opened the package, probably rewrapped it, and already told Joe of its contents over the phone. "Why would there be writing all through them?"

I have answered this question before. So far, all Reynard's packages have been alike. "That's why they were free. Who wants magazines that are written in? But Belle will still like them."

"The postmark is Richmount, like all the others." Joe is mollified, and disappointed. Reynard, then, has not slipped, has not inadvertently provided Belle with my real identity.

I put my music away, rise to go with Scaddegood in my arms, but Joe has turned reluctant. He takes the monkey from me and posts himself across the top of the stairway, barring my exit. He has lost interest in the mystery package. I notice for the first time that he is carrying a rolled poster under his arm. Leaving Scaddegood to cling unaided to his shoulder, Joe now unfurls the poster with delight and begins to explain it to me, his captive audience. It is a shiny, colorful picture of circus horses pulling a beer wagon, an advertisement. He found it posted in a bar, he explains. The owner of the bar gave it to him, believing it was suitable memorabilia for the circus museum. It is not; the poster is not old enough to be a vintage artifact, but the photograph has enthralled Joe. He wants to tell somebody about these horses and this beer wagon. "Those are Clydesdales," he says, changing to a dry, scholarly voice. "Not Percherons. Percherons are usually gray, dappled. These are ginger brown, don't you see?"

"With the big, white hairy feet." I wonder if it is conceivable that the authorities have traced Reynard's package, are even waiting for me at Belle's farm by now. My imagination goes wild for a moment. With my bad leg, I cannot run. I picture myself awkwardly stumbling off across the stubbly winter fields. If I returned to the farm and discovered an ambush, perhaps I could shout, The lion is loose! Create a diversion and buy a little time. Find the toy gun and draw it ominously, stage a standoff. This is ridiculous. What is a little writing in a few magazines? Indiana is cold in January. I stare at the fuzzy feet of the horses in the picture, hear the hum of Joe's voice rolling on. Maybe no one cares about my whereabouts anymore. I am twenty years old, no longer a minor. For the moment, the calliope loft seems safe. A warm lethargy slips over me. When Joe's voice stops, I say, "Tell me about the horses. Tell me all of it. Were they harder to drive than elephants? Than camels?"

Comparing Clydesdales with exotic animals does not interest Joe. He has no easy repertoire of answers for these odd questions and so ignores them, goes on with the story he is already telling me. "April, nineteen thirty-three, Prohibition went out. They wanted circus horses to celebrate, for parades, pulling beer wagons. Trucks wouldn't have done it. Not that they didn't have trucks then, motor trucks. Sure they did! They could've had trucks, if you see what I mean." He pauses now, a little helpless, searching for words to express the enormous feeling that possesses him. "It was a celebration they wanted, you see, so it all went together." Scaddegood raises one hand to his mouth, grooms it daintily with his agile tongue, manipulates his tail in sweeping motions, a bit like an orchestra conductor waving a baton. "They wanted circus horses."

I slip comfortably into the refuge of Joe's story, a temporary shelter, warm as a fuzzy blanket. The Clydesdales in the photograph are dressed out in bright blue and silver harness, red and white ribbons. It is an eight-horse hitch. Two drivers in green circus livery sit atop the wagon's box. Joe studies the picture intently, dangling it at arm's length with one hand, idly stroking the monkey with the other. Scaddegood is content enough, slackjawed now and relaxed. Perhaps he is weary from his day's adventures. "Using horses," Joe continues, "was ceremonial. There weren't more than a dozen men in the world could handle an eight-horse hitch." It is as if some detail of the picture has eluded him. "They wanted circus horses," he says, growing more and more animated, a little frantic.

I think of Ezra. "I once had a friend who said both sides of the soul merge in the horse," I tell Joe. "It's an animal suited for both drudgery and ceremony, work and play, dark and light. He said the figure of the horse admits all dark genius into workaday sunshine."

Joe appears to understand perfectly. "Circus people work hard. Folks seldom appreciate that part of our lives."

"And he said man and the machine merge perfectly in the motorcycle. Perhaps it's the same thing."

"Motorcycles." Joe nods, relieved of his anxiety, grateful for my support. He pats his polished hair with satisfaction.

But I have inadvertently put an end to his story, and I am not yet ready to return to Belle's house. "Joe, this monkey doesn't like music," I say, stalling. "Watch this." I raise my hands above the keyboard as if to play. Scaddegood has been chewing idly on the collar of Joe's shirt. Now, swiftly, he drops the collar and claps both hands over his ears. He grimaces and sways precariously on Joe's shoulder while he regains his balance.

"Look at that!" Joe exclaims in dismay. "He's been tethered to a calliope, or maybe a big organ." Joe has finished with the poster. He rolls it up and turns his attention to Scaddegood. "Monkeys are abused more than any other animals. Once a publicity man from Cole's had one shaved in a barber shop to get a newspaper story. Had him shaved clean."

"Tell me the story, Joe."

"He caught cold and died," says Joe, but he is done with stories for now. "Belle says to come," he remembers, "come right away."

"I can walk. There's no hurry."

"No need. We don't want this monkey to take a chill. If I drive him back, you might as well ride, too."

* * *

Belle is waiting for us, peering through the window. No one else is in sight. I feel swift relief.

As I suspect, the package has been carefully re-wrapped in brown paper and tied with raffia. The original creases in the paper are visible. Belle proffers it at the door, now torn between her relief at recovering the monkey and her curiosity over the package. "The mailman brought it," she says.

"The monkey followed Norma," says Joe, handing Scaddegood to Belle. "He was sitting in her lap up in the calliope loft. He's been tethered to one. He covers his ears when he sees her start to play."

I accept the package. Across the front of it, in my father's careful hand, replete with misspellings, is written, "To the girl with the bad leg who playes music at the lion farm." Followed by the name of our village.

Belle is comforting Scaddegood but now turns to me eagerly. "Well, open it up! Maybe it's a nice present!"

Inside the wrapping are four copies of *National Geographic*, the magazine available in most plentiful supply in Reynard's dayroom. "The Swiss Alps!" I exclaim. "What a treat!"

Joe says, "She got them for you, Belle. For free, like before."

Belle sends him a sharp glance for betraying the fact that she had already opened the package. "Who are they from, Norma?" she asks.

"A dealer in Richmount." I turn the pages of the first magazine, pretending that my interest is only casual. In the margins, in careful script, Reynard has copied out the Book of Leviticus from the Bible. I skim through the words looking for significant insertions or deletions, but the text appears to be unaltered. To Belle and Joe I read, "And the Lord called unto Moses, and spake unto him out of the tabernacle of the congregation, saying, 'Speak unto the children of Israel, and say unto them, If any man of you bring an offering unto the Lord, ye shall bring your offering of the cattle, even of the herd, and of the flock.' " Instructions for orderly worship in the tabernacle. More intriguing perhaps, for my father, lessons in hygiene and sanitation. Beside a photograph of mountain climbers in the Swiss Alps, almost as a caption, Reynard has inscribed the treatment for leprosy. "Listen to this, Belle. 'And the priest shall look on him the seventh day: and, behold, if the plague in his sight be at a stay, and the plague spread not in the skin; then the priest shall shut him up seven days more.' " Perhaps Reynard now believes he has been shut up in the hospital for leprosy. It is the King James version of the Bible, graceful and flowing, secretive, rambling, lending its meaning in a grudging, circuitous fashion. Like my father.

"You haven't been to Richmount," Belle presses on. "Who do you know there?"

"Someone who knows me only as a girl with a bad leg." I set this forth for her consideration. "If the person had known me, wouldn't he or she have written my name on the package?"

Belle sees the logic of this and sighs. Despite her curiosity, she will not betray me. No surreptitious phone calls will be made, no letters to authorities written. I am a little giddy with relief. "Actually, Belle, they're from my father. He has second sight. That's how he found me, but he can't remember my real name."

She sniffs her disdain.

It amuses me to trail traces of the truth right under Belle's nose and watch her reject them as too preposterous to be true.

Belle proceeds methodically. "You say someone in a shop promised to send you magazines, but they didn't know your name?"

"They probably just forgot my name. The magazines are free because they're written in. Who wants to buy written-in magazines?" I have decided not to worry about the package. I will simply be cautious in the next days, watch for new developments, but I am always cautious. "Here's Birmingham," I say, turning to the second magazine. Its margins are filled with the poems of Robert Browning. "My Last Duchess" leads off on the table of contents page.

"Birmingham, Alabama or England?" Belle asks.

"Alabama."

Joe says, "I was robbed once in Birmingham, Alabama." He has been preparing to leave. Darkness has now settled over the farm. But he decides to linger, to remember Birmingham, Alabama.

"I once played there with the Cooper show," Belle offers, beginning to prepare our supper. "While we were there, all of the camel men quit in an argument with their boss, a man named Childers. He wanted them to dress up as fake Arabs. They all walked out and there was no one to look after the camels. Then the manager told everyone to sleep in the camel tent that night, to watch them, but I refused. I never lowered myself to such things."

"Birmingham, Alabama," says Joe warmly.

The margins of the photographs of Birmingham have

been illuminated with lines from "Pippa Passes." Scaddegood joins me, bends over the magazine with apparent interest, then swings his head swiftly to bite my thumb. This attack seems meant in play, but still manages to break the skin. "Joe," I say with sudden resolve, "if this animal is going to keep biting me, I'll take him in for inoculations. Can you drive me into town in the morning?"

"That's nonsense!" Belle scoffs. "He's a nice, clean monkey."

"Can you, Joe?"

"Sure," he replies, "be glad to. Belle, let her do it. You know it's a good idea. We've never been able to keep a monkey."

Belle and her friends usually doctor their animals themselves. During their working years, they were always strangers passing through strange towns. They mistrusted the local people they played to, wanted no outsiders handling their beasts. Often they could not afford veterinarians and consulted them only at times of real emergency. Sometimes local veterinarians were not trained to treat circus animals, or were fearful of the big cats, the colorful snakes, the rhinos, the larger apes. The circus folk are masters at preparing poultices, lancing abscesses, suturing wounds. Skillfully they minister to the bloated and flatulent. They deliver the pregnant, abort the unwanted. They deworm and unconstipate, force fevers up or down as desired. When they must, they execute, with cool deliberation, knowing the exact path a bullet must take in each exotic animal to bring swift and merciful death. But their mistrust of outsiders causes them to ignore vaccinations. A working circus administered its own inoculations, had a full medicine shelf. But the vials and syringes of Belle and her friends were empty long ago. Pharmacists will not hand over the medications without prescriptions; veterinarians insist on administering injections themselves. The circus folk make do, and do without.

Belle agrees to my plan by simply ignoring it.

"Will you stay and have a bite with us?" she asks Joe.

Reminded of the hour, he declines and hurries on his way. "Keep the place closed up good or you'll lose that monkey again," he cautions.

"He's calming down," Belle announces confidently. "I doubt he'll go off again."

When Joe has gone, Belle sets before us a supper of fried potatoes and smoked sausage. From somewhere, bananas have appeared. The arrival of Scaddegood has been acknowledged and heralded in the circus community. In the next days, many offerings will be brought to the door for him. A monkey brings luck.

Scaddegood is, indeed, settling in. As we eat, he moves about us languorously, taking bits of food from our plates and eating daintily. In the middle of the meal, he locates the box of cat litter Belle has prepared for him and defecates noisily.

"There's a good boy," Belle says approvingly. And to me, "He has a little gas but his bowels are open. That's a good sign."

The litter box is located in a corner of the kitchen, and now the heavy, sour odor of Scaddegood's accomplishment drifts to us. I wonder if this monkey is humiliated by his confinement, or if he accepts it with grace and rises above it. As if to demonstrate the latter, Scaddegood now sails up into the air and settles on a high shelf.

"Cover it up," Belle tells him firmly. "Scritch, scritch." She makes a small, clawing motion with one hand. To my amazement, Scaddegood comes meekly down, returns to the litter box, and covers his excrement.

"Did someone teach him to do that?" I ask.

"Not well enough," says Belle, "but he'll catch on."

"Where will he sleep?"

"With me, I expect," says Belle.

The cat litter does its work and the odor disappears. I am surprised, as always, at how easily circus people live with animals. Impressed by Scaddegood's intelligence, I make one more gesture of friendship toward him. I offer him a bit of sausage from my fingers. He approaches carelessly, then without warning, snatches the sausage from me and again sinks two teeth into the back of my hand.

"Stop that!" Belle cries, but Scaddegood has once again sailed upward, out of reach. This time he clings to the top of a doorframe.

"He doesn't like me, Belle. Yet he sat on my lap in the calliope loft."

"That was work," says Belle, "or he thought it was. He thought it was an act, and he's been trained to behave in acts."

"But when he's off duty he's his own man?"

"I expect so."

"It's the music he doesn't like, Belle. Music and musicians. Yet he followed me. He must have already known I was a musician."

"I imagine he did," says Belle without further interest.

"I'll wash up," I offer, and Belle quickly accepts. She is eager to be at the stack of *National Geographics*.

"I won't cut them up yet," she assures me. I suspect she is as curious as I am to peruse Reynard's carefully copied lines, but if this is her goal she is quickly distracted from it. "Here's a picture of zebras!" she announces with pleasure. "I once worked over a pen of zebras. I wore a striped outfit. I guess I looked like one of them all right. It was a big hit."

When the dishes are washed, I join her, find a *National Geographic* featuring British Columbia. The third magazine is embellished with the Book of Esther, the fourth with essays by Ralph Waldo Emerson.

"New York," says Belle, wistfully turning a page. "The Staten Island ferry." Her voice softens; she extends the photograph for my examination. "Once Alexander and I had a free day and New York was such a delight, so filled with novelty. Europe was the center of all real culture, of course, but New York was so pleasant."

"And Alexander?" I mask my curiosity by returning my attention to my own magazine, and staring resolutely at the page before me.

"In New York," Belle continues, "you could find all the fancy, frivolous little things. Thread in every color. I sewed all of my own costumes. On the Continent, I wore mostly pure white, but in New York I found more colored fabrics. I could have been a dress designer, you know."

"What did you wear on the ferry boat?" I urge.

"A simple little shift. It was yellow. And a big hat, white lace with a yellow ribbon. I always wore a hat for protection from the sun. Alexander said the hat made me look even smaller. He could never believe how tiny I was." She laughs lightly, remembering. "We took a picnic and slipped away one day." Scaddegood, as if drawn in by the tale, comes quietly down to nestle in Belle's lap, and she falls silent.

"What was Staten Island like then?"

"Oh, there were lovely open fields with wildflowers blooming, goldenrod and chicory. But on the ferry coming back, I lost my hat. The wind caught it and it sailed out across the water. We never saw it sink. It floated away, carried by a wave, until it was out of sight."

"What did Alexander say?"

But the tale is over. Belle muses, then looks up from the page with genuine surprise. "What did he say? You won't believe this latest story he is telling, to everyone but me. He says he's firing Danny Brundage and hiring a new drummer. Everyone's talking about it. It's all for my benefit, of course. He thinks if he threatens me over Danny I'll agree to his moving the calliope." She pauses to give me a contented smile. "Danny Brundage was drumming for me when I did my first triple. Alexander would never dare fire him. Norma, do you know the problem with the triple? The audience cannot really count that fast. It looks no harder to them than a double. The ringmaster must always announce a triple. The two-and-a-half, where the flyer is caught by the legs, is much more impressive to watch."

But I did not want to hear about triple somersaults, nor about Danny Brundage. I wanted to continue dreaming of the white and yellow hat sailing on forever over the sea.

In the morning, when Monumenta has been fed and

Belle and I have eaten breakfast, I fasten a leash and collar on Scaddegood.

"Shots are not necessary," says Belle, "not necessary at all. In a healthy animal community like ours, isolated from diseased animals, there's absolutely no danger."

"What about the sick horse?" I ask. "What about Scaddegood himself? How can you say we're isolated?"

"Not at all," Belle murmurs, but she locates her purse in a kitchen drawer. "If you insist, I'll pay for it, of course. He's my monkey." She presses a fifty-cent piece into my hand. "If that's not enough, you tell me."

"Thank you, Belle, I'm sure it will be enough."

At the sound of Joe's truck, Scaddegood comes to life in my arms, wriggles to look past my shoulder and out of the window. "He remembers riding in the truck," I say to Belle.

"Of course," she replies.

"He's just like a child. He wants to go for a ride." Despite the bites, I do not dislike this monkey. I venture to stroke his head and he responds with an affectionate pat to my cheek.

When we are under way, Joe turns solicitous and conspiratorial. "Norma, I know Belle doesn't go for shots, but you're doing the right thing. Monkeys are delicate." With two fingers he retrieves a dollar bill from his shirt pocket and extends it to me.

"That's not necessary, Joe."

"I know, I know, but I want to. Let's just say I'm buying an interest in the little fellow."

"Thank you, Joe."

The veterinarian, a woman in her sixties, sturdily built, with bobbed gray hair, is curious. "How is the lion?"

"Old and nearly toothless."

She smiles. "A lion doesn't need many teeth to do damage."

"No, not many."

"They have mostly dog acts?"

"Mostly, yes."

"And they don't bring their dogs in for shots. Do you realize many of the skunks and raccoons in this area are rabid?"

"The dogs are usually confined. What do you make of the monkey?"

"His lungs are congested. I'm going to give him an antibiotic along with the vaccinations. I doubt he's ever had one before, and in that case they work very well, almost miraculously. Otherwise, he looks good. It's probably just a heavy cold." She administers a series of shots and charges me thirty dollars. "You strike me as an intelligent young woman. Tell them to bring the dogs in, persuade them."

"Couldn't you just sell me the rabies vaccine? Circus people know perfectly well how to give injections."

"I'm not allowed to do that."

"They're wary of doctors, of all outsiders. Couldn't you bend the rules?"

"No, but I could drive out there and vaccinate the dogs. I'd do it free, charge them nothing. Try to persuade them."

"Yes, I will. I'll try to persuade them."

Scaddegood is rubbing his bottom from the sting of the shots, but as I pick him up to go, he suddenly extends his right hand to the veterinarian. "So, you want to shake hands!" She laughs, taking the small, wrinkled hand.

"I seem to be the only one he bites," I venture.

"I had a monkey once," the woman offers. "They're peculiar little beasts, very peculiar."

12

WHEN EZRA received his check, he thought he was rich.

The capo is not a new device. It is as old as fretted instruments, as old as stiff fingers and sluggish minds. A few years ago somebody persuaded most of the people in the world they should play the guitar. Reynard's appraisal of the guitar craze, repeated frequently over the years, goes straight to the heart of the matter: "It is the paradox of our time that the ungifted, the rank amateurs of the world, have chosen for themselves the most difficult instrument human cunning has ever devised. The guitar? I don't believe it! Department stores are selling more guitars than refrigerators!" He discouraged students who appeared at our door asking for guitar lessons. "Unless you are prepared to devote the rest of your life to this instrument, don't even consider beginning."

There is a school of classical guitar. It consists of players who exploit the instrument to its fullest capacity. These people play scales, melody lines, harmonies with plausible counterpoint, and a variety of rhythmic patterns. They play in several keys—A flat, for example, and F sharp minor. They take lessons in a traditional fashion, study for lengthy periods of time, often with many teachers. They are dedicated. They play Bach and Villa-Lobos, Albéniz and Brahms. This school is a very small one. Almost everyone else plays, with luck, three chords.

Venturing beyond simple chords in easy keys quickly leads the player into the treacherous realm of wrist-wrenching hand positions and mind-boggling finger combinations that must be committed to memory. Sharps, flats, key changes, enharmonic equivalencies—the difficulties increase geometrically. A capo is a movable bar that is attached to the fingerboard of a fretted instrument to uniformly raise the pitch of all the strings. With a capo, a player can continue to use simple fingerings in unsimple keys. The instrument is changed rather than the hand position.

The design of Ezra's capo took into consideration the most important point about these devices: no one wants to be seen using one. All guitarists would like it to appear that they know what they're doing. His capo was a slender, streamlined object of dull color that was almost invisible from a distance of only a few feet. It could also be attached, removed, or shifted with a minimum of fuss.

The letter he received shortly after Reynard's prediction came from the manufacturer of the capo. It had been forwarded from the prison. While Ezra had been languishing in his cell, the capo had earned him several thousand dollars. A note consisting of a single sentence was folded into the check. "In accordance with your request," it read, "we have reissued the check with today's date."

"Whose request?" I asked. Ezra and I were standing on Mitch's small, lopsided front porch, beside the mailbox.

Ezra's smile was peevish. "The prison held up my money all this time. They were afraid I'd use it to hire a good lawyer, so they didn't give me my mail. Now they want to keep me happy."

"Do you have a patent on the capo?"

He shrugged. Once his initial surprise had passed, there was really no anger in him. Even pique was too strong a word to describe his attitude. "I don't think there's a patent," he said. "I really don't remember. The manufacturer fixed it up. I think I have a licensing arrangement."

"I don't think you can have a licensing arrangement without a patent to license," I said.

He began to laugh. "Look, Ada, they gave me the money. I'm rich! Okay?"

"Ezra, you aren't making sense. You take a stand on an impossible cause like Reynard's, then turn passive in a situation like this, where you could take some reasonable action. Talk to Mitch about it. Go back to the prison and straighten out your affairs. Maybe you could clear your name."

"There isn't time now," he said.

"Going back would make more sense than drawing maps of Chicago."

"But Ada, look what my experience is doing to the legal system. It's causing people to look at their policies. They're afraid of what I might do. I'm much more powerful if I do nothing and let them wonder. Their concern now about me could make them more cautious the next time they deal with a man's life."

"Maybe," I said, "but it could also make them very eager to find some reason to put you behind bars again, so you can't make any trouble for them."

But the subject did not interest him. "I'm going to cash this and buy Schutzie something nice," he said, "for looking after all of us. Then I'm going to Chicago and hire private detectives."

"That could stir up Edlyn if she found out. Things are bad enough already."

"Things will improve now," he said confidently.

In the excitement of Ezra's proposed trip, the matter of a patent for the capo was not taken up again, but a local police detective dropped by to see Ezra. "I understand you served time in prison," he said.

"And you've been asked to watch me?" Ezra said with amusement. "Watch all you like. I'm a performer. I like being watched."

When the man had gone, I said, "I told you so."

"Ada, don't say 'I told you so,'" he answered with a grin. "It isn't charitable." The money had put him in high good humor.

I went with Ezra to say good-bye to Reynard. The Chicago trip was planned for the following morning. "Here is cheesecake," said Schutzie. "Take it along for Mr. Cunningham."

My father had been moved back to his old ward. The orderly greeted us warmly. "We're glad to have him back. We all missed him."

Ezra asked, "Did they need his room for someone else?"

But the man would not answer; he turned and walked away.

Even Reynard's violin had been returned to him, but he was not playing. He was bent over a table in the arts and crafts room, with his back to us, painting a picture with a large brush and bright poster paint on coarse newsprint. Ezra told him about the money.

"Yes," Reynard said without turning around. "I've something here to show you."

Always hopeful, Ezra said, "William Blake painted."

Reynard nodded. "That's a good place to begin. You see, I realize the concept of second sight is troubling you both a good deal. You think it is the invention of an insane mind—and I don't deny I'm insane—but it's really a concept that has been with us for a long time. The subjects in medieval church art see visions all of the time. For centuries, you know, the supernatural was used to explain phenomena that are now understood through science. Disease, for example. But there's more to it than that, much more."

I said, "Schutzie sent cheesecake, Reynard. Do you want a piece?"

"The X ray would seem supernatural to someone who did not understand it," he continued, "so we have further to go with our science. Coming at it differently, isn't all art really second sight? What visions did Bach see? Beethoven?"

"She put blueberries on it," I said. "I'll cut you a piece."

Reynard turned to face us and gestured toward his

painting. "I'm talking about the invisible world. I've painted this to illustrate to you the invisible world, its reality."

"And you painted it now," Ezra said with growing interest. "I mean you painted it this morning, because you knew without our telling you that we were coming."

"Of course," said Reynard.

"You come every day," I said to Ezra.

The invisible world was mostly green. It consisted of intersecting circles in clusters and chains, large circles and small. One was red, two were yellow, the rest—a dozen or so—were green. The picture looked a little like a drawing of atoms and molecules; it looked like the diagrams of test questions in logic that are given to school children: A will walk to school with B but not with C. C will not walk with B. D will walk only with C. Which of these students can walk together in a single group? I said, "Ezra, find the largest common area of intersecting circles." He glanced at me sharply and did not reply.

"Just let me play it for you," Reynard said. He moved to the sink and washed his hands, took a large bite of the cheesecake I had cut, and raised his violin. He began with a long, vibrant open G, swept into a G minor arpeggio rising over two octaves, played a rapid series of double-stops, all in fourths. Then he stopped abruptly. The sweep of carefully articulated sound was a pattern of harmonies that suddenly lost its center. The fourths sounded arid, bitter. The passage hung in the air, unresolved and unfinished.

Ezra asked, "What about the ending?"

"It's invisible," I said.

Reynard turned his attention to fine-tuning his E

string. His chin was flattened on the violin to hold it securely while his right hand worked the small, silver tuner at the bridge. With his left hand, he held his bow suspended, pointed carefully at the floor, in the manner of an orchestra player who must always take care not to strike the players on either side of him. He looked like a busy squirrel bent over a nut. His eyes, above the warm gleam of the wood, were angelic.

Guilt assailed me. "I'm sorry, Reynard," I said gently. "I was only teasing. It's a lovely picture."

"Thank you," he said. "I may do another in yellow."

The weather warmed suddenly; the ice melted. Ezra took it as a good omen. "Great bike weather!" he said. He gassed up the motorcycle and headed for Chicago.

Because he was so confident he would succeed, Ezra took no precautions to conceal his efforts from Edlyn. She must have discovered almost immediately that his detectives were questioning people about her. Within a week of Ezra's departure, Edlyn sent us a copy of a letter she had written to the court in Richmount, which held jurisdiction over both Reynard and me. In it, she restated all of her concerns for my physical and mental well being. She recalled in detail the events surrounding my mother's funeral, including her disbelief and sadness at finding me unable to dial the telephone or feed myself. The picture she drew was of a severely handicapped, imbecilic child. Then she turned her attention to Schutzie. "Mrs. December lacks the cultural background and education to be a proper mother for this child."

Mitch was angry, but Schutzie was livid. "Why can't she say straight out I got the wrong color skin!" she cried.

"She want everybody white! White as her son of a bitch car!"

I felt personally responsible for this hurtful attack on Schutzie. It was Saturday and the bank was open until one o'clock. I walked down and withdrew my money; I had almost three hundred dollars. That night I dreamed I was very small and my mother was dressing me for a special occasion. She buttoned me into a pink coat that resembled a baby's nightgown. Her fingers toyed with the top button and then began to stroke my throat. I looked up into her face and saw that it was not my mother at all, but Edlyn. Then she looked away from me, and tears began to roll down her cheeks. I woke suddenly, a knot of terror in my throat.

A few days later Edlyn appeared in person. I had just come in from school. Mitch was at his office. The warm temperatures had melted the snow. "That aunt of yours is here!" Schutzie said, peering out the front window. The afternoon sun glanced off the white Lincoln as it drew to the curb. Edlyn stepped from it, resplendent in a pink suit. "She looks like an Easter egg," said Schutzie. "I'm not gonna let her in."

"Don't be ridiculous, Schutzie," I said. When Edlyn rang the bell, I squared my shoulders and opened the door.

"Ada, it's good to see you!" Edlyn began, giving us her small, tight smile. "And you, Mrs. December. Is your husband at home?"

"No!" said Schutzie. Then, abruptly, "You are a bitch!" She stood very straight and tugged at the points of her jerkin. "Go away!"

"Schutzie, it's all right," I said. "Please."

But Schutzie would not be calmed. She picked up a vase and raised it above her head as if to throw it.

Edlyn looked startled, and then amused. "I need to speak to my niece as well. Ada, perhaps we could go for a walk."

"Don't go, Ada!" Schutzie cried. "You hear me?"

"A walk sounds fine," I said. "Schutzie, calm down."

Reluctantly, Schutzie lowered the vase. "You stay in broad daylight," she cautioned. "You don't go down alleys."

"Right," I said. I found a jacket and followed Edlyn down the steps.

"How can you stand that?" she asked, annoyed and yet making a joke of it. "Living with that Japanese." We set off down the sidewalk. "We were always a well-bred family, Ada. Your mother and I were raised in a lovely home, you know. Everything was very clean."

"Schutzie is clean," I replied. "She's a better housekeeper than Grace ever was. You really can't blame her for being angry. You've done some ugly things to us." I wondered why she had come and if we were at last to have a confrontation.

"Nonsense!" Edlyn declared. "The ugliness comes from that disgusting folksinger your father has set on me."

"Ezra is harmless."

"Of course he's harmless!" she replied. We had walked to the end of D street. Edlyn now turned down Main Street. "I want you to understand one thing very clearly, Ada. There is nothing at all any of you can uncover that will harm me. There's simply nothing to be uncovered. Do you understand?"

"Then why not just ignore Ezra and Reynard? Why not let us alone? We're happy as we are."

She sniffed. "With a Japanese woman that throws vases? I hardly believe you're happy."

"You've been embarrassed by Ezra and Reynard. I can understand you feel harassed." In fact, I could see Edlyn's side of it clearly enough. A madman had chosen her as his target; a convicted murderer, Ezra the Wild, lay in wait for her at every turn. And that was just the beginning. Whatever Grace had done to her, Edlyn saw it as betrayal. She probably thought I was mixed up in it, too. Beneath the bright Indiana sun, with the subtle swish of the elegant pink suit moving along beside me, I could not picture Edlyn committing any sort of misdeed, large or small. I felt certain Reynard was wrong about her, dead wrong. In spite of everything she had done to us, I felt sorry for her. My pity was of the most perverse sort, of course. If Reynard could set all of this in motion, it meant his resources weren't played out. He had strength reaching beyond the hospital walls; wit, and a certain kind of logic. All of it had a hopeful aspect. This mix of feelings exhilarated me. I felt grave and also capable, and I walked on determined to console Edlyn for her misfortunes, but to my surprise, she changed the subject.

"Just ahead," she said, a note of anticipation slipping into her voice, and I realized she was leading me to the statue of the Madonna of the Trail. It was civic art of the most ordinary kind, set in place to commemorate pioneer women. "I want you to see this statue, Ada. You'll like it."

If I'd been suspended between sympathy and hostility,

the false tone of her voice put me off and pushed me away from her. "I've been seeing it all my life," I said.

The statue rose several feet in the air from a shoulder-high pedestal. It portrayed a pioneer mother in a long gown and sunbonnet. She carried a baby in her arms while a child of two or three clung to her skirts.

"I expect this reminds you of your mother," said Edlyn, smiling widely now, "considering the historical significance. I mean it combines the ideas of Mother and History."

"I really can't say it reminds me of anything." She was leading up to something and I had decided not to help her.

"In addition to that," she continued, "it is so very touching, don't you think?"

"Touching?" I asked, obstinate and glum.

"You see, Ada, we could be a real family, you and I. You could be helped; you could get treatment. Then we could make a fresh beginning. I would buy a little place for us, and you could have friends. I'd get you a fine piano."

Goods were being offered, bargains going fast. "There's nothing wrong with me, Aunt Edlyn, nothing that can be fixed. I don't need any treatment, and there's nothing I want from you."

"I'm prepared now to make a cash settlement to the Decembers," she said.

"They don't want your money. Mitch returned your checks."

She sighed. "Ada, he was merely biding his time, hoping for more. You'll see. You'll see how quickly the Decembers change their minds when I offer them real money." She raised one arm to the stone figures, as if appealing to them. "I was hoping you'd see the . . . rightness of all of this. It would have made things so much easier."

"You were hoping I'd concede without a struggle? And allow myself to be put in the hands of your doctors and psychiatrists?"

Her arm seemed frozen, poised in midair. Then an expression of complete perplexity slipped over her and she turned her face away.

In profile, Edlyn looked most like Grace. There was a certain roundness where her neck rose to meet her jaw, a small area of flesh that appeared inexpressibly tender and vulnerable. I thought for a moment that I would cry, and then discovered I wanted to laugh. Grace would have made the statue into something and wrapped it up. She would have walked off with a victory, but Edlyn couldn't put it together. I seemed to be looking at Edlyn through some old tribal memory, some fluke in the genes that told me more than I deserved to know and gave me an edge. Edlyn was slippery because she had no heart of her own. She chalked it up to thievery, some mischief on my mother's part. A thing like that was never strictly true, but Edlyn went where the wind took her, and felt abused in all circumstances. She'd outwit us just by being unpredictable. I knew I should have been afraid, but the part of me that was Grace was amused. With overt cruelty, I laughed out loud. Then I walked off and left her standing there. When I glanced back, she had begun retracing her steps, walking slowly back toward the December home.

13

I WALKED briskly, feeling virtuous and hollow, and very much a child. For years I had played the role of Grace's prodigy. I had probably believed all of her Ada nonsense, put it on like a shining mantle. All that silly vanity, playing grown-up. Now the other side of me surfaced, welling up like something held under pressure. I was the little girl offered great riches and fine things, and I had turned them down on principle. I wanted to believe Edlyn. I could picture the little place she'd buy for us, see me in it handling her, filling in all her gaps. I could see the fine piano and feel its perfect unmarred keys beneath my fingers, more than that, even—the jewel to end all jewels, what we'd never had and would never come close to—a good fiddle.

On impulse, I turned away from the house and entered the Pendle campus, walking to the far side, where an old cemetery, nearly hidden in a grove of oak, crept up to the gravel path. In fact the cemetery had no connection to the college; it belonged to an earlier time. The juxtaposition of the two disparate things, this violation of order, suited my fastidious sense of injury.

All of the headstones seemed to bear the name Williams. Referring to the cemetery, my mother had said, "It is as if a complete family was wiped out with a single disaster." There were babies, young people, adults, old people. I sat down unceremoniously on a flat stone rising a foot or so from the earth and put my face in my hands. Then, sheltered by the trees, I cried. It seemed to me I was crying because I had never had a cat. Or that I had, indeed, had a cat who now lay buried beneath the stone on which I sat. As I cried, this cat became more and more real to me. It was a small animal with soft black fur. It seemed to me then that I could have talked Reynard into having a cat, despite his abhorrence of them, and that in fact it had been Grace behind the scenes who had forbidden it, or even destroyed the cat. Hadn't she made a cat die? I saw the name Jethro Williams on a nearby stone and concentrated on the shape of the letters. No, it had not been a cat but a doll that had died. I saw that Jethro Williams had died at the age of nine. I wondered what things he had hoped for in those nine years, and what image had flashed in his mind at the moment of death. Then I sat on a little longer, giving Edlyn time to leave, to load her bargains and specials into the Lincoln and take them back to Chicago.

When I returned, the white car was gone and I saw Mitch coming hurriedly down the sidewalk. "Ada!" He had been walking the streets, searching for me. Schutzie appeared on the porch. She had been monitoring the phone.

"I'm sorry," I said. "I'm okay, I was just walking. I should have let you know where I was." We moved into the house; Schutzie pulled the door closed behind us and locked it.

"I came right home," Mitch began. "Schutzie phoned me that Miss Simmons was here and I came, but you had gone."

"Did she offer you money, Mitch?" I asked.

He considered and then nodded. Schutzie said, "I told her to go to hell."

"We told her we didn't want her money," Mitch said simply.

"Thank you," I said. "I thank you both for that."

"You goddamn welcome," said Schutzie.

"What will she do now, Mitch?" I asked.

"File her custody suit," he replied. "She'll see it as the only avenue left to her."

"To stop the harassment," I said. "And it will seem a charitable act, done out of concern for me."

"Yes," he said. "Ada, there is something else I'd better tell you. I will do everything I can, of course, but I think she has a good chance of winning. You see, since she has made all these claims about your health, the first order of business would be an evaluation by impartial doctors."

"And they would find nothing wrong with me, Mitch!" I countered. "Nothing requires treatment!"

"That's true," he said, "but the court might well look at potential costs."

It was not necessary for him to continue. I understood. "Money, Mitch?"

"I'm afraid so," he said.

"The court could see me as a person who might need a great deal of medical care in the future. The person with the money to pay for that care, to keep me off Richmount's welfare rolls, would receive custody."

Reluctantly, he nodded.

"And her drinking?"

"We'll pursue it, we'll pursue every possible angle."

"But we have only one isolated incidence of drunkenness," I said.

"And only the three of us as witnesses to that," said Mitch. I knew what he would say next before he spoke. "Ada, the time is growing short. In less than two years you will be of age, and there's no real evidence your aunt has done anything wrong. At the very worst, you would be in her charge only a short time. And when you're eighteen, you'll still be welcome here. You know that, I'm sure."

"Yes," I said. "Of course."

That night I sorted out the smallest and most delicate of Reynard's tools—tools meant employment—and put them in a canvas bag, but when I closed it, the little bag looked ominous, terrifying, like the last remnants of a life. Around midnight, the false spring vanished. The wind came up and it began to snow; I decided to wait for the weather to clear.

Ezra returned in a blizzard. We awoke to his pounding on the door at four in the morning.

"You better sell that motorcycle and buy a car," Schutzie said, putting on coffee. "You rich now."

When Ezra had warmed himself, he told us what he had learned. We were gathered expectantly at the kitchen table. "It was almost too easy," he began. "Edlyn had an illegitimate child eighteen years ago."

The numbers interested Schutzie. "Two years older than Ada," she said.

Mitch half rose from his chair. "Where is this child now?"

"Dead," Ezra said. "It was a girl. She lived only eleven days and died under mysterious circumstances."

"What kind of circumstances?" Mitch asked.

"They thought at first she had been strangled," Ezra continued. "A coroner's inquest was held. Edlyn was under suspicion for a time but . . ." Ezra paused and looked steadily at me. "Grace and Reynard Cunningham testified on her behalf. They said they had been present with Edlyn in her apartment when the child died. On the strength of their testimony, Edlyn was cleared. No funeral was held. The body was cremated. That's Edlyn's past."

"And the real estate dealings?" Mitch asked.

"The detectives are still working on that, but everything appears to be in order. It all looks legitimate. Edlyn is a respected businesswoman. In the last few months, she's begun to drink heavily, but there's really no law against that."

Mitch looked puzzled. "But you said it was easy, almost too easy. What do you actually have against Edlyn then?"

"She murdered her own child," said Ezra.

"Because it was illegitimate?" Mitch asked with growing annoyance.

"No," said Ezra, "because there were birth defects.

Ada, I'm sorry. There's no way to make this easy for you. From the hospital records, it appears Edlyn's child had exactly the same disabilities you have—nerve damage affecting both hands and one leg." He handed an envelope to Mitch. "There's a copy of the record. It was obtained surreptitiously, but you can subpoena a legal copy if you want one."

Schutzie came and sat beside me, took my hand. "It's all right," I said. "I'm all right. I'm glad to know, Ezra. This means Grace knew from my birth I was crippled. I've always suspected that. It also means it's hereditary, doesn't it?"

"It . . . appears to be hereditary," Ezra said quietly.

Mitch sighed and tossed the hospital report onto a table. "It's an interesting story, a sad story, but it doesn't prove murder. You're saying Edlyn killed her child and Mr. and Mrs. Cunningham lied to protect her."

"To prevent a family scandal," Ezra said. "Remember, they were both teachers in a small college, as well as being in the public eye. But Grace never forgave her sister. She never spoke to her again. When Ada was born, Grace's hatred of her sister became even greater."

"That's only speculation," said Mitch.

"Of course," Ezra replied, "but it all fits. Then Reynard became ill and started writing Edlyn letters, threatening to disclose the thing that had happened years ago. Edlyn has no fear of Reynard. He's insane, not a credible witness, but she fears Ada. She's afraid Grace, being a writer and hating her, might have left a written record somewhere, a record Ada knows about or may someday discover."

"This is nothing but speculation," Mitch said again.

"You've got to give me something I can present in court. And just consider what you've said. You've impugned both Mr. and Mrs. Cunningham. I can see that, in view of what's happened, Mr. Cunningham would be an unreliable witness, but Mrs. Cunningham was a respected historian. I'm sure we can all agree that Mrs. Cunningham's honesty was above reproach."

I said nothing, but I found it a strange statement. I knew perfectly well my mother had lied often, to create interesting books and articles, to protect my father, to protect me. I could believe Ezra's accusation of my parents. The idea of murder was harder to accept. It had the flavor of Ezra's folk songs, of tense major seventh chords straining for the octave, of half diminished harmonies, and Gypsy tales transmogrified for coffeehouses. Still, my ambivalence toward Edlyn lingered; I could make a case on either side. If I began with the cats and the dying doll —the memory of the tale now squeezed my throat shut with alarm—a thread could be found leading to the statue, where a stone mother clung to a lifeless infant. When Edlyn first beheld her imperfect daughter, had she looked upon the child with the same perplexed face she had shown to me at the statue? Perhaps after all we were nothing but folk-song characters, melodramatics plucked from some fiction and dropped into the quiet life of Richmount. Nothing in all of my life validated any other scenario. Ezra, patient and determined, hysterical and newly rich, had used his money to buy us all identities. His efforts were generous beyond measure. Of most immediate interest, he had provided me with an excuse to stay in Richmount a little longer. His story was both gruesome and preposterous. Yet, perversely, it filled me with hope.

Mitch had been studying his hands, trying to absorb all of it. Now he said to Ezra, "I admit that much of what you've said sounds plausible, but I don't see how I can get a case out of it."

Ezra was not discouraged. "I think we should talk to Reynard," he said. "Lay all of this before him."

"I agree," said Mitch. "Perhaps I can arrange a weekend furlough. Since they've moved him back to his regular ward, they must not consider him dangerous. He might be able to tell us something we *could* corroborate. I will admit we really don't have much of anything else to go on at this point, and time is running out." He paused and looked at each of us in turn. "I suppose I should have told you this before, but I received notice today that Miss Simmons has begun formal custody proceedings through a local lawyer."

"You mean yesterday," Schutzie said quietly. "It's past midnight, another day. How many days do we have left?"

We went to bed but I could not sleep. A little before dawn, I rose and began sorting through the clothes in my closet, making a small pile of sturdy, practical outfits, pushing Schutzie's brighter creations to the back of the rod.

A weekend furlough was granted without objection. Mitch had filed a countersuit. He believed the granting of the furlough reflected some sympathy for our side. "We have friends," he said on his return from the hospital. "Everyone there was very sympathetic toward us. Perhaps we've underestimated the value of that."

My father had no illusions on the matter. "They've simply forgotten my last trip out," he said when we arrived to pick him up. "They've had a dozen people since more violent than I, perhaps two dozen." It was Saturday morning and we had come in force; Mitch, Schutzie, Ezra, and I. Reynard's suit was neatly pressed, the knot of his tie was exactly centered on a clean, well-mended shirt.

"Mr. Cunningham," said Mitch, ushering him into the car, "we're delighted to be able to have you with us."

"And I am grateful to you for sheltering my daughter," Reynard replied, "more grateful than I can say. I have meant to send a note of thanks to you and your wife, but my affairs have been very pressing."

For the first time, the five of us gathered in the house on D Street. Reynard had brought his violin. He played a Beethoven sonata, and I played the piano accompaniment, while Schutzie completed preparations for lunch. Ezra and Mitch listened attentively.

"Mr. Cunningham," Schutzie said, ushering us into the dining room, "I know you are a better cook than I, but I have done my best."

"And you have done gloriously!" Reynard cried. "I can almost identify the meal by its marvelous aromas!" Schutzie had prepared cream of asparagus soup with cheddar cheese, a chicken and almond casserole, fresh spinach salad, peach torte. More than an hour was spent eating and discussing the food. We were delaying the afternoon's business as long as possible, pretending this was merely a pleasant gathering of old friends.

It was Reynard who finally brought the happy interlude to a close. "Now," he said, rising from the table, "let's go into the living room and talk. There's much to be done and little time."

We moved obediently after him, with only Schutzie remaining behind to clear the table. We had not yet told Reynard of Ezra's discoveries in Chicago. We might have wondered exactly what it was Reynard was planning for us to do, but no one questioned him.

My father had never lost his poise, even in the hospital. I had thought him at his finest then, his learned manner juxtaposed with the setting of an insane asylum, but I had been wrong. He was at his best here in the December home, against a backdrop of books, in a setting of genteel poverty. A stranger would immediately have identified him as a wise and gentle man.

The afternoon sun slanted through the small front windows and fell on the old piano. The chipped veneer gleamed like solid walnut. In the soft light, everything looked finer than it was. I watched the shadow of a passing car move silently across the room, and I thought, they are going to believe every word he says.

"I'll tell you what I learned in Chicago," Ezra said. He proceeded cautiously, relating first the fact that Edlyn was a reputable real estate agent, respected by other business people. Reynard sat quietly, listening. Then Ezra began the rest of the story. "Edlyn had a child," he said, "a little girl—"

He got no further. "She strangled the baby," Reynard broke in. His voice was calm and level. "For a long time, Grace did not tell me the complete story. She said at first that she had been present with Edlyn when the child died, and I testified to that at the inquest. Then she broke with Edlyn. She told me it was because she had learned her sister was a criminal, guilty of unscrupulous dealings in real estate."

"Real estate!" Ezra exclaimed. "And that's the part of the story you remembered."

"Yes, real estate," said Reynard, as if he were raising the subject for the first time.

"After Ada was born, Grace said Edlyn had to be kept away at all costs. She would be a bad influence on Ada. Then when Ada was three or four, Grace told me all of it. We had learned of a treatment that might help Ada, a rather complicated surgery. It was expensive and we did not have the money for it. Grace asked Edlyn to pay for the surgery. Essentially, it was blackmail. Then we learned the surgery was of no value, was actually fraudulent. The doctor at Children's Hospital in Indianapolis told Grace that. Ada, do you remember the visit?"

"Yes, I remember the dress I wore, and Grace with all of her jewelry."

"So we never pursued it. The doctor said there was no real treatment, that physical therapy might help a little. We believed her music lessons were the best therapy. And we hoped, always, for a miracle. Since the disability was hereditary, and had been identical in both Ada and in Edlyn's child, we chose not to have any more children."

"Good Lord!" Mitch said in a hoarse whisper.

Silently, Ezra folded his hands, clasping them together so tightly that the knuckles turned white.

In fact, nothing had been proved, but the effect of my

father's story was electrifying. Very softly, Schutzie said, "The Chinese restaurant with the sukiyaki."

I waited for Mitch—the attorney, the naysayer, the pessimist—to demur, waited for him to say, This really puts us no further ahead. In that pained, weary voice. But he did not.

Schutzie said, "You will tell them everything, Mr. Cunningham, right away."

Reynard laughed lightly. "I am not a reliable witness. Unfortunately, I am insane. The evidence you need is Grace's own account, written in her own hand. My wife wrote everything out in longhand. Ada will remember that."

Everyone turned to look at me, as if a great deal depended on my answer. "Yes, she always wrote first drafts in longhand," I said.

Mitch grew animated. He was being offered what he valued above all else, a piece of paper, perhaps a substantial document. "Where is this account?" he asked.

"In Grace's coffin," Reynard said quietly. "I buried it with her."

"But why did you do that?" Ezra asked.

"So that Edlyn would not find it and destroy it," Reynard answered. "Had I not, it would have been lost in the fire."

The three of them nodded, as if placing a document in a coffin were a perfectly logical thing to do.

Mitch said, "I can ask for an exhumation order."

Ezra took a pencil and notebook from his pocket and began to make rapid notes. "Let's get as much as we can first, get it all down, as many details as possible."

The project now resembled a religious undertaking;

they were going forward on faith. The stone would be rolled away; the tomb would yield its treasure. I lay my head back in my chair and closed my eyes; the sharp, sweet memory of my mother's warm flesh leapt suddenly into my mind. Then a wave of revulsion swept over me. I opened my eyes to find Mitch bent over Ezra's notebook.

Schutzie brought us tea and Reynard went off to wash his hands before drinking it.

"Mitch," I said, "Reynard was very distraught at Grace's funeral. I don't think he could possibly have done anything that wasn't seen by other people."

"But you don't actually know that," said Mitch. "You don't remember it clearly yourself, do you?"

"No, but . . . ."

"But what?" Mitch asked.

A vague memory hovered at the edge of my mind. "As I remember, the funeral director was everywhere, hovering. Reynard was so upset. . . . I don't think the man ever took his eyes off Reynard."

"The business with the rings," Ezra recalled.

"Yes," I said. "I wonder if a call to the funeral director would turn up anything. He's still in business. He might remember something."

"Of course!" said Mitch. He wasted no time in making the call and directed me to pick up the extension phone.

"Yes," the man told him, "I placed a sealed packet in Mrs. Cunningham's casket, at her husband's request. It's not at all unusual. Families frequently request that a memento be buried with the deceased." He did not know what the packet had contained.

Our hopes were high. The weekend proceeded without incident. On Sunday night, we took Reynard back to the hospital.

On the strength of the funeral director's statement, Mitch obtained his exhumation order. We learned that two weeks preparation would be required for the opening of the grave. Part of this time was needed to satisfy legal requirements, part was required to arrange for equipment to break the frozen ground. It would be an eventful two weeks.

Buffered by Mitch and Schutzie, I had become indifferent to town gossip. Our enemy was Edlyn. By comparison, the idle talk of neighbors, which had caused me much concern when Reynard and I lived alone, seemed a minor matter. I had not imagined that its venom could reach past the sturdy figures of the Decembers and pierce me. Yet, it was not Edlyn's attack that eventually ruined me but the desperate fears of Richmount.

Opening a grave did not suit the tender sensibilities of the town. Mitch said, "No one can recall that it's ever happened before." His "no one" referred to the circle of men in the courthouse. Mitch was tense now. We'd forged ahead toward a confrontation and there could be no retreat. Later, I would understand his fears were well-founded. He was shielding us. People did not find the exhumation simply unusual; they considered it monstrous.

I had believed that in the time since Reynard's commitment I'd earned a good reputation in the community. Playing in churches, teaching students, repairing instruments—surely these activities had established me as a solid citizen, but my respectability vanished quickly as news of the planned exhumation spread through Richmount. I found my name linked to imagined black deeds, criminal activity.

Ezra's contribution, in retrospect, was predictable. In every situation he was too much, too soon. Believing the manuscript we required would be in our possession within days, he fashioned our story into a ballad, which he sang at a local tavern. His lyrics were rife with allusions to murdered children and black hands rising from graves demanding justice. The song was medieval in character and borrowed heavily from the old English ballad, "Lord Randall." Richmount was scandalized.

Schutzie was first to report the stories to us. "Nobody in the supermarket gonna speak to me!" she cried, setting her bag of groceries on the table and glaring at Ezra. "Why you sing like that?" With tenacity, she had found someone to repeat the stories to her. "They say we devil worshippers, trying to raise evil spirits! They say that grave opening gonna be a black sabbath!"

Ezra was delighted. "There's the power of music to rouse the heart!" he said with satisfaction. "Now you see how thin the veneer of this thing we call human reason really is!"

Mitch was badly shaken. "This is not a time to cast doubt on anyone's reason. We have to go forward in an orderly way."

Ezra only laughed at our protestations. "We've won! We've nothing else to worry about!"

The day of the exhumation was bright and cloudless, a perfect winter day. By noon we had learned that Reynard's packet contained fourteen violin strings, and nothing more.

That afternoon, encouraged by the sunny weather, eleven-year-old Bobby Brenton pedaled his new ten-speed bike across the Whitewater River bridge, slipped on a patch of ice, and plunged into the river. At seven that evening, I was ordered to undergo psychiatric examination. An angry, determined Schutzie had a full account of events within a few hours. The sober citizens who had been reluctant to speak to her earlier were now eager to unburden themselves.

Bobby was one of my students, neither better nor worse than any other. He had been instructed by his parents not to take his bike out until spring, but the parents had been away and he had found the sunshine irresistible. He was not badly hurt and even the bicycle survived the fall with only minor damage. When firemen fished him from the water, his first words were "They're gonna kill me!" Certainly this was a reference to his fear of his parents' wrath.

Who can say what forces moved Bobby, and in exactly what manner? The shock of the fall and the icy water, the appearance of the fire truck, the swift ride in the ambulance with the siren blowing, the awesome sight of the hospital emergency room, of police officers in uniform, the fear of his parents' anger over the damaged bike—it was a potent recipe for hysteria. He may have felt he had committed a terrible crime from which he had to extricate himself at all costs. When Bobby's father had satisfied himself that his son was not seriously hurt, he demanded, "Why did you do such a foolish thing?"

And Bobby, caught up in the most exciting and terrifying events of his short life, confused and inspired, cried, "Ada Cunningham put a curse on me! She made me do it!"

Bobby's father accused the hysterical boy of lying. The father was a practical man who earned his living laying brick. The words *upright* and *square* fitted him as much as they fitted the well-made walls he created. There was no room in him or in his work for notions edging off into the absurd. He told his son—reported by a nurse and then quickly forgotten by almost everyone—"I won't punish you for wrecking your bike, but I will punish you for lying." Had the father been in charge, I believe the accusations would have been disposed of quickly.

But Bobby's mother moved swiftly into the breach. Mrs. Brenton had a spiritual side. She brought to mind the old hymn tune, "Almost Persuaded." Her heart and conscience pulled her into charitable deeds and then, halfway through, abandoned her.

I believe she had brought Bobby for lessons as an act of charity to me, probably with misgivings from the beginning, and at some level she had expected to be repaid for her kindness. I think each gold star I placed on Bobby's music assured his mother of her own high mark in heaven. But she had wanted more: to be thanked, praised, and paid in some substantial earthly way. It was all in her injured tone when she telephoned me to say, "You let me down. You let me down very badly."

The precise details of my supposed offense were not clearly defined. They were not needed. Nudged into recognition, the citizens of Richmount could catalog and recite their charities to the Cunninghams, their long suffering, their generosity in overlooking our eccentricities. They felt betrayed. The exhumation followed by Bobby's accusations gathered all of our scurrilous affairs into one place, assembled our oddities into a recognizable pattern. How tolerant our neighbors had been! And now they had found out everything at once.

When a police officer appeared at our door that evening and told Mitch, "Bring in the girl for an intake interview in the morning," quick tears sprang to Mitch's eyes. Then he nodded in solemn, silent assent.

I went to my bedroom and packed a suitcase. At three in the morning, when Mitch and Schutzie were sleeping, I rose and dressed, putting on the warm coat Schutzie had made me. I carried the suitcase downstairs, picked up my fiddle case, and let myself out the back door. I walked to the bus station and sat outside on a bench until the waiting room opened at five o'clock. The first bus out of town went to Cincinnati. I bought a ticket and boarded it. In Cincinnati, I drank a cup of coffee and looked through a dirty window at the snowdrifts. Whatever lay ahead, it would be easier in a warm climate. I bought a ticket for Los Angeles.

14

POPCORN JOE is not cold working in the drafty museum barn. Enthusiasm warms him. With the assistance of the Calabrias' capable hands, he is transferring our stationary calliope to a circus wagon. "Moving this machine," he tells me as I arrive, "won't change a thing." He loves restoring old circus equipment above all other jobs. He is suffused with such purpose his ancient, lined face has taken on a soft ivory glow. A plank across sawhorses is his workbench. Parts of an undercarriage dressed with fresh grease are scattered across it like the mechanical carnage of some accident. "Moving this machine will improve everything, Norma," he declares. The argument may yet come right if he stays with it. He does not grasp the inconsistency of his statements because he is busy watching me for treachery. My arrival has caused his eyelids to lower ever so slightly.

"I'm sure you'll do your best," I tell him gently, because he is my friend, but my level tone does not deny that I am here to watch matters closely. Belle and I have been outvoted in this democratic community. Alexander will have his mobile calliope, fired by its original and portable coal boiler. Belle's objections to the change are personal. She sees it as a disruption of her household. Mine are technical. I fear the old instrument may not hold up to all this earnest hammering and wrenching. I've grown fond of the calliope, and playing it is my only bona fide reason for continuing to live in the circus community.

Daviso Calabria salutes me with a dripping paintbrush and a grandfatherly smile. "Do not frown so!" He is kneeling on a carpet of newspapers. Before him lie the defeated wheels of an old circus wagon, their spokes and inner rims showing dim traces of red and white paint. Under his clever fingers, the old wood is coming to life with yellow sunbursts and blazing red circles, designs of bold ocularity that suggest irises and pupils. Perhaps these are Ezekiel's wheels, full of eyes, so our calliope will not lose its way. "Norma," he cajoles, "what is the worst that can possibly happen? If the calliope is ruined, we'll get a little organ and set it in the wagon. You will be our organist! There is a church here in town that has in its basement an old organ. It is no longer used, and it is perfectly good!"

"He knows!" Mike Calabria calls down from the calliope loft. He is removing my little bench from its anchor of screws and bolts. "Daviso likes that organ! He almost won it in a poker game. The members of that church should know what their priest does nights!"

"Preacher!" Daviso counters, stung by the taunt. "He is not a priest. He is a preacher, you old fool!" If you are a Calabria you have to win every time. Any loss sends you home to zero.

"Preacher!" Mike concedes. Then he sends me an easy smile, assurance that I am not the target of his jibe.

"Restoration," Joe struggles on, "doesn't do any damage." He is a capable workman. He has restored circus wagons, even cage wagons, which must be very strong. He has built show props. He is responsible for most of the home repairs that keep the circus folk from freezing to death in their shabby rooms in winter. But he has never before attempted to restore a musical instrument. He is encroaching on my territory, and he knows it. He fears I will come at him with book learning, theoretical arguments and vocabulary complaints that might impede this project. He has seen my repair manuals, sitting on their shelf, lying open on our kitchen table. Their pages bristle with exotic words and cunning diagrams. I believe Joe is more frightened of books than he is of wild beasts. All of this fear is in his heavy-lidded eyes as he struggles to persuade and contain me. All of this and more. I have been seeing eyes like these for years. The able-bodied are never certain about the capabilities of cripples. They credit us with some advantage: to plead, to usurp, to insist, to spoil; and the obligations of the firm to the infirm must be honored. With Joe, my advantage is even greater: Joe used to be a dancer. He wonders why I was chosen for this disability rather than he, and how that choosing empowered me. You never know when a cripple is going to file a claim.

A small burst of profanity erupts in the loft. Then Mike

calls down to us, "It is nothing! Nothing at all!" But even thirty feet away I can see the sad crack that has opened in the back panel of the calliope bench. The flash of raw white wood plunges me into inexpressible sadness, like a nearly forgotten grief leaping out from the past.

"A little glue!" cries Joe. "A little glue, it will heal right up!"

His voice restores my equilibrium. What, after all, is a crack in a piece of wood? The curious moment passes as swiftly as it came.

"Nothing in wood I can't handle!" Joe persists.

I offer him the same objections I gave Alexander. "What about rust and corrosion, Joe? What about metal?"

This is what he wants to hear, a straight-out challenge. Rust and corrosion are fairer competitors than repair manuals and bad legs. "I don't see any yet," he counters. He takes up a wrench, himself restored, and leans happily on a frozen bolt, grateful for my sense of fair play.

The wagon that will house our calliope, de-wheeled now and sitting on blocks, formerly carried animals. Joe believes they were elephants. "Once in Tiffin, Ohio," he tells us, "we had an elephant get loose. He just ran off and lost himself. We searched for two days and couldn't find him. Then the owner of the show offered a hundred-dollar reward to anyone who found him. That brought the people out! But those farmers didn't know the first thing about the shape of an elephant's foot. When we finally captured him, we found out all those people had been tracking him backward."

The construction of the old animal wagon is devious. The solid panels along both of its sides are divided into three hinged sections running horizontally. In the days before zoos, before television and movies, the only exotic beasts many people saw were those that arrived with the circus, to be paraded down the street and displayed under the big top. Circus folk, with an eye toward ticket sales, liked to whet public curiosity. Why display all of a tiger or zebra in the free parade when turning back a single section of the wagon's side would reveal a tantalizing head, a middle, or a set of nervously pacing feet? Young and old stretched or crouched to see the missing parts as the wagon lumbered by, and followed the calliope at the parade's end to buy tickets to see the animal entire. The old wagon seems an appropriate choice for all this dedicated labor. Under Alexander's direction, Joe and the Calabrias are after the animal entire. They want the past in the present, stasis in motion, reality in transcendence.

"Help me lift this!" Mike calls down to his brother.

Daviso climbs the steps to take one end of the heavy structure Mike has just loosened. It is the ornate cover enclosing the calliope's interior. "Holy Jesus!" Daviso cries a moment later. "Norma, here's what you came to see! Come and look!"

Joe and I hasten up the steps to view the exposed guts of the instrument. Joe whistles softly in admiration. The mechanism is in perfect condition, miraculously free of rust, of corrosion, even of simple dirt. A melodious stream of Italian bursts from Mike's lips. I believe it is a prayer of thanksgiving. Three old men gaze with rapture on this shining display of immortality.

* * *

The sight of Joe's pickup truck parked in an inch of snow makes Alexander Sandler reflective. He is arriving at the museum barn as I am leaving.

"Alexander!" I greet him. "They have opened the calliope and the mechanism is perfect."

"Good!" he cries, his huge smile exhibiting large white teeth, the mouth of a trumpeter. He is on foot. His bare ears are pink from the cold.

"Aren't you going inside to look at it?"

"In a moment, Norma." He sees Joe's truck every day but this morning it has enthralled him. Perhaps it is the way the false winter sun glances off metal and glass, suggesting warmer climes. "In New Orleans," he tells me, "I bought a truck like that. I was not with a circus then. The truck was to carry black musicians. Many times we had to meet and play secretly. All black bands could play in public, or all white bands, but in some places mixed groups were not allowed." He laughs and shakes his head. "Often I did not know what was permitted and what forbidden! I was new to the country, new to the language. I depended on black men to tell me the rules. The man on the bottom understands rules much better than the man on top who makes them. The black men always knew what was allowed, and when they rode in my truck they were safe. They looked like laborers. You can go anywhere in the South with black men if they are sitting in the bed of your truck!"

This is a tale I have not heard before. Because I am also a musician, Alexander has regaled me with the music and stories of his native terrain—the Prut River, Moldavia, Bessarabia, Bucovina, the Carpathian Mountains— but I have never heard the story about a Russian Jew carrying a black band through New Orleans in a pickup truck. It is irresistible. "What did black men make of you, Alexander? With your glass of tea? What did you say when they offered you pork and beans?"

"I am always able to eat," he says. "I always find a way. What they saw in me mostly was the trumpet. At that time there were many cornets. Some people said the cornet sat better beside the clarinet. But once I had heard the full, open song of the trumpet I had no wish to step down to a cornet."

"And they let you play? With the trumpet?"

"Of course!" he says proudly. "They never told me not to play, black men nor white. And in New Orleans I heard for the first time everyone improvising at once."

"Collective improvisation?"

"Exactly, and the real thing. In Chicago, people thought they were improvising together, but the music was really accompanied solos, very close to swing, and often sliding into four beat. In New Orleans, you could hear a pure two beat, and the blues was always present in the music. The blues is the root for the black man, and for all American jazz."

"And you liked New Orleans best?"

"Certainly I liked the climate!" he says with a laugh, pounding his gloved hands together and studying the snow. "I liked New York until the piano took over. For awhile there was nothing but stride piano. It was very popular for a time. They wanted the horns to hold a note forever while the piano improvised. But when you went west, sometimes the piano disappeared from bands completely. In St. Louis, I saw few of them. The piano was not flexible enough, and musicians there were in a mood to change everything. In St. Louis I saw for the first time the string bass used for melody and harmony, instead of being only a string drum. But do you want to know the strangest thing about St. Louis?"

"Of course."

"They wanted the trumpet with no vibrato. They told me I would be old and shaky soon enough! Now I will go and see the calliope."

"But you haven't finished your story. You didn't like St. Louis?"

"I liked it better than Kansas City. In Kansas City they wanted to use the harmony line for melody. Sometimes they got a beautiful sound, like a feather, like a dream, but it was music with no roots. It belonged to nothing. Then when I went back to New York, everything was changing. First they wanted the trumpet to sound like a French horn. I liked that very much. Then they brought real French horns into bands, and tubas, too. It was a much better time than before. You cannot say one city is best because everything changes. It must always change. If it does not, it begins to imitate itself. Then the life is gone. Now go home or you will be frozen."

But the evolution of music is a subject that compels me even more than black men in Alexander's truck. "I'm not cold. You are right. Music wears out. I want you to tell me how it happens, and why."

He chuckles and shakes his head. "You are a girl who loves stories! Yet you tell no story yourself. When you repair instruments, you know what you are doing. That work is not like sewing, the work of a simple girl. And when you pick up your fiddle, I hear exercises only violinists know, from the books of professors."

"I had a few lessons. Lots of people have a few lessons."

"This circus is not a place for young girls. It is a place people come when they are ready to die."

"Not Joe," I counter, "not Mike and Daviso. Those three are planning to live forever."

"A girl cannot make a life only of stories. Why do you stay here?"

"I am in hiding because I am a witch. If the police discover where I am, they will come and take me to jail for practicing witchcraft."

Alexander throws back his head and laughs, delighted at my apparent nonsense. "My girl, all women are witches! Every one. A man has no chance at all with them!"

"Tell me *that* story, Alexander."

"Wouldn't you like that!" he cries with wicked merriment. "You will get no such stories from me! But go, you are freezing. I am freezing you with stories."

"I'm not cold. I think this involves music. Why are all women witches?"

"Because of their secrets," he says with a wry smile. Then, turning serious, he asks, "What music would you play if you could? If you had a fine piano and perfect hands? Would you play only for the dead?"

"You found my music." I removed my manuscript from the calliope shelf before Joe's restoration began, but Alexander has been making plans for the instrument for months, examining it with an eye to taking it down.

"Don't worry," he replies. "I cannot read music, and I will not betray you. But you cannot live only among the dying, writing for the dead."

"And your drummer?" I ask to distract him. "How is

your drummer? Danny Brundage says he doesn't mind being fired."

"Retired," Alexander insists. "He is going to donate his drums to the museum. They will be displayed, along with his scrapbook. Danny understands he is being honored, and he agrees that the new drummer is excellent."

"Belle says you have humiliated Danny."

"Belle sees only what she wants to see. Norma, you know the true facts. Can you not persuade her?"

"I see no way. I see no point in trying. Go and look at the calliope."

"Yes," says Alexander. "Yes, I will go."

Walking in snow always makes me think of endurance, of shoe soles that last beyond all reasonable expectation, like gifts, and of shoe soles that fail, like promises nearly kept. My mother taught me to count in Latin by marching me around the living room to music—step, step, step —because, like my father, I can memorize most easily any information tied to a tune. Mnemonic melodic curve. These are the words I call forth to hurry my chilled feet: *Unus, duo, tres.* Learning is an enterprise filled with hope, fraught with heavy purpose. *Quattuor, quinque, sex.* But heavy purpose did not keep Grace from laughing and clapping her hands to the music. *Septem, octo.* When I could count all the way to twenty with every hard consonant in its proper place, she bought me a lavender satin bedspread as a reward and read me the story, "Cornelia's Jewels," first in Latin and then in English. The mother of the famous Roman Gracchi gave up wealth and position to devote her life to her children. Ever after, I would picture Cornelia's "jewels," her sons, wrapped in lavender togas that resembled my bedspread. *Novem, decem.* Grace and I were making the future, my future, a magical time and place in which all of my learning would be dedicated to projects of high seriousness. Where did my mother fancy I would march while shouting out Latin numbers? Who employs Latin-speaking marchers with bad legs? Alexander is wrong. We do, indeed, live by stories. *Undecim, duodecim.* Because I have never been offered a job speaking Latin or marching does not mean such jobs do not exist.

When Grace began driving a car, she was terrified of reverse gear. "Ada, never go backward!" she commanded with laughing eyes. She drove from Indianapolis to Philadelphia and back without putting the car into reverse, driving in a circle each time she wanted to change direction. Eventually, she learned to use reverse gear. The felicities of chance are everywhere this morning, like a pepper of soot on the crusty snow. *Reversal.* Joe's elephant tracked backward. Joe and the Calabrias turning back time. And Alexander? One should be fair. He is going back only to gain momentum to go forward. He is more honest than the other old men. Joe and the Calabrias are improvising on his tune. Alexander improvises only when the trumpet is pressed to his mouth. Must one be fair even in stories? Lies that carry the truth? *Tredecim, quattuordecim.*

Lo, cried Isaiah, I am a man of unclean lips. And an angel flew down with a hot coal to burn all sin from those lips, all lies. A glowing coal, hot as scalding tea. Some things endure, like strong shoe soles, like trumpeters' lips. But there is also suddenness in life, death as swift as a board snapping in two, exposing the whiteness of pure grief. Shoe soles that fail. I do not think Alexander has factored failure and consolation into his equation. *Quindecim, sedecim.* Even Isaiah is a story.

"I've poured you coffee," Belle greets me. "Take off your shoes and I will rub your feet."

Her small hands have lost none of their strength. There is delicate perfection in the coordinated movements of her fingers. It occurs to me that hands like these could have played the violin. "Thank you, Belle."

"Now drink your coffee. Norma, Danny is gone. They found him dead in bed this morning. Teddy MacKay is going to tell the men at the barn."

"Belle . . . I am so sorry." My reaction to this news is purely personal. I am too cold for any more confrontation, too weary. "If you think I am going to defend Alexander, you are totally wrong."

"No defense is needed," she replies, her voice solemn but sturdy. "No defense and no accusation. While we live, Norma, we are duty bound to show kindness to one another, but it is not in our power to take life. It's fortunate Alexander saw this coming, or we would not have been ready for opening day."

Why does this amaze me? If Belle did not espouse such fatalism, she could never have climbed to her swing, never launched forth. Not once. Her hands, strong as they are, would not have been enough to carry her down the years. Sometimes the felicities of chance are so artful they tempt you to see pattern everywhere and profess certainty. This is accomplished more easily, of course, if you are on the winning side. Like Belle. Like Alexander. Grace and I believed we were on the winning side.

Scaddegood rouses himself from the easy chair where he has been sleeping and bounds over to examine my stocking feet. I tense against attack. This morning has left me edgy. "Belle, if he bites me again, I am going to turn him over my knee and spank him." But the monkey is all cordiality, still warm and heavy with sleep. He concludes my feet are acceptable and then settles in my lap. After a moment, I take up his hands in my own.

"For the funeral," says Belle, "we were thinking of a little violin music, just a simple hymn. Do you know 'He Leadeth Me'?"

"Of course. It's a lovely choice, exactly right."

"And the new drummer?"

"He's excellent."

"Then we'll be all right," says Belle.

15

I GOT off the bus in Kansas City and cashed in the rest of my ticket. My leg had begun to ache furiously and I needed to walk. I also knew I would soon need money. Hanging on the wall behind the ticket seller in the Kansas City bus station was a calendar. I realized with a start that it was my seventeenth birthday.

It was evening, nearly seven. I put my suitcase and the fiddle in a locker, buttoned Schutzie's warm coat, and set off down the windy Kansas City sidewalks. I walked for several blocks and then began looking for a bar with a piano. I had decided that the fiddle, which had served my father so well, would not do for me. First, I did not really play well enough. Second, the figure of a lame girl fiddling was too odd; it would attract attention.

Eventually, I found the Dew Duck Inn, a pleasant enough establishment that was as much restaurant as bar. Through the window, I could see an old upright piano. A sign over the door featured a plump mallard with raindrops cascading down over its body. The duck's face was grim and unsmiling, the raindrops looked like tears.

My father had begun his career begging; I had heard his stories often enough. Perhaps a little of his street sense had even been passed along in the genes. Fortifying myself with these thoughts, I entered. "Hi!" I said to the bartender. "My parents are still getting our bags at the station. They'll be along soon for dinner." The man smiled. Not waiting for a response, I plunged on. "Your restaurant was recommended to us, by someone who lives here in Kansas City." I had no idea what the state's bar laws were, and could only hope I looked old enough. "I don't want to order anything yet. If you don't mind, I'll wait."

The bartender accepted the story. I pretended to discover the piano, removed my coat, sat down and played, "A Foggy Day in London Town." The dew on the duck had suggested it. I laid a dollar bill on the far end of the piano, out of the bartender's view, for seed. Reynard had said, if people see quarters, they'll leave quarters. I had seen the same technique used often in church collection plates. When I had finished the song, a plump woman in tight pink pants untangled herself from a bar stool, came over and asked if I could play "Darkness on the Delta," and laid a second dollar bill on top of the first. As I played, I surveyed the room. There were a dozen customers scattered about; cigar smoke drifted up from shadowed booths and tables. A sad young man in rumpled clothing, who had been drinking alone in the back, approached the piano. He asked for "You Light up My Life," looking as if he wanted to cry. I played and he cried; then I played the song in the minor, with ornaments. He cried harder and left two dollars. The bartender was busy with a sudden flurry of business, customers escaping the wind that had grown fierce and blustering outside the door. A five-dollar bill now seemed a good bet. I laid one on top of the stack and tried two Chopin mazurkas, always crowd pleasers, keeping them a bit subdued, to rouse enough interest to attract customers without disturbing the bartender. By the time he became curious and then suspicious, more than an hour later—glancing at me frequently with a tight, unfriendly frown—I had nineteen dollars. When he reached for the telephone, I had to assume he was calling the police. Except for Reynard and the engaging stories of his childhood, I would have attempted to leave by the front door. Instead, I walked toward the ladies' room, went on out the back door into an alley, and returned to the bus station.

Going to Los Angeles in steps, exercising my leg at frequent stops, now seemed my best course. I bought a large bottle of aspirin for my aches, and a ticket to Oklahoma City. As I waited for the bus, I realized I had not eaten all day and that I was famished. I went into the coffee shop, ordered pancakes, and ate them greedily. The shop's busboy was a young Japanese. He could have been Schutzie's brother. I needed suddenly to hear his voice. "Do you live near here?" I asked as he passed.

He turned, surprised at the interruption, and looked annoyed. "Not far."

I thought of Schutzie, awakening and finding me gone. Had she felt betrayed?

The coffee shop was crowded. An elderly man with unkempt gray hair and a paper shopping bag sat down to share my booth. I had not intended to speak to him; when I did, the sound of my own voice startled me. "Did you ever hear of people opening a grave?" I asked abruptly.

He looked up, busy with some other thought; then he seemed to find me in the cubicle of seat and space. "Where did you hear that?" he asked.

I found I could not stop talking. "Oh, I just read it in a story. These people thought something valuable had been hidden in the casket, so they went out and dug it up."

"What did they find?"

"It wasn't there."

"Wasn't that on television?" he asked.

"It probably was."

He warmed to the subject. "I saw on television how they opened a grave to find out how a man had died. He'd been poisoned, but there wasn't anything about hiding things in the casket."

"And you thought it was all right to do that? On television, I mean?"

"Well, they had to find out how the man died, to catch the murderer."

"But it didn't bother you? You didn't feel it was disturbing the dead or committing a sin? Nothing like that?"

"Oh, no. I've always been interested in scientific things. I had a neighbor once who worked at a hospital.

Sometimes he'd tell me what went on there. He had a jar of alcohol with a human kidney in it. I've always liked things like that, scientific things. I suppose a religious person might look at it differently. Are you religious?"

"No."

"Well, there's always been a conflict between religion and science," he said.

"Just those two?" I asked.

"What?"

"Maybe there are other ways of looking at things. Why should there just be religion and science? Maybe there are other categories." This was ridiculous, but I could not stop talking. "Neither religion nor science offers an adequate explanation of the universe. Nor does any theory of goodness. All religion is postulated on goodness. Or obedience. But the good and the obedient fare no better than the rest of us. And science is a brute!" I could not account for the passion that had seized me. I sounded like Ezra.

"Finding more categories would be in the realm of science," he said stubbornly. "I think religion and science cover it all."

"What about second sight? What category would you put that into?"

"I don't believe in things like that," he said, sipping his coffee, "but I know young people are fascinated by the supernatural. Like astrology."

To stop my tongue, I looked away and studied the back of the Japanese boy as he cleared a nearby table. My hands had begun to tremble and I grasped the edge of my seat to steady them. I told myself a small attack of nerves was a matter of no concern. In view of events, I was even entitled to it, but my hands continued to tremble and a troubling thought slipped into my mind. My concern should have been for the living—for Reynard, for Schutzie and Mitch, even for Ezra. Yet it was the specter of my mother that had seized me with such force. I rose to go and discovered that my odd declaration was not yet finished. "My mother believed everything written is written in code," I said, "and that each person speaks a different language." I fled.

The man looked puzzled but called after me in a kindly voice, "Good luck to you, miss!"

I found a snack counter, purchased milk and crackers for the trip. I had gone too long without food, slept too little. Surely these accounted for my strange behavior. I determined to take better care of myself.

But on the bus to Oklahoma City, I slept and dreamed of the house on D Street. In the dream, Schutzie was trying to set out asparagus plants in the little front yard. Large tears fell from her eyes, dropped onto her hands, and ran down over the plants. Her solemn face resembled that of the duck in the tavern sign. The plants were being washed away by her tears while Schutzie struggled to anchor them in the soil. I said, Dig a trench, Schutzie. But she answered, I cannot dig here. This is a grave. Then she looked up at me and became the man crying in the bar. I awoke in the close air of the dimly lit bus, faint and covered with perspiration.

A young black woman was shaking my arm. "Are you all right, miss? You were moaning in your sleep." Weary and disheveled from traveling, she sat across the aisle from me cradling a sleeping child. A profusion of boxes and bags filled the seat beside her. "You on the run?" she asked softly.

The question brought me fully awake. "I'm fine, just fine. I'm sorry I disturbed you. I'm on my way to visit my sister."

She withdrew her hand but continued to glance at me from time to time, perhaps with suspicion. I thought for the first time that I was now a missing person. I determined to be more cautious, to carry on no more peculiar conversations with old men in restaurants. When the bus reached the station in Oklahoma City, I put my possessions in a locker and lay down on a bench to sleep, but a memory of my father surfaced. I sat up, put my money and the locker key in my sock. Then I slept until noon.

I woke to Sunday in Oklahoma City. Midday. Brilliant winter sun and warmer air revived me. I walked awhile and finally settled for an organ in a hotel dining room. They were serving brunch to late risers and the after-church crowd. I could see a priest at a table near the window. Drawing on Reynard's experience, I found a phone and the local directory in the hotel lobby. A moment later I had the name of a church prosperous enough to hire a staff and list their names in the yellow pages. The church's organist was Harold Martin. I hung up Schutzie's coat, straightened my hair, and approached the restaurant's hostess.

She was a stout, pleasant woman, well corseted beneath a black dress. Her blond hair was done in an intricate beehive style. She had blue-tinted glasses that caused her to squint. "Hello," she said, taking in my rumpled appearance with disapproval, but smiling nonetheless.

"Mr. Martin sent me," I said. "I hope I'm on time."

"Who?" she asked.

"Mr. Harold Martin, the organist at Trinity Church. To play organ during lunch. I'm his student. I hope he remembered to call and say I was coming." I produced a sturdy smile. The woman reminded me vaguely of the beefy boy I had intimidated on the sun porch. "Do you know anyone who attends Trinity?"

"My niece," she replied.

"Of course. I thought so." *Trompe l'oeil.* The intensification of the reality of components by juxtaposition, a new creation feeding on carefully rendered detail.

There was only one question left to ask and she asked it. "Are we supposed to pay you?"

"No, students play for the experience, but the church accepts donations."

The organ stood behind the salad bar. My dollar bill was out of the view of both the hostess and the cashier. To my surprise, the instrument was a lovely old Wurlitzer with draw bars. As I sat down, I looked directly into the face of a pink-cheeked elderly man with white hair. "Play 'Lady of Spain'!" he called out. The draw bars gave the organ a fine range of color; I was able to keep the song going for five minutes. When I finished, the old man came over and leaned on the organ. "You ever play any accordion?"

"No, but I'd like to," I replied. He asked for "Up a Lazy River" and left a dollar.

A young couple ignored a malicious toddler throwing custard on the carpet and asked for Tony Bennett songs. "All of them!" they said, and generously left a five-dollar bill.

Eventually, the circulating hostess saw the money. "Isn't that lovely?" I asked with swift enthusiasm. "You have wonderful people here today, Christian people."

The hostess considered and seemed to decide this was a personal compliment. "You certainly have a lot of songs memorized," she said. "I took piano for about a year when I was a child but I only memorized one song."

And eventually, a man asked, "You know Harry Martin?"

"Yes," I answered guardedly, "he teaches music."

"Well of course he teaches music," the man replied, "at the high school. But they say you know him."

"Many school teachers also have private students."

"I guess I never thought about that," the man said. "My name's Grimes. You tell Harry I said hello."

"Grimes," I replied. "I certainly will tell Mr. Martin I saw you."

Customers drifted in and out. I played for almost three hours, until the crowd had thinned to a handful of coffee drinkers. I took away sixty-two dollars, a spectacular profit.

"Will you be back next Sunday?" the hostess asked as I departed.

I gave her my most engaging smile. "Unless you turn in a bad report on my playing."

"Oh, I wouldn't do that," she said. "It sounded all right to me."

I walked several blocks to another restaurant and ordered scrambled eggs, but when the plate was set before me, my appetite vanished and a wave of panic seized me. I looked about cautiously, thinking perhaps I had been followed, that some imminent disaster threatened, but the handful of customers ate on peacefully, seemingly unaware of my presence. Then I recalled how often my mother had taken me to restaurants and ordered scrambled eggs. Eggs had been among her favorite foods. My panic subsided, then edged into melancholy. I picked up my fork, determined to throw off the sensation, but the eggs tasted like cardboard. It came to me then that I had never really grieved for my mother. My days had been too busy, my existence too precarious for a luxury like grief. Until now. The melancholy grew intense, then shifted and was transformed into guilt. I slipped the paper place mat from beneath my plate and turned it over. I took a pencil from my pocket and wrote:

My dearest Grace,

I have had no chance until now to tell you how sorry I am you are gone, how much I miss you. [As I wrote, one part of my mind looked on fearfully, even frantically. Writing a letter to a dead woman made no sense, was perhaps an insane act, the first symptom of an illness like my father's: Reynard, the family letter writer. Yet my hand continued to write.] I have failed with both Reynard and myself, but those efforts have taken all my time and energy. Only now do I begin to see the real tragedy of your death, stretching beyond Reynard and me. The unfinished life. The unfulfilled promise. Grace at age fifty. At seventy. Lines of invisible energy radiating into the world. Interacting. Experience modified. The energy gone now. Wires dead. The modifier that will not modify. For music, you loved poems most, Whittier the balladeer who wrote,

"Maud Muller, on a summer's day, raked the meadow sweet with hay." And who concluded, "For of all sad words of tongue or pen, the saddest are these: It might have been." But you also honored music, for Reynard's sake and mine. It was you who told me that music helps us organize our lives. Did you mean all art? I sound like Ezra. I was four or five and I had asked you why we played music. Do we play to organize our grief as well? To fortify us for our own ·death?

Then the fit stopped as suddenly as it had begun. In the remaining space, I began to list all of the musical compositions I could think of that took death as their theme: *Kom Susser Tod; Guisto Cielo; Massa's in de Cold, Cold Ground; Bach's St. Matthew Passion; Go Tell Aunt Rhody the Old Gray Goose is Dead; Pavane pour une Infante defunte; John Henry; Hang Down Your Head Tom Dooley; The Damnation of Faust; The Old Rugged Cross; The Egmont Overture; Siegfried's Death Music; Swing Low Sweet Chariot;* Mozart's *Requiem* written for his own funeral; Ravel's *LeGibet* with its evocation of gallows and church bells; Falla's *Sicilienne* on the death of Melisande.

A third of the paper remained. I wrote, *On the Death of Grace Simmons Cunningham,* followed by the word *Allegro.* But why was it always necessary to begin with an allegro? I crossed out the word and wrote *Adagio,* then crossed that out and wrote *Largo.* And a moment later understood why I had made this choice. When Reynard had been teaching me tempi, he wrote out, "Largo, a slow, broad tempo, almost as slow as grave." But I had not known the Italian gra-*ve,* the slowest tempo of all, and committed the word to memory initially as the English *grave*. Further, the Italian *largo* was related to the Latin *largus:* generous, abundant. A measure of my mother's determination, her splendid courage in the face of an insane husband, a crippled child, perhaps a murderous sister. I drew five lines, a treble clef, entered four flats and a four-four time signature. A theme came almost immediately: four stately quarter notes followed by two half notes, outlining a melodic curve. A suspension on the third note leaning into the fourth created a pleasing dissonance and motivated a consequent to follow my antecedent. I wrote several measures, until the paper was filled, amazed at what the nether reaches of my mind had created. Had my brain been preparing this music while I sat at the Wurlitzer playing "Lady of Spain"?

I walked to a nearby park, the place mat folded in my pocket; paced the gravel paths; sat on a bench with green, peeling paint; watched the sun disappear, the lights of the city emerge. I was afraid to take the paper out and look at it, hounded by my father's admonitions: Too much music has already been written. The time is wrong as well. Our sensibilities have been fractured and fragmented. A community of belief no longer exists. The twentieth century belongs to technicians, not composers.

When the light of day was completely gone, I took out the paper, unfolded it, and carried it to a nearby streetlight. My worst fears was immediately realized. My melody was a hackneyed, derivative line without interest. Alone in the darkness, I felt my cheeks flush with shame. A passage from Rilke, barely remembered, slipped into my mind, his scathing appraisal of young girls sketching: "They do not notice that with all their drawing they still do nothing save suppress within themselves the unalterable life." I crumpled the paper, then reconsidered and tore it into shreds and left the pieces in a trash bin: My pretensions. My silliness. My humiliation. I walked rapidly back to the bus station.

I continued by the scenic route, through Hobart, Sweetwater, Midland, Odessa, and first saw the inside of a jail in True Point, New Mexico.

I was playing an old upright that had been painted silver, in a bar called Sunup, when a deputy sheriff appeared beside me. "You can't solicit in this town, lady." He was a grimy giant, young, with coarse black hair, hard farmer's hands, scuffed boots. His only mark of authority was the sudden reserve of the garrulous bartender at his appearance.

"My husband's getting the car fixed," I said. "He told me to wait in here. We broke down."

"Ain't no broken car in this town," he replied, a twitch of amusement beginning at the corners of his mouth. "Ain't no husband. I been cruising all evening." It was a game, a gamble and—to his surprise, it seemed—he had won. His big, slow eyes moved over me, the piano, the line of bottles behind the bar, and paused to study his own face in the mirror beyond. "You're a whore," he said at last.

The bartender, fat and breathy, green-faced in the dim light, approached guardedly. "She's crippled. I run a clean place, Jim. You know that. Maybe her husband's out on a side road. I don't give you no trouble, Jim. She's crippled."

Jim ignored him and looked steadily at me. "You're a crippled whore."

Four dollars lay on the end of the piano. "I should have gotten a permit to play," I said. I handed Jim the bills and glanced at the door. "Here's my husband. He'll pay you the rest of it. It's fifteen dollars, right?" I asked, improvising. "State of New Mexico permit, fifteen dollars." I slid off the piano bench on the opposite end from him and took a tentative step toward the door. "These folks just wanted to hear some songs."

Jim accepted the four dollars but he did not even glance at the door. One large hand shot forward and captured my wrist. "Ain't no husband," he said. And to the bartender, "I'm gonna fine you fifty dollars for keeping a disorderly place. You pay up right now."

"Jim, I ain't got fifty dollars," the man pleaded. "You known me all your life. Your daddy known me all his life."

"I have to go to the bathroom," I said. "I'll be right back."

Jim did not look at me but his grip on my arm tightened. "Every day you don't pay, fine's gonna go up," he told the bartender.

The man withdrew money from his pocket and handed over five ten-dollar bills. "You're breakin' me. I known your mama and daddy all my life."

Jim propelled me to the doorway, across a rutted parking lot, and into a squad car.

"Perhaps you haven't been a police officer long," I said

as he slipped the car into gear. "Musicians are protected by state statute: *Omnia tempus habent.*"

"I'm deputy sheriff," he replied, unmoved. "Sheriff went to Tucumcari for a wedding."

"Tempus nascendi et tempus moriendi. A violation would be a black mark on your record." I ventured a guess—and lost. "It could prohibit you from holding public office."

"I ain't runnin' for nothing," he replied.

The jail was a square building that, except for its barred windows, looked like a large house. "This is a nice place," Jim said, steering me up the steps. "You'll like it here. Some jails got rats. We got a nice clean place." The building appeared to be empty. A single dim light glowed above the doorway, another in the empty office. Jim marched me past the reception area without stopping.

"You have to book me," I said.

"You gonna get a shower," he replied. "We got a clean place here." He thrust me into a bare room with four shower heads and another single light bulb, this one protected by wire mesh.

"You can wait for me in the office," I said, but he shook his head, suddenly somber, and leaned against the doorway to watch.

He accepted my clothing piece by piece and placed it in a pile beyond the reach of the water. "Lord, you're an ugly little frog. Wash your hair, too."

Then he turned a faucet and water shot out in an icy spray. "I've been sick most of my life," I said. "Infections, one after another."

Jim did not move and continued to watch solemnly, as

if the scene were somehow sad. "Here's a towel," he said, shutting off the water. "We got clean towels here." He approached in two swift steps, wrapped the towel around me, and pushed me to the floor. "You gonna tell me how I do," he whispered, fear now edging his voice. "You lie to me, I'm gonna crack your ugly neck." I clawed at his face, jamming my fingers into his eyes. Angered, he brought a huge fist down against the side of my face. My head struck concrete painfully. One powerful arm shot forward across my torso, pinning me to the floor. Blood pounded in my ears like a swarm of crazed insects. He smelled vaguely of dust, of red clay carried on a hot wind, an acrid scent settling to the floor through air dampened by the shower. As he moved above me, sweat poured from his face and ran into his eyes. Dazed from the blow, I could not clearly see him. It seemed to me he was crying large, soiled tears.

I rolled from him and reached to cover my abandoned shoes and socks. In his passion, he had not seen the bills hidden there. "You're just like everybody else," I said. "No better, no worse."

He sat back on his heels and worked his jaw as if testing it following a blow. "Get out of here," he whispered, sweeping damp hair from his forehead. "We don't want no whores in this town."

I threw on my clothes and stumbled from the building, running beyond the dim circle of light from the jail to the sheltering darkness of a nearby yard. Then I fell to my knees, retching violently. Rage and nausea made the black air electric blue. From the open window of a nearby house came music from a tinny radio, the jangle of a country song. Beyond and above the sound, an infant cried. When the nausea had subsided, I moved my head gently, testing for damage, and discovered I had no hearing in my right ear. Moving my head brought back the dizziness from the blow and I lay motionless on the ground for several minutes, unable to think.

A rough, moist touch against my cheek roused me. It was a marauding cat examining the dried blood that had trickled from my ear. I drew the animal into my arms, holding it so tightly the pulse of its heart throbbed against my hands. But the cat wriggled free, drawn forward by impulse stronger than friendship, by the dark mission of bone and sinew, of survival. When it had gone a few feet, it stopped and looked back at me with condemning yellow eyes.

I rose and made my way along dark streets back to the tavern. My bag and violin case had been set out on the sidewalk, objects disclaimed. I bathed in the rest room of an all-night diner and, fearful of returning to the local bus station, began walking through the night to the next town. A rancher gave me a ride to a truck stop where I would be able to catch a bus. There, I slept for an hour behind a storage shed.

I woke to New Mexico sun and the incredibly beautiful sounds of traffic. My hearing had returned. I was bruised but whole.

I traveled fifty miles to the village of June, where I stepped off the bus and directly into my second jail. To my surprise, the sheriff was a woman. "I'm Mildred," she said, ushering me into a cell. "Sit here and cool off. I'm locking this door for your own protection. A runaway girl is her own worst enemy." It seemed she took coffee at the bus station café several times a day. It was the best coffee in town and she also kept an eye on things.

"I'm going to visit my sister," I said.

"They all are." She told me she had moved into her job when her husband, the previous sheriff, had died. She was a large woman, buxom and florid. Her red-veined eyes had peculiar irises the color of ripe wheat. "That violin gave you away," she continued, hooking her keys to the belt loop of men's trousers. "Tramps don't play the violin. My brother's girl took violin lessons and played in a youth symphony orchestra in Texas. Girl like you, your folks will be glad to get you back." Mildred wheeled and walked smartly down the hall with a tapping step remarkably light for so large a woman. She disappeared into her office and, presumably, set about discovering my name and place of origin.

I sat back on the narrow single bunk, surveyed the empty and silent cells around me, and discovered I was thinking about dissonance in music. Why did some modern compositions almost without recognizable melody and harmony please the ear while others, nearly identical in form, carry no meaning, fail to rise above the simple condition of disorderly sound? I studied the two scarred faucets on the cell's small sink, found their twoness grim and devoid of hope. Dark–light, sin–virtue, old–new—the polarity that always undermined certainty. A previous prisoner had left an inscription on the wall above the sink. When my eyes discovered it, the eerie appropriateness of the message to my condition left me quite shaken: YOU CAN'T TRUST NO ONE.

Music publishers were fond of compiling anthologies in which two or three lovely tunes appeared among twenty-five or thirty pieces of mediocre or worthless music. The practice was most common with twentieth-century music, where problems of copyright, surviving relatives, or questionable editions were most prevalent. Customers would pay for the entire book to secure two of Kabalevsky's *Pieces for Children,* a Scriabin prelude, a bit of Rebikoff or Satie. Frustrated by such publishing tactics, Reynard had liked to say, "If these people know the difference between good and evil, what makes them think I do not also know?"

The disclaimers in the introductions to these anthologies, with charming and inventive variants, were always essentially the same: "In addition to popular favorites, we are pleased to present here music previously unpublished"—just written, neglected, found in a trunk, shut out by the establishment, lost at sea, discovered in a remote country. Yet the results were always the same. The lost music should have remained lost, the just-written left unwritten. Sitting in my cell in June, New Mexico, I could not think of a single instance in which a gem had been found among the dross. Both my father and I had been denied this experience promised so glowingly by publishers again and again. Yet Kabalevsky had once been new, young, unknown.

The publishers, of course, set up an impossible situation, one doomed to failure. By their own hand, they presented new pieces in the worst possible manner, framed by masterly works in whose shadow they could only seem shabby. And why, actually, were they shabby, when, technically, the two things were so similar? I had spent all of my life amid the teaching of music principles ("It is the shaping of the phrase, the energy of the rhythm, the whimsy, the delight, the depth of emotion, the classical order, the arrangement of intervals . . .") without discovering why the good was good. "One knows," said Reynard, and of course he was right, but it was a rightness based on shifting sand, on the judgment of a community of so-called informed persons. In my jail cell, it had no reality. The glowering faucets were monuments to my uncertainty.

Then in solitude, in exactly the manner Ezra had described in his declamations on prison life, I reached beneath these mad imaginings and brought forth the real question: Was new music good only to the degree in which it remained connected to the past, trailing clouds of glory into new territory? If so, creativity was nothing more than subtlety, the dressing out of the old with novelty, dressing it out so cleverly that listeners could experience all of novelty's delights without surrendering even one of their old gods. If this were so, the cacaphonists without recognizable significance, moored to nothing, were the true inventors. Unless you held the notion that the constant redefinition of a handful of ideas was the only true business of the world, and a good thing. Did I love Charles Ives for his "Yankee Doodle" or in spite of it? Or even simply for the sea changes he wrought upon it? The dull, scarred faucets, unmoved and uncompromising, glared back at me.

After a time, Mildred returned bearing the news that she could learn nothing about me—"You covered your tracks"—and carrying a large Bible. She opened the cell door and sat down on the bunk beside me. While she leafed through the book, I speculated on her failure: Had no one reported me missing? Had Mildred simply been inept or perfunctory in her search? Had Mitch, under the influence of Ezra and fearing Edlyn, departed from his principles and deliberately given out erroneous information to prevent my being found?

Mildred paused in the twenty-ninth chapter of Proverbs and began reading aloud. "The rod and reproof give wisdom, but a child left to himself bringeth his mother to shame." Then she sent me on my way. Six hours after my arrival in June, I was back on the bus.

In Phoenix, luxuriating in the city's warmth, I stayed almost four months. "I'm looking for a job playing piano," I said to the bartender at an establishment called The Library.

He studied me warily, his gaze lingering on my lame leg. "How old are you?"

"Eighteen."

"You got anything catching? Any disease?" He was a thick-bodied man with black hair cut in a short, stiff brush. He looked like a boxer.

"No," I replied. "I was born crippled, my hands and one leg."

"How are you going to play the piano with crippled hands?" He nodded at the instrument, an aging upright.

I played "Rhinestone Cowboy," "Snowbird." "Anything special you want to hear?"

"Nothing," he said. "I'm not musical. Trouble I have with piano players, they get drunk."

"I won't get drunk."

"What's your name?"

"Norma," I replied. The name had simply come to me. It sounded like normal. A surname presented itself immediately. "Norma Bellini," I said.

When we had settled on salary, he asked, "What really happened to you?"

"I married this guy and he beat me."

The explanation appeared to satisfy him. "He crippled you."

"Yes."

"Just don't get drunk on the job. I don't give a damn what you do in your spare time. You'll get Mondays off." His name was Tom and he called himself Tico. "You want a room upstairs?"

"Okay."

My room on the second floor opened off a hallway. It was accessible from a stairway rising out of the barroom, and also from outside stairs used when the bar was locked. The room was small, a bare cubicle with worn linoleum and a single window overlooking a used car lot. There was an iron bedstead painted a sickly yellow and a desk Tico assured me would also serve as a chest of drawers. A folding chair was mated to the desk. A curtain on a string shielded a clothes rod and four hangers. At the end of the hall was a toilet and a rusting shower. Folded on the end of the bed was a neat stack of surprisingly clean sheets and towels. Reynard had neglected to tell me that a concern for clean linen is often the mark of a brothel.

I retrieved the suitcase and fiddle from the bus station locker where I had left them and moved in. That night I played for a clientele built around Tico's two prostitutes. Olive was black, past forty. Tall, pencil thin, she had large moist eyes that gave her face a sad, dramatic expression. She carried a small white poodle with her at all times. Olive loved jazz. Joleen was white, fair and shapely, but with coarse, irregular facial features. Clients frequently remarked, "It's a shame about her face." She was young, perhaps twenty, but already a business-woman. She looked out at the world over her bulbous nose and protruding upper teeth with the speculative gaze of a banker.

On my first evening, Joleen approached me between songs. "You get the joke about this place?" she asked solemnly.

"The joke?"

"They named this place The Library so guys could tell their wives they were going to the library and then really go to a bar."

"That's a great joke," I concurred.

"I've known bars called The Office," she continued, "even one called The Post Office."

"Very clever, all of them."

"I don't mean anyone really believes it," she said. "It's a joke."

"Yes, I see that. They're all great jokes."

Satisfied, Joleen nodded and, unsmiling, wandered off.

My music was received well enough, and when I was able to produce two obscure melodies for a valued cus-tomer—"How Ah Ya, Hawaii" and "Redwing"—Tico glanced at me with mild interest and carried a bottle of Coke over to the piano.

Olive, cruising, looked narrowly at the Coke, circled the piano, and finally settled on the bench beside me. The dog nuzzled my neck and chewed at my ear with polite interest. Between songs, I stroked his head and he responded with a dainty howl of pleasure. We were in-stant friends. Olive asked for Ella Fitzgerald songs, then said, "You finish that Coke, you carry the bottle back to the bar yourself. Let everybody see you walk."

"Walk?"

"Look, honey, these johns see you crippled, they let you alone. Nobody want a crippled girl."

"Thanks, Olive. What's the dog's name?"

"Invention. The john that gave him to me claimed he was an inventor with a string of patents as long as your arm. The only thing he ever invented was that story. Look, I warn you about this dog, honey. He gets excited, he pees."

My room lay between Olive's and Tico's. The following morning I awoke to the sounds of Olive's all-night customer making a confused exit. Invention barked as the man pounded on the locked door to the inner stairs and eventually found his way out at the end of the hall. It was almost six o'clock; the beginning of a pink sunrise touched my window as the man clattered noisily down the outside stairs. I heard Olive's delicate feet pad softly into the hall to retrieve the dog, then the heavier steps of Tico rising to investigate the disturbance. He paused in front of my door, then bellowed at Olive, "That goddamn dog craps in this hall again, I'm gonna rub your nigger face in it!"

Olive screamed back, "Man, you blind? Why don't you look where you puts your foot?"

Above it all, Invention barked a melodious obligato. I had been dreaming of Grace, wished now I could tell her that here in Arizona, at The Library, the sun came up like thunder.

I became accustomed to nights filled with the amorous groans of Olive's clients, interspersed with the faint, provocative sounds of Olive herself, tender sighs and gasps, delicate squeals, snatches of whispered conversation; her imitations of delight. She seemed the heroine of a long-running play who strives, performance after performance, to be eternally fresh, always entertaining. Olive was a veteran, drawing on a repertoire of tricks and surprises I found astonishing. I wondered why she bothered. Her customers varied from night to night, were unaware of her prior and subsequent performances. Most were too coarse to appreciate her art in any case.

Joleen, in the room beyond Olive's, seemed to function in virtual silence, although the intervening walls muffled sound, preventing me from forming a reliable critique of her work. Joleen was also filthy, usually odorous. Her skin was often ornamented with foul eruptions. These she picked at daintily with long crimson fingernails. Suspicious of The Library's seemingly clean linens, I purchased my own, and arranged to shower at the YWCA.

Tico remained cool toward me, professional and taciturn. I found his complete indifference to music remarkable. No melody moved him, no rhythm delighted him, no repetition annoyed him. Our first altercation came in my second week when I refused a patron's request to sing an obscene song. "I don't know it," I said, "and I don't sing."

Tico's thick body loomed up beside me almost instantly. "She didn't hear you, maybe," he said to the customer. And to me, "You know every goddamn song there is! Sing!"

At this, Invention leaped from Olive's arms and sprang into my lap as if to defend me. A small, heroic growl rippled from his lips.

To my surprise, it was Joleen who intervened. "We don't want that cheap-shit porno in here," she said to Tico. "It drives away quality people."

Tico considered and then agreed with her. "You do what Joleen tells you," he said to me. "She won't steer you wrong." His voice was almost fatherly. As Tico withdrew, the dog sent me an apologetic glance, and I felt his warm, wet trickle soaking my clothes.

Although music had always been a prominent part of my life, I had never before performed publicly every night, six nights a week. I began at six in the evening and, except for occasional breaks, played until one in the morning. While the repetitions of popular songs did not appear to bother my audiences, the relentless monotony began to torture my own ears. I discovered early on that only a handful of people actually listened to the music, that I could switch from a movie theme to a Mozart sonata with impunity. Tico, at the bar, was totally indifferent to my programs so long as my periods of silence did not stretch out for an unseemly length of time.

I devised ornaments and variations to rescue the pop songs from their syrupy thirds, the merciless thud of the seventh falling into the tonic, the dreary cadences. I supported the melody lines of country songs with fugal voices and cross rhythms; but after two months, no amount of tinkering could dispel their howl in my ears.

To my surprise, classical music died almost as quickly: Mozart; Chopin; the Beethoven sonatas; the Schumanns, both Robert and Clara; Schubert's songs. Even such moderns as Kabalevsky, Poulenc, Fauré, with their irregular harmonies, their dissonances, their humor, their freshness, expired quickly under my industrious fingers in the marathon repetitions. The inventive rhythms of Stravinsky became as dull and gray as the drumming in a high school band. I thought of my lazy father who had always played only enough music to get by, never enough to tire of it.

One evening in my third month at The Library, as I struggled to make something of "Time in a Bottle" in F-sharp minor, using the melodic minor form of the scale —a ridiculous task a little like playing music blindfolded —a wave of revulsion passed over me, and sudden hot tears sprang to my eyes. I realized that in three months my ears had grown jaded to five hundred years of music, not only to specific compositions but to styles, harmonies, melody contours, and rhythms. New music in these same modes would have been no better. Obscure Mozart would have given no respite, unpublished Dvořák and Ravel no delight. Gone was music's power to stir, to evoke, to calm, to cheer, to console. I felt stunned, the victim of a cruel robbery.

That night, as Olive writhed and sighed in her imitation of passion, I took out the fiddle and tuned it. I plucked the notes of the theme I had written at the restaurant in Oklahoma City. Then I plucked them again. Was the sentimentality I had heard before in the phrase and which still clung to it actually parody? The sharp sense of dismay that had overpowered me as I stood under the streetlight in the park returned immediately. It was presumptuous to attempt the craft of Bach, of Mendelssohn, of Debussy. Preposterous. The certain mark of a fool, perhaps of a lunatic. But this time I was driven forward by the racket of barroom music still echoing in my ears. I found paper and wrote again the title,

On the Death of Grace Simmons Cunningham. The development of the theme came almost immediately. Put over into six-eight time with an icy, bitter underpinning of fourths and tritones, the music became a caricature of a barcarrolle, a syrupy Venetian boat song gone mad. I wrote rapidly, pausing only to pluck the fiddle strings from time to time to check my peculiar sonorities. When a second theme emerged—indeed a largo, the first tempo I had envisioned—I saw the composition would stretch beyond a single section. I went back and wrote under the title, Part I, The Dead Shall be Transfigured. Then, perhaps because I had so recently christened myself Norma, a fragment of libretto from the Bellini opera slipped into my mind, the libretto Reynard had sung so joyously from my earliest memory: *Dormono entrambi, non vedran la mano che li percuote.* They sleep, they will not see the hand that strikes the blow. From this, my new, cockeyed sensibility leapt forward to the last act of the opera, to Norma's final confession before the funeral pyre. *Son io, Norma!* It is I, Norma. I crossed out the title bearing my mother's name and wrote, *Suite for the Dead.*

Olive sighed deliciously in counterpoint to the scratching of the pencil. As silent and single-minded as Joleen, I wrote on. I returned to the first theme again and again, each time with skepticism, but it was made of sturdy stuff and held up against all of my onslaughts. This meant that the peculiar modality had already been in my mind in Oklahoma City. The marathon playing at The Library had only hastened a process that was already under way, had perhaps been growing and forming itself for years. I wrote on until dawn. When the sun rose, I had six pages of an orchestral suite. They were ragged, imperfect pages needing pitiless revision. I had given my barcarolle a double exposition, acceptable in concerto form but redundant in music without a soloist. I had carried the French horns out of their best range. My key was terrible for violins and violas; neither the open A nor the open D strings could be used, sacrificing resonance, and the material for the first entrance of the violins was too brutal for the lyric character of the fiddle. I thought of the charge leveled against Brahms, that he did not write for instruments but against them. Still, I had six pages of music that did not hurt my ears. I crawled into the yellow bed and slept soundly, dreaming I was a small child sitting under the mock orange in our yard in Indiana, digging in the soil made fragrant by falling, rotting blossoms, singing the song of the ladybug. Midway through the dream, Reynard appeared and asked, Where are you going to get an orchestra? You no longer have even a name. But perhaps there's one around. Look behind the chimney in the attic.

My fourth month at The Library was my last. Each night after the bar closed, I sat at the desk on the folding chair and wrote. I had treated myself to staff paper and with the broad dimensions of an orchestra score quickly filled several tablets. I did not find the writing a wholly pleasurable experience; sometimes the frustrations I encountered were almost unbearable. Yet the challenges I set for myself were exhilarating enough to carry me through the dreary hours of playing. In my dreams, I explained to my father it was not my task to worry about the music's ever being played or published, but only to write it. Awake, I gave myself the same advice.

I had almost forgotten Los Angeles; Phoenix was warm enough. I told myself I lived as well as Schubert, and probably ate better.

Then, on what had begun as an ordinary Tuesday evening, Olive, from halfway up the stairs, beckoned to me. I finished the song I was playing. Tico gestured, indicating I should follow her. At the head of the stairs, I was met by a stout, sweaty man, one of Olive's clients. "This man want you," Olive said without preamble. There could be no doubt about her meaning. When I did not answer, she drew me aside and whispered, "Look, sometimes a guy a little kinky. He want a crippled girl."

"No," I said. "Olive, I thought you were my friend."

"This business," she said. "Honey, he all worked up over you. Won't take five minutes out of your life."

Tico appeared beside me. His hands shot out suddenly and pinned my arms behind my back. "Move right along down the hall," he said. At this show of violence, Invention leaped from Olive's arms and attacked Tico's leg. Tico threw the tiny dog off with one vicious kick. The customer smiled, a wild, damp grin. But the dog was back immediately, a small, white knot biting and growling at feet and ankles.

Tico put his face close to mine and whispered harshly, "You want me to call the police? Send you back to that husband?"

Invention's courage was of heroic proportions. He came at Tico again, this time leaping against his shin. At this, my memory—or perhaps my father's—clicked. "The dog's peeing on you!" I cried. Tico loosened his grip for an instant and I slipped away from him. Fearing I could not take the steps quickly enough, I lunged into the open stairway, and landed in an unceremonious heap at the bottom, bruised but unbroken. Briefly, I glimpsed above me the figure of Tico examining his trouser legs.

"What happened?" cried one of the handful of customers at the bar.

"Fire!" I offered and, nursing a bruised hip, hobbled out of the front door.

I walked to the bus station, washed my bruises, and slept on a bench until early morning, when the occupants of The Library were most likely to be asleep. Then returning, I mounted the outside stairs quietly and slipped down the hall to my room. I retrieved my belongings, returned to the bus station, and bought a ticket to Los Angeles.

As I waited for the bus, I went to a telephone and, on impulse, dialed the Decembers' number. The sound of Schutzie's voice stirred me more than I had expected. "Hi, Schutzie," I said with effort. "It's me, I'm okay."

"Ada!" she cried. "You sure you okay?"

"Yes. I'm fine."

"Kiddo, you never gonna guess. I'm pregnant!"

It was wonderful news; I should have been pleased. I was truly surprised at the sharp pang of jealousy that assailed me. I would be replaced in the little house by a baby. "That's wonderful," I managed to say.

"Betcher boots! Ada, if you're okay, you better stay away. That aunt got it all over that you're crazy. You come back, she find a way to lock you up."

"Are the police looking for me?"

"Not much, I think. Ada, you want to know a strange thing? Nobody ever took your picture since your mama died. All they got is a small, fuzzy school picture."

"You and Mitch didn't tell them anything?"

"What we gonna tell? They say, she got friends? I say, when she gonna have friends? Work all the time. They ask your father, you got relatives? He say, we all descended from William Penn. Then he change it to William the Conqueror. Then he change his mind and say Hungarian Gypsies."

It was simpler than I had imagined. Reynard and I had been so isolated there was little information to give the police or to withhold. "How are Reynard and Ezra?"

"Ezra moved out," said Schutzie. "That agent got him a tour of England. We gotta call him Larry Lederman now."

"Good for Ezra."

"Your father tell Mitch you're in New York City, but Mitch won't tell."

"Reynard said that?"

"Your father say he saw a lion and a library. Mitch say that's the New York Public Library."

"It was a dog," I said, "with the heart of a lion."

"What?"

"Never mind, Schutzie. Mitch is right. I'm in New York City, near the public library. I'll watch out for the lion. Reynard's okay?"

"Fine. Last week I took him a cherry pie. Look, kiddo, if you're in New York, I'll tell everybody you're in California."

"Make it Alaska," I said. "That's the biggest state. It will keep them looking longer."

"Sure, Alaska!" said Schutzie. "And Ada . . . we love you."

"And I love all of you," I said. "Good luck with the baby."

"You gonna keep in touch?"

"Betcher boots," I said.

16

I GOT off the bus in Los Angeles and started walking, thinking vaguely I would go and look at the Pacific Ocean.

I met Kyle Hawkin when I took a job as a cashier at Ralph's Supermarket in the suburb of Lawndale. It was late afternoon when I saw the Help Wanted sign in the window. The idea of working in an ordinary grocery store was appealing: no more bars, no prostitutes, no songs banging in my ears.

Kyle was a painter, a witch, a religious fanatic, and a recovering mental patient. She stood behind her cash register, looking on in silence, as I was hired. When the manager asked if I was ready to start immediately, Kyle said, "Of course she is. I'll begin training her this afternoon." When he had issued me a green smock and departed, Kyle said, "Norma Bellini, I'm pleased to meet you. Let me help you find a room. This isn't a good neighborhood for girls." She found a spot for my bag and fiddle case in the office, and we took our places behind twin cash registers.

Kyle was fragile and dark, pale as if from illness. Some disorder in her face made one side of her mouth lifeless and turned all of her facial expressions wry and lopsided. She had long black hair and the quick, bright eyes of a clever cat. I did not know for some time that a bizarre diet and the peculiar medicines she made for herself had dried her skin and aged her prematurely. Her maternal manner and low, husky voice also made her seem older than she was. She had injured her throat and vocal cords in some experiment with her homemade medicines. I took her to be middle-aged. In fact, she was barely twenty-five. "I believe I can get you a room about three blocks from here," she said, "with an old lady who has a cozy little bungalow. Nothing fancy. There's nothing fancy around here anymore. Maybe there never was."

"It doesn't have to be fancy," I replied, grateful for her help.

"The only drawback is, the woman's a Christian Scientist, and she gets a little pushy about it. I met her at a healing service."

"That wouldn't bother me."

"There's a spark of truth in everything," Kyle said, "even Christian Science. Please hand me my purse from back in that corner." Kyle's large purse weighed several pounds. When she opened it, I saw it contained a curious assortment of objects: bottles of liquid, feathers, a scout knife, seashells, pieces of colored chalk, a number of rocks. She withdrew a small stone and handed it to me. "This is opal," she said. "Carry it with you at all times to ward off thieves and muggers."

"Is it valuable?" I asked.

"It's good quality Australian opal," she replied, "but not really valuable."

Kyle was as open as I was secretive. After she had explained the operation of the cash register, she told me she was from Butte, Montana, where her father had once run for mayor and been defeated. He was an automobile dealer. Before that, he had been a missionary in China. "In the old Pearl Buck days," Kyle explained. Her mother was much younger than her father. "I was born very late in my father's life. That was the real cause of my illness. Human germ plasm becomes exhausted. I could have been a Mongoloid."

"I've read about it," I said, "but it's only ova. Sperm don't age."

Kyle smiled her half smile—it was the wry expression that accompanied most of her pronouncements—and said, "Do you think they're telling us everything?"

I nodded, uncertain if the question had been sincere or a subtle joke. I soon learned that such peculiar utterances were Kyle's favorite tactic. Even when we had become close friends, I was seldom certain if she really meant the things she said.

Her illness, she told me frankly, was schizophrenia. She had only recently been released from a mental hospital, which she insisted on calling the Montana Lunatic Asylum. "My mother's a sweet little thing," she said, "but having a lunatic in the house is bad for my father's business."

Again, I was uncertain how to respond. "Did they send you out here?"

"I volunteered. Graduates of the Montana Lunatic Asylum often go far in the world."

I despaired of understanding her tone. "Why don't you just call it a hospital?" I asked.

"Being a lunatic is much like being royalty," she replied. "You always keep your identity, even in exile."

I felt she was confiding in me, and a confidence given invites one in return, perhaps demands it. "My father is in a mental hospital," I ventured, and then added, "in Connecticut." It was my first attempt at creating a new personality for myself by simply telling large portions of the truth, changing only names and places. I found the technique immediately liberating. It enabled me to take back large parts of my life; it also eliminated the wearing task of constantly inventing my past and trying to remember my own inventions. The technique worked well for me.

"Destiny is fan-shaped," Kyle said. "At any given moment, the future is completely preordained in lines of energy flowing from a single point. Yet, one lateral step creates an entirely new constellation of forces. At the base of the fan are constants. And you surely must see the constant in our meeting like this. Lunatic asylums."

"I'm not sure I believe in destiny," I said.

"You should not associate with me at all," she continued. "If you had free will, you'd run from me. Flee! Another mental patient in your life? Indeed!" She paused and laughed softly. "But you won't, you can't."

Kyle was incredibly bright. Before her illness, she had already completed college and traveled in Europe. She was a Phi Beta Kappa from the University of Minnesota, with a double major. "In art and political science," she told me. "All art is political. Look at Paris. Architecture is especially political. Every government builds buildings that reflect and enhance one political point of view." She carried her Phi Beta Kappa key on her key chain to gouge out the eyes of muggers. It dangled from the chain along with her rape whistle and a Celtic cross.

After work, Kyle drove me to look at the room. Her car was an ancient English Austin, a relic from her father's used car lot in Butte. My first thought was that the decrepit machine could not possibly have made the trip from Montana to California, but the Austin was remarkably serviceable, and in the months I spent with Kyle, it never failed us.

I rented the room and prepared to resume the habits of composition I had begun in Arizona, writing each day after work, but my landlady, as Kyle had predicted, was evangelical with her Christian Science. Evenings, when I refused to join her in her living room for religious discussions, she played tape-recorded lectures at high volume and aimed them at my door. The lectures were expositions of the writings of Mary Baker Eddy.

Days were better. Side by side at our cash registers, in free moments, Kyle and I chatted. Our topics ranged from Carl Jung to comic strips, wholistic health to charismatic healing, Virgil to vitamins, Paul Klee to St. Paul, Minnesota. When I told Kyle I was composing music, we fell into a heated discussion of the etymology of the word *fugue,* which in music means to follow but in psychiatry means a flight from reality.

Before her illness, Kyle had had one art show in a small

gallery in Minneapolis. She produced a clipping from the Minneapolis *Tribune* to verify this story. The show had been well received. The reviewer declared her oils expressed exciting new ideas against a background of tradition. He felt a bright future lay before her. "But no one wants paintings with religious themes today," she said, "and that's all I paint now."

"We no longer have a community of belief to support religion," I said, paraphrasing Reynard. "Our sensibilities have been fragmented."

"And must be mended!" she replied with the wry grin.

When I told her I could not play the music I was writing, because of my unreliable fingers, she asked to see my hands. "But you play that violin you carried in here?"

"Fairly well."

The following morning, Kyle arrived at the store carrying a small bottle of black, vile-smelling liquid. "Drink it," she said, "to rejuvenate your hands. Don't be afraid. Christianity has its roots in witchcraft." When I refused, she drew a cup from her purse, poured some of the liquid into it, and set it on the floor between us. "The vapors will help a little," she said. I could not persuade her to remove the cup, and we worked all day with the foul odor wafting about us.

After two weeks, I gave up trying to work in my room and accepted Kyle's offer to share her apartment. She called for me at the bungalow in the Austin, and together we loaded my meager possessions into the small back seat. The landlady pressed religious tracts into my hands and we set off, wheeling around the corner and down Hawthorne Boulevard.

As Kyle drove, I tore up the tracts and let the pieces

flutter out of the window. Suddenly, we were in a holiday mood. "We're saving on rent by doubling up," Kyle said. "We have to celebrate." She stopped and bought a bottle of whiskey.

I had not seen Kyle's apartment, but it suited me perfectly. It was three rooms and a bath assembled erratically at the side of a garage on a narrow lot in Hawthorne. The landlord's house sat in front. The apartment opened onto the alley. While the vista was not impressive, the privacy was glorious. The entrance door led into a kitchen of uneven plasterboard walls and a floor covered with a patch of loose linoleum. Rusting metal cabinets were placed about here and there. They looked like objects set out for the junk man to cart off. Beyond the kitchen lay the living room. It held a studio couch, a chair, orange-crate tables and, incredibly, an old upright piano.

"You didn't tell me about the piano!" I cried.

"I wanted to surprise you," Kyle said. "The landlord moved the old wreck out of his house. All of this furniture is his junk, but fate intended this piano for you. Try it."

"It isn't an old wreck at all!" I said, when I had run over the keys. To my amazement, it was a vintage Chickering. Except for a scarred case and strings that needed tuning, it was an excellent piano. "What's your favorite song?"

" 'There is a Balm in Gilead,' " she answered promptly.

I played the old hymn, and Kyle, in her low, rasping voice, began to sing, first softly, then with growing fervor, louder and louder, her injured voice straining at the notes. She closed her eyes and raised her hands as if in supplication. It all seemed some ceremony designed to lead her into religious ecstasy, but at the song's end she smiled and resumed her former composure. "Let me show you the rest of the place." There was a bedroom with a single cot, and a small but clean bathroom.

"Where are your paintings?" I asked. She led me to the bedroom closet. Kyle's oils were abstracts in brilliant colors. Religious symbols were sprinkled liberally through the ovals and boxes, the wandering lines, the harsh, lightninglike explosions of jagged color: eyes, burning suns, crosses, and especially fish. Kyle seemed able to depict an endless variety of fish. "They're beautiful," I said. "I know very little about painting, but they're vigorous. In music, that is a term of praise."

"I accept it as such," she said, smiling, "but I haven't been able to paint much here. Vandercrap in front is full of the devil. I can't paint on the property of Satan."

"The landlord?"

"It's actually Vanderhoven. Do you want the cot or the couch?"

"The couch. You paint in the bedroom." A card table held her paints and brushes. She seemed to have no easel.

Nothing in the apartment was level. When Kyle poured a can of beans into a pan to warm for our supper, they rolled to the side of the pan. "It's like being on a ship," I said, "on the ocean."

"The ocean is the holiest of all places," Kyle replied, finding glasses and pouring out the whiskey. Then she peeled a raw onion and chopped it into the beans.

Living with two excellent cooks, Reynard and Schutzie, had made me conscious of food. "If you put raw onion in beans that are already cooked, the beans will be warm before the onion is cooked," I said, and then wondered if I had offended her.

But she smiled. "It's good anyway. Sort of Chinese. Al dente."

"Al dente is Italian," I said.

"Try not to let your mind become cluttered with things of no importance," she said, taking frequent sips of whiskey. "Food's only purpose is to nourish the body. There's much too much pretension on the subject of food." She proceeded to chop and add other items to the beans: seaweed, bay leaf, fresh garlic, and a brown substance she told me was cattail stem. She made toast with a fork over the gas flame, set the table. By the time we sat down to eat, she was quite drunk.

Cautiously, I tasted the beans. "Delicious!" I said out of courtesy. They had a gray, gritty taste.

Kyle took one bite of the beans and then began removing them from her plate with her fingers, one by one, and arranging them on the table in a pattern. I got up and emptied her glass down the sink, refilling it with water.

"That's a helluva thing to do to good booze," she said, but she made no attempt to stop me.

I scraped the rest of the beans onto her plate. "Eat. If you drink any more you'll start throwing up."

"How does a sweet little girl like you know that?" she asked teasingly.

"I worked in a bar. What's that noise?" The hum of a motor had begun outside the window.

"That's the windmill," said Kyle.

"You're drunk," I said. "They don't have windmills in Hawthorne, California."

"We do!" she said, waving one finger playfully.

I was beginning to feel the whiskey myself. "In Hawthorne, California, they don't even have wind," I said, and suddenly discovered tears rolling down my cheeks.

"Why are you crying?" Kyle asked.

I began to sob, and could not answer for a moment. "Because my mother loved Nathaniel Hawthorne," I finally said.

"Hawthorne accepted the supernatural," said Kyle.

"It isn't really a windmill, is it?"

"Of course it is!" Kyle replied. "It's Vandercrap's. He retired out here from Holland, Michigan. He makes a big thing of being Dutch. Come on, I'll show you the windmill. You're right, we're in a hollow and there's no wind. He turns it with an electric motor."

Kyle took my hand and we stumbled out into the alley and crept around into the dark yard. In the space between the landlord's house and the garage there was, indeed, a windmill, a home-built structure about twenty feet high with four spinning blades turning at the top.

"Why does he run it at night?" I asked.

"That sound lulls him to sleep. It's really a form of devil worship, to attempt to copy the Lord's handiwork."

"Kyle, the Lord didn't make windmills."

"But he made the wind," she answered. "Do you want to climb up this windmill?"

The whiskey made me daring. "I certainly do," I answered.

Kyle went first, pulling herself up from strut to strut. I followed, until the two of us were poised just below the spinning blades, and the artificial wind was blowing our hair. "It's wonderful!" I cried. "Just like being beside the ocean! The holy, holy ocean!"

"At the ocean you feel spray!" Kyle cried, and raised her hand. I saw for the first time that she had brought the bottle of whiskey with her. She dribbled whiskey against the blades, sending a fine, stinging mist into our faces.

"Just like the beach!" I cried.

"Dover Beach!" Kyle shouted back. " 'Ah love let us be true to one another, for the world which seems to lie before us like a land of dreams, so various, so beautiful, so blue—' "

" 'New'!" I corrected. "Not 'blue'!"

A light flashed suddenly in our faces. Vanderhoven had heard us and come out with a flashlight. "You girls get down off my windmill!"

I looked down into the face of an angry old man, dimly lit by the flashlight. " 'We are here as on a darkling plain!' " I cried.

"You're drunk!" he shouted. "I can smell it! You're both drunk!"

" 'Swept with confused alarms!' " cried Kyle. "My friend is moving in with me!"

"I raised two girls myself!" Vanderhoven cried. "Two fine, decent girls! I want you out of here tomorrow! Both of you!"

"I'm paid to the end of the month!" Kyle shouted. "You are a devil-worshipping son of a bitch!"

"The week!" Vanderhoven cried. "You're paid to the end of the week, not the month! Saturday you go!"

"Saturday!" Kyle agreed. Then she took aim and, tipping the bottle carefully, poured the rest of the whiskey on Vanderhoven's head.

As we fell drunkenly into bed, I called out from the

living room couch, "Why is Vanderhoven a devil wor-
shipper? Really?"

From the bedroom, Kyle called back, "His lousy mate-
rialism!"

"I think I liked the wind story better!"

"Go to sleep, Norma!" said Kyle. "Give your liver a
chance to cope with the alcohol!"

The next day we started house hunting. Shaker's
Beach was a village a few miles from Hawthorne. It was a
community of abandoned gas stations, aging motels, and
crumbling houses. A haven for transients, it sat like a
bruise between the affluent beach communities on either side of it. Kyle chose Shaker's Beach for us after
meditation and a session of automatic writing. "We need
a place to work," she announced, looking out at
Vanderhoven's windmill with disgust. "This will be it,
and it will be a house." To her credit, we located a small
house in the village almost immediately. She did not tell
me she was planning to steal Vanderhoven's piano.

17

THE PRODUCE manager at Ralph's was a fatherly Italian named Angelo. He hated all forms of governmental authority. A few years earlier, he had attempted to bring his elderly and ill mother to the United States from Italy. Some bureaucratic entanglement delayed her papers and, while Angelo struggled to resolve the matter, his mother died in Italy. Angelo had never forgiven the government. In his forties, he was six feet tall and barrel-chested, with powerful arms and shoulders. He carried heavy lugs of fruits and vegetables about as if they were children's toys, was often called over into the meat department to shoulder sides of beef.

The light of Angelo's life was his family, a wife we never saw and two teenage sons who stopped in at the store from time to time. Both boys were replicas of their father, gentle giants. Angelo drove to work each morning in a sturdy pickup truck. Without telling me, Kyle chose Angelo and his sons to steal the piano. The story she invented was simple and direct: The piano belonged to Kyle; it was an heirloom that had come down to her from her grandmother. Vanderhoven had ordered her out of her apartment, but he refused to let her take her piano unless she submitted to his advances. In his fatherly indignation, Angelo asked no questions. Predictably, he did not suggest that Kyle call the police.

On Saturday morning, when the Austin had been packed with our belongings, Kyle announced that we could not leave without ministering to Vanderhoven. "I am a lay priest," she said. "It is my duty to try to persuade this man to abandon his Satan worship."

"Let's just go," I said, but she refused, and also insisted that I accompany her to call on the Vanderhovens.

We were received with suspicion, but I believe Vanderhoven was intrigued to find Kyle carrying a Bible. Reluctantly, he admitted us, and for an hour we sat on straight chairs in the Vanderhoven living room. Kyle read from Ecclesiastes, then began preaching on verse from the first chapter: "The wind goeth toward the south, and turneth about unto the north; it whirleth about continually and the wind returneth again according to his circuits." She told Vanderhoven the wind was the breath of the Holy Spirit. To create wind artificially was to make a graven image. She told him his windmill was a pagan idol. The old man listened, frowning; from time to time he raised one tentative hand as if to protest, but Kyle was too glib for him. He seemed unable to find a pathway into the argument. Eventually, he gave up trying and sat listening in amazement. Mrs. Vanderhoven, a

quiet, white-haired lady, seemed perplexed and apprehensive, but I think she finally decided her husband had
somehow converted both Kyle and me to Christianity.
Eventually, she brought us all glasses of lemonade. While
Kyle was preaching, Angelo and his sons quietly removed the piano, loaded it onto the family truck, and
drove off down the alley.

The piano was sitting in the living room of the Shaker's
Beach house when we arrived around noon. Angelo and
his boys were gone, but they had left us a bottle of Chi-
anti to wish us well in our new home. The bottle of wine
sat atop the piano.

Kyle, triumphant, told me of her coup.

"The police will be here in an hour," I said.

"No, they won't," she replied confidently, picking up
the wine and searching through her purse for a cork-
screw. "Angelo hates the police. If anyone questions him,
he'll lie."

"Kyle, how can you reconcile lying and stealing with
Christian principles?"

"Destiny meant you to have this piano," she replied
with the wry, inscrutable grin. "Why else would the Lord
have sent us Angelo? Norma, that truck even has heavy-
duty springs. When the Lord makes his will known as
clearly as that, it would be a sin to go against it. Spiritual
law stands above human law. Try and understand that.
Besides, Vanderhoven had already thrown the piano out
for junk. What will it cost to have it tuned?"

"I'll buy a tuning hammer and do it myself."

I still had a little money saved from my employment at
The Library. A few days later, I put a hundred dollars in
an envelope and mailed it to Vanderhoven anonymously.

A knowledgeable dealer would have paid him more for the old Chickering, but the average buyer, seeing the scarred case, would probably have offered less. I was in no position to discuss the fine points of the transaction with either Vanderhoven or the police.

Kyle was correct about Angelo. We lived at Shaker's Beach for nearly a year and, when trouble came, it did not come from the accommodating Italian produce manager.

The house, for all of its deficiencies, was a bona fide house, not a garage apartment, not a room over a bar, and for Kyle, not a hospital. It was small, barely a cottage, with peeling paint that had originally been yellow, sagging doors, a weathered and leaking roof. One side was raised on rotting pillars to level it into the sandy hillside. But a large west window looked out at the ocean, half a mile away, with a kind of threadbare gentility, and the stiff, salt breeze was the same wind that blew across the luxurious estates in Palos Verdes, a gray prominence we could just see pushing into the bay to the south of us.

Moving filled Kyle with exhilaration. When we had carried our boxes into the house and unloaded them, she scrutinized our small pile of belongings so intently that they seemed to take on great value. "Finally we have a house," she said with deep feeling, as if our move had been a matter of long and careful planning rather than precipitous flight.

Having a house meant a great deal to her. When she spread her paintings out in good light, I saw that all of them had hard, bright edges. Many were squares within squares. She hungered for space. "This place is spiritually pure," she said. "We'll both be able to work here."

She went outside to study the house, planting her feet in the sand and setting her hands on her hips as if to argue, or to defend herself from attack. "It's autonomous," she said. "We can live here without contingency, in an open mode."

"It's only a house, Kyle, for heaven's sake," I said.

"You're right. It is a house for heaven's sake," she replied with the lopsided smile.

At the front of the house, a sandy path led to the rutted street; in back was a small rectangle of scrubby yard populated by large numbers of land snails who collected around the clumps of sparse, tough grass. The front door was hazardous because the porch was missing. There was a drop of nearly four feet to the ground. The back door was a little better. Part of a porch was still in place. By stepping over broken boards we could reach dependable wooden steps that carried us up to the door.

Kyle brought her paints out into the yard and began a picture on the side of the house. Her subject was a lizard, a large beast nearly two feet long with a broad, scaly snout that curved to a delicate point, and four carefully wrought feet. As I worked about the house, sweeping out the rooms and carrying the worn rugs out to shake them, I watched the lizard grow. Its feet were excellent; the claws appeared to sink deeply into the wood and hold it tenaciously. The mouth was closed, set in a somnolent smile. She painted the lizard bright orange, gave it a brilliant purple eye and an overlay of black detailing. Sensuous, serpentine scales that looked like curving flower petals flowed down to the tail.

The next day she turned her attention to the inside of the house, ignoring the cleaning I had already done. The house was mostly a single room with a folding divider separating sleeping space from a small living room. Adjoining was a scarred kitchen, and beyond that an ancient bathroom with a high, old-fashioned tub on rusting iron legs. Someone had left furniture. It was badly worn but we welcomed it; a large overstuffed chair, a wicker settee, three folding cots, a dresser with a cracked mirror, end tables, pots and pans, even a broken ironing board, and in the kitchen—the miracle of the place—a beautifully made glass and wrought-iron patio table. The metal was painted white; the glass top was unscarred, uncracked. The table looked so hopeful, we took it as a good omen. When we sat down to eat we could see our feet through the glass. Our soiled sneakers assumed new interest, like objects in a shop window. Looking at them, we could believe anything was possible. The episode with the beans, I learned, had not been an isolated incident. As Kyle ate, she was often overtaken by inspiration. She would spill portions of her food onto the table and arrange it into designs; not only beans but corn, odd-shaped scraps of bread, grape seeds, and noodles were pressed into service. Under her hand, they became daisies, deserts, mountain ranges. Often, they took the shape of the lizard. If she liked a creation, she left it on the glass tabletop, often for days, and we ate around it. If a design did not work out well, she simply scooped the food up with nimble fingers and ate it.

Angelo and his sons had pushed the piano into a spot along the north wall of the living room. Because of its weight, we had no choice but to leave it there. I wondered if he had checked under the rotting house to determine if the floor was strong enough to support it.

Sometimes at night, when the roar of the ocean carried in to us on the wind, and the doors rattled, I wondered if the piano might fall through the floor, but it stayed securely in place.

From the inside, the large west window gave us a view of one tall eucalyptus rising from the yard of a neighbor below us, and the ocean beyond. Our panorama, interrupted only by the tree, began with the tip of Palos Verdes and swept to Malibu on the north, with Catalina Island slumbering like a scaly old whale in the middle distance.

Kyle arranged the house to her satisfaction; it required several days. She created additional shelves from cardboard boxes, pushed the little tables around endlessly, scrubbed and swept diligently, washed and polished the windows. Then she sprinkled everything with holy water. I learned she had been stealing it from Catholic churches in a sponge. She had nearly a cup of water in the bottle in her purse. She poured a small amount into a saucer, dipped an aluminum tea ball into it, and swung the tea ball around on its little chain as if it were a censer. When she had finished, she took her paints into the bathroom and began a mural on the wall above the toilet.

This time it was a large fish done in brilliant yellow. It swam against a background of pale, undulant blue. The fish was edged in orange and resembled a sunburst, but the creature had been injured in some manner, and as it swam blood spurted from a wound in its side and splattered over onto the blue background. Its single black eye was dull, half closed in pain. Below and to the side of the fish, she painted a miniature of the orange lizard. This time it was standing on its tail, looking up at the fish thoughtfully.

"Is that the Crucifixion?" I asked.

She said that of course it was.

Because we had stolen the piano, we had to look for new jobs. Vanderhoven would be watching for us at Ralph's in Lawndale.

The job change turned out better than we'd hoped. We found a supermarket in Redondo Beach, only a mile from the house, and the pay was twenty cents an hour more than we had earned at Ralph's. Even better, the manager let us share one job. This gave each of us half days to work at home.

"My sister and I have an invalid mother at home," Kyle told the man. "She's had a stroke. One of us must be with her at all times."

The manager accepted Kyle's story. "I'm for family," he said. "You're good girls."

Sometimes he gave us the day's leftover fruit as a gift for our mother: brown bananas, molding oranges, sour and bruised peaches. I would take mine and walk home by the beach, hurling each piece of fruit in a great arc out over the breakers to watch the gulls gather and sweep down curiously. But Kyle always carried hers home. She washed it, cut away the rot, and made us little salads and compotes, seasoned with her own peculiar herbs. Sometimes her concoctions were delicious; sometimes I found them totally inedible. We took turns cooking, and I kept a loaf of bread and a jar of peanut butter in the kitchen. When Kyle's recipes became too bizarre for my taste, I fell back on these staples.

Between us, we could usually put in forty hours a

week. With this income and Kyle's frugal ways—which included, I believe, shoplifting—we managed quite well.

Kyle began to paint furiously, even frantically. She scoured secondhand shops and rummage sales for old oil paintings, which she painted over. These were often cheaper to buy than new canvases. As fast as she carried them home, she filled them. Her abstract creations often looked odd in the elaborate frames that had recently held a great-grandmother, a romantic landscape, or a sailing ship. "All aspects are favorable in this house," she said often, squinting at her work. The west window, for all of its charm, could hardly have been worse for painting. The sun's glare was merciless; but Kyle never complained. "This house was given to us," she said.

"It's the power of suggestion," I offered one day.

"The Lord doesn't care what you call it," she replied, "so long as you don't blaspheme."

I wondered if she would find the raucous noise of my music blasphemous, but she took in stride the major sevenths, the syncopations, the banging sforzandos; she even went out of her way to invent pleasant things to say about the music.

"That sounds like a bagpipe, Norma. I like it."

"It's a musette, a single sustained tone."

"All of your music is righteous because it's an expression of God's wrath."

I conceded that all modern music probably sounded a little wrathful. "But I think it's my own wrath, not God's."

"It's the same. Your're only a channel," she said. "But I like those sweet little things."

"The thirds. It's an exhausted interval. Here they function only as parody."

"Be careful with parody," she advised. "God is not mocked."

"And was that the real problem with Vanderhoven's windmill?" I asked.

She sighed as if despairing at my ignorance. "It was such an ugly windmill!"

"Kyle, if you mean what you've just said, and if you're right, then the only people in hell are bad artists."

"Where else would you put them?" she asked, close to anger. "Go eat some peanut butter! Your blood sugar's dropping and your brain is starving!"

At the beach house, the suite took shape, but if Kyle found her work easier, I found mine more difficult. My fluency seemed to disappear as I worked my way more deeply into the material; I encounted problems I had not known existed in the earlier, more superficial work. Could music be merely a collection of fortunate sounds? A collage? Or was a deeper unity required? Reynard's notion of a framented consciousness tormented me. I went to a university music library and studied the scores of Mahler, of Wagner, and especially those of Anton Bruckner: the music of the long, arching line. Were these lines essential unities? Victorian excesses? The pedal-point habits of an organist turned composer?

I consulted Kyle. "Do you think music is nothing more than fortunate moments?" It was Sunday morning and we were sitting over coffee. I was looking at my feet through the cereal patterns Kyle was arranging on the glass tabletop.

"Certainly," she replied, "so long as the fortunate moments are not mere empty display."

I was surprised at her acuity. "Paganini is mostly display," I replied.

"But you're wrong in asking me," she went on. "Consult your dreams for direction. Get back to Adam and Eve. The dream life is the only authentic source of creative principles. And the real answer to your question is no. The dream life always has unity and integrity, but its parts always seem like only fortunate moments. It's just as well to treat them as if they were."

"You're talking in circles," I said.

That night, predictably I suppose, I dreamed of Adam. In the dream, I was shoveling away the dirt from Grace's grave. I worked alone, digging with an orange shovel that was the color of Kyle's lizard. As I worked, a sense of urgency came over me. It seemed my mother was still alive and I had to reach her before the air in the casket was exhausted and she suffocated. But when I got to the coffin and frantically tore off the lid, Grace lay dead. It was the figure of Adam who emerged from atop her body. He rose threateningly, then sat down on the edge of the coffin and grinned at me. I woke trembling in the half-light of dawn, and found Kyle beside me.

"Hush," she said, taking my face in her hands. "It's all right."

"What happened?" I asked.

"You were dreaming."

When I had related the dream to her, Kyle said, "But surely you see the meaning of that. Your mother is the origin of your life, and Adam is the origin of all life. The coffin is the womb. All creation is *the* creation. This is a good dream."

"My music began as some kind of history of my mother," I said. "Then things got out of hand. I thought it was my own history. Now I'm not sure. Maybe it's nobody's history."

"Or everybody's," Kyle said.

"My mother was a liar."

"And so are you," she replied, "and so am I, because we're creating a history of the future."

"You're playing with words, Kyle."

"Schizophrenics do that," she said with her half smile.

I could not stop trembling. To calm me, Kyle boiled water with paprika and leeks, and gave it to me to drink. In desperation, I accepted the steaming cup, and the brownish, onionlike broth did have a soothing effect. I fell back into a peaceful hour's sleep.

When I awoke, I found Kyle mixing her paints beside the piano. "What did Adam look like?" she asked.

"What do you mean?"

"Describe him to me!"

"I can't. This is ridiculous."

"No, it isn't. Just tell me what he looked like. It's good material. If you can't use it, perhaps I can."

This struck me as enormously funny and I began to laugh. "He was young, younger than my mother. His hair was in ringlets, a soft, light color, nearly gray. But his face was fierce. He looked rather classical, with a good nose and prominent bones, and he was muscular. Kyle, this is stupid."

"Was he wearing a fig leaf?" she asked.

"No, a toga, to the middle of his thighs, lots of drape, and anklets laced up his calves."

Kyle began a picture on the wall beside the piano. It was my morning to work. As I departed, she was mixing daubs of paint into a pink flesh tone.

When I returned at noon, the painting was almost completed. Kyle had Adam in profile, in a half crouch with a length of stick in his hand, as if he were about to lunge at someone. She was in high spirits. "How did I do?"

"Very well!" I said. "It's marvelous! I think he was a bit stockier in the neck."

She corrected to my specifications; then she put in Adam's single eye. It was huge and white with only a fleck of color toward the nose. It made him look almost blind with rage. Kyle was good with eyes. "Look at the lips," she said. They were thick, sensuous, slightly parted. "He wants to sing."

"And what does all of this accomplish?" I asked.

"Give it a little time," she said.

In the end, and by a circuitous route, Adam served me very well. As I worked at the piano day after day, forced to look at him, it came to me that his beauty was only remotely related to theory. Staring at the drapery of his toga one evening, I said to Kyle, "You're really a fine painter. Your effects are never cheaply won." The strength of the painting came from a balancing of opposites: the raw and the polished, the profound and the fanciful, the familiar and the obscure. Her audacious juxtapositions threatened tradition while forgetting none of it, undermined it, and in the undermining, energized it. Emotion was always restrained, bodied forth subtly through distortion of form. She resisted every easy thing. The genius of the picture was Adam's eye. Nearly blind, it saw everything.

Kyle said, "The point is to impose perfect order on forms assembled by chance. Except there is never really any chance, only the appearance of it."

I thought of Emily Dickinson. " 'After great pain, a formal feeling comes.' "

"Painful things can become too studied," Kyle countered. "What appears to be chance comes out of your own vision, and you don't study for it. You slip up on it. Poor little Norma. You're bent on having it all spelled out for you. You never learned to play."

"Play?"

"Playfulness. You never give in to whimsy. Do you know what Paul Klee said when he began a painting?"

"What?"

"He said, 'I'm going to take a line out for a walk.' " She laughed, a little puff of breath rasping through her injured throat, then said, "Very well, give me your hands." She took my right hand and turned it palm up. "Come and sit beside me." She took the left hand as well. "All of the past and the future is written in the hands."

"For once I agree with you completely," I said. "My hands are my destiny."

She studied me, letting a smile begin and grow slowly. "We mean different things, of course, but it makes no difference. Isn't it remarkable how often people can communicate when they're talking on completely different subjects? To understand thought, you must consider it graphically, as a grid, with impulses carrying messages every which way, but always by the shortest possible route. This factor of efficiency creates intersections of unlike ideas that for a moment have related meanings, or even the same meaning. This is inevitable. The result is a sub language, many sub languages."

"You don't actually believe in palmistry," I said. "You're too bright."

Her brows shot up with amusement. She enjoyed my discomfort enormously. "Everything is in motion," she continued. "Never forget that. But who's to say in which direction things travel? Does fate move inward from the hand to the brain? Or does the brain dispatch directions outward to govern the design of the hand?"

"My disability is genetic," I said. "My mother's sister had a child with the same dysfunction."

"Not the same," said Kyle. "Identical, perhaps, but not the same. Your dysfunction serves some purpose. You chose it, even to manipulating the genes. Everyone who is sick chooses to be sick. I developed schizophrenia to avoid confronting the issues I found in painting. I worked it through my elderly father and his exhausted germ plasm."

"But you believe everything is preordained, that there is no free will," I argued. "That was one of the first things you told me about yourself, back at Ralph's."

"Choice and predestination," she replied. "Yin and yang. Why are you grinning at me?"

"Because I think your answer is an evasion, but I will agree that duality rules the world. Dark and light, dissonance and harmony."

"Our sub languages are merging again," she said, undeterred. "I see everything—including palmistry—as motion with the initial direction of movement, the impetus, unknown and unknowable. But you chose to have crippled hands to prevent yourself from becoming a performer. You are forced to compose. You knew how great the temptation to perform would be if your hands were normal." Her pale cheeks warmed with conviction, the hot blush of mad debate. "Norma, can't you help yourself even a little bit? I'm doing all I can, but I can't do it all! Your father back in Connecticut—the violinist?"

"Yes."

"They've locked him up. I'm talking about time! We don't have forever." Then she turned her attention to my hands. "The ring finger or finger of Apollo governs talent. You crippled it worst of all. That was taking a terrible chance. You could have sacrificed everything, lost it all. The fifth finger matters less. It is the Mercury finger and governs discernment. I should think its crippling accounts for your distorted perception, your confusion in seeing a direct path to your goal. But that is secondary. For the most part, the small finger is simply under the influence of the ring finger. Well, you've devoted most of your life to managing your father's insanity. Perhaps it's inevitable for you to be so literal, so thing-y about life. In any case, the crippling of the fingers is compensated for in the thumb. The thumb is the real master of the hand."

"I have large, prominent thumbs because I use them so much," I said, "to compensate for my weak fingers."

"Of course. There's the direction of the motion again. Which came first? It doesn't matter; it's all here. At the base of the thumb is the mount of Venus, where a gathering of all the emotions is found. Because the thumb controls the mount of Venus, it dominates the personality.

Your thumbs are very long, a factor that could not be altered by exercise. This indicates intelligence. But because your thumbs are so very long, they overpower the qualities in the mount of Venus."

"My head rules my heart."

"Don't laugh! That's exactly right."

"Two hands," I said, "the two-ness of life."

"Please don't interrupt," said Kyle. "All of this is corroborated in the palms as well. The head lines are much deeper than the heart lines, much stronger."

"So am I to be a composer or not? What does my future hold?"

She sighed, despairing of me. "This is only potential. Don't you understand anything at all? Of course you're going to be a composer! You're a composer already."

"All of it works out to be the 'try harder' theory of creativity, doesn't it?"

"Not all of it," she replied. "Some things are given, by grace. But now I'm hungry. These sessions always burn so many calories. We need to eat potatoes, good quality carbohydrates."

I retreated to the refuge of my earliest training. "In any situation of doubt," said Reynard, "sing the music. The voice is primary. All instruments imitate the human voice."

The jumble of notes sorely taxed my vocal cords and carried my voice into novel and eerie stretches of dissonance.

"You're not much of a singer," Kyle observed, "but since your purpose is to raise a dead spirit, I suppose it's appropriate. But I am surprised at the degree of rage in the music. I didn't hear that in the piano version."

"Why don't you just shut up and paint?" I asked. "Why don't you just for once shut your mouth?"

"I was moved by the music," she said solemnly, mischief lighting her eyes. "I was moved to testify, like a Quaker . . . whose silence has been violated."

I relented. "Somebody said modern music won't succeed until someone comes along who can whistle Prokofiev's *Promenade.*"

"Try whistling," said Kyle, in high good humor now. "But I'm right about the rage."

"Yes, I suppose that's what made me shout at you."

"And does that insight solve your problem?"

"No. The issue is something like phrasing. All phrasing is based on the length of one breath, one human breath. The music pauses when the singer draws breath."

"I like that." She had now decided to console me. "It's not just a fact of music, it's really a world view. So just mark the pauses on the score, tone down the rage, and you're done."

"Something *like* phrasing . . . but not precisely that. Phrasing involves breaks. I have to find connections."

"Now look who's playing with words," said Kyle.

I went to the library to study scores.

Like Reynard, Kyle was occasionally on target with her hocus-pocus. One morning she peered into her bowl of cereal and exclaimed, "See this!"

Dutifully, I looked, and saw only cornflakes swimming in milk.

"Everything has pulled to the east, in the direction of intuition! This will be a propitious day."

"I don't think this table's level," I offered.

"This omen is for you," she said. "The cereal is in the southeast area of the quadrant, the lower portion. Music is at a deeper, more abstract level of consciousness than painting."

In the library after work, I sat leafing through scores by Erik Satie, pausing at his *Gnossienne Number Two,* a brief composition of only two pages, without key or time signature, without bar lines, and opening with a peculiar triplet formed from an eighth note and a quarter note. The pattern of the triplet suggested to me a foot slipping on ice and then righting itself, a slight stammer inter-rupting a flow of speech, a ripe plum glancing past a tree branch as it fell to earth. These images recalled one of my father's dicta: "The skills needed to perform music are numerous, but only one skill is needed in listening to it, a grasp of what it means to be human."

Satie's performance marks were printed above the staff in lieu of tempi. The sections were marked succes-sively *with astonishment, don't leave, with great kind-ness, more intimately, with a light intimacy, without arrogance.* Here was the wit of twentieth-century music set free to range, a strategy of no strategy where the performer became an aleator spilling dice in random patterns, and the listener completed the loop of specula-tion . . . with ripe plums and slipping feet. And all of it happened with only the notes and Satie's amusing in-structions for guidance. My gaze lingered on the conclu-sion of the piece, an E-minor chord in its first inversion. Then I raised my eyes to return again to the beginning, and in the act of returning understood everything at once. Because music existed only in time, the listener could never go back to rehear a passage as a reader leafs back in a book, nor pause to listen longer as one hesitates before a painting. A composer got only one chance. If I substituted the word *shape* for *phrase, gesture* for *drawing breath,* the real strategy of the piece came clear. The music itself instructed the listener in how to listen by forming coherent shapes signaled by gestures. The instructions Satie had written out were clever, perhaps useful, but in the end they were not really required. All that was needed was in the notes, signaled by the peculiar triplet which was repeated at critical junctures throughout the piece.

I went home filled with hope, and found myself confronting a skeptical Kyle.

"You already knew that," she declared. "You're telling me music exists in time, not in space, and I'm supposed to get excited?" She walked to the living room window and stood gazing out at the ocean, turning her back to me.

"Maybe I did know. Yes, of course I did. I think it was just a matter of raising that knowledge to a conscious level."

"That's a bit too Freudian for my taste," she replied, "but if it serves you, use it, of course."

I sat down at the piano and began to play the Satie. "Shape, signaled by gesture. That is all I know and all I need to know."

"Keats wasn't writing music," said Kyle. "You've missed something. Stop playing; come and look at the ocean."

"Why should I? Kyle, really."

"Do as I say. It's important."

I obeyed, rose and moved to her side.

"Now, what do you see?" she asked.

"Water," I replied, "the moon, the South Bay Furniture Company, the drugstore."

"The ocean is a repository," she said. "What you have left out is memory. No one can listen to music without memory. Maybe you should raise that idea to a conscious level."

I watched the line of automobile headlights coming up the coast highway below us.

"Do you agree?" Kyle pressed.

"Perhaps I do, but when I tell you why, you won't like it."

"What does it matter whether I like it or not? It's your own sensibility that matters."

"Kyle, I think your concept of memory involves history, of the individual, of the race, of humankind; but memory to me, for now at least, means musical memory."

"In order to play a piece without the score," she said. "Yes."

"There are two kinds of musical memory. The first, as you say, is knowing all the notes, a performing technique. The second is the ability to hold a complete musical idea in your head from beginning to end. It's a function of hearing, and we don't all have it in equal measure. There are tests you can give to small children to determine how much musical talent they have. Actually, they aren't very good tests; children nearly always reverse your expectations, and hearing will improve with practice. But the tests are based on musical memory in terms of listening."

"You play something and have them sing it back. I see."

"No, that won't work. Not all people are singers, especially children. You play two pieces of music and ask the child if they are the same or different."

This idea caught her fancy. "Of course! You get a pure, intuitive response, untainted by conditioning."

"It's a listening exercise," I said. "That's all. It's not a world view, okay? For me, right now, it's a footnote to the concept of shape and gesture. If a shape is too long or too complex, or if a gesture is not distinct enough, the listener will lose the idea before it's completed."

Clearly, she was disappointed. "Make the simple shapes long and the complex ones short."

"I knew you wouldn't like it."

"Use a bass drum to signal things."

"Kyle, do I tell you how to paint?"

"We'll celebrate in any case," she said. "If you find all this technical business useful, it represents growth. Tomorrow we'll take a picnic and go to the beach. We'll have a campfire. I had hoped you would find a relationship between the shapes of your music and your memories of your mother. After all, those memories were the initial impetus of the music."

"Be honest," I said. "In your own work, you're very concrete. All the eyes and lips, Adam's toga—none of that came from raw intuition, raw memory."

"It's just that I had expected a little more."

"From your cornflakes?"

I went out and sat in the dark on the back steps. The

single frail light of a ship far out moved slowly across the bay. In fact, Kyle's observations had stirred many memories, but they were of my father rather than my mother. Reynard had always felt there was no point at all in composing music. "There's too much of it already," he said, "and only the tiniest fraction of that is worth keeping." I believed much of this came from his preoccupation with perfection. He would cut compositions mercilessly. "Dispense with the nonessential!" Frequently, his targets were the Romantic composers, with their elaborate and interminable endings. "The melody comes to rest here. Anything else trivializes it." Many people shared this view of the Romantics, but Reynard carried things further. He felt no compunction at all in cutting Mozart, Beethoven, Haydn, Handel. Nearly all solo or chamber music that crossed his path suffered excision, sometimes literally, with a scissors. Only orchestra music had been exempt. As a fiddler in the ranks, he'd had no authority to undertake cuts. Had he been a conductor, I'm sure he would have attempted it. Reynard believed in the complete work present in the detail, all the instructions for a life in a single cell. "All truth," he said once, "probably reduces in the end to one word." It was hardly a useful idea for a composer.

I had been trained to economy, yet I knew very well that many musicians expanded the compositions they played. Baroque organists worked from a figured bass, creating music from numbers indicating the harmonic structure. Early harpsichordists were expected to introduce ornaments into music without benefit of performance marks. Nineteenth-century performers improvised their own cadenzas for written concertos. They were expected as well to create almost endless variations on themes, often without preparation. Jazz expanded simple ideas into something larger. Folksingers added verses. In all music, refrains gained in importance with repetition. Reynard never expanded music; he contracted it. In a long career, he had written only one composition. It was a Spanish dance in two parts. In the first, a succession of dotted eighth and sixteenth notes cascaded in a downward spiral like objects cast off, barely worthy of notice. The second part opened broadly and sweetly with an A-major chord, like a single bright moment before a storm, but it, too, soon fell off into agitated downward motion. Written out, the piece would barely have filled a page. It survived only because friends had persuaded him to record it. Watching the single freighter, silhouetted now by a rising moon, I found myself haunted and divided by the memory of the Spanish dance. I knew Reynard was nearly infallible in his musical judgments. Yet there is nothing on earth so worthy that its merit can survive scrutiny by a certain aesthetic sensibility. Fault can always be found. Did the melody contour of the Spanish dance trace the pattern of a critical awareness that destroyed everything in its path? Did it predict years in advance that the man who possessed it would eventually find himself talking to Jesus? I had wanted to tell Kyle that excursions into memory always turned up wildly unmanageable polarities, but I had had neither the heart nor the energy for a debate.

After a time, she appeared in the doorway. "What are you doing out there?" she asked.

"Planning how I'm going to play the Satie. You interrupted me."

"I'm sorry."

"No you're not," I said.

"You're right," she replied. "I'm not."

At the beach the following evening, we ate sandwiches and plums, then walked barefoot beside the lapping water, gathering wood for a fire. Kyle wore a smock; she had transferred much of the contents of her purse to its large pockets—vials, tins, feathers, pieces of root, powders. As we walked, the bulging pockets clacked and clattered. "Are we going to hold a coven?" I asked.

"Musicians play etudes to improve their skills," she replied. "All rituals are exercises to improve mental discipline. What do you say to that?"

"I say the English language is a very slippery proposition."

When we had a supply of wood, Kyle located a secluded spot beside a small, low outcrop of turf. With her pocketknife, she shaved slivers of wood for tinder and soon had a fire going. "First you must give thanks for the insights you have received," she said, drawing a piece of crumpled paper from her pocket. I saw it was a sheet of discarded staff paper, salvaged from my wastebasket.

"I don't have to do anything, Kyle."

She smoothed the paper and held it out to me. "You must burn this. All of your previous errors will be erased, carried away in the flames."

"And will it prevent the militarization of African tribesmen as well?" I asked.

"What does that mean?"

"Nothing." I had never told Kyle about Reynard's fires. I set aside my troubling memories, took the paper, and threw it into the fire. There seemed no point in spoiling her party.

Kyle began to remove objects from her pockets, setting them in a line on a flat rock. In a metal cup she combined ingredients, explaining as she went. "Comfrey root for healing, calendula for a sunny mood, ginseng for memory, rosemary for cleansing, willow bark to ease pain." There were a dozen or more items in her recipe. She then added enough sand to fill the cup, mixed the concoction with the feather of a grackle, and set the cup into the fire to heat. "Herbs often have contradictory uses," she said. "If you are agitated, ginger root tea will calm you. If you are depressed, it will rouse you."

"There's mental discipline for you," I said.

But she was no longer listening to me. "All supplication is related to fertility," she said. "It doesn't matter if you're growing barley or children or paintings." On her knees by the fire, holding her hands before herself as if to warm them, she began to chant. "Be not a terror unto me. Thou art my hope in the day of evil." She repeated the words again and again, swaying now, her cheeks growing pink. Whether the color came from the heat of the fire or from passion, I could not tell. I sat back in the sand and watched, fascinated and also repelled.

Then without warning, the chanting ceased. Kyle pulled the hot cup from the fire. Before I could grasp what she was doing, she had plunged the ends of her fingers into the heated sand. "My god, stop!" I cried, but it was too late.

She sat on her heels, smiling, silent, watching ugly blisters form at the end of each of her fingers. "They are purified now," she said quietly.

I was astonished. I had been so involved in my own affairs, I had not realized her work was going badly. "I am so sorry . . ." I began, intending to give solace, but she brushed my words aside with a superior smile that broached no intrusion. Annoyed and revolted, I left her sitting beside the fire and walked home.

By morning, the strange breach between us had healed, but my revulsion lingered. Because of it, I did not clearly see for some time that Kyle's health was deteriorating.

With Satie's triplet before me as a meritorious example, I revised the music. In the end, I changed little of what I had written. Kyle said, "The Satie merely confirmed you in your own instincts."

"I don't know if I can believe that," I replied, "but it sounds wonderful." I decided the work was essentially finished. I began copying my hasty scribbling into a readable autograph. Awash with optimism, I visited a neurologist for a complete physical examination. He told me essentially what Mitch's doctor in Richmount had said: that my disability had been present at birth, that it was untreatable, and that it was unlikely to become worse. He also told me how fortunate I was, that many people had handicaps worse than mine.

Kyle's fortunes and mine seemed at opposite ends of a seesaw. Her work pace slowed and then stopped altogether. She continued to pursue witchcraft in an effort to reverse her luck. I was uncertain if her peculiar behavior came from artistic frustration or a return of her illness.

We had been in the Shaker's Beach house ten months when Kyle began offering sacrifices. One dark night, she crawled between the rotting pillars of the house and buried a silver dollar deep in the sand. "Rejecting material things is the beginning of vision," she said as she emerged, brushing the sand from her clothing. "I can't work at the store anymore. I can't earn money."

I began working the job full time myself.

A few days later, Kyle asked me if I knew how to snare a rabbit. "There are no rabbits here," I told her.

"The rabbit symbolizes the leap of the imagination in the presence of fear," she said.

She began to fast and lost weight rapidly. No argument I could invent persuaded her to eat, and she was dead set on the rabbit. In the end, I brought a package of frozen rabbit home from the store, thinking that when she had finished her ceremonial nonsense, she might be cajoled into eating the meat.

The ceremony she devised was simple, and revolting. She placed the pieces of meat on the table and left them to rot. "The mortification of the flesh," she explained. When I could no longer tolerate the smell of the meat, I threw it out, expecting an argument, but she did not seem to notice it was gone.

One day she came home from a rummage sale wearing a trench coat that was much too large for her. "What do you have in your pockets?" I asked. "They're bulging." She smiled enigmatically and refused to answer, but she made no objection when I looked into the pockets. They were filled with pieces of chalk. "Tell me what you're going to do with these," I demanded.

"Watteau drew with chalk," she replied. "He lived three hundred years ago. You would like his work,

Norma. All color and light. They call him the Mozart of painting."

"And you're going to draw with chalk?"

"It is the impermanence of chalk that attracts me," she replied. "It is much less intimidating. Do you see that it would be quite impossible for anyone to be frightened of a simple piece of chalk?" She studied me for a moment, then threw back her head and laughed. It was a coarse, hideous sound.

"I want to know what you're doing," I said.

She turned away and stared out the window at the ocean. "There isn't much time now. The missionary work is all that's left."

"Kyle, you're ill," I said gently. "I think you know that."

"Of course I know it," she replied.

"Then let's get you to a doctor, get you some real medicine, instead of all this hocus-pocus."

"Poor little Norma," she said quietly, "you want to cure me, but it's too late. This has nothing to do with painting, you know. The genes are catching up with me. It's as simple as that."

She began going out each morning wearing the trench coat, its pockets stuffed with chalk. Our existence now depended on my working. I had to wait for a day off from the store to follow her. When I did, I discovered she had a map of the greater Los Angeles area. She had set for herself the task of writing on the wall of every public rest room within five miles of our house, writing simply the words *Stop, Look, Listen.*

I telephoned her parents in Montana, and learned that the woman Kyle had described as her mother was actually a young stepmother. Her own mother had been insane and hospitalized for many years. The stepmother, busy with her own life, clearly wanted nothing more to do with her troublesome stepchild. The elderly father looked to his young wife for direction. He promised vaguely to send a check, but did not ask for our mailing address.

Kyle began to wear the trench coat night and day, even sleeping in it. It was soon filthy. When I pleaded with her to take it off long enough for me to wash it, she replied, "I am Joseph, the child of my father's old age. This is my coat of many colors."

In the eleventh month of our life together, Kyle made her final sacrifice. Despite all I had undergone with my father it took me by surprise. One night, she stacked her paintings in a pile on the living room floor, climbed atop it, doused the trench coat with gasoline, and set herself on fire.

It was past midnight and I was sleeping ten feet from her. I woke to a nightmare of fire and screams, the heavy smell of gasoline. Kyle died, arms raised, as if she were blessing the flames. I saw her for an instant, then dense smoke blackened the air. When I heard the large west window explode in the heat, I leapt through it, past the jagged edges of the glass, and landed in the cool sand.

The California authorities were the most sophisticated I had ever encountered. By daybreak, I was sitting in a police station. Within hours, they had located Kyle's father. "He is hiring a crematorium to finish the job she started," said the jail matron when I questioned her. "Her ashes will be returned to Montana." The woman provided me with clothing: clean but worn jeans, shirt, and sneakers. Then she led me into an office where most of the particulars of my life lay spread across a desk in the form of police reports.

The officer behind the desk was a tall black woman who reminded me a little of Olive. "Your house burned down around you once before," she began, studying me with unblinking hostility. Whatever her life experiences, they had left her single-minded and pitiless. A deep scar on one cheek suggested violent encounters. "Your father is suspected of setting that other fire but his mental condition has prevented a clear determination of facts."

"My aunt was also a suspect," I ventured.

"No one has ever seriously believed that idea," she shot back, never changing her expression. Kyle's act had been a classic case of self-immolation. I don't think I was ever seriously suspected of arson. This was strategy. "You are also accused of abusing a child and suspected of being mentally unstable." She drew a paper toward her and glanced at it briefly. "Casting spells. Your employer at the grocery tells us your friend Kyle also spoke of casting spells. Do you consider yourself a witch?"

Sitting in the police station, with Kyle newly dead, her pictures lost forever, I found these words bizarre and unspeakably cruel. Perversity seized my tongue. "I consider myself a composer, but all artists are witches, all art is witchcraft."

Almost imperceptibly, she sniffed. "Your attempts to appear worldly do not impress me. What happened to your leg?"

"It's a deformity I was born with."

For some reason, this idea amused her. "And were you born a witch as well?"

"Perhaps I was."

"Your mother believed you were a child prodigy. Do you think genius is close to madness?"

The conversation had evolved into a petulant struggle. "My mother was a persuasive writer."

"She has also been dead for several years. Yet you told your employer you cared for an invalid mother. Was that your friend's mother?"

I met the challenge head on. "Kyle's mother has been in a mental hospital for years."

"So it seems," she said, unimpressed with my candor.

"What crime am I charged with?"

"That's the problem," she said with heavy scorn. "I'm not sure what to make of this circus."

I flared into anger, as I am sure she had intended me to do. "I don't consider my friend's death a circus!"

"Then tell me what it is!" she cried, urging me on to greater rage, probably hoping I would incriminate myself.

"I'll tell you the moral of this story!" I shouted. "You had better lock up all artists, because they start fires!"

She smiled, enjoying my discomfort. "I see you've come to enlighten me this morning."

Eventually, I was led out of the office to be driven to some holding cell while California and Indiana discussed how best to dispose of me. The man escorting me, a youthful and muscular officer, clearly did not consider my frail person a serious security risk. He walked along beside me whistling softly under his breath. To put him further off his guard, I exaggerated my limp. As we neared the squad car, I saw a man passing on the other side of the street, and stopped abruptly. "That's my husband," I whispered, "the man who tried to kill me before. He must have followed me here." I grasped the officer's arm tightly as if for protection and moved a little behind him. "He carries his gun strapped to his thigh." I believe it was this bizarre detail coupled to my tight grip on his arm that confused the officer. For a moment, he was disconcerted. I wondered briefly if a violent encounter lay before him, waiting to complete his education, some interchange that would produce a scar as profound as that on the black woman's cheek, or if simply meeting me would be sufficient to destroy all of his appealing, youthful trust. Then I bolted. He glanced once at my frail body and chose to pursue the innocent pedestrian across the street. The first haven I saw was a small café. I ran in the front door and out the back. At the next corner, a bus presented itself. I rode two blocks before the driver tired of my elaborate search for a transfer and put me off.

I spent half the day walking back to the house in Shaker's Beach. I approached cautiously but the place was completely deserted. The little house was a total loss. I found the fiddle tools, black and mangled from the heat, and buried them in the sand. Finally, I crawled under the house and retrieved the silver dollar Kyle had hidden there. The Austin still sat in the driveway, waiting for the family in Butte to decide its fate. It yielded four more silver dollars Kyle had left in strategic places to ward off accidents and auto theft. Then I walked down the hill to the highway and hitchhiked to Long Beach. Before the day was out, I was a waitress in the Circus

Café, a small restaurant decorated with circus posters and run by an elderly man who had once been a clown.

"I was a bareback rider until I fell," I told him. "My leg."

Hungry for any sort of association with the circus, he hired me. Before he could question me closely, I asked, "Were you with Cole's?" and pointed to a poster. I discovered I had little to fear. The man was so eager to relate his own life, he had little interest in discovering mine. The material on the posters and in circus publications piled on a back table provided me with enough information to invent a fairly credible past.

A few weeks later, leafing through a circus trade paper, I came upon an ad: "Wanted, Steam Calliope player. Must have authentic circus experience." The address was a town a scant seventy miles from Richmount. I discovered I was homesick.

Except for the owner of the Circus Café, I would probably not have been given the job in Indiana. From this talkative, open-hearted man, I learned that circus folk accent the first syllable of *calliope*, pronouncing it to rhyme with *cantaloupe*. Or lucky stroke.

18

MONUMENTA IS dying. Day by day, roar by roar, her morning bellow has lost its zest. In these weeks, the winter landscape has not changed, yet this day, her last (all acknowledge it except Belle), is a propitious one; February twenty-ninth, leap year day. Like Kyle's rabbit, Monumenta will leap out of life into the void of imagination, perhaps in the presence of fear. Still, there is no fear in the cat's muted roar, only exhaustion. Day after day Belle has administered a series of nostrums. This morning she diagnoses bronchitis, cooks a beef broth laced with hot peppers and patent medicines. This brew is intended as an expectorant. "To get her phlegm up," says Belle, stirring and seasoning. Watching, I think of the cooks I have known: Reynard, Schutzie, Kyle, and now Belle. Say what you will about religion, the real business of life and death is negotiated with the stomach.

Beneath Belle's shelf of potions is my own work shelf. Surveying the objects there—the glues and varnishes, the tools I bought to replace those lost in the California fire—I expand and restate my observation, which is somehow intended as a benediction for the lioness on her last day. The real business of life and death is negotiated with the stuff of the earth. I jumble all of this once more, like shaking dice, and try again. Although the violin tools I now have are finer than any Reynard ever owned, I do not hold them in high esteem, because they still seem unfamiliar, and already Monumenta is dying. This clumsy metaphor is also immediately discarded. It is no doxology hymn for morning and evening, no kyrie for a cat. The habits of composition have warped my mind; my ear is hell-bent on connecting everything in the world to everything else; friction and juxtaposition to generate . . . what? *(Life chain-chain reaction-chain of being,* chants the mad voice in my ear. *If true things are not true, why do the plays of Shakespeare make such great operas?* Grand *operas?* Hush, I reply. I am not writing an opera. Put away your toys and go to bed.)

Belle controls her mounting anxiety but does not hide it from the monkey. Scaddegood cowers in a chair and moans softly, a high-pitched, eerie sound we have not heard from him before. Between moans, he sucks one finger with incredibly precise and delicate movements of his lips. He looks exactly like someone playing an oboe.

When Monumenta's soup is ready, its temperature checked by a quick dip of Belle's elbow into the brew (Monumenta will not die by scalding), Belle pours it into a pail and heads for the back door. At this movement, Scaddegood screams in dismay. Perhaps believing he is about to be abandoned, the monkey leaps onto the table, and from there to Belle's shoulder. He clutches her neck in panic, nearly strangling her. "There, there," she tells him gently.

"I'll go with you Belle," I say. "Let me carry the pail."

She accepts my company but refuses to yield up the soup.

In the freezing air of the backyard, Popcorn Joe and a handful of other friends have gathered, awaiting Monumenta's end: two old women in brightly colored, ill-fitting coats—Joseph coats for dwellers in a strange land; three grizzled old men with wasted shanks, hands thrust into the pockets of boys' cast-off jackets. Enduring the cold they despise seems some sort of sacrifice for the lioness, a blend of penance, superstition, homage, hope. They break ranks to let us pass on our solemn journey to the barn.

Monumenta's nostrils catch the scent of beef. She rises on her front legs to greet us, looking a little like a clumsy puppy. "Poor baby," coos Belle. With Scaddegood still clutching her neck, Belle opens the cage, enters, stoops to set the pail before the groggy lioness. A faint but certain flicker of excitement crosses the cat's eyes; the quivering nostrils freeze. One paw lashes out and the monkey is toppled into the purplish maw. Scaddegood's anguished scream is cut off in a sickening slash of teeth. Monkey fur and monkey blood explode like the popping of a child's balloon. "Oh God!" howls Belle. She falls to her knees as if to pray before the lioness. "Oh God, oh God!" I grab her arm unceremoniously, drag her from the cage, slam it shut.

"Come on," I urge, "let's get out of here." I move

between her and the lioness to shield her view, but Belle rises and brushes me aside. With glazed eyes, she watches Monumenta devour the monkey, until the last dribble of black guts has been sucked into the thick lips.

"I'll call the veterinarian!" Belle cries suddenly. This decision is an acknowledgment of the enormity of our disaster. Calamity is upon us all; here is Armageddon.

"I'll call," I offer.

But she sweeps past me, hurrying now to the house.

"Jee-sus," exclaims Popcorn Joe in a rasping whisper, "there's never been a way in the world we could keep a monkey! Never once! They go on you every time."

But Scaddegood, beloved though he was, is dead, and these circus folk are superstitious. They look through their grief for omens. While Belle secludes herself in the house, her friends peer into the barn curiously, a bit hopefully, perhaps believing the sacrifice of the monkey will restore the old cat's stamina.

Shortly, the veterinarian arrives. This sturdy woman clad in jeans and mackintosh, we soon learn, has not been told the true purpose of her mission. She alights from her van believing she has been summoned to vaccinate dogs. Belle stalks from the house to meet her with a gray, belligerent face. "If I'd told you it was a lion sick would you have come?" she challenges.

The veterinarian gives us a cunning smile, shows neither shock nor disappointment. Her eyes look everywhere. Perhaps it is victory enough being invited to these forbidden premises. "Where is the lion?" she asks.

But before she can take a step toward the barn, the roar of a motorcycle explodes in the driveway. All eyes turn to see a blaze of red hair arriving out of the winter sun. It is Ezra! Perched on the seat behind him, white shirt and neatly knotted tie showing above his overcoat, blue from the icy wind, is Reynard. Almost before the machine has stopped, Reynard slips nimbly from it and rushes toward me. "You are live!" he cries. "I am in time!" Quick tears spring to his eyes.

"Reynard!"

"My little girl!" We clutch each other in an ardent embrace.

Ezra, looking sheepish, approaches, stares at me, then almost in a whisper says, "Reynard believed you would die today."

The veterinarian, still wearing her smile, stands frozen as if in fascination. Belle and her friends stare at us with open, curious faces.

"My friends," I announce warily, "these are . . . my friends."

"It is your father!" Belle cries triumphantly. "I see the resemblance!"

"Where are the dogs?" asks the veterinarian.

"You ever ride that bike in a show?" Joe asks Ezra.

"It's the lion that's sick," says Belle.

Only Reynard sees any pattern in all of this. "It is the lion!" he cries. "Of course! The lion is dying! Not my little girl!"

"She's not dead yet!" Belle says staunchly.

"How did you find me, Reynard?" I ask.

"By monitoring the lion," he replies. "The lion population of Indiana is quite small. First I picked up the library. That signal was weak. But the lion came through very strong."

"But you thought I was in New York, at the public library. A lion and a library."

"Mr. December postulated that," says Reynard. "I never believed it, of course. I knew where you were, and that you were safe, but I did not know your name." He glances warily at the assembled group. "Your *stage* name." It is the only explanation I will ever get. "But it is the lion who is dead!" Reynard concludes. "Not you!"

"She's not dead yet!" Belle insists.

"Yes she is," says Joe who has wandered into the barn and back out again. "The old girl's gone."

Belle's hands fly to her face in dismay; she begins to weep. The veterinarian strolls into the barn to look at the dead lion.

"I broke him out," Ezra now remembers to say. Mischief is building in his eyes. "Reynard called me in Chicago and I came down and broke him out."

"Actually, I just walked away," Reynard says. "My record was excellent. I doubt they'll look long for me. There will be enough others, more troublesome than I, to keep them occupied. And no one saw Ezra. His reputation has not been compromised."

At this, Popcorn Joe, who has been listening, extends his hand to Reynard. "Norma's father is welcome here, and her friend. Belle will say the same, you watch. We've been in jail a few times ourselves. Are the two of you show people?"

Reynard looks at Joe's grimy hand, smiles wanly, finally takes it. To me, my father says, "I will get over these things . . . my hands . . . I will get well." A new expression sweeps over him, a blend of black terror and gritty resolve. He whispers, "I will not go back to that place. I cannot."

"What happened?" I ask.

He cannot tell me, but I see this is a new, determined Reynard. I have no illusions, see only that I have been given a second chance with him.

But my father's cheer returns as quickly as it vanished. "Who is Norma?" he asks Joe.

"Well, Larry Lederman," I say to Ezra. "I thought you were in Europe."

"I go back and forth."

"Are you rich?"

"From time to time," Ezra replies. "The capo is still earning money."

"Here are the dogs!" cries the veterinarian. Word has spread that a lion and a monkey are dead. Superstitious fear is everywhere. Fourteen dogs and their owners have appeared in the yard. This group includes Teddy Mac-Kay, who smiles past his scarred but cancer-free lip and chats knowingly with the veterinarian about medical matters. She sets joyfully to work.

"Your father tells me you're composing," says Ezra.

"He knows that?"

"Reynard knows everything," Ezra replies confidently.

"Yes," says Reynard, "where is the music? We will edit it and then Ezra will find a publisher for it."

"But you hate composing!" I remind Reynard. " 'We have lost our community of belief! Our consciousness is fragmented! We live in an age of technicians, not composers!' "

"Marvelous!" He laughs lightly. "Did your mother write that speech for me to promote my career?"

"You wrote it! You preached it!"

He lays one gentle hand on my heaving shoulders. "Ada, the most rational father will alter his view when an eager child draws him in a new direction. Can a father who has lost his reason do less? The points you raise are provocative, nearly persuasive, but they are too easy. You must resist every easy thing."

This homily thrills Ezra who nods eagerly. "Ada, I can put your music into the hands of the best agent in the business."

"What about Edlyn?" I ask Reynard.

"Dead more than a year." he replies, "drinking and driving. Most unfortunate."

"And you didn't tell me!"

"Nor me!" says Ezra. "Are you sure, Reynard?"

"Of course I'm sure," Reynard tells him. "It was in the Chicago papers. While you were in Europe, I should imagine. A nurse brought it to my attention. She thought I might inherit from Edlyn's estate. I did not, of course."

"Reynard!" I am close to exasperation. "You could have written me that instead of copying out the Bible in the margins of magazines!"

Reynard considers this possibility with real interest. "You never seemed to get on with her, nor did your mother. Ezra, of course, never knew her at all."

"But the Chicago business!" cries Ezra.

Reynard raises bright, untroubled eyes. "What Chicago business?" he asks.

Belle has struggled heroically to vent her grief and overhear our conversation at the same time. "Ada's family and friends are welcome here," she now offers, pronouncing my real name with satisfaction.

Popcorn Joe glows with hospitality. "We do pretty well here," he declares. "Like they say, keep quiet or keep moving."

"I have to go back to Chicago," says Ezra, "but thank you."

"Perhaps my father and I can get a little place of our own," I tell Belle.

But Reynard feels otherwise. "I like it here," he decides. "This place seems propitious. If the lady will have us, let us stay."

"Reynard," I caution, "look around you. There are many animals in this community. Dogs. Cats."

"Yes," he replies with a sigh, "my perplexing, perhaps consanguineous relationship to animals. I suspect it is the cause of my illness, the denial of the primitive. And here's the paradox! My life is now arranged so I must confront the issue. And I shall do it! I am determined!"

"I knew it!" Belle cries with delight. "I knew immediately that your daughter came from a cultured and educated family!"

"Belle, what he said was—" I launch into this sentence, and then think better of it. "You might say my father is allergic to animals."

Belle nods wisely. "The fresh air should take care of that."

The veterinarian completes her task and, giving us all a cheery wave, drives off in her van. Ezra must also be on his way. He embraces us and departs, the motorcycle roaring and belching beneath him.

"May I look around?" Reynard asks.

"Of course," says Belle. She and her friends retreat into the house to plan Monumenta's burial.

Reynard wanders off into the barn and is back in barely a moment. "Grace," he whispers, "that lady's lion was very large."

"Yes," I tell him, "she would never fit into the trunk of a car."

He nods, bemused. "It was the bars on the cage that caught my eye." Then, "Do we still have a fiddle? I brought nothing from the hospital, and I am determined never to go back."

"I have one I picked up at a secondhand store when I first came here," I tell him. "I've worked it over. It's not bad. Let's go inside. You're freezing."

"Culture," says Belle, seating Joe, Reynard, and me for supper, "was always important in my family. When I was a little girl my mother said, 'Belle, always keep yourself in good company.'" She beams at Reynard, exulting in his neat shirt and coat, his carefully knotted tie.

"That pie you made looks first rate, Mr. Cunningham," says Joe, who has not been able to drag himself away from our company, who accepted Belle's supper invitation almost before it was offered. He smooths his shoe-polished hair with one hand and asks, "Were you ever in the jail in Dayton, Ohio?"

"Dayton!" cries Reynard happily. "Yes, when I was thirteen or fourteen. The pie there was marvelous. The sheriff's wife made it."

"I remember the pie," says Belle, "but I didn't know the sheriff's wife made it."

"A little woman with dark eyes," Joe recalls.

"Yes," says Reynard, "but there is something else I must take up with you. Unfortunately, I set fires. When I am not being watched, I must be locked up. With the lion gone, perhaps her cage could be made into a studio and sleeping room for me. It would have to have a heater for winter, a remote heater I could not reach. I think I would like the acoustics. There's no drapery in the barn at all."

"I'm the handyman here," Joe volunteers. "If Belle agrees, I'll do it for you."

Belle agrees. "It seems fitting," she says solemnly, "a memorial of sorts to Monumenta, having a gentleman in her space."

"In Topeka," says Joe, "I knew a juggler with fetishes. Besides setting fires, he ate sand. It never seemed to hurt him, but his teeth were ground down to nothing from it. He thought the sand helped his balance. Every night he had a friend search him for matches and tie him to his bed."

Belle remembers the juggler with a nostalgic smile.

After supper, Reynard plays Italian songs for Belle on my violin: "Santa Lucia"; "Funiculi, Funicula"; "O Sole Mio"; a cornucopia of Verdi hits. In response, Belle weeps ecstatically: for Monumenta, for Italy, for culture. At the conclusion of his recital, Reynard asks, "Ada, can you support the two of us with your repair work until the music is edited?"

"Yes," I reply, "if we live simply."

"There is plenty for all of us," Belle promises. "Without Monumenta to feed, we will be quite prosperous."

"The editing should take about two months," says Reynard. "Then I shall find employment."

"Playing in a bar?" I ask.

"Yes, a regular job, like yours in Philadelphia."

"Phoenix," I correct him. "You saw that?"

"I saw Philadelphia. Sorry. Then there are barber shops, perhaps dances. And we'll look into finding more repair work from schools, perhaps even start a few students."

"No, Reynard," I say, "no more students. A witch and a mental patient? Our teaching is over."

He considers and then agrees. "You're right, of course. We'll have enough without teaching. No matter. And when there's time, I want to make a small violin for the Decembers' little daughter. Ezra can mail it to them anonymously, perhaps the next time he is in Europe. Then we must have no further contact with them, for our own security."

"They have a girl, Reynard?"

"Of course. Named Grace, for your mother. Didn't you know? But first your music."

"You haven't seen it," I remind him. "And it's modern. I think you'll hate it."

"Didn't I teach you Bartók?" he counters with a merry smile. "Gretchaninov? Copland? Ives?"

"The music is all about Grace's lies," I declare; to provoke him, to prepare him in every way, to cushion myself from disappointment.

But his smile does not waver. "Every lie is somebody's truth," he replies. "New lies for a new age. The only question left to settle is your name."

"My name?"

"Yes," he continues, "perhaps someday your reputation will be weighty enough to overcome the petty concerns of Richmount. In the meantime, you must adopt a pseudonym for our protection. An easy solution would be simply to publish the music under Ezra's name, since you will be marrying him eventually."

"Reynard, I have no plans to marry."

"Even Grace spoke of it, years ago," he continues. "After you are married, Ezra will want to move away, but I shall persuade him to stay in Indiana. This will be a good place to raise your child."

"Stop, Reynard," I command. "This nonsense has gone too far. I will never have children. My faulty genes will die with me. Be perfectly clear about that."

"There is no cause for concern," he replies. "I have been educating myself on the subject, with the help of a very nice lady in interlibrary loan. Your disability is sex-linked, manifested only in girl children."

"Reynard, are you sure? Interlibrary loan?" This is too easy. This is too fast. "Please tell me the truth."

"It is the truth!" he declares, his voice blending triumph and compassion. "The mystery of a lifetime solved in a single entry in a medical journal, the research of the last couple of years." And that solemn face, so much like my own, lights with wonder. "How the truth walks before us in disguise! In any case you will have a son, a fine, perfect little boy. You will name him . . . P . . . P . . . Parsifal, I think. Yes, Parsifal, the innocent made wise through compassion." And Reynard begins to sing the Wagner:

"Here thou art in a holy place,
No man with weapons hither comes.
With shut-up helmet, shield and spear.

This day, besides! Dost thou not know
What holy day hath dawned?"

I am grateful the music has distracted him from predicting more of my future. "Where did you learn the English translation?"

"From an old recording I found at the hospital, a gift from the Salvation Army, I believe. The English sounds more felicitous than the German, don't you think?"

"Parsifal," Belle muses. "I knew a ringmaster by that name in Trenton."

"Indeed!" says Reynard. "Well, I will get on with the animals tonight, get that out of the way."

"What animals?" Belle asks.

"Don't fret," says Reynard, "I shall only draw a picture."

With my glue powder and water, Reynard mixes a thick paste in a saucer, stirring it with his finger. "What is that?" I ask.

"Camel color," he replies. "May I have a large sheet of paper?"

Belle fetches paper and as Joe, Belle, and I look on Reynard quickly creates the shapes of two camels, painting with his right forefinger. They are daubs of glue with scrawny legs, done in profile. When the glue has set, he adds eyes with drops of mahogany varnish. Then he considers, returns to the glue, and makes each hump larger. And with this, the camels are complete. He studies them thoughtfully, then with a ballpoint pen, letters above the first the name *Bach*.

"I trained a camel once in St. Louis—" Joe begins.

But Reynard silences him with one sternly raised finger, as if Joe were a student. "If you please, one moment." Then, after the name *Bach*, Reynard writes, *Did Not Washe His Handes*. "That should do it, yes," he says. "Now, please go on about St. Louis."

At the end of the evening, with only one hour left of leap year day, I walk with Joe to his truck. "I cannot guarantee that my father will stay well. His behavior is completely unpredictable."

Beneath the winter moon, Joe pats his hair and puts on his cap. "We're friends here," he says. "We handle things. Is keeping a fanciful man harder than keeping a lion? You watch. You just watch."

The following morning, Reynard and I prepare to leave for the museum barn. Only a plank on sawhorses will provide a desk large enough for a bulky orchestra score.

"You will both be frozen," Belle cautions.

"Indeed, no!" cries Reynard. "Belle, this scarf you have given me is wonderfully warm, and the gloves, and the overshoes."

I behold my father. "You look exactly like one of us."

Halfway to the barn, we meet Alexander returning on the road. News travels quickly here. He greets my father with a welcoming smile.

"Your face," says Reynard above their handshake, "is familiar. I believe we have met, but I cannot recall the occasion."

"Yes," says Alexander. "You have the same face as your daughter, but there is something more. Perhaps it will come to us." Then he turns to me. "Norma—Ada—I urged you to go into the world, but the world came to you. It is the same. Good luck to both of you with your editing. The calliope is finished. You will have the barn to yourselves."

"And good luck to you with your opening!" says Reynard. When Alexander is beyond hearing. Reynard looks after him with a bemused smile. "His epigram was lovely, about going into the world. Is it a famous proverb?"

"We never know. He doesn't tell us."

In the barn we spread out the pages of music and, warmed by March sun through the high windows, bend over them. "All music," says Reynard, "can be viewed as movement in relation to a fixed place, rising or falling, toward or away from, impulse and return. Everything else is posturing. I shall employ this principle in the editing. Cuts are needed. You have six parts. Much will be left over. The dalliance will have to go."

"Pruning?" I ask.

"Yes, pruning. But you already knew that, didn't you?"

"Yes. Reynard, tell me about the camels."

He raises his face and gazes at the calliope, gleaming with fresh paint. "Do you think we could fire that thing up?" he asks. "Just once? I've never played one."

"I believe we can," I reply. "We'll do it for Monumenta, a calliope recital for her burial."

Reynard's genius is intact, untouched by time, by illness, by events. Before the lioness has been laid in her secret grave, two pages of music are finished. "Ada," says Reynard, "you must never forget that I am insane. You must concur in this work, you must verify."

"I understand. You would probably go on cutting until nothing at all was left, but I believe I can stop you at the critical moment."

Under the hand of this seasoned orchestra player, notes are pulled back into the ranges of instruments, ornaments are slashed heartlessly, doublings are eliminated, harmonies are pushed left and right, up and down, to support melodies. A clean shape, profound as a camel's hump, emerges. Spring is coming.

On an afternoon when we have finished our day's work and are walking back to the farm, a precocious breeze from the south touches our faces with warmth, giving us great hope.

"Should I go back to Richmount, Reynard?" I ask.

He considers only a moment. "No, I think not. You need only imagine you have gone back and cleared your name. Play all of that through the emotions, through the central nervous system. The emotion is as good as the act; it's actually more authentic than the act, because we can only experience the world through feeling. And you would clear your name only temporarily in any case. Each new measure of music you compose is a criminal act all over again. You will always be an enemy of the state. Consider Edlyn. She passed out of our lives like a dream. Yet her passing did not redeem us. She stirred eddies that remain to torment us. One thing always touches another. Nothing is resolved except in art."

In these weeks, the inquisitive Ezra uses his resources to learn many things. He tells me by telephone, "No one seems to be looking for either you or Reynard. Of course, that could change at any moment."

"Yes. Then Belle and her friends would hide us, just as they have hidden Monumenta's corpse."

"You'll be cautious?" he asks.

"I will be cautious," I promise, but when am I not cautious?

"No one is ever guaranteed a safe ride in this life anyway," says Ezra. His deep, rich voice colors this observation, making it seem enigmatic and profound. "The Decembers do indeed have a child," he continues.

"A girl?"

"Yes, a girl. And I located Reynard's article from the medical journal. Then I telephoned the people directing the research and talked with them for nearly an hour. The report Reynard gave you is completely correct."

"Incredible. And Edlyn?"

"Her death appears to have been a suicide."

"An automobile accident?"

"Yes, she drove off the road, but she left a long, rambling letter on the seat beside her. It made no sense to the authorities."

"You saw it?"

"That wasn't too hard to manage. She had come to believe you were her own child, and that she was her sister. The letter was addressed to Grace and also signed Grace. She apparently lost all sense of her own identity."

"Did she mention a doll dying?"

"Yes, she did. Is that significant?"

"It would depend on who told the story. Grace could have written it ten different ways."

"But what was the truth?"

"Grace's truth? It would have depended on whom she had decided to save, whom to sacrifice—a doll, a child, a sister."

"If you're trying to say your mother destroyed Edlyn, you're dead wrong. Edlyn left her estate to the Quakers. That indicates the depth and complexity of her guilt."

"That's only speculation."

"Of course, but the pattern is perfectly clear," says Ezra, who knows everything. "Have you settled on a name for yourself?"

"May I pose as your sister?"

"Of course," says Ezra. "Ada Cantor, then."

19

THE FIRST of May, a morning of timid sun and cool breezes. Our tent is up, a blazing curtain of red and yellow stripes. Overnight, our hired acts have arrived, outsiders booked for the summer to augment the skills of our elderly performers. The field behind the tent is a sea of trucks and house trailers. Their license plates announce Texas and Oklahoma, Missouri and Florida. The followers and fakers are here too. Their sideshows and vending trailers fill nearly all of the space between the tent and the museum barn. Everyone is welcome. Our residents wander among the new arrivals looking for familiar faces, listening for news. The grounds are fringed with budding locust trees, the beginnings of wild grape and milkweed, a greening assemblage bent on parallel adventure.

I am here to superintend my portable calliope, resplendent now with gold figures on a field of red: eagles and gargoyles, the head of Neptune blowing ropy wreaths of sea spray, winged Roman soldiers with the voluptuous breasts of women, all joined with sensuous, serpentine golden vines, a fanciful coat of arms with a lurid and eclectic past. The calliope has been drawn into position before the big top. I fear jostlers and vandals, but with only this thin sprinkle of early customers, I can circle and wander while standing guard.

It is barely eleven o'clock when the barkers start up: "Tarantulas, tarantulas, tarantulas! They are here. Boas and anacondas! They're here, too! Don't go home without seeing them! Spiders and snakes! Spiders and snakes! They are here! They're alive. Those giant spiders and snakes! Tarantulas, tarantulas, tarantulas! We are open now! There is time before the big show! They are here! Bring your girlfriend! Bring your boyfriend! Spiders and snakes! Spiders and snakes! They are here! They're alive! Tarantulas, tarantulas, tarantulas!"

"World's smallest horse! No higher than a man's knee! Bring the children to this educational display! It is open now! World's smallest horse! Scientifically bred as a house pet! Featured in the national press! Bring the children to this educational display! World's smallest horse! We are open now! There is time!"

"Popcorn! Funnel cakes! Corn dogs! Cotton candy! Get them before the show! Do not let your pleasure in the performance be interrupted! Popcorn! Funnel cakes! Corn dogs! Cotton candy! Get yours now!"

"Peanuts salted and roasted in the shell! Inside selected packages are wristwatches! Genuine wristwatches! Peanuts salted and roasted in the shell! This gentleman has found a wristwatch in his package! Hold it up, sir! Hold it up high! Peanuts salted and roasted in the shell! Inside selected packages are wristwatches! Peanuts salted and roasted in the shell!"

Fully assembled on opening day, our company is one third Hispanic. The soft accents of Mexico hum through the staging area.

Belle's authentic Italian flyers, who call themselves Luigi and Cosica, are man and wife. They chat quietly together.

"Se van a fines de la semana que viene."

"Sí. Documentos. Siempre documentos."

"Sí. A fin de cuentas, todo se resolvió sin dificultad."

"Too much money. Dollars, never pesos."

Behind the snake show, our high wire man stretches through a series of warm-ups. "What is your name?" asks a roaming early customer, a lady with blue-white hair.

"Wolfgang, madame. I am from the National Circus of Germany."

"Germany! How interesting."

"Sí, madame."

In their holding pen, Teddy MacKay's poodles, coal black, dressed with red ruffles around their necks, yap frantically. Over the winter, they have nearly forgotten the stench of our rented-for-summer animals: a pinto pony, five smallish scruffy dromedaries, and most odorous of all, an elephant.

Belle has left off currying the pony to chat with a group we have not seen before, a family of Vietnamese tumblers. Of the parents, two daughters, and two sons, only the youngest child, a precocious boy of perhaps nine, speaks understandable English.

"Good horse!" he tells Belle, touching the pony's nose, then reaching up to capture its neck in a fervent embrace. He looks like any child yearning to ride a pony, and also like no child I have ever seen. His difference—I am a bit startled—is not in his powerful young body but in his face: eyes that watch everything without seeming to move; a smile dancing out from sinewy cheeks, bringing some message about resolve; yet a supple, spontaneous mouth, merry now with delight over this horse.

Belle has seen it too; her face is alert. "Come up, then!" she commands, patting the pony's bare back. The boy springs; in barely an instant he is astride the horse, shoulders squared, one hand swept out in a theatrical gesture. "Little love!" Belle cries in admiration. "Precious little man!" The boy's parents look on with tentative, courteous smiles; the other children, eager and hopeful, watch the pony.

Joe arrives with the local boy he has hired to keep the boiler on the calliope fired. He lingers, not quite willing to put this gaudy chariot into a stranger's care. Joe started the fire early; it must be continued all day to have steam at the ready. Orange coals flare beneath the tank. A curl of black smoke dances from the stack.

The boy is perhaps fourteen, lean and eager. He looks at the head of Neptune and then at me. "You play this thing, miss?"

"I do."

"I guess you've been with the circus a long time. You fall off of something? Your leg?"

"I guess."

There is something in this interchange that pleases Joe. He looks at the boy with new interest. "What do you do, son?"

"Nothing."

"No," Joe insists, "what do you do?"

"My folks think it's crazy. I mean they like to come and watch the show, but they think it's crazy."

"Tell me what you do."

"I ride pretty well. We have horses. I can do almost anything with a horse. My folks think it's crazy."

"The circus," Joe tells him, "began with the horse. If you take away everything else, that's what you have left —the horse."

"The horse?" the boy asks. He has not expected this news. His face registers surprise, and then pleasure. "The horse," he says again. "I'm not afraid to fall."

"You can break ribs," says Joe, "as many ribs as you like. Only a neck or knee injury is serious, especially for riders."

"The neck," says the boy, "the knee," recording this information, prepared to cast away all of his sound ribs with heroic abandon.

"Keep this boiler going," says Joe, confident now. "Don't let the fire go out."

"I will," says the boy. "I won't. You can depend on me."

Reynard appears in a Gypsy costume provided by Belle. Beside the entrance to the tent, he takes up his fiddle and begins playing Romany airs. On the ground, his open violin case is seeded with two one-dollar bills. But when half an hour of plaintive Hungarian tunes has stirred no interest, he glances down into his case with a practiced eye, and switches to "The Flight of the Bumblebee." Almost immediately, his bills are peppered with a fine sprinkle of silver. He smiles and nods his thanks at his benefactors.

Joe reappears as an Abraham Lincoln clown, a new concept. I had thought it inappropriate, but children squeal with pleasure and recognition at the sight of his tall hat and beard cruising the ticket line. I realize I have no feel for this business after all, no true instinct.

The pace quickens. Joe takes up a stack of circus programs. "Souvenir programs! Circus programs! One dollar! Inside the big top they will be two dollars! Get yours now! Circus programs! Souvenir programs! Illustrated in full color! One dollar!"

Alexander, the Calabrias, and Rick Ross file by in full costume—black pants, red vests, white shirts, and red captain's hats. Shiny black bow ties complete their outfits. The sight of the uniforms stirs excitement. We are building, from tarantulas to the calliope. Alexander gazes at the restored instrument, then sends me a satisfied smile.

I mount the steps to the calliope and insert my earplugs. "The Saints Go Marching In" whistles forth in earsplitting grandeur. The crowd falls back in stupefaction at this miracle of noise. Children shout and clap their hands over their ears. Infants scream.

Customers now hurl themselves into our tent, where they immediately confront Reynard, a red vendor's jacket covering his Gypsy garb, standing beneath a sign that proclaims PREFERRED SEATING, ONLY ONE ADDITIONAL DOLLAR! Bills are torn from pockets and thrust at him. "The Saints" blends into "Dixie," and then "Happy

Days Are Here Again." The tarantula man, looking bored, slides a Closed sign across his ticket window. The vendors move inside. "Over the Waves," sings the calliope, and beyond its perimeter, beyond Reynard's shoulder, I see waves of customers scrambling up into the bleachers. En route, they buy popcorn and cotton candy, which have now doubled in price. Arrogant vendors refuse to change ten-dollar bills, and customers, in a panic, make change among themselves in stressful camaraderie. Popcorn and cotton candy are passed down long rows of people, dollar bills are passed back. "In the Good Old Summertime," whistles the calliope, and I see the peanut man's shill hold up a wristwatch. As a second chorus of "Summertime" hurtles to a close, I watch Alexander. Across a sea of hands, he waves his trumpet at me. I dismount and straggle inside, leaving our stoic boiler boy a lonely figure on the nearly deserted grounds.

Rick Ross produces a mighty drumroll. Alexander and the Calabrias, who have also taken up trumpets, play a fanfare. The ringmaster, in tall black hat and red cutaway coat, steps into our circus's single ring. "Ladies and gentlemen! Children of all ages!"

"The tickets were worth every penny of the price," says Reynard, as I slip into the seat he has saved for me. "I'm so glad I could bring my little girl to the circus." He is a courteous but persistent voice-over. "I only wish your mother could have come."

"From the corners of the earth!" intones the ringmaster. "Death-defying acts!"

"Do not be misled if feats seem effortless," Reynard instructs. "The master always makes the difficult appear easy."

"Hush, Reynard."

But a hush is unnecessary. The ringmaster concludes his speech, waves his hat, and folds himself into a deep bow. "The Entry of the Gladiators" thunders from the band, the curtains open, and Belle appears astride the pinto pony to lead the grand processional around the perimeter of the ring. Rouged and feathered, in a brief leather dress, she is an Indian maiden. The bare legs and bare pointed toes that slip gracefully along the horse's flanks are those of a young girl. She is followed by the rented camels, draped in crimson and gold, led by Teddy MacKay, who will work them. On the back of each camel perches a poodle. The dogs are settled now, professionals eager for performance. Teddy MacKay is dressed as a sheik.

After the camels comes Joe, borne by the elephant. In pith helmet and khaki safari garb, he sits just behind the animal's head, saluting the crowd with a trainer's baton. Four of our residents are clowns, their old faces anonymous behind makeup. They are still sprightly in baggy pants and ballooning jesters' suits. I am amazed at how grand our shabby company has become.

Lest our enthusiasm wane for a moment, Alexander's trumpet samples the glorious repertoire of circus music —"Gentry's Grand Triumphal," "Georgia Girl," "The Billboard," "The Thunderer," "Bombasto"—and the performers file by.

The Vietnamese children march sedately behind their parents, all of the family now in billowing lime green shirts. The children are Asian princes and princesses.

The band plays the grand processional out of sight and into the spotlight steps our first act, a girl who performs on a low trapeze. The blue velvet robe and pink boa Belle has provided do not mask her clumsiness. Casting them off, she stands in the circle of light, a straight, wooden figure, graceless and unmuscled. Our budget for hired performers is limited. It will buy us one or two top acts, and a complement of the less skilled. From the trumpet's rich middle range, "Deep Purple" unrolls like satin. But even underwritten by voluptuous music, the girl cannot succeed. With mechanical movements, she hangs upside down, arms thrashing, and then forms a lopsided bird's nest. She skins the cat and does a backward pullover. The trapeze wobbles erratically. But our warm crowd is still caught up in its early frenzy. Excitement will carry them mesmerized through the initial acts. Alexander picks up the tempo and launches "Ecret's Galop" to cover the girl's awkward departure.

The ringmaster introduces the poodles. "No animal," he cries, "enjoys performing so much as the dog!" The poodles bound into the ring, then abruptly stop and arrange themselves in a semicircle. Teddy MacKay skips in after them, glittering now in a suit of silver and blue. One of the riggers flies by him to set up props, inverted tubs in graduated sizes, a set of steps, a frame-mounted hoop. "How Much Is That Doggie in the Window?" asks the band, Daviso's trombone yelping playfully. With barely a flip of his hand, Teddy sends balls of black fur hurtling through the air, somersaulting, leaping, dancing through intricate patterns. The horns have fallen silent. Rick Ross's snare follows the accelerating feet of the dogs as they sail upward; his bass proclaims their safe return to earth. A poodle on its hind legs slowly climbs the steps, and the band remembers "Old Dog Tray." Teddy's modest signals belie his role in all of this geometry, and the self-important poodles claim everything for themselves.

"Dogs . . ." muses Reynard. He looks wan but hopeful.

They are followed by a Mexican juggler, introduced by the ringmaster as Herr Heinz of Hamburg. To help preserve the man's cover, the Calabrias take up tuba and sousaphone, and a German band is born. *"Muss I Denn,"* sings the trumpet. The juggler, his dusky Latin skin showing beneath brief lederhosen, progresses from rings to pins to china plates to daggers. Gravity has been tamed. Objects shower and cascade. The band sends him off with the "Olympia Hippodrome March."

Joe appears, carried into the ring in the curl of the elephant's trunk. A rented elephant has a limited number of stock moves, but Joe exploits each one. This elephant sits on its rump, rises on its hind legs, lies down and rolls over. For a finale, it lifts Joe and swings him in its trunk. Joe exits sitting on the elephant's head, both arms raised in triumph.

"Keep back!" cautions the ringmaster. "The elephant is coming all the way around!" To "Burma Patrol," Joe and the elephant circle the dirt path at the ring's perimeter.

Then Teddy MacKay is back to work the camels. In his sheik's garb, he runs them in a circle, masses them to left and then to right, while "Caravan" screams from the band.

Joe, flushed with success, comes to sit beside us. "Wait until you see the Vietnamese!" he cries. "I was watching them warm up behind the tent."

But it is another half hour before the tumblers appear.

The crowd's euphoria has waned. To hold them, we must give them our meager best. The Vietnamese, fierce with makeup and slicked hair, march sternly into the ring and cast off silver capes. Their slight bodies are taut. Even the mother is firmly muscled. Gone are the smiling children. These are warriors of the East.

Alexander's horn searches through the Mediterranean, through the Middle East, and finally locates China. An angry, harmonic minor sails through the tent, the father shouts a command, and suddenly bodies are whirling. Lime green shirts bounce and somersault, twist, and fly above the earth, separating and merging again into symmetry. The mother leaps to the teeterboard and sends a son somersaulting into the air to land on his father's shoulders. The crowd cheers.

Belle, queen mother of us all, now with a cape of feathers over her Indian dress, slips into the seat beside Joe. "Look at the baby!" she cries with delight. "Do you see? He is not afraid!"

The smallest son, the one who sat upon the pony, is coming to life. It is as if exertion has warmed him. He is slipping into a new role. Smiles flicker on the small face. As the crowd's enthusiasm grows, his eyes light with joy. He has passed beyond himself into another existence. He is going farther. He has discovered the secret of performance. He will work this crowd himself. After each trick, as the tumblers bow, this child bows deeper, puts the faintest wiggle into the motion. The crowd loves him. He bounces between tumbles, rising two feet off the ground, arms thrown out as if to embrace his audience. The others are helpless to stop him. They hew even closer to their rigid roles, as if their discipline could pull him back to them. But it is no use. He steps to the teeterboard, grinning broadly, arms outstretched, fingers wriggling suggestively, drawing the people to him. His mother sends him sailing up to his father's shoulders as if he were completely weightless. The father catches him neatly and seems to hold him tight for a moment, as if he cannot bear to give him up. But the child is free in an instant and somersaults quickly to the ground.

From the bandstand, Alexander is watching. The trumpet calls, from Moldavia to Vietnam, and finds its answer. Across miles, across years, across language. Alexander and the child own the crowd. Time has stopped. The boy could somersault forever. But the father has begun the pyramid that will end the act. The mother leaps to the teeterboard and a brother is sent skyward, then a sister, and another sister. Then it is the boy's turn. He hesitates and, in an outrageous gesture, drops to kiss the ground. The crowd roars. Only the smallest flicker of doubt crossing the mother's face gives warning. Then she leaps to the board and the child is sent sailing, sailing. He grazes his sister's arm and sails free. For a moment, the small limbs fly out, then he gathers himself into a ball and falls almost silently to earth.

Belle, the world's expert on falls, is beside him in an instant. She requires only the briefest second of time. Then she sends Alexander a wretched glance. The trumpet explodes into the "Stars and Stripes Forever," our secret signal of distress. The clowns burst into the tent. The Vietnamese family with frozen, stricken faces, stare out at the crowd. Then, perhaps insane with fear, they bow stiffly as the child is carried out.

In another moment the ringmaster appears and the

band falls silent. "We are pleased to tell you the child is
not seriously injured!" he cries. "It is only a sprain! And
now, on with the show!" The crowd cheers.

But Belle's white face and slowly returning step pro-
claim disaster. As she reaches us, I see the pain in her
eyes. "Oh, Belle!"

"Sit down, Ada!" she commands in a steely voice I have
never heard before. There is an icy smile across her face.
"Stay where you are. The boy is beyond help. We must
think of the living. A crowd in panic now would injure
many people, and it would ruin us. A horde of police
descending on this place? Ada, do you think your father
is the only fugitive here?"

Grim and shaken, Joe comes to her assistance. "The
tumblers are professionals, new to the country but not to
performing. They will leave quietly."

"And grieve in private," says Reynard, whose mind has
always been quicker than mine, more canny. His eyes
are bright with tears.

"But Belle—"

"Hush, Ada," she orders.

Alexander is blowing grief in a cascading wail. Then he
seems to remember he is responsible for this crowd, for
these clowns. The music rises as quickly as it fell. The
tune is now a Yiddish *freilach*. The clowns join hands to
dance, stepping lightly, then tumbling over each other.
Grief and necessity ferry Alexander from Russia across
the Prut River, into Rumania, the Transylvanian Alps,
Bulgaria, Greece, and Turkey. They drive him through
New Orleans and down Broadway. But he cannot es-
cape. He backtracks, reworking the tunes, adjusting
them. The Calabria brothers, on cornet and trombone,

follow as their aging lips allow. Rick Ross drums frantically, demonically. And now the songs return transformed. They seem to remember each of the boy's movements, his incredible joy.

"And always back to the minor," says Reynard. "A
music that forgets nothing."

"What did you say?"

"Ada, I suspected it from the beginning. He is a
klezmer."

"A klezmer, Reynard?"

"It means itinerant musician, from Yiddish. First in
Russia, then here. Everywhere, really. The everywhere
is in the music. When Donald and I were young and
traveling, we sometimes encountered them. They came
from places with lovely musical names, Czernowitz,
Smyrna, Anatolia, Salonika, Beltsy. I though they were
all dead. I wonder if he is the last one."

"The last klezmer?"

"Shh, Ada. I was never able to determine exactly, but I
don't think they use the word themselves. Listen, he is
playing a Hebrew service for a Vietnamese child. There
is always a scream when he rounds the A. I don't know if
the music is crying for the past or announcing the future."

Riggers have run forward to erect nets. Only the high
wire act and the flyers, our grand finalists, use nets. On
the wire, the agile Mexican named Wolfgang lifts his
balance pole and launches forth. Even twenty feet below, we can see tears glistening on his cheeks. He crosses
and returns while Alexander, throwing caution aside,
reaches out to console him with Spanish music: "In a
Little Spanish Town," "Lady of Spain," "In My Adobe

Hacienda." Wolfgang mounts his unicycle and shoots forward uncautiously onto the wire. Then back on his feet, hands outstretched, he reaches to pick up a handerchief with his teeth. He is unwilling to let a child die with more courage than he gives to life. He runs, he skips! The audience is enthralled, gasping now. "Cielito Lindo," plays Alexander recklessly, unwilling to be surpassed. The walker comes down to thunderous applause.

And already Luigi is swinging upside down, legs locked, hands ready to catch his wife. Cosica, in blood red, chalks her hands, catches her swing, and sails toward him. "Fascination," sings the trumpet in strictest three-four time. Cosica sails into space and is caught in Luigi's grip. The ringmaster announces a somersault, then a double. Cosica and Luigi sail flawlessly. The crowd is enraptured. Their heads move to and fro with the flyers. It is several moments before we are aware of a commotion outside; it is Reynard's instincts that come alive. "The accident has brought the police," he tells us.

But his intuition is scarcely better than that of the flyers. In an instant, Cosica has dropped to the net and somersaulted to the ground, with Luigi only seconds behind her. They streak from the ring and disappear beyond the curtain.

Then—whether by second sight or street sense, we will never know—Reynard looks over his shoulder and assesses our situation with what will prove to be complete accuracy. "There are only three officers. They are not really concerned at this point. They have heard only that there was an accident. The Vietnamese need a little longer to get away, and the flyers are illegal aliens. We must protect all of them."

The ringmaster has rushed forward to take charge. He declares our abrupt conclusion was completely planned to enhance pleasure in the drama of our performance. Then he concludes, "May all of your days be circus days!" pitting a single voice against a crowd that is growing restive.

"Look at them," says Belle. "They don't like the way the flyers left. They're putting it together, remembering the accident. We have only a minute."

Two police officers stride into the tent. "Less than a minute," says Joe.

Alexander sees it too. The band explodes into the "Washington Post March." But the crowd knows Alexander now. With the instincts of children and animals, they have seen him for the sorcerer he is, and no longer trust him.

Then some old rumble rises out of the past. How do the young ones know the mix? Is the modus operandi carried in the genes, in the dark green night of the cell? The boiler boy is at my elbow, terrified but loyal. The promise of circus savvy Joe saw in him earlier is now fully realized. His young face is alive and canny. "You gonna play that thing, Miss?"

He hurries me out of the tent. Before I am halfway up the calliope steps, he is handing me my earplugs. At the keyboard, high on the old animal wagon, I survey the world of possibility, the whole creation in an instant: a roiling crowd framed by the broad mouth of our tent, the bandstand beyond flashing brass, the proud barn rising. The opening measures of the suite whistle forth like demons released from hell. Pared down for this small keyboard, the music is a raucous, eerie plaint; but the chaos of the galloping notes inspires its opposite in the crowd. Startled and curious, they are already slipping back into docility. Below me, a police officer shouts and gestures against my noise, ordering me to stop playing. The boiler boy, with hand signs and mobile face, declares to the officer that he, too, has been driven to his limit by these queer circus folk. The officer accepts the declaration as a show of support and is mollified. The two fall into easy, mute camaraderie. I am amazed at the boy's virtuosity.

Time is the same thing in music that it is everywhere else in nature. Time is what passes while history is being made. Belle and Joe lead another officer into the seclusion of the barn where conversation will be possible, and close the door. Just inside the tent the Calabrias have taken charge of the third officer. How pleased they are he has come! They want to show him the clever construction of our bleacher seats. This is vital information that will immediately body forth all the mystery of the circus in bold relief. Has he not come on a tour of inspection? But before the man can focus on the joint of board with board, the Calabrias discover that it is, after all, the electrical wiring that requires the immediate inspection and approval of the police. They pass the silver ball of the man's attention between them.

The suite whistles on. Stripped of its auxiliary voices, it has assumed an alien life of its own. I am as curious about it as my audience. We live, after all, to know God. Beyond discovery, there is little worthy of our attention. All the seeming multiplicity of things falls into place under a single heading. On the bandstand Alexander, looking old and tired, packs instruments into cases. These performances take more out of him than he admits. He pauses to wipe finger marks from brass, to peer into the bells of horns. How much of this is meant to calm the audience, he will never tell us. He lives in our world and not in it, picking his own path through the vocabulary: con, entertainment, transcendence, oblation. Who in the crowd could be alarmed when the leader of our band looks so totally bored?

The suite, however truncated, has for the first time an audience, and by it is transmogrified. The loop of speculation it casts forth is completed now by another presence, silent but sentient. When the boiler boy turned me out of my bleacher seat, my best hope was for a novel sound to control an anxious crowd. Sometimes a question can be masked by a bigger question, a noise by a larger noise. With the bawdy instrument, the popcorn-sated crowd, the innocence of soft May sun stretching toward dusk, I did not envision a serious performance. Such is the vanity of composers. A crosshatch of response carries back to me on the gently rising wind, a cat's cradle of yeas and nays. The suite is getting mixed reviews, but it is holding together. With beginner's luck, more instinct than design, I have succeeded at the first rule of music composition: The Law of Good Continuation. My tumbling notes produce instability, and a concurrent hope for rest, a pattern laid up in our collective memory from infancy. What is holding the crowd, drawing them from the tent to the calliope, is the promise of resolution.

Reynard appears below me and raises one hand in brief salute. Trained to sound, he is not as eloquent with gesture as the boiler boy, but his meaning is clear enough. He is telling me the flyers and the Vietnamese have safely departed.

Resolution. Drawings in caves show primitive musical instruments. Who was the first man to play his ragged, abrupt grief smoothly into history? The first woman? Music, said my mother, helps us organize our lives. The suite lurches on, imagination striking a bargain with experience, giving me back what was taken from me.

Reynard conducts the closing measures of the music with speculative nods of his head, then announces, "It reads quite well, I'd say."

"There are a dozen things wrong with it, Reynard. A hundred. But I know what I have to do."

"No," he says, "you've done enough. You must move along now to the next composition."

Alexander is searching through the thinning crowd. Belle and Joe emerge from the barn, their business accomplished. Joe smooths his polished hair and shakes hands with the departing police officers. Alexander locates Belle and falls into step beside her. After a moment, he takes her hand in his own. Our opening day is over.

20

IT IS full summer when Ezra appears at the farm in person, bringing the news that a market has been found for the suite. Reynard, seeing the motorcycle, believes his brother has arrived. "Donald!" he cries, rushing from his studio in the barn, arms open in eager love. By the time Belle and I reach the driveway, he has realized his mistake and is chatting happily with Ezra. "Good news!" Reynard cries. "The suite has been sold! It will be played by an orchestra! Published!"

"Welcome, Mr. Lederman!" Belle says to Ezra.

Looking dubious, Ezra gives me a huge hug. "It's not quite that way," he says. "They want to use your suite as background music for a television film, a documentary on space travel for young people. The money is good, but how do you feel about background music?"

"It's perfect!" Reynard declares. "Into the ears of children! Where else can new music go?"

"You'll be famous!" Belle croons. "A celebrity, Ada!" She glances warily at the mounting sun. She has forgotten to bring out the parasol that protects her white skin.

"Famous, Belle?" I chide. "From a documentary? I doubt that, but I will abide by whatever decision my father makes. In music, I have never known him to be wrong."

Ezra says, "You can always write more music, Ada. This is just a beginning."

"She is writing more every day!" says Reynard. Then, always courteous, he remembers to ask, "And what of your own music, Ezra?"

"I've finished with Blake," Ezra replies. He straightens his shoulders, sets his head at an angle, and begins to sing an exotic, melancholy song:

"Animals ferocious with hunger to swim rivers,
Greater part of the camp will be against Hister,
It will have the man carried in an iron cage,
When the child watches the river."

"Bravo!" Reynard cries, clapping his hands in approval. "Bravo, indeed! But—forgive me—my late wife would have recognized your poem. Grace knew every poem ever written, every song, but my own memory is often deficient."

"Nostradamus," says Ezra.

"Of course!" says Reynard. "Your new enthusiasm, then? And very fertile soil."

"What I have come to realize," says Ezra, "is that destiny is fan-shaped. At any given moment, the future is completely preordained in lines of energy radiating from a single point. Yet, one lateral step creates an entirely new constellation of forces. At the base of the fan are constants."

"Is that in Nostradamus?" I ask.

"I don't think it's in Blake," Ezra replies.

"But," says Belle, "it's very lovely all the same."

Reynard, always eager to help, smiles merrily, raises one hand as if to bless us. "I believe it was first in Ecclesiastes, phrased only a bit differently: 'For to him that is joined to all the living there is hope, for a living dog is better than a dead lion.'"

"True," Belle intones solemnly, "so true, Mr. Cunningham."

"I knew that dog," I recall. "His name was Invention."

Ezra is filled almost to bursting with joy for all of this success, all of this wisdom, all of this poetry. "Let us not lose our simplicity," he cautions. "William Penn said, 'Do not walk in the light of your own fire.' He meant self-indulgence."

"Perhaps," says Reynard, "perhaps. But isn't it possible he was simply telling us to be alert, lest we miss the next necessary thing?"